ALEX DRYDEN'S
RED TO BLACK

"One of the more intriguing novels
of the year in any genre."
Daily Telegraph (London)

"Prescient . . . [*Red to Black*] depicts a frightening and
ruthless Russia, which answers to nobody."
The Economist

"An absorbing debut, a spy thriller that exposes the
links between the 'old' Russia of the Cold War and
the 'new' Russia of Vladimir Putin. . . . Dryden's fact-
based scenario provides worrisome food for thought."
Publishers Weekly

"[Alex Dryden] wants us to know we're still not
safe. . . . And Dryden has written a superb spy novel
to prove it. . . . The warning bell that *Red to Black*
sounds against Putin's Russia has a powerful ring,
especially when it turns to the KGB. . . .
Mixing espionage and romance in equal measure . . .
[it has much] in common with the elegantly
paced books of John le Carré."
Richmond Times-Dispatch

"An exceptional novel by any standard [that] readers
who enjoy a love story mixed with their espionage
(à la le Carré's *The Little Drummer Girl*)
will appreciate."
Library Journal (★Starred Review★)

By Alex Dryden

MOSCOW STING
RED TO BLACK

Coming Soon in Hardcover

THE BLIND SPY

RED ★ TO BLACK

ALEX DRYDEN

HARPER

An Imprint of HarperCollinsPublishers

This book was first published in Great Britain in 2008 by Headline Publishing Group.

This is a work of fiction. References to real people, events, establishments, organizations, or locales are intended only to provide a sense of authenticity, and are used fictitiously. All other characters, and all incidents and dialogue, are drawn from the author's imagination and are not to be construed as real.

HARPER

An Imprint of HarperCollins*Publishers*
10 East 53rd Street
New York, New York 10022-5299

Copyright © 2009 by Alex Dryden
Excerpt from *The Blind Spy* copyright © 2012 by Alex Dryden
ISBN 978-0-06-208587-0

First Harper premium printing: December 2011
First Ecco paperback printing: June 2010
First Ecco hardcover printing: September 2009

Printed in the United States of America

Visit Harper paperbacks on the World Wide Web at www.harpercollins.com

10 9 8 7 6 5 4 3 2 1

To 'J' and to the
Russians who want their freedom

'. . . On a huge hill, Cragg'd, and steep,
Truth stands, and he that will Reach her,
about must, and about must go'
John Donne

Thank you to the many people in Russia and the former Soviet republics, who helped with this book and who wish to remain nameless.

1

I **DON'T KNOW WHO I'M** writing this for but perhaps it's for you. If that makes it sound like a confession, you may wonder what I'm expecting in return. A small part of me, I admit, seeks forgiveness, or at least understanding. But that part of me is less important than the forgiveness I wish to give myself, and which I find elusive.

I am writing to draw a line under the past, with its rot creeping into the present. I know now that if I had done this a long time ago, the present would never have been postponed and things would be different today.

In one of his more fatalistic moments, Finn said to me: 'Anna, you know our story can never be written.'

'Why not?' I asked him.

'Nobody would believe it,' he said.

But I'm here now, sitting in a medieval vault in a

house in Tegernsee on the southern borders of Germany, reading Finn's story – our story – and I'm aware that all I have between me and the hostile forces that swim up at me from the pages is the Contender handgun and the twelve rifle shells on the table by my hand. And now that I've found these notebooks of his, or books of record, as he calls them, buried in this vault along with all the other material of our secret profession, I see his fatalism was short-lived. As I sift through the piles of notebooks, oddments, scraps and sheets of paper, documents and microfiches – their edges stained with cellar dampness – with only the heat of an oil burner to keep me warm, I can see that he has practically written our story himself.

The notebooks certainly contain the facts and, without these facts, my feelings would be drifting in a vacuum, unmoored to the reality that at any moment I may need to use this gun and all my years of training to kill my way out of here. Feelings need to be clothed in reality and the facts – this story – supply the clothes. For days now, I have been reading and rereading Finn's prose, notes and observations – over and over. I'm reading them sitting in this dark stone vault and my eyes are running from the fumes of the oil burner and I strain in the dim light to follow the thread of a story that began long before I met Finn.

According to one note Finn made, our story begins in 1998, when Boris Yeltsin's Russia reached its nadir. A later scrawl in Finn's undisciplined handwriting names 1989 as the beginning, the year the Berlin Wall came down at last. But another, perhaps more thoughtful, observation says that it all started in 1961, when we Russians erected the Wall in the first place.

Whatever the true beginning, however, everything Finn and I have experienced will continue to unfold into a dark and uncertain future, with or without us.

As I read all his disparate and complementary records, the thing that strikes me most deeply about what Finn experienced in his long quest to have the truth accepted in his own country is his sheer obstinacy, the relentless autopilot of individual human endeavour when success seems impossible.

What also strikes me is that Finn's past has dictated his life, much as my past has dictated mine.

'You cannot escape your past, Anna,' he once told me. 'But you don't have to live in it. You don't have to build the present in its image.'

If only Finn had been true to his own belief.

Finn could have had a quiet life. That is the point, I realise, as I sit here shivering in the damp cold. He told me that he chose to pursue this quest, not just for the truth, but to have the truth accepted by his masters in London, and their political masters in the British Government. But did he really choose? Or was it his deep-seated need for acceptance that fed his stubbornness and single-mindedness?

For my part, I know I'm looking for someone or something to find responsible for my own actions, but I can't escape my part.

Oh yes, Finn could have had a quiet life, a beautiful life. He had a great talent for doing nothing, which he called happiness, but he chose to go alone down the Tunnel, as he calls it here, and I hope I'm not deluding myself when I say he would not regret that now, whatever's happened to him. For Finn has disappeared and, as I wait for the crash of sledge-hammers against the door upstairs, I'm looking for a clue to tell me something, anything that might help me to find him.

There is much, too, about Finn himself in these notebooks which distracts me from my increasingly urgent task. There are details of his internal strug-gle to understand his motives, a struggle which I never fully understood, and that he never told me, despite the fusion of our love. During all the time I've known Finn, he never wanted to bring his own past like an evil spirit into our house. So he wrote it down in the notebooks and buried it with our secret story in this vault, which has hidden many things and many people in its long history.

And there is much in the notebooks about his feelings towards me.

'There are three distinct spirits in our relation-ship,' Finn once said to my grandmother at the da-cha in Barvikha. This was back in the freezing winter weeks leading up to the millennium, when perhaps he and I were at our closest, and when trouble seemed far away. 'There's Anna, me and the spirit that joins us.' My grandmother, with her peasant background, was comfortable with the world of spirits. She laughed with mirth and hugged him. Like many people whose lives he touched, Nana loved Finn.

Finn had just given me a charm bracelet. It con-tained two charms: a rabbit for me and a monkey for him. It was his nickname for me, Rabbit.

'The silver circle that links the charms,' he said, 'is the spirit that joins us.'

'I'm not sure I believe in spirits,' I said.

'I find I can't do without them,' he said breezily.

'How sentimental,' I replied.

But it was typical of Finn instinctively to sense the language, the context, of whoever he was talking to. Nana appreciated his inclusion of spirits. Nana was very superstitious and, my mother told me, she was also psychic. With her deep grey eyes that glinted over her sharp, hooked nose, she even looked witch-like. When Finn described his relationship with me in this way, she replied as if foreseeing the future.

'If only that were true,' she said. 'If only you, Anna and the spirit that joins you both really were the only three things in your relationship. God bless you.'

At this moment, in the cellar, I pause over another scrap of paper he wrote about us, on some Luxembourg hotel notepad. I'm mesmerised by what he's written and can almost feel his presence here, through the words.

'When we make love, and we look into each other's eyes, I see the child in you, Anna, the spirit in you, and in those moments you are me and I am you.'

It is these brief, aching glimpses of our intimacy that distract me from my task and, to keep my mind away from such thoughts and focused on the present danger, I sit and listen for the slightest sound. Then I slot the gun's firing pin into the mechanism and slide a single round of green spot ammunition into the chamber. With this weapon, I can kill a man at over two hundred yards.

It is hard enough to keep love safe. In my own experience it is prone either to snap suddenly, or to dwindle and fade to a monotonous daily exercise that is not so different from filling the dishwasher or taking the dog for a walk. I have passionately kissed a man at the start of a film while out on a date at the cinema and, by the end, found him physically repulsive to touch. I have also watched other affairs dwindle imperceptibly to the banal, the everyday, the meaningless.

But neither of these fault lines is true in the case of Finn and myself. We have, or is it had? other troubles. Whatever the truth of our love, we allowed too much to come between us. And the past sneaked into any available crack and fissure in our relationship as frost enters the cement courses of a house.

We had the malevolence of others, with their huge forces arrayed against us, but it was we, ultimately, who allowed their hostility to disrupt the peace we might have found.

We had microphones, watchers, tails, people in every corner. We had two of the world's most experienced intelligence services tracking our every movement. We had shining slivers of time to snatch for last minute walk-ins in hotel rooms across the city. At reception desks, Finn would call me his wife.

'I'm not your wife,' I told him at the beginning. 'I'm a colonel in the SVR. Doing a job, that's all.'

'OK. Colonel,' he might say. 'Allow me to undo the buttons of your shirt.'

'Please.'

'Please, then,' he'd say.

Do I mean that we had the malevolence of others, or do we still have it? Where is Finn? What has happened to him? Is Finn now the past or is he still in the present?

2

I MET FINN for the first time back in January 1999. Our meeting had been at the Baltschug Hotel, across the Moskva River from the Kremlin. The hotel was to remain a place of good memories for us throughout Finn's residency in Moscow. As he put it, rather unnecessarily, 'It was the venue for our first official fuck, Rabbit, endorsed by Her Majesty and the KGB.'

Finn was sitting at the head of the table in a private meeting room at the Baltschug, in his role of Second Secretary of Trade and Investment. He was holding court with a dozen or so business and security acolytes and their boss Pavel Drachevsky, the billionaire aluminium tycoon. Drachevsky had invited some of his managers: his leaden ex-KGB security boss Chimkov; Alexander, the poet, translator and KGB snake who had worked at the United Nations in Geneva for several years; and my friend Natasha, who tried to act in Russia's confused public relations world as Drachevsky's PR assistant.

Whether Finn knew the lunch was a set-up or not, he didn't show it. When I arrived, deliberately late, he looked completely relaxed. He was sitting in a high-backed chair at the head of the long table. He wore a slightly creased blue suit and a tie, which could have been tied by a schoolboy, with a large thick knot and one very short end. He had brown hair, brushed straight back over his head and greying slightly at the temples, and his face was lined from laughter. His eyes, which changed through various shades of green and brown, depending on the light, as I discovered later, contained a kind of merry amusement that stopped just short of scorn. Finn always seemed to be enjoying himself.

I noticed that he addressed more of his conversation to Natasha, who is very pretty, than to Drachevsky, who was the reason Finn was there and who can't claim good looks as his forte.

Whether or not Finn knew who I was, I couldn't tell, but as I entered the room dressed in black leather – it embarrasses me now to recall this – I immediately had his attention. Of course I did. That was the idea. Finn's reputation for womanising in Moscow was always considered to be the hook to catch him with, despite our consistent failures up till now, and in the crude logic of the KGB it was considered that Finn would be more of a pushover if I, the youngest female KGB colonel, wore black leather.

I took my seat next to Natasha so that Finn would now look at both of us, and the conversation continued in a relaxed and businesslike way.

And then, at the appointed moment, Natasha looked up the table towards Finn. It was all rehearsed. In her lazy seducer's voice which she and I would practise to our increasing amusement in her apartment over a bottle of wine, she came out with the line we'd told her to say.

'Tell me, Finn, are you a spy?'

This was the signal for the whole table to stop talking and look directly at Finn. I was supposed to read his face.

There was dead silence. It was a foolish, old-fashioned Cold War moment.

But all I saw in Finn's eyes was his continued relaxed amusement. And then, startlingly, he put up his hands like a pickpocket caught in the act.

'How did you guess?' he said.

It was brilliantly done.

It was certainly not what anyone had expected. It threw the business officials at the party into barely concealed consternation. One or two of Drachevsky's managers looked around, breaking the injunction to stay staring at Finn, as if they were personal witnesses to a great diplomatic scandal. 'The Second Secretary of Trade and Investment at the British embassy in Moscow admits to being a spy.' These managers were almost there, at the interview with ORT News, telling the story of the headline with knitted brows and the melodramatic seriousness beloved by TV interviewees.

But I saw immediately that to look at Finn was

not to look at a man who appeared to have confessed to anything at all.

At least silence was maintained in the confusion and the rest of us stayed staring at Finn, hoping, I suppose, to unsettle him. Finn, however, treated us like an audience he had spent hours trying to win. This was his moment of triumph, not defeat, he seemed to say.

'I'm double O zero,' he said, and smiled that open, guileless smile that still makes my stomach tighten when I think of it.

There were a few unrestrained grins around the table; Natasha actually laughed out loud. The brain-dead Chimkov and the snake Alexander kept their blank, trained expressions in place. Drachevsky just looked mildly curious. And as for me, I could not help smiling but I resisted aiming it at Finn and looked down at my plate.

The tension, which we thought we would create, but which Finn had effortlessly usurped, was broken. I suspected then that I had been promoted beyond my ability. I was charmed by him.

Finn pressed home his advantage, supremely confident, every inch the willing entertainer. 'I do know some spies,' he said, as if to compensate for the drudgery of his trade job, and again he rocked those managers who, a moment before, had thought they were at a crucial moment in contemporary history.

'What, here? In Moscow!' one of them said, outraged.

'No,' Finn said, apologetic now that he might have led them to expect too much. His face said how embarrassed he was that he didn't know any spies actually in Moscow. 'No, they're retired now. I only know them socially, I'm afraid.'

Later in the day, Finn called me and asked me to dinner, just as my controllers at the Forest had expected. I accepted, of course. It was my job, after all, but it was easier than I'd feared.

We went to a sushi restaurant which had recently opened up near the church where Pushkin got married; Finn said it was the most expensive dinner he'd ever bought anyone. He'd booked our first room at the Baltschug that night because, as he made clear, he had a discount. I remember I was annoyed by his deliberately aimed presumption. But already he knew I had my orders – we both had our orders – and he decided to make the most of it.

I remember that evening clearly and things Finn said still play over in my mind. He was incredibly indiscreet. He made no attempt to pretend we were anything other than what we were. Looking me in the eye, he said, 'There wouldn't be any need for spies if there weren't any spies, Anna.' And later, in bed, he said, 'You're completely wasted as a colonel, you know. You're the best honey trap there ever was.'

He knew just how to get a rise from me at that first meeting.

One of the reasons why we'd always failed to trap Finn with the spectacular list of professionals we'd lined up for him was because he was so amused by the idea of honey traps. He'd talk to them for hours in order to waste our time, just as some men want only to talk to prostitutes. In this as in other things,

Finn was quite childish and the girls we threw at him were a source of hilarity and disdain for him.

Afterwards, when we'd made love, he said, 'You do realise I'm going to have to use you. I can't kick the youngest female colonel in the KGB out of bed. I'm going to have to sleep with you a lot, if that's OK.'

'Keep up,' I said. We're not the KGB any more. 'We call it the FSB these days.'

But Finn always called us the KGB to the end. 'It's the same thing, isn't it,' he said. 'It's just an old dog with a new name. There's no difference, except that now you've all been to business school as well as Honey Trap High.'

'Are you trying to ruin the evening?' I said.

He turned to me and it was the first time I saw him not play-acting. 'No,' he said. 'No, I don't want to ruin anything.'

We made love again, and afterwards it felt so strange, like we were two lovers who'd known each other for years.

'We've met before, I know it,' Finn said.

'And in what incarnation would that be?' I replied.

He held my hands above my head. 'No incarnation. You were pure dust and so was I.'

I undid his fingers. 'Why don't you do something to jog my memory?' I murmured. But he'd fallen asleep.

Anyway, that's how I first met Finn.

3

NANA'S DACHA AT BARVIKHA had always been my home, in as much as I've ever had a real home and, once our affair began, it became the symbol of home for Finn and me. At any rate, Barvikha was the home of my heart and it became so for Finn too. I now see this symbol we had as part of the spirit that joined us.

In the seventies, when I was a child, I spent more time at Barvikha than anywhere else. Or is it just the happy memories that have expanded those times in my head? My parents lived abroad and Nana brought me up at Barvikha, taking me out of Moscow to the dacha as often as my schooling would allow.

My mother was the daughter of a career diplomat who later became the most favoured economic adviser to the Politburo in the now forgotten days of the Soviet Union. He had one of only a thousand or so personal passes to the Kremlin. But whatever economic advice he gave I don't think he could ever have told his masters the truth; truth consisted of what they, the Politburo, wanted to hear, and my mother's father, Viktor, was their well-trained, patriotic parrot.

My father served in the Foreign Intelligence Service; he was in the KGB's First Chief Directorate, to be exact. This exclusive and privileged organisation, whose agents pursued their intelligence activities abroad, is called the SVR. My father speaks Arabic fluently and he and my mother lived for several years at the embassy in the Soviet compound in Damascus.

We were very privileged but, like most privileged people, we didn't realise it. My mother's family, through Grandfather Viktor, had access to every foreign product available in the Soviet Union and my father's position ensured a comparatively spacious apartment in Moscow, in a well-guarded, well-heated, modern housing block on Leninsky Avenue. The KGB and Military Intelligence had a quota of good apartments there, but our block contained a deliberate mixture of people from other ministries, from the Soviet news service TASS, and so on, so that no one could identify it as an SVR foreign intelligence residence, not even its own occupants.

But everyone knew who the SVR people were, from the licence plates on their cars and the higher standard of the Volga cars themselves, not to mention the military habits of these members of the elite. And then there was their pride. My father was far too proud of his role in the SVR to hide it convincingly from the neighbours.

The apartment block next door to ours was run by Military Intelligence and was for the sole use of foreigners – mainly diplomats, journalists and trade representatives from developing countries.

There were fixed militia posts dotted around this diplomatic block and operatives from KGB counter-intelligence shadowed the two buildings round the clock. When I was six years old my father told me, 'Never, ever approach the diplomatic building or any of its inhabitants.'

Teachers at my school backed this up by telling us that to approach foreigners was 'way outside Soviet rules', so we were all scared of, and fascinated by, contact with foreigners.

But then we had the dacha at Barvikha to escape to. It stands in the beautifully still, evergreen forest south of Moscow, near Yasenovo, the SVR training centre. Yasenovo – a lyrical name – was the SVR's cold heart. But inside the KGB we just called it the Forest.

For Nana and me, Barvikha was a place of great peace, despite the armed guards. Their presence was somehow dwarfed by the great forest. The forest breathed its quiet timelessness and rock-like calm into us both.

The dachas were spread discreetly among the trees, out of sight of each other, and ours was a short walk away from a deep green pond, soft and brackish in the summer, hard-iced and covered with snow in the winter. There was a high fence around the perimeter of the forest, of course, but we didn't notice we were in a special fenced area once we were inside.

'Maupassant always took lunch in the Eiffel Tower,' Finn once told me, 'because he hated it so much, and it was the only place in Paris he couldn't see it.'

So it was with us at Barvikha, though of course we loved the place. But we could somehow look beyond the ugly presence of guards and fences and the instruments of repression because we were on the inside.

'That's what it's like to be on the inside of the KGB,' Nana said. 'If we look out we can't see where we are.'

She was right. From inside the KGB, from inside the KGB's forest, we had the view of the world outside, but we couldn't see the ugliness of our position in the Soviet apparat. And as I sank deeper and deeper into the Russian secret state, I observed less and less of what I was actually doing on its behalf.

Nana preferred to be at the dacha rather than in Moscow and would grumble bitterly when she had to take me back to school after the weekends. She would hurry me out of class on a Friday afternoon and, unless we went to the circus or the fairground, both of which she loved, we would go straight out to Barvikha in one of my father's official cars, just the two of us.

Nana distrusted our KGB privileges more than she disliked them. She was of a generation where nobody was safe, regardless of how exalted they were in the system. But the one privilege she wholeheartedly enjoyed were the two chauffeurs and the official black Volga cars with their special plates and flashing blue lights which could whisk us out to the forest on a Friday night, or back from Barvikha into the centre of Moscow on a Sunday night at high speed, without militia interference.

But in Barvikha she was at home, and so was I. Other than the official cars, she rejected all the elite services we had in Moscow and could have had at Barvikha. She spent her days shuffling across the dacha's worn parquet floors, yellow dusters under her carpet slippers, endlessly buffing the polished wood with her feet. I don't remember that we ever ate with the other residents at the central restaurant block. This block served all the dachas of the elite and you could find every kind of caviar there and other delicacies on demand.

She triumphantly rejected the luxury, mainly foreign, goods we could have brought to the dacha from Moscow, and she and I would go instead into the forest, for mushrooms in the autumn or for berries to make jam in the summer.

We had the pleasing illusion of being self-sufficient when we were at Barvikha, and that illusion was what Nana trusted. She guarded this illusion closely in her jam making and mushroom picking. We lived in a country which was a concrete box of illusions within illusions, topped with barbed wire to protect us from reality, and no one knew that better than us.

My father and his colleagues in the SVR were the only ones in a position to see the truth, the disparity, and could compare us with the outside world.

Nana, like everyone else, had to find the source

of her power elsewhere. She found it in the making of jam and cakes and bread, or foraging for mushrooms and berries.

'The Party doesn't control the wild things,' she said.

'What about the guard dogs?' I asked her in childish innocence.

'They're not wild,' she explained. 'They've been brainwashed too.'

I was confused by this. Three times a week Nana scrubbed my body mercilessly, but the prospect of washing my brain too conjured up many nightmares later.

'What about your cat then?' I persisted.

'She answers to no one,' Nana replied.

And neither did Nana. She answered to no one. To me, she was as real as the bark of a tree, as real as stone, as rainwater. She was of the wild herself.

In 1976, when I was seven, I asked Nana why our leaders always looked so cross. The reason, she said, was that no matter how hard they tried they could never completely take away everyone's power. The impossible task naturally made them very angry. The biggest, most ruthless secret service in the world couldn't control the inner lives of its own people.

'Tyrants become tyrants by force of will,' she said. 'By imposing their power on others. But that's the easy bit. They can never be truly powerful, however, unless they also take away every last morsel of power from other people. And that, as far as I know, is not possible until death.' And she laughed with triumph. 'But then they lose that power anyway to God!'

Nana, like many others, didn't accept the illusions handed down by the state, by my grandfather Viktor, the economic adviser, or my father. Nana chose her own illusions. And she made her chosen illusion her own reality, her power, and in this she was free. It was a lesson I haven't properly understood until now.

In 1976, I went to a school in Moscow reserved for the elite, but, thankfully, not one of the schools attended only by children of KGB officers and which my father considered to be academically slothful and run solely on the basis of privilege. I was lucky in this.

With true Soviet panache, the school was called Number 47. I met a more interesting mixture of people there, many from our apartment block, though I was aware even at that age that I was different, one of only two pupils in the school who was the child of a senior SVR officer. The headmaster was always deferential and I knew of his instruction to other teachers to 'go easy' on me, 'to be careful', to treat me with kid gloves.

I was supposed to make friends with Vladimir, a boy two years older than me, whose father was also in the SVR, but I disobeyed my father's instructions and formed a crush on Misha who was in the same class as me, and the same age. I wrote Misha a letter.

'Dear Misha, I think you are wonderful and I am going to marry you. I am not going to let Eugenia marry you. I hope you still love me. Who are you going to marry? With love from Anna.'

'God, you were bossy,' Finn said when he saw the letter one day as he leafed through my scrapbook that Nana had kept. Afraid of my father, I had never sent it.

Misha had learned to be afraid of me because his parents were afraid of my father. I'd go to his house for tea sometimes, or to play games, and his parents' behaviour towards me was a combination of hope and dread. So I learned that I was apart. As an only child, the solitude of specialness was greatly reinforced by my father's position among the secret elite.

In very different circumstances to mine this is what Finn, too, learned as a child.

It was the summer holidays that, oddly, I dreaded most. I went to see my parents in Damascus and was bored in the confinement of the Soviet compound. We called it the 'colony' and referred to our homes as 'white houses', a typically white, racist Russian expression; in Russia anyone with even a faintly dusky skin – which included everyone in the Soviet southern republics – was considered inferior. But I yearned to be outside the compound, to meet people other than embassy and KGB children with whom I played endless games of table tennis. I felt more like I was a prisoner in our own privileged compound than one of the elite.

It was during one of these summer holidays, when I was fourteen, that I lost my virginity to a teacher from my school in Moscow who my father had paid to come to Damascus to give me private tuition. The teacher and I flew first class from Moscow and, as he was a nervous flyer, he bought a bottle of vodka. He recounted a number of near air crashes he'd been in, then drank three-quarters of the vodka and fell asleep for the rest of the flight. I drank the rest and was sick.

A week later, our chambermaid saw him as he emerged from the laundry room of our house in Damascus. He was reeking of vodka, she said, despite not being airborne. I had fallen asleep in the unwashed clothes, also reeking of vodka.

Though both of us denied everything, he was sent home, lost his job and disappeared. If I am honest, it was I who had seduced him and I tried to blot his fate from my mind.

That summer, in an effort to improve my holiday moods, I was given a Persian kitten by one of my father's diplomatic friends in Damascus and he became my main companion. I called him Genghiz and played with him all the time, eventually taking him back to Moscow. He was a cat with magical powers. He would patrol the neighbourhood around Leninsky Avenue frightening the stray dogs and making the militia's guard dogs whimper. At Barvikha he took over the forest and cowed the KGB guard dogs there too, but he was the best of friends with Nana's Siberian cat whom he protected.

I was eleven when I first learned my father was a spy. He told me why our lives were different from those of the others on embassy territory. Even the ambassador, I'd noticed, treated my father with unnatural respect. And my father was always working.

'The SVR are the workhorses of the Soviet state,' he told me, as though reading from some thirties manual of appropriate slogans. 'Diplomats are there thanks only to their Party connections.'

With little attempt to disguise it, he despised my mother's father Viktor for his diplomatic status.

But to me his remark was a terrible insight into who ruled in Russia and who still, effectively, rules today. Nobody ever mentioned the people at all then, except as an ideological abstract. Nor do they now. But wasn't it our people who worked in the factories and fields who were the workhorses of the state? No, they were just glue. Try asking a Russian MP today what the people would like and you'll be met by the blankest stare of incomprehension. It is not even cynicism, in my opinion. The people are actually invisible.

'The people are the grease in the machine,' my father said once.

Russian elitism remains unchanged from the Middle Ages and is far worse than anything in the West.

When my father wasn't toiling as a workhorse of the state in a 'normal' way – in other words, engaged in the SVR's fight against the waves of truth that threatened to wash over the Soviet Union – I remember him sitting in an upholstered red leather swivel armchair in his private study. I was forbidden to enter, but on the occasions when I broke into his sanctum, I always saw him drinking. Even as a child, I thought 'Why does he always drink? What is he hiding? He's trying to avoid the truth.'

These drinking sessions often went on long into the night. Scotch whisky was what drew his drinking partners, who came and went unannounced, and he always had a ready supply from Grandfather Viktor, though he still despised Viktor for these 'unearned' privileges.

My mother, intelligent, educated, witty, would do stray and unchallenging embassy jobs as a typist or telephone operator. The position of the housewife was revered in the Soviet Union, rather as the cow is revered by Hindus. It was a state policy that clumsily blundered over, and then blunted, a natural instinct, I thought. They nationalised some normal human instincts, while others they simply crushed.

So as a housewife my mother's unused degree in philology became merely a status symbol for my father and lay mouldering in the attic of her past.

Sometimes, very rarely, there'd be something to cause a ripple of excitement in Damascus – for me, at any rate.

One July day when, as usual, I was playing table tennis in the hot dusty compound, my father's secretary ran outside to tell me to come immediately. Inside the house, my father and mother and a man I didn't recognise were standing around a beautiful cello, which my father had bought for my mother a few months before. They were standing at a safe distance, as if the cello was an unexploded bomb. Everyone was silent, my father was frowning, my mother looked scared.

'Is this certain?' she said faintly, and my father grunted.

He'd bought the cello from a colleague of his, at our embassy in Libya.

As I stood and watched, curious at this tense scene, I learned that, on the day before, the colleague of my father's had defected to the Americans. We all stared at the cello in horror. My father finally covered it up with a bedsheet, as if it were a corpse.

For weeks afterwards, KGB counter-intelligence officers came down from Moscow, unable to comprehend how my father could have bought a cello from someone who would, at some future date, defect. In the eyes of these officers the cello was a clue. It somehow contained the virus of defection. So it was taken to pieces, deliberately broken, and never fixed and put back together. My mother never played a cello again.

For two weeks my mother and I and Genghiz had to stay in our house on the compound, with the windows and blinds shut in the stifling heat, while KGB officers raked over everything and guarded all the entrances, in case the cello made a dash for it, or had the power to make us all defect too. Suspicion and fear ruled the house. My mother went grey, my father's anger revealed the fear behind it more than usual. But I found it comical that a cello could cause so much panic.

After the incident with my tutor, my parents realised they'd be happier without me unhappy in Damascus and allowed me – as if it were solely for my benefit – to stay in Russia during the summer holidays.

'It's better for her education,' I heard my father say from behind their bedroom door. My mother complied, though I knew she didn't want me to go. For many years – and despite the fact that I was overjoyed to spend my summers with Nana at Barvikha – I blamed her for giving in to his will. He felt judged by me, perhaps, by my silent looks that questioned his behaviour, and wanted me out of the house. But she was too weak to stand up for me, or for herself. I vowed I would never be weak like her.

After that, all my holidays were spent at Barvikha with Nana and Genghiz and I only saw my mother and father two or three times a year when they came on leave to Moscow or I spent a few unwilling days over Christmas with them in Damascus.

From then on, I devoted myself to my studies, determined to become a workhorse of the state, instead of a 'weak woman'. I was top or near the top in my class and I learned to speak fluent English. I read everything I could, including the banned foreign books my mother's family had access to. I wrote poetry and short stories and dreamed of travel to foreign countries and I passed my exams with flying colours. As the Soviet empire began to totter in the middle of the eighties, I was a young trainee in the KGB.

From a thin, gangly, sulky schoolgirl, I grew into a woman. I let my black hair grow long, down to my waist, and it accentuated my height. Slavic cheekbones appeared out of the puppy fat on my face. And my green eyes, Vladimir told me, could be seen from across the street. I became, Vladimir said, a classic Russian beauty and, in response to this flattery of Vladimir's, I chose not him but my fencing trainer as my first real lover. Occasionally I would be approached at a party to play some Soviet heroine at the Mosfilm studios outside Moscow. Of course, I could never accept these offers.

By the time my parents returned to Moscow on long leave, they'd become estranged from each other. My father stayed in a separate apartment, although careful to maintain the fiction of their marriage. To my father's disgust, when Gorbachev came to power in the middle of the decade, my mother began to work for the Sakharov human rights organisation.

My parents' false marriage affected me in unexpected ways. My father began to take me out to official functions in place of my mother. I knew it was because my youth and beauty reflected well on him. And I hated him for it.

By the beginning of the eighties the Soviet Union was nearing the end of its irreversible decline, and then the genial Ronald Reagan raised the stakes still further by placing a new missile system in Western Europe. This decline had been going on for a long time, of course, but nobody really understood it except the SVR – our agents abroad – who could see the outside world most clearly. The truth had become so devalued that it had effectively ceased to exist. Even the Politburo had to be told by the KGB, who learned from the SVR, that things weren't what they wanted them to be. Like anyone else, the complacent Communist Party bosses in their closed enclave of the Politburo chose to believe their own illusions.

In 1982, mainly for this reason – a final recognition that decline was irreversible without change, and that the intelligence services were our country's only hope of survival – the Politburo appointed the KGB boss Yuri Andropov as leader, and our first KGB president. Where before the KGB had been a servant of the Party, this fateful move was the beginning of a reversal of that hierarchy. My father was very pleased.

'At last we've got someone who knows how to run the country,' he said angrily. 'A real professional, not some politician.'

Years later when I told Finn of my father's remark, he said it almost exactly mirrored what was said in Britain when someone with a life outside politics became a minister in the British Government.

'But at least in England it's always someone from the business world, not a spy chief,' Finn said. 'Spies in England work for Her Majesty's Government.'

For some reason I'm always amused by this expression.

But the phrase 'At last we've got someone who knows how to run the country' became a running joke for Finn and me whenever someone in a foreign country came to power. At the diplomatic parties we attended together in Moscow, an official would say, 'I see that chap Berlusconi has got in in Italy', and Finn or I, or worse still, both of us together, would say, 'At last they've got someone who knows how to run the country.' And then both of us would burst out laughing at our private joke. It was a child's game and we upset a lot of pompous old diplomatic bores that way.

And that was one of the first things I noticed Finn did for me. He lifted me out of my hitherto serious, even repressed, behaviour. He eroded my solemn and determined ambition to be a workhorse of the state with his gleeful, carefree frivolity. I found it – the recklessness of his behaviour – new and exciting.

'You know, Rabbit,' he told me, 'your seriousness exposes the disguise of my frivolity, and my frivolity exposes the disguise of your seriousness.'

And so we played with and reacted to each other's character opposites – in this and other ways – like two dissonant musical instruments which, combined, made sweet music. We slowly lured each other out of our inner hiding places. We dropped the emotional barbed wire that we'd both used to protect ourselves. And we fell in love with the differences we saw revealed in each other. I looked in the mirror of Finn and he looked in mine, and we began to see who we could be, who we really were.

Finn used to list the things he loved about me, in a sort of league table of characteristics that changed positions according to his whims. But I remember one true and beautiful thing he said, from early in our relationship, which stuck in my mind more than others.

We were in a corner suite at the Marco Polo Hotel, north of Pushkinskaya and our room looked down on to the ice park.

'I forget how to pretend when I'm with you,' Finn said to me.

And I felt the same way about being with him. I'd fallen like a stone, but what I said was: 'You think you're good at pretending?'

'Are you?' he said, smiling.

'Yes. Better than you by a million miles.'

'Pretend this, then,' he said, and he kissed me.

But Finn's reckless frivolity got him into trouble with others, particularly his masters at the British embassy, on more than one occasion.

'It is symptomatic of your behaviour,' was the way Finn's head of station put it. 'You don't seem to take anything seriously any more.'

But he was wrong on both counts. First, Finn hardly ever took anything seriously.

'There's hardly anything worth taking seriously,' he would say.

And, second, when he did take something seriously, he took it more seriously than anyone, his head of station included, could possibly have imagined.

4

I T WAS NOT ONLY my father who was delighted when Andropov came to power, but also the whole of the KGB. And as soon as he had power, the old spy pursued a two-pronged policy. He ruthlessly put down dissent, including punishing people who committed economic crimes, and simultaneously he set about loosening the same reins a little by allowing a small, KGB-controlled experiment in free trade.

This was hugely significant in terms of how Russia has developed. A few carefully chosen so-called *buzinessmen* – traders with their own semi-legal *tzekhs*, or workshops – were allowed to conduct business while at the same time being closely monitored by the security services.

What Andropov and his cronies failed to see – or, more probably, exploited – was that the only people who could take advantage of these little windows of opportunity were the criminal elements, the mafia, the men who had conducted business throughout the history of the Soviet Union. They were the only people who knew what to do.

And so the mafia were the first to benefit from perestroika when it finally arrived under Gorbachev in 1985. They were already in pole position, the only ones with money. By the nineties they had completely entrenched their power. And with them were their allies in the KGB who watched over them and shared in the spoils. Thus the secret state and the mafia state were married in a devil's pact.

'It was the KGB itself who managed perestroika right from the beginning,' Finn said. 'Perestroika was an invention of the KGB's.'

But from inside the KGB I couldn't see it.

For my final exams, I wrote a short story, which won me a prize at school. It was a fictional tale about the last man to be executed in the Soviet Union for possession of more than ten thousand dollars; holding more than ten thousand dollars was still a capital offence under Gorbachev.

The story was called, 'Not a Great Start to the Day', a tongue-in-cheek title that echoed the thoughts of the condemned man as he looked out of his cell window on to the execution yard on his final morning on earth, and saw that it was snowing. My father was furious that I appeared to see injustice in the man's execution.

After my parents returned to Moscow, all the years I'd spent with Nana in the capital and at the dacha in Barvikha, with only brief visits from them, hadn't prepared me for the fact that my father evidently felt he still had complete power over my future.

Like our leaders, my father always looked angry. Sometimes his crossness spilled into rage and that always terrified me, until I learned to suppress my fear. My mother, however, never seemed to lose her nerve.

'He has a very stressful job,' she'd say. 'He has to think about everything.'

I couldn't understand, if his life was so bad, why he didn't simply change it, get another job – retire, even. Fearful now of the change in my relationship with him, as he demanded I accompany him to functions, I didn't fully understand that he endured a constricting fear that killed his self-expression. He lived in fear from the past, too; a fear that would eventually infect me.

What I also didn't know, until much later, was that he worked in the most secret department of the SVR that dealt with *nelegali*, illegals. These were foreign nationals who had come to train in Russia in order to strike against their own countries. This department was called Department S. My father was a major recruiter of citizens of Syria and neighbouring countries and ran a vitally important network in the Middle East. He was a personal friend of Yasser Arafat.

But to me he was just a dangerous, lonely, angry man, who had, therefore, to be manipulated carefully. I remember one terrible night, when, after a state function, we had returned to one of the several apartments in Moscow that seemed to be at his disposal. He was drunker than usual, and began to manhandle me, though I couldn't say for certain that it was molestation. I gave him more and more vodka until eventually he fell asleep. When I confronted him the next day, he said I had imagined the whole thing.

Twice he tried to marry me off to the sons of colleagues, including Vladimir, the older boy from school Number 47 whom I'd been instructed to befriend and with whom I'd maintained a distant friendship throughout our schooldays. Vladimir even asked me to marry him when I was seventeen and my father went into a fury when I refused. I didn't want to end up like my mother, a necessary addition to a husband's career. I didn't want to be a woman whose job was to 'understand' her husband.

In avoiding that trap, I ended up in another.

Perhaps it was compensation for my refusal to marry Vladimir or any of my father's choices that led me, subconsciously, to try to please him in other ways. And that was *my* weakness, believing I could still have a proper relationship with a man like him at all. But it was for this reason that I applied to study at the secret KGB training establishment at Yasenovo – the Forest – to the south of Moscow.

My application pleased my father. I did it without thinking, through a compulsion that was stronger than my base instincts. All the years of Nana's sharp but gentle influence were swept away by obedience to the powerful hold I allowed my father to exert on me. If anything, the years of absence from my parents increased my desire to please him.

Nana never said a word when I told her – and that told me all I needed to know. Nana couldn't have passed a KGB exam to save her life, but she despised the organisation. She used to tell me jokes about the KGB, in the woods, with a carelessness that old people so magnificently grow into. Nana and Genghiz saw eye to eye on the subject of our intelligence services. While Genghiz mocked their guard dogs, Nana mocked them.

But Nana made one far-sighted remark, an illustration of the visionary or psychic power behind her watery grey eyes. And even though I didn't understand her at the time, I see it now.

'Something good will come of it,' was all she said.

As I drifted almost in a dream state into the arms of our security services, I wondered how anything good could come from joining the KGB. And yet that was how I would meet Finn, my one true love.

5

THE KRASNOZNAMENNIY INSTITUTE, or KI, was where women trained for the KGB. I studied there for three years, and then went on to put my training into practice at Balashiha-2, in the forest to the east of Moscow. There I trained foreign female subversives, the *nelegali*, whose eventual role was to return to their own countries and undermine them with terrorist activities.

During this time, I also lectured to the male KGB students in Vishka, or the Tower, as it was called.

Balashiha-2 is both the strongroom of the Kremlin and its arsenal and training ground for covert and subversive operations, hidden in the vast forest fifteen miles east of Moscow. To keep the capital's population obedient it hosts the notorious Dzerzhinskaya army division, but Balashiha's real usefulness lies in its highly secret training camp for KGB units involved in foreign operations. They call this the Centre of Special Purposes. It is where the paramilitary *spetsnaz* are based, or special forces units like Vympel, the Alfa Group and the *nelegali* in the 'Foreigners' Area'.

To all of us the SVR, Russia's foreign intelligence service, was called the Forest. The Forest then and today is the centre of Russia's subversive operations abroad.

My admission to the Forest was not as easy as my impeccable background would suggest. Though my father had friends there, they could only facilitate interviews, not help me through them. I was interviewed intensely for weeks and what caused me most trouble was the short story I'd written at school, 'Not a Great Start to the Day'.

Was I sympathetic to the condemned man in his cell awaiting execution, as my father had accused me? Did I believe in American free-market activities, which the condemned man was guilty of pursuing? Was I critical of the law and the arm of the law that executed the guilty criminal?

The interview when the subject of the short story was raised took place early one morning, out at Balashiha. One of my three interrogators asked me: 'Why do you sympathise with the guilty man in your story?'

'I make him seem convincing,' I answered. 'That isn't the same thing as sympathising.'

'But he should not seem convincing!' he demanded. The man had thick lips, and eyes like shale.

To their consternation, I stood up and drained my glass of water. Then I looked him in the eye.

'The guilty are never convincing, Comrade. Were you convinced?'

I found that manipulation came effortlessly. I convinced them that the story was the opposite of what I knew it to be, that it was in fact highly unsympathetic to the condemned man. They were pleased. I realised then that great manipulators are themselves susceptible to manipulation.

Some of the assessment was absurd, like something out of a KGB manual from Stalin's time – which, in some cases, it was. Despite my impeccable linguistic qualifications, they tested my English language from a schoolbook written in 1941. The first three lines were, 'Long Live International Youth Day! Long Live the Communist Party! Long Live Comrade Stalin!' – conversational gambits that I've never found particularly useful.

The book was a story concerning two schoolchildren, Sasha and Misha. My favourite chapter in it was called 'Two Little Patriots', in which Sasha and Misha go for a walk in the woods near the border and see something behind a tree, which turns out to be a man. He is wearing white clothes and is carrying a white bag, and is all but invisible against the snow. The boys realise he is a spy. They alert the border guards and the man is arrested. 'He is a spy!' the KGB officer, who dashes to the scene, proclaims. 'Well done, boys!'

'Well done, boys!' later became another coded phrase between myself and Finn. We uttered it whenever we wished to indicate a disastrous decision by our respective leaders.

My time at Krasnoznamenniy taught me to speak English like a native, to handle weapons, to make IEDs – or improvised explosive devices – and most of the arts of self-defence. And my time at the Forest put this training into action as I then trained others.

I also endured the increasingly unconvincing political 'education', which nobody seemed to take seriously any more. Few people really believed what they were told about the West. Once, it had been necessary to induce a fear of the West so great that it overshadowed the fear ordinary people, at any rate, had of our own system. But not any more, not by the late eighties. By 1989, we didn't even use the title 'KGB' among ourselves, so discredited had the organisation become.

As Gorbachev dismantled the Soviet Union, morale in the organisation was lower than ever and it reached rock bottom under Boris Yeltsin's presidency. Our training went on, just as before, but without the ideological underpinning.

But the Forest had its entertaining aspects, if, like me, you were given to silent mockery. I particularly enjoyed the company of Dato and Zviad, a Georgian and an Armenian. They were in a special division of mainly Georgian and Armenian men who were training to be homosexual honey traps. Finn loved my stories about this division and he used to glow with the gleeful enjoyment of joking about homosexual honey traps when he was at Moscow's diplomatic parties even when, once again, he was warned to stop by the British embassy.

'Practising being a practising homosexual,' Finn called it.

In 1991, just as I was finishing my training, Gorbachev was put under house arrest at his villa in Sochi on the Black Sea. I came back to Moscow that August, just before the coup took place. I saw the Dzerzhinskaya division enter the city in the early hours of the coup and watched with foreboding as the new and short-lived 'President' Yanayev visibly trembled as he promised us Russians that Gorbachev's reforms would continue.

Yanayev and the KGB general at the head of the coup, Kryuchkov, were clearly way out of their depth and received little support, even from the special forces. The coup leaders had seized power in a haze of nostalgia for the 'good old days', which they were perhaps too drunk to realise had never gone away.

This inept coup set back plans that, unknown to all but very few in the KGB, were well under way. These plans had been drawn up to manage the transition from Communist Party rule to a new Russia. Instead, however, Boris Yeltsin filled the vacuum left by the bumbling coup leaders. Yeltsin became the hero. He stood on a battle tank and won over the people and the army. The coup was crushed and three days later I watched from the Lubyanka as crowds advanced on our old KGB headquarters. At the last minute, as we held our breath before wreaking death on the streets, the mob turned away and toppled the statue of Felix Dzerzhinsky, the founder of our secret police.

I was twenty-three years old and it was the oddest time to be starting a career in the KGB. Freedom, real freedom, at last seemed within reach of us Russians for the first time in our history.

By the time I met Finn seven years later my career path had accelerated me to the rank of colonel. He had been Second Secretary of Trade and Investment at the British embassy for those eight years, under surveillance by us and confidently marked down as SIS, MI6, a British spy.

My father, remote, claustrophobic and sinister, was pleased with my swift rise and the good reports of my progress, which he read avidly. My mother didn't seem to care. Nana just laughed and called me 'Colonel' when she wanted to annoy me.

When I met Finn I had grown out of my affair with my fencing trainer, because – I'm ashamed to admit – he was too nice. I was having an affair with a 'Hero of the Soviet Union' called Alex. A hard man, forty-eight years old and from the Vympel *spetsnaz* group, Alex was one of the small team that had entered the presidential palace in Kabul on Christmas Eve in 1979 when the USSR overthrew the regime in Afghanistan.

'The Russians always choose the most inconvenient times to do their evil deeds,' Finn always said.

Alex had lost his leg during the Afghan campaign afterwards, but the presidential raid was highly successful, with several key murders accomplished. It plunged Afghanistan into the chaos that plagues it to the present day.

Alex was twenty years older than me. Finn was only twelve years older. Nana said I had a father complex, 'but at least you are showing signs of improvement,' she said.

6

DEAR RUSSIANS, very little time remains to a momentous date in our history. The year 2000 is upon us, a new century, a new millennium. We have all measured this date against ourselves, working out – first in childhood, then after we grew up – how old we would be in the year 2000, how old our mothers would be, and our children.'

Boris Yeltsin's wandering voice faded and rose from our new television screen, like that of a man talking in the wind.

'Back then,' the President continued, 'it seemed such a long way off to this extraordinary New Year. So now the day has come.'

Finn shifts on the sofa. 'It's certainly a miracle he's made it,' he says facetiously, as we watch Yeltsin's face on the screen, a face with all the mobility of botched plastic surgery.

Finn and Nana and I have just finished a late supper and are curled up in front of the fire to watch the New Year speech Yeltsin has made a habit of delivering. Finn is drinking brandy on the sofa, munching peanuts, and stroking Genghiz. He is over-engaged as so often. I am lying with my head on his stomach. Nana, who rarely sits down because of her arthritis, is sliding on her slippers across the dacha's parquet floors like a robotic vacuum cleaner.

'This is like being back home,' Finn says. 'Watching the Queen making her speech on Christmas Day. Except with Yeltsin you have the added excitement that he's going to die in mid-speech. You never get that with the Queen,' he says with mock disappointment.

Outside the windows, a snowstorm is raging; it is wild weather, and Finn insists we keep the curtains open so he can watch the wind and snow in the light of the porch lamp. Eight years in Russia hasn't diminished his fondness for snow.

After a year of knowing Finn, Nana and I are used to his remarks. He always enjoys providing a running commentary to whatever is on television. There is a part of Finn, I think, that secretly yearns to be an entertainer and the television is the perfect instrument to heckle without the risk of any comeback.

Yeltsin's voice emerges from his old Russian face, puffy and sick from heart problems and alcohol. The tricks of the television studio don't really do it justice. Make-up conceals much of the problem but still the ailing president gives the impression of being propped up on a Kremlin film set, with our new Russian flag displayed regally behind him. In this respect, he looks like so many of our past leaders from Soviet times, cardboard cut-outs propped up on platforms to watch troops and tanks and missiles file past through Red Square. Unlike them, however, I've always thought Yeltsin's face was essentially kind, not angry.

We are at Barvikha – me, Nana and Finn. It is the last day of the millennium. By this time in the evening the sky has darkened behind thick winter clouds. A wind ruffles the trees and the end of a hanging branch scratches back and forth on the wood-tiled roof of the dacha.

By now I have begun to know Finn personally, intimately. Of course I knew everything about him as a target of intelligence long before. I've read his KGB file many times while sitting in the sealed ante-room of General Kerchenko's office. Kerchenko was the old KGB hardliner from Brezhnev's day, who was my case officer on Finn. I would sit in this heavily disinfected room at the Forest – I never knew why so much disinfectant was necessary – and pore over the photographs of Finn on his own or with a string of women in Moscow's nightclubs, many of whom were our own honey traps. I read the transcripts of his conversations and looked for hours into his strange eyes, trying to see the mind behind them. In these photographs, he seemed constantly amused, carefree, knowing. I'd got to know the muscles in his face and tried to fit the transcripts of his conversations to its changing expressions.

I got to know his mannerisms and his accent and his conversational tics, his habits, and his likes and dislikes. I knew his history, or that part of it we had been able to piece together in order, we hoped, to use it against him. I had been briefed endlessly on the subject of Finn, and I'd read his file a hundred times, so that when we finally met it was like meeting a character from a favourite book.

'Dear friends, my dears,' Yeltsin stumbles on – not at all like the Queen, Finn says – 'today I am wishing you New Year greetings for the last time. But that is not all. Today I am addressing you for the last time as Russian President. I have made a decision. I have contemplated this long and hard. Today, on the last day of the outgoing century, I am retiring.'

Finn puts his glass down on the small cherry-wood table next to the sofa and Nana stops her shoe shuffle. She and I look at the screen in shock. I can't see Finn's face from where I'm lying. I had no idea beforehand of the contents of Yeltsin's speech but this was not what any of us had imagined.

'Many times I have heard it said,' the President continues, '"Yeltsin will try to hold on to power by any means, he won't hand it over to anyone." That is all lies. That is not the case. I have always said that I would not take a single step away from the constitution, that the Duma elections should take place within the constitutional timescale. This has happened.

'And, likewise, I would have liked the presidential elections to have taken place on schedule in June 2000. That was very important for Russia – we were creating a vital precedent of a civilised, voluntary handover of power from one president of Russia to another, newly elected one.'

Not sure now what we're watching, all three of us are suddenly enthralled. Even Finn is silenced. I see his hand stop stroking Genghiz and now it weighs down heavy and immobile on the cat's stomach until Genghiz struggles free from it and walks off in a huff, shaking his flattened fur.

I lift my head from Finn's lap and sit up and look at the screen at that electrifying moment. My long black hair is tousled where I've been lying on it and Nana distractedly untangles it from behind the sofa, as she's always done since I was a little girl.

'This is great,' Finn says. 'Yeltsin always knows how to grip an audience. It's just like eight years ago, when he stood on the tank outside the White House.'

'Turn it up a bit,' Nana says, and Finn reaches for the remote control.

Yeltsin talks on, about the surprise of his decision, its unscheduled nature, and says that Russia should enter the new millennium with younger men at the helm. He says that he has done his job and that, now the worst is over, Russia will always be moving forward, never returning to the past.

'The past is already here, that's why,' Finn says. 'The past is dictating the present.'

Finn is right. The past that haunts Russia in all its terrible identities, and that haunts Russians, is standing behind Yeltsin's veiled words like the shadow of Death.

'Why hold on to power for another six months,' Yeltsin continues, 'when the country has a strong person, fit to be president, with whom practically all Russians link their hopes for the future today? Why should I stand in his way?'

'Oh God,' Finn murmurs. 'Oh no.' I look at him, but his face is fixed to the screen.

Yeltsin rambles now, about his desire to be forgiven for not fulfilling some of the hopes of the Russian people; of the huge difficulties he'd faced in taking the leap from a grey, stagnating, totalitarian past into a bright, rich and civilised future in one go.

'Today it is important for me to tell you the following,' he says. 'I also experienced the pain which each of you experienced. I experienced it in my heart, with sleepless nights, agonising over what needed to be done to ensure that people lived more easily and better, if only a little.'

Dimly, from outside the dacha, the muffled sound of a car starting its engine filters through the falling snow and the forest's trees. And then another follows, and another, one by one and slowly, like the staggered start to a long cross-country race.

'Everyone now goes to Moscow,' Nana remarks. 'To pay homage to Yeltsin's heir.'

Finn pours himself another brandy.

'So,' Finn says, 'that's it, then. A civilised, voluntary handover of power from one president of Russia to another,' he echoes Yeltsin's words. 'In other words, Putin gets to be president if he gives Yeltsin immunity from prosecution.'

We look at the sick man on television like awe-struck children.

'I am leaving,' Yeltsin continues. 'I have done everything I can. I am not leaving because of my health, but because of all the problems taken together. A new generation is taking my place, a generation of those who can do more, and do it better.

In accordance with the constitution, as I go into retirement, I have signed a decree entrusting the duties of President of Russia to Prime Minister Vladimir Vladimirovich Putin.

'For the next three months, again in accordance with the constitution, he will be head of state. Presidential elections will be held in three months. I have always had confidence in the amazing wisdom of Russian citizens. Therefore, I have no doubt what choice you will make at the end of March 2000.'

This bitter flattery of Yeltsin's to deceive the Russian people, this endorsement of the man who has, as Finn predicts, given him immunity from prosecution, is the real beginning of the new era when Yeltsin's attempts to lead Russia to democracy are finally abandoned.

'In saying farewell, I wish to say to each of you the following,' Yeltsin continues. 'Be happy. You deserve happiness. You deserve happiness and peace. Happy New Year, happy new century, my dear people.'

Before the national anthem has finished there is the sound of more official cars crunching across the snow towards the main road to Moscow.

And that is how, on New Year's Eve in 2000, we Russians learned we had a new president. Vladimir Putin, only the second KGB boss after Yuri Andropov to achieve this, slips quietly into power. But this time, unlike back then, it takes place in our bright, new, democratic Russia.

7

FINN GETS UP, walks over to the window, stretches, and looks out.

'So they're all leaving for the city,' he says. 'I suppose I should hurry along to the embassy like a good boy too. They'll want to code a special British welcome to the new chief.'

He pauses by the window and carries on looking out at the heavy snow falling in the pitch darkness and lit only by the porch light. The track from the dacha is always kept clear and the road out to the motorway into Moscow is open even in extreme conditions. I watch him watching the red tail-lights streaming towards the motorway.

'Why would anyone want to leave a little wooden house in the forest, with a warm fire blazing inside, to go to the city on New Year's Eve?' Nana asks him. She approaches Finn to put a hand on his arm.

'Typical bloody Russians,' Finn says to her and forces a smile. 'Why do you always choose our holidays to change the world? Why don't you use your own bloody holidays?'

'Telephone them at the embassy,' Nana urges him. 'Say you're sick. Say you've been poisoned,' she giggles.

We are always joking about poisoning Finn, Nana and I, ever since he'd told us he'd been warned by the embassy to be on his guard against it. Now, it seems like a bad joke. But back then, there was still some light in the East, as Finn put it. I had taught Nana the English words, 'Doing him in', and she would go around the dacha when Finn was staying, muttering about 'doing him in' to his face, and cackling loudly.

But the idea of Finn being poisoned seemed to have lodged itself in the mind of Finn's station head at the embassy.

'I don't see any reason why you shouldn't see this girl Anna,' Tom, Finn's station head, had told him.

'OK, Tom.'

'In fact, it might be useful if you do. If we can learn something from it. We're trying to get a profile on her for you. She's new, she's young, no record, but she's straight out of the Forest, we know that much.'

Tom thought for a moment.

'Only thing is, what if they grab you, Finn, when you're in Barvikha? Poison you, and you spill out all our lovely secrets?'

'I'll eat only off Anna's plate,' Finn told him.

'We'll have a watch on you, of course, but we can't follow you in there.'

'I'll wave from the end of the road every hour.'

'Just remember, Finn. You're supposed to be tapping her, not the other way round.'

'Oh, don't worry. I'll tap her all right,' Finn said, but this rare crude allusion was lost on his boss.

In retrospect, Finn and I saw the window that had briefly opened for us to be together in the year leading up to the millennium as one of those fleeting moments in history when two opposing sides seem temporarily to be struck with amnesia about why they are fighting.

The British would never have allowed Finn to come on to KGB territory, either before that brief historical moment at the end of Yeltsin's presidency or after it. The end of the Yeltsin era, the final years of the 1990s, opened the window to our relationship for a camera-flash instant, before it was slammed shut again under Putin. At any other time, we would have seized Finn immediately to suck out the marrow of his professional life, before handing him back – empty, soul-destroyed, useless – in exchange for some similar unfortunate from our side whom the British possessed.

Our luck – Finn's and mine – was to benefit from that moment when history paused, like the crest of a wave, before gathering its force to move on again.

'It's a moment,' Finn once said, 'like the one in the First World War when British and German troops stopped killing each other for a day and played football instead.'

Finn and I took advantage of the moment given to us.

One of our early meetings was at the Tretyakov Gallery in Moscow where Finn was particularly fascinated by Petrov-Vodkin's painting, 'The Bathing of a Red Horse'.

We walked around the gallery together until we stopped at this painting. Both Finn and I noticed the man in a black fur hat and black coat and the woman wearing a rabbit-skin hat and a thick Scandinavian herringbone coat. They were behind us, apparently looking at other works on the walls, but not really seeing what they were looking at.

'Guess which one of them is your side,' Finn said and grinned at me. 'Or do you know?'

'I don't know what you mean,' I said.

'Come on, Anna.' Finn grinned more broadly at me. 'I bet you a thousand roubles the man's one of ours.'

Even though Finn and I had already openly discussed our own roles in this seduction, I still tried to maintain the pretence that we had met casually, that our affair had nothing to do with anyone but us.

As Second Secretary for Trade and Investment, Finn had long been marked down by us as a member of the Service. He'd been in Moscow too long and he practically had 'spy' written all over him. He would joke in public about his job, a ruse he called a double bluff and which, admittedly, confused us for a while. In fact, it was only when, in late November

1998, we eavesdropped on a recording of his station head telling him to stop joking about being a spy that we knew he was a spy.

'I'll have to go,' Finn now says unenthusiastically, standing up. 'Putin!' he chokes. 'How perfect is that. The put-in. God! And God save Russia.'

'Is that the view of your government or just your own?' I ask him as I lean in a mockingly seductive way with my back to the fireplace. He grins at my pretence to be doing my job.

We have a game, Finn and I, saying one thing we each know about the other from our professional research. I'll say, 'You were brought up in a hippy commune in Ireland by your mother and her hippy lover.'

He'll reply, 'You went to school Number 47 and were brought up by Nana because your father was stationed abroad with the SVR.'

Then I might say, 'At the age of twelve you were taken by an uncle away from your drug-addict mother and sent to a crammer near Cambridge.'

Usually he's the first to say something below the belt. 'At school when you were fourteen you were caught having sex with a teacher. He was punished, you weren't.'

'On our files you are a notorious womaniser. Despite your age,' I'll add.

One of us eventually attacks the other physically and the game will end with us wrestling on the floor, or on the bed, or in the forest.

When we make love, Finn says afterwards, 'I

don't know what sort of crap we've got as researchers these days, but I've read a hundred times you're not a pushover.'

'Whereas you are such an easy lay,' I say.

Now, Finn's face is troubled.

'What's the point?' he says, and slumps back down on to the sofa. 'I can't sit in the embassy discussing Putin on New Year's Eve. We'll all have plenty of time to talk about the little creep.' He turns to me. 'Anyway, Rabbit, you can tell me all about him, can't you? Give me something to justify my staying at Barvikha. Throw me some bones so I can impress them all tomorrow. I have to do some intelligence work. It's my job.'

Nana cackles delightedly.

'Let's toast Vladimir Putin,' she enthuses mockingly. 'Long live the KGB!' She boosts Finn's glass of brandy and pours a glass of vodka for herself. She rarely drinks alcohol. And we all, in our own ways, drink to forget.

8

WHEN FINN AND I had met a year before, at the end of 1998, our now new and unelected President, Vladimir Vladimirovich Putin, was prime minister under Boris Yeltsin. Nobody knew anything about him outside his close St Petersburg circle and the KGB. He had an approval rating well below twenty per cent among the population.

So he decided to wage war against Chechnya, to avenge the earlier Russian defeat there under Yeltsin. It was a hugely popular war. Chechens died by the tens of thousands and the Russian dead were flown back home secretly. Putin's ruthlessness soon tripled his popularity rating among the Russian people.

In a rare moment at a news conference in Belgium, Putin's mask slipped. When a Western journalist questioned his murderous tactics and the

Russian atrocities in Chechnya, Putin snapped back at him.

'Come to Russia,' he said, 'and we'll circumcise you so that it'll never grow back.'

This was our new president.

But now in the listlessness that grips us at the dacha, instead of pressuring me to tell him what I know about our new KGB president, Finn begins to tell us what he knows about Putin. It's a strange moment, theatrical, even, and Finn talks half to himself, as if he's reading a story.

It's a story that, in truth, begins in 1961. As he tells it to us, Finn sits by the fire, cradling his tumbler of brandy. He knows he's being recorded from somewhere in the room. My people, much to Nana's annoyance, have of course wired up the dacha to catch his every word.

Much later, at the vault in Tegernsee, I realised – too late – that this was the turning point. At this instant in the dacha at Barvikha, Finn made his decision. The stand he chose to make began here, in the home of our hearts. Sitting by the crackling fire, he began to throw away his secret life and, as I now realise, he was throwing it away for my sake.

When Finn decided something, he decided it quickly. And events would then unravel very fast. He had the capacity to think fast and very far ahead on these occasions. As it turned out, the telling of this story put into play all that was to follow. From that afternoon at Barvikha what has happened to Finn and me was set in motion.

His aim was later to become clear to me, but it wasn't clear at the time. He had a plan, for far into the future, to make sure we could share our lives together without the artificial, professional barriers preventing it. And it was for that reason alone that he began the process of burning his boats.

Six years later, picking up Finn's first notebook and reading it by the light of the oil lamp in the vault at Tegernsee, it is an eerie experience. The first lines written in Finn's hand are word for word what he said on that evening, the eve of the millennium.

'For me,' Finn begins, settling a cushion behind his lower back and tickling Genghiz under the chin, 'the story began in January 1989. Although it really started back in 1961.

'In 1989, I was stationed in West Berlin. One grey middle-European winter night an East German citizen by the name of Anatoly Schmidtke landed on a flight from Geneva at Berlin's Tegel airport. The flight was less than half full and he was easy to spot. He was stopped and arrested immediately by the British. We controlled the zone around Tegel. Berlin was still divided into four zones. The Soviets had East Berlin, and West Berlin was divided between the British, the French and the Americans.

'We swiftly moved Schmidtke to London where we put him in a high-security cell in Belmarsh prison. It's where we keep awkward foreigners out of sight from the press.'

Finn bends down to stroke Genghiz who is curled up at his feet, ancient now like Nana, and who seems, unusually, to have given Finn his stamp of approval.

'I was sent with a senior officer from the Service

to interview Schmidtke,' Finn continues. 'I was an up-and-coming officer and my station head considered this to be a golden opportunity to introduce me to a real Russian – or East German – spy.' Finn grins like a schoolboy at the word.

Then he looks at me and I see for the hundredth time how his eyes become completely different from each other when he's focusing on something. One of them, the left one as I look at him, is soft and gentle. The other is hard, cruel even. He is like two different people in one pair of eyes. I've never seen a man's eyes like this, eyes that could express two completely separate expressions at the same time, as if they were operated by two different sides of the brain.

'So off we went to Belmarsh prison,' Finn resumes. 'You knew him?' Finn says to me. 'Schmidtke?'

'Only by name.'

'Yes, Schmidtke was a bit before your time.' Finn smiles. 'Anyway, back in eighty-nine, I was sent to Belmarsh to interview him about what he'd been doing in Geneva, not to mention what he'd been doing in the other twenty-eight years of his operational life.'

'He wasn't Russian?' Nana asks.

'He was – is – a Russian German, originally from the East. He became a Stasi officer. He was even Foreign Minister for a short time. But mainly he headed an organisation just over the Wall on your side called KoKo, for short. Kommerzielle Koordinierung. Of all his positions and centres of power, KoKo was the gold seam of his influence. It was KGB, of course, but it was run on a day-to-day basis by the East Germans.'

And now Finn barely pauses.

'KoKo was set up in 1961, just after the Wall went up. It was a hybrid trade organisation the purpose of which was to get hold of foreign currency to fund KGB and Stasi operations abroad. Foreign currency wasn't so easy to obtain for your people after the Wall went up. Your own Wall made traffic from East to West more difficult for the KGB, too. So Schmidtke's mission was to find new ways to get hold of valuable foreign currency. The rouble was useless, unconvertible, of course.

'It all started pretty crudely with Schmidtke's thugs combing East Germany for works of art the Nazis hadn't hidden – antiques and so on. They just confiscated stuff from their owners and sold it through various dealers from Switzerland and Belgium, London and other places. Schmidtke set up a secret financial pipeline from East Germany to Switzerland in order to launder the money and he learned from Soviet sympathisers and illegal financial operators in the West how to set up offshore accounts, wash money, avoid tax. What he learned about capitalism was how all the grimy underside of it worked, the illegal side, the side used by organised crime. So his main contacts in the West were by and large criminal. But there were bankers too, and lawyers, who operated above the line.'

Finn looks up to the ceiling at this point, as if to make sure that the microphones are picking up his every word.

Nana disappears into the kitchen and comes back with a tray of *pelmeni* – thin dough pancakes filled with minced lamb – that she's made, despite dinner

being so recent, and puts it on the table next to Finn.
She shakes flour from her apron on to the crackling
logs in the fireplace and holds on to the mantelpiece
for a moment.

'Are you all right, Nana?'

'Yes, yes, I'm all right. Just a dizzy spell, Anna.
They come and go quickly.'

'Sit down, Nana,' Finn says and stands up to plump
a cushion on the chair opposite him, but she remains
standing. In the corner of the room the Russian flag
still flutters on the televison in front of the Kremlin's
cameras, but I've turned the television down. Nana
can hear only if there's no background noise.

'So, in the West, did nobody ask where these
artworks came from?' Nana says.

'No. There was money to be made. On all sides.
In 1961 Europe was in disorder after the Wall went
up. There was a lot of movement across the line still
and we were encouraging people to come over. Of
course, that's when the KGB put many of their people
in place in the West. It was the end of free movement and everyone was trying to get their pieces in
position.'

Finn looks at the clock on the wall over the mantelpiece. It is half an hour before the New Year. He
gently touches the side of my face in a gesture that
Nana says later is the one that wards off evil spirits.
Nana has all kinds of superstitions like this from
God knows where. To me, Finn's hand on my cheek
feels like protection of sorts too, so maybe Nana is
right.

'You want me to continue?' Finn says, and a
line of worry creases his eyes. He says it as if we

are going through some door, some magic portal of no return, or over the brink of a precipice. And in a sense we are.

'Yes, why not? Go on.'

He brushes the hairs on my temple as he takes his hand away and then continues, as before, carefully laying the words down as if they are a ball of string along which we can find our way back.

'Well, soon, of course, Schmidtke's theft of art ran out of steam. There wasn't anything left. Who knows how much money KoKo made? Millions? Certainly. But new ways had to be found to fund the KGB's increasing presence in Western Europe and elsewhere. They were funding the Communist parties in France and Italy, for a start. But that's another story. So Schmidtke turned to what was practically the only thing the Soviets had to offer of their own. Arms.'

Finn now spreads out on his back as if the smallest effort of movement might result in the end of the world. To me, trained observer that I am, it is a position of deliberate vulnerability, of 'I'm taking a big risk.' It is the psychiatrist's couch and the 'patient' is peeling off one layer of the onion of his hidden self to test the effect it has.

The fact that we all know about the microphones adds a surreal touch, I suppose. We're all playing, to some extent, to the third ear in the room – Putin's Ears, as Finn refers to the microphones later. But while Finn, it seems to me, wants my masters to hear what he is saying, he nevertheless and unnecessarily looks straight at me as if to convey a deeper meaning that cannot be known by anyone outside the room.

I know he's conveying a message to me beyond his words, but that the message in some way includes his words too.

In retrospect, I now realise that it was an appeal, an appeal to me to understand his real motives, the unexpressed, the unsaid.

'KoKo became one of the biggest illegal arms sales operations in the world,' he continues. 'At its height it was selling shipments of weapons all over Africa, the Middle East, South America, China, rebel groups in the Far East . . . Schmidtke even sold a cargo of small arms out of Rostock to the Americans for their covert war in Nicaragua. Good, solid Soviet-made weapons and East German optics could soon be bought throughout the world. And Schmidtke funnelled the profits down his secret financial pipeline into Switzerland. Two banks in Geneva friendly to Schmidtke and the KGB washed the money and a friendly bank in an obscure Swiss canton invested this laundered money into all kinds of business ventures.'

Finn smiles at a memory. 'I remember once when I was on a skiing holiday I was sitting on a ski-lift in a canton in Switzerland. I suddenly realised that this ski-lift was, in fact, a KGB investment,' he says. 'The technology was Swiss,' he adds, as if concerned that we might be worrying about his physical safety.

But then he's serious again.

'So. When we arrested Schmidtke in Berlin in eighty-nine, several billions of dollars had been laundered by KoKo and invested in all kinds of ways. When we brought him in, Schmidtke was returning from Geneva having deposited over a billion dollars.

We were a few hours too late to stop him divesting himself of the cash and bonds. We knew the money was held in an escrow account belonging to one of Schmidtke's Western agents, a Belgian arms dealer living in Switzerland. We wanted him too, but missed him that time and every time since then.'

'What does this have to do with Putin?' Nana asks. 'Our new President, God bless us.'

'Putin was one of Schmidtke's colleagues. He also worked for Schmidtke's KGB controllers in the eighties,' Finn says. 'That's the connection. Back in the days when he was based in East Germany, Putin and Schmidtke met regularly.'

'And Schmidtke was clearing out the accounts before German re-unification,' I say, 'which is why he was depositing these billions in Switzerland.'

'Yes. There were a lot of traces to be covered in a very short time,' Finn replies. 'Everything happened so quickly after the Wall came down. It wasn't just Schmidtke and the Stasi and their KGB allies who had a clearout. Every KGB general and some regular army generals in East Germany were stripping the place. Huge Russian air transporters were flying out cargoes of Mercedes stolen in the West and bound for Moscow. The rapaciousness was unbelievable. Do you know that when Mercedes opened a dealer-ship in Moscow at the beginning of the nineties, they couldn't sell any cars, there were so many already there? Instead, they opened a service centre; they made good money, thanks to Russian driving.'

'And Schmidtke?' Nana says.

'We questioned him for a few weeks in London. We knew he knew everything, all the skeletons, right up to the very top of the political leadership in Bonn. But the West Germans naturally wanted him, too, and they had a greater claim. We let them have him. Perhaps that was a mistake,' Finn adds.

'Why?' I ask.

'Why was it a mistake? They questioned him for two years. At the end they found he still knew more about them than they knew about him. He held all the secrets. Their secrets, secrets they didn't even know about their own political leaders. Don't forget, for nearly thirty years Schmidtke was at the heart of East Germany's infiltration of West German politics, banking and business. He knew it all. I'm amazed he wasn't killed in prison, actually. There were plenty of people who would have appreciated him more if he were in the grave. But he had very powerful allies. And still has. After two years of interrogation, the Germans let him go, under their surveillance, into a quiet, paid retirement in a village called Tegernsee in southern Germany.'

Finn rolls over on the sofa and puts his hands on my knees and seems to study them as they stroke my skin.

'Tegernsee,' he says, lost in the movement of his hand. 'It's a charming little place on a lake, you'd love it, Rabbit. And it's very convenient for the Swiss border. The town has a number of interesting residents, in fact, as well as Schmidtke.'

Finn's hand moves around the inside of my knee. I take it and move it away. 'Go on.'

Finn pauses and sighs and drinks from the brandy glass until it's empty. Nana hobbles to the sideboard and brings the bottle over to refill it. Finn thanks her by blowing a kiss. He's half sitting up. It's as if he's pretending to be drunk. And then he lies back again, sliding his hand across my stomach, and continues.

'The German intelligence service, the BND, put a watch on Schmidtke's apartment in Tegernsee from a field across the river at the back. It was a good spot with a clear view. In winter, that is, when they set it up. In the spring, however, a wall of leaves sprang up from the trees that grew up on the riverbank, and all their beautiful Zeiss lenses were met with this thick green wall that cut off Schmidtke's apartment completely. Famed German intelligence. *Vorsprung durch* kockup.'

'But the British, they . . . you'd already got something out of him, hadn't you?' I say. 'You knew the secrets the Germans wanted to find?'

'He told us only a little of what he told the Germans,' Finn corrects me. 'It was plenty, believe me, and they knew we knew. We waited for them to act on it, but they didn't. It was too costly for them, of course. Schmidtke was starting to unravel thirty years of KGB successes in West Germany right up to the highest level, so they put the lid on everything he told them and eventually they didn't want to hear any more.'

'Did the British tell the Germans everything Schmidtke told them?' I ask.

'We share all our intelligence,' Finn replies straight-faced.

I laugh. 'But not in this case.'

'No. Not in this case,' Finn says and smiles. 'Or not as far as I know.'

He finally unrolls himself from the sofa and

throws the two remaining logs from the basket on to the fire. He begins to put on a coat and hat, and the white felt boots Nana had brought back for him from a tourist trip she'd made to Nizhny Novgorod. Then he picks up the log basket. He looks at me and I get up from the rug to get dressed for the cold too.

We walk into the forest far away from where we keep the logs at the back of the dacha. It's pitch dark, the first hour of the New Year, the new century, the new millennium. The snow is falling weakly inside the wood, like the last of the seed dribbling from the bottom of a packet, but when we emerge into the clearings beside the pond, it is robust, the big flakes driving down unimpeded with an apparent urgency to bury everything deeply and for ever.

Finn chats nervously. He tells me about a Vietnamese refugee he and some friends had sponsored when they were at university. The boy had arrived at a military airbase in Scotland in mid-winter and three days after he'd arrived he'd woken up to see the landscape white with snow. He'd called Finn in a panic, believing there'd been a nuclear attack.

'Perception is sometimes a traitor,' Finn says to me after he's finished this story. 'And sometimes it's the truth. How do you distinguish when it's one or the other?'

'Instinct maybe,' I reply. 'That's all we have, isn't it?'

'But we're afraid to use it most of the time. For most of us, truth is merely facts. That's where we feel safest.'

We walk further into the forest and stand by a pond which is seamlessly coated with snow so that it has become one with the surrounding land.

'What do your instincts tell you now?' he asks me.

'About what?'

'About where we're going, you and I. Us.'

'I don't think about it. I don't think about you much when we're not together,' I say, and it's true. 'I have my survival to think about.'

He holds my hand through our thick gloves.

'And what if you did think about us, Rabbit, about where we both want to go?'

'I can't think about it,' I say.

'Or won't,' he says.

I am silent.

'Let me tell you, then. My instincts say we should get out of all this. Retire, if you like. Remove the obstacles, our work, these forces around us, everything that conspires and will continue to conspire against our future. Let go of everything that restricts us from being true together. My instinct says we should reduce us to just you, me and the spirit that joins us.'

I consider what he's saying. I fear the treason he's suggesting. His to me, or mine to my country? I don't know. And if Finn is true, what might it do to me, this treason? And I have other fears too. But these fears are of the wrong things; they are fears of a change in my life so massive I can barely imagine it. My fear is of leaving everything familiar to me, everything in my life up to this point, in exchange for Finn and uncertainty. It is a base and useless fear. I know that what I should be afraid of is the opposite. I should be afraid of not leaving everything familiar to me. I should fear not changing.

We walk around the trees now, there's no path, and step over broken branches with a coating of snow that bulges over them like baggy trousers and dwarfs the things it settles on.

'It's the flexibility of snow that pleases me most,' Finn says. 'The way it joins the most uneven surfaces together in beautiful, soft curves. It unites the whole landscape. It seems to heal the earth.'

But I'm not really listening. I coldly assess the thought that Finn has put into my head, the thought of him and me, with nothing to disturb us. Then I look for the familiar and bring us cruelly back to the present.

'Who is Vladimir Putin?' I ask. 'I want to know what you think.'

Finn looks at me, to give me the opportunity to reconsider, perhaps.

'That's the question,' he replies at last, and a shadow crosses his face; a shadow of grief, maybe, that a moment devoted to us and us alone has lost a rare opportunity.

He picks up a stick and dusts off the snow to reveal fungi still clinging to its rottenness.

'History is a broken toy,' he says, carefully handling the stick. 'It breaks and gets fixed and breaks again. Bits fall off and are replaced. It breaks over and over again and everything is replaced and everything remains the same. History is like the axe that has its handle replaced over and over. Is it still the same axe? It functions in the same way. History is just a toy in the sense that people want it to function in the same way, and it does. It still breaks and is still mended in just the same ways.

'What happened with KoKo in 1961 in East Germany sowed the seeds of a plan and the Plan grew and grew in ambition but it was always interrupted, thwarted by events and forces. When the Wall came down in 1989, we in the West thought it was all over. The Cold War was won. That's how it seemed. The end of history, some idiot called it. But like so much in history our thoughts were coloured by our hopes – and our ill-conceived perceptions. You see, the past wouldn't go away. The Plan only lay dormant. Yeltsin, he was the real hope. But he himself and events around him conspired against a truly new Russia. In the nineties, you know this, Anna, Yeltsin could have got rid of the KGB for good, stuck a knife through its heart. But there was so much turmoil in the country that he didn't quite make it. He didn't have the time, or the will to make the final push. Perhaps he didn't dare. Whatever. And now? Well, now the KGB is back and it will be stronger than it's ever been. Putin's Russia will be the KGB's Russia, just as it's been for the past seventy years. But it will be so with a major difference. This time, economic chaos will be replaced by economic abundance. The KGB will be richer than any organisation on earth, richer than the CIA. And the Plan will rise from its bed, nourished by the new men of power.'

'What plan?' I ask him.

'You don't know?' he says, looking hard at me, and I feel for one moment that all he wants me for is this. And I don't know the answer he wants.

He looks away, apparently relieved that I don't know what he's talking about, and beyond that, he doesn't expand, however hard I press him.

Even for him this monologue is rather melodramatic and portentous, yet there's something so powerful emanating from him as he speaks that my initial urge to laugh is quietened. He stands there in the dark forest, with the snow falling around us, like some kind of shaman possessed by a supernatural force. I wonder what I'm doing even considering trusting this man.

Yet I know we have missed a chance for us, an opportunity, and it was me who rejected it. This time there will be other chances, but one day we will run out of chances to save ourselves.

I realise that, despite the inevitable searching somewhere out there in the darkness. Finn has chosen to absent us from the microphones for this moment.

I wonder what General Kerchenko and my two case officers will think of Finn's theatrical eloquence when I submit my report later. This Plan he talks about . . . Will they think it fiction? Bathos? Madness? To my surprise, they thought it was none of them. They ignored it.

9

IN THE SPRING of the year 2000 Vladimir Putin moved into the Kremlin and began to cement his seat of power.

At the British embassy across the River Moskva from the Kremlin, Finn slowly undermined whatever power he possessed. He told me he'd argued with his station head about the direction in which Putin was taking Russia. He was uncharacteristically truculent and morose.

One afternoon the two of us took a trip out to New Jerusalem, the seventeenth-century Orthodox monastery on the River Istra west of Moscow, and afterwards we had supper with friends of mine who lived nearby. Finn usually drove when we went anywhere, but this time he asked me to bring my car. He was in a foul mood.

'I've been given a formal warning,' he grumbled.

'Accept my government's policy, work with the status quo, or get out.'

'That seems reasonable,' I said. Then we both laughed that it was I who was telling him to be loyal to his country. The rest of the trip revived his spirits and he seemed like his usual self.

But he told me as we walked around the huge monastery later that behind the scenes they were going to get him out anyway.

'I'm finished with Moscow,' he said finally, and we lit a candle to us.

He held my hand.

'And I don't want us to be separated,' he said.

'No,' I said.

'So if it's going to be one thing or the other,' he said, 'us together, or you staying in Russia without me, which is it to be?'

I didn't reply. And after the night by the pond, this was my second denial, a second opportunity lost.

In the weeks after our trip out to New Jerusalem, Putin first gathered round him the trusted members of his St Petersburg KGB clan, people who had worked with him when he was deputy mayor of the city, and from earlier when he was stationed in East Germany before the Berlin Wall fell.

Simultaneously he summoned the men who had been the real rulers of Russia in the shadows behind Yeltsin's presidency.

I heard from a colleague based at the Kremlin that they came to him one by one. These shadow rulers were known to us Russians and to the world as the oligarchs. In the words of Boris Berezovsky, the oil, metals and media billionaire, they were the 'seven bankers who ruled Russia'. These immensely powerful men had formed an uneasy alliance between themselves – one that transcended the clash of their own business interests – in order to put their support behind Putin to win the presidential elections. First, they had persuaded Yeltsin as the millennium approached to hand his crown over to the younger man and now they supported Putin to ensure that he won the contested election. They were backing him with their huge resources as the best candidate to protect their own interests.

One night Finn and I went to see *American Beauty* at the cinema in Tverskaya. Finn fidgeted throughout the film and when I tried to talk about it afterwards he appeared not to have seen it at all.

'They're afraid for their prospects if Evgeni Primakov wins the presidency,' Finn said.

'Who?' I asked him, thinking about Kevin Spacey's dead-looking face in the movie.

'The oligarchs! They're so afraid of Primakov that they're going to jump straight into the fire and support Putin!'

Primakov was my chief, the boss of the SVR, who was running against Putin in the elections.

'Are there really people like that in America?' I asked, thinking still about Spacey's character. But Finn was obsessed. For once it was me trying to introduce some levity, not him.

'It's just the same as it was five years ago,' Finn went on. 'Then it was the Communists they were afraid of. They thought the Communists would turn back the clock and deprive them of their wealth. So they formed an alliance between themselves for as long as it took to see off that threat and make sure Yeltsin was re-elected.'

'Are we going to get something to eat?' I suggested. 'Or are you going to rave on out here? I'm freezing.'

So we went into Yolki-Palki on the other side of the Bolshoi from Tverskaya. Finn always liked it there. The restaurant was dressed up in peasant decor with straw bales and wooden farm animals and checked tablecloths. Finn stopped talking about the elections for a moment.

'This place has never been the same since the city banned the real animals,' Finn said.

Back in the early nineties, when it first opened, the restaurant had real chickens and ducks that wandered about inside.

But then Finn was off again before we'd even ordered.

'Putin is essentially the oligarchs' choice,' he said. 'He's reassured them somehow. Why do they believe him?'

'Because it's what they want to believe.'

Later we walked in the freezing night to the Kremlin and watched the black Mercedes and four-wheel-drive Porsches enter and leave the Kremlin with their windows blacked out, and I told him, one by one, which rich Russian baron had come to pay his respects to Putin.

'They come like boyars to a medieval tsar,' Finn said. 'They pay their respects and hope to exert their influence.'

And in the course of those weeks up to Putin's election victory in March, they all came: the oligarchs, the richest, most powerful men in Russia. Preceded, some said, by lavish gifts or suitcases of cash, they came to ensure that their choice for the elections was an ally. They were confident, powerful and richer than the rest of Russia put together.

But once he'd got their money and once their media outlets had ensured his victory, Putin was not the man they thought they'd voted for. To their dismay, having funded his rise to power, what they found was a president unlike the weakened, pliant Yeltsin.

While Putin had the decor of Yeltsin's Kremlin bathroom changed from whimsical *trompes l'oeil* of twittering birds and fluffy clouds to a formal burgundy, 'like dried blood' as one of the oligarchs put it, he also changed other, more important, matters. From now on, he told them firmly, only if they stayed out of politics could they run their businesses and continue to enjoy the wealth they'd seized. It was not what they wanted to hear and many of them, to their cost, didn't actually believe it.

When Boris Berezovsky confidently went off to his French château on the Côte d'Azur in the summer of 2000 to rest and recuperate after the successful but gruelling spring election campaign, he left his protégé Stepanovich with a list of names to give to the newly elected Vladimir Putin of those he wanted to see in positions of power around the President. The list was Berezovsky's hold on power.

But at the Forest, I watched my bosses and they

laughed at the names on it. The Kingmaker had made a serious error.

By the end of the summer, Berezovsky's television stations were confiscated by Putin and he, with Gusinsky, fled into exile – Berezovsky to London, Gusinsky to Tel Aviv.

'I told you, didn't I, Rabbit?' Finn said triumphantly.

I don't know what role Stepanovich had in the fall of Berezovsky, if he had a role at all. But we all saw that from then on he was very close to Putin and, later, Berezovsky cursed his protégé's betrayal. Stepanovich, who only a few years before served the drinks on Berezovsky's private jet, had made a separate peace.

'Watch what happens now,' Finn said. 'Berezovsky and Gusinsky are examples *pour encourager les autres*. Just watch.'

It was true. With Berezovsky's fall, the others quickly saw which way the wind now blew from the Kremlin and they bent their knees to the new chief and his KGB entourage.

Only the richest of them all, Mikhail Khodorkovsky, took a stand against Putin. He lasted until 2004, when his private jet was stormed by masked special forces on a Siberian runway. Tried in a kangaroo court, he was put away to rot in a Siberian uranium mine that still serves as a prison camp in our new democratic Russia. For disobeying the President's instruction to stay out of politics, he received eight brutal years in Russia's old gulag, with the promise of more to come.

Between Putin's appointment to the presidency on New Year's Eve and the March elections, on the other side of the Moskva River from the Kremlin, the British embassy prepared for a visit to Moscow by Tony Blair in February 2000, to endorse Putin as candidate.

'Blair's come smiling to Moscow,' Finn said. 'He's been strolling in the grounds of Putin's dacha, describing Putin to the lapdog press as a reformer, a man we can do business with. The little creep wants to be Margaret Thatcher and casts Putin as his Gorbachev.'

To return this endorsement of him, Putin graced Blair with the rich reward of making London the venue for his first official foreign visit after he was elected. In London, Putin was given the red-carpet treatment and dined with the Queen. The massacres of Chechens in Putin's war there were brushed aside by Downing Street. Putin promised the hopeful world a 'dictatorship of the law'.

But whose law, we asked ourselves in Russia, if not the law of the KGB?

During this time, Finn and I often met at the Baltschug Hotel on the river, a few doors away from the British embassy, and we enjoyed its fine view of the Kremlin over lunch or a drink or in bed. Despite me telling him archly that the Forest would gladly pay for our room, Finn somehow obtained these rooms at what he called 'diplomatic rates', and said he didn't want our lovemaking being listened to.

'I'm supposed to persuade you,' I said.

'Then you've failed.'

'Thank God for that.'

We could never trust Finn's apartment, nor mine, and to the irritation of Kerchenko, visiting random hotel rooms was the only way to keep our most private moments to ourselves.

At the Forest, General Kerchenko and my other case officers on Finn, Yuri and Sasha, ignored Finn's talk about a plan which I had written up in my reports. They just seemed fixated by Finn's disaffection with MI6 and the ridiculous notion that Finn was ready to come over to our side. But how could he defect, I tried to tell them, when there was no apparent ideological difference between the two sides?

I remember now that Finn had bought and then framed a collection of stamps which had been issued under Gorbachev and which featured the British spy and traitor, Kim Philby. It amused him enormously that Philby should be celebrated even in Gorbachev's Russia, at the time when both sides in the Cold War were laying down their differences.

But when I told my controllers about the stamps, they failed to see the irony, preferring instead to believe that Finn admired Philby. And every time my reports informed them how Finn railed against Putin, they said it was cover. Kerchenko and Yuri, certainly, really believed he had begun to unburden himself in preparation to defect, that he was a crumbling figure.

Finn certainly gave a very fine impression of crumbling in those times, but I knew it was a feint.

Finn didn't crumble in public. He was a person who crawled away to be on his own if he had so much as a head cold.

Finn's self-destructive behaviour began to undermine his position at the embassy very fast. At the Baltschug Hotel one afternoon in early summer two months after Putin's election, over a bottle of extremely expensive champagne, Finn told me he had been sacked. It was an eerie conversation. I knew it wasn't true and he knew I knew. We'd grown to know each other well in the intervening months and I could sense the guile in his claim. If he'd been sacked he would never have been allowed to meet me, or to go anywhere outside the embassy in Moscow. They'd have had him on a plane back to London before he could pick up his laundry. They'd have given him leave to get out of the country, and then sacked him back in London.

So I knew only that he knew he was going to be sacked. And that could only mean he had engineered it himself. I recalled our conversation at New Jerusalem and how Finn had asked me what I would do if we were separated. During our conversation I realised that even the British didn't know they were going to sack him yet.

'I've told them I can't work for a government that backs Putin,' Finn said to me.

He then went on to reel off a list of evidently rehearsed remarks about Putin; rehearsed for the benefit, I guessed, of his station head. They were mostly things I'd heard him say before, but this time he was using me to get his story right and I played along with him even though my mind was in confusion.

He said Putin was the worst type of KGB insider, and always would be, and that the West was duping itself with its wishful thinking about a new Russia. He said that the British were mad to trust him, even to do business in any committed way with him. And that Putin had showed his spots with the Chechen war and then continued to emerge from the KGB chrysalis in his policy towards the oligarchs.

'Surely London can see that if Putin really cares about changing Russia he'd force the oligarchs to bend before the rule of law, not before the KGB's version of it?' he said angrily.

All Putin was doing, he said, was confiscating the oligarchs' assets and giving them to his own cronies, not putting them up for auction for the good of the state.

'But Putin's clever,' Finn admitted. 'By both making war against the Chechens and reining in the oligarchs he's appealed to the popular tastes that guarantee him the support of the people, which he needs until he tightens the noose. He'll discard the people when he's done that, you watch.' Finn leaned back in his chair. 'Putin's won his domestic audience in two simple, brutal moves,' he said.

I remember Finn's fist striking the table a little too hard while he was making one of his points, so that other occupants of the bar noticed.

'It won't stop there,' he said. 'The end of freedom and the confiscation of property for the rich few is just the beginning. There'll come a time when the KGB will be in control of everyone's lives again, right down to the minutiae. Doesn't anybody in Russia care about that?'

He ordered more champagne and I drank so that there would be less to fuel his anger.

'If London's going to support Putin in public, it might just as well have supported the Soviet Union throughout the Cold War! It's worse than that! Russia will be far more dangerous now than it ever was with thousands of nuclear missiles it would never have fired.'

'Let's go for a walk,' I said, worried that too many people were overhearing him. But he didn't seem to hear me.

'Remember the Plan,' he said. 'I told you about the Plan by the pond at Barvikha on New Year's Eve.'

'I remember, Finn. I don't know what you mean.'

But he seemed to check himself, and said no more about this obsession of his than he had back then.

Finally, he looked at me with his strange, schizophrenic eyes and said that it wasn't his conscience that was forcing him to say this, but his common sense, and that it would be hypocritical of him to continue supporting a national policy he totally disagreed with.

I was taken aback by his outburst. It was so public.

'I'll only ever tell you the truth,' he suddenly said. 'I want you to know that.'

'Why should I believe you?' I said.

'Only you can decide that,' he replied.

And when I looked at him, I knew that I believed him, even though he was lying about being sacked. I knew that he was speaking to me suddenly from his soul, and that he would only tell me the truth. And in that moment I discovered something that I'd never known; that when someone truly believes in you, a door is opened and you automatically believe in them, too.

I realised then that I felt more for him than I'd dared to think before and I didn't like to watch him apparently destroying himself. For that's what he seemed to me to be doing.

I told him that all his high-minded talk about common sense over conscience was simple sophistry, and that it sounded like a contradiction.

And then a strange thing happened. He leaned back in his chair again and a gleam of interest came into his eyes, as if this was the first thing I'd said that he'd noted. In fact, I had the distinct impression he was about to make an actual note of my remark so that his argument could be refined for the real performance of it later.

It was then that I knew for certain this conversation with me was a rehearsal and that he was deliberately engineering his own fall from grace.

But he just smiled. When the rehearsal was over, he was more relaxed than I'd seen him for months. Crises made Finn calm. I'd seen it in him before. They were what he knew and understood. His childhood years had been spent in always having to form his own resolutions to crises.

But I didn't show that I knew what he was about. I didn't tell my bosses about this aspect of the afternoon or that I thought Finn was engineering his own dismissal from the Service. He didn't ask me not to tell them, but it was as if he knew I wouldn't reveal it to them. And that, I guess, was the first time that I betrayed my country, if only in the small print.

'I'm going to follow my own path,' Finn then said, rather grandly. 'I'm going feral.'

He poured me another glass of champagne. For the first time that afternoon there was an awkward pause. I realised we were entering something he hadn't rehearsed, something in the real world, and Finn always looked as if he was in a bit of a muddle when his personal reality got too close.

'Look,' he said and smiled broadly. 'You see . . . darling Rabbit,' he said, 'I want to ask you something. I want us to be together. I want you to come with me, Anna.'

His eyes, one beautiful and kind, the other hard and a little frightening, looked into mine.

'We've known each other for such a short time,' he said.

'It's been more than a year,' I said.

'You're the person I want to share my life with.'

I couldn't speak, and he smiled into my eyes.

'You don't have to say anything now,' he said. 'Or ever, in fact.'

'Ask me something else,' I said at last.

Finn didn't ask me anything else. Normally, he would have said something like, 'OK, what time is it in Ouagadougou?' or something equally facetious. But this time he fiddled with the stem of his glass. We were both, I saw, circling the dangerous territory of acknowledging a need rather than just a desire for one another.

He looked up from his fingers on the champagne stem.

'When they ask you,' he said, each word coming out of his mouth like a heavy object, 'if I said anything out of the ordinary at this meeting . . . when they ask you that, tell them that I told you I loved you.'

I looked at him in astonishment and then I laughed out loud. It was so perfectly typical of Finn. To be so obtuse, to confuse, to disguise – that was always the geography of his mental processes until time and our knowledge of each other had helped him drop his defences. Whoever he was speaking to had to draw their own conclusions from his riddles.

'Wait a second,' I said. 'Tell them . . . you told me . . . that you love me.'

We stared at each other before Finn broke into a smile once more. He knew I was laughing at his in-ability to just say it. I love you. And then, to the alarm of the other people in the bar, we began to laugh. We laughed and laughed until the laughter itself made us laugh. We stood up and hugged each other closely, and when we pulled away I saw his eyes were watery.

'You're leaving, then,' I said.

He said nothing, and I knew he wouldn't be drawn by such a direct question.

'I bet you,' I said, 'that you tell me you love me before I tell you I love you.'

'You're on.' He grinned.

It would be a year before I saw Finn again.

10

IN THE AFTERGLOW of our mild hysteria, I walked alone back across the river from the hotel and descended into a depression that was bound to follow. I didn't want to take a taxi, so I walked past the Kremlin on the far side of the river and up towards Pushkinskaya Square. I stopped briefly and drank half a cup of coffee behind the Bolshoi and watched the slow flow of summer passers-by, window-shopping in the expensive fashion shops for objects that would have cost many of them a lifetime's wages.

I shook myself out of the crash in my mood by buying something myself. And I thought about what Finn had said. I even briefly entertained the idea of doing my job by telling my superiors what I believed was the truth, that Finn was deliberately getting himself the sack. But I dismissed it quickly. Finn had drawn me into . . . what? Complicity? No. He had, in his strangely awkward way, opened his heart completely.

This decision to omit something from a report was the first certain sign that my personal relationship with Finn was gaining ground over my professional one. It hurts me now to think that this shocked me. I realised I was going to lose him and I knew I had to harden my heart.

I questioned his feelings for me, and then I remembered his invitation, which I hadn't answered. It seemed like a moment of reality that glittered as a patch of water thousands of feet below glitters briefly when it catches the sun.

I want you to come with me.

I couldn't imagine how I could or would leave Russia. I couldn't conceive of such a step at the time. Things – defences – began to pile up in my mind to prevent me from leaving: my job and the fateful result of walking away from it. I would be branded a traitor. Then there was Nana; not to mention the brave new Russia with its hope for the future, despite Finn's misgivings. I counted up all the reasons, no matter how trivial, for not accepting his invitation – anything, in fact, but face what I really wanted to do, which was to go with him. I was hooked to my past, shackled by fear to the familiar. I was afraid of such momentous change. To walk away from the Forest in itself was an unimaginable step.

As I walked I tried to imagine what it would be like to be a traitor. On a street in London, perhaps, how would it feel? Would I always be looking over my shoulder? And if all failed with Finn? I would never be able to return.

It flashed across my mind that treason would be the perfect revenge. But revenge for what? My father? The evils of the organisation I had chosen to work for? The injustice of something or other in this imperfect world?

And yet somehow, in my conflicted state, I sensed that Finn understood that I couldn't leave with him. Not yet, at any rate. That realisation opened up new questions. Did his understanding make his question insincere? It wouldn't be beyond Finn, by any means, to ask for something that couldn't be given but that, in the asking, somehow absolved him from guilt or responsibility for it.

But I didn't believe his invitation to go with him was insincere. I believed he wanted me to go with him, that he knew I couldn't and – most intriguingly – that it didn't matter. There was something else he hadn't said, something missing that would make everything right between us when it finally appeared.

I looked back at our relationship and tried to find a pattern that clarified what was happening.

As long as we had had a professional reason to see each other, to be lovers, we never had to ask ourselves how we really felt about each other. We were like two people in an arranged marriage who grow towards each other without seeing it happening. Finn had crossed this line, although I hadn't. In his invitation he had shattered the mirage. How did I feel about Finn when the arrangement was broken, when the professional reasons for seeing him disappeared? I wanted to expose him then, a foreign intelligence officer working against my country. Finn was everything I had been trained to destroy.

The answer caused me a moment of anger.

As I read his notebook for this period in the vault now, I see three entries for that day, the last time we met at the Baltschug Hotel. 'Pick up trousers' is the first. 'Call Bob about the flat' comes next. And finally he writes, 'Asked R [for Rabbit, presumably] to come with me.'

Strangely, I feel great warmth at the juxtaposition of these thoughts that dispels the dank cold of the vault. To be included with his trousers and his flat is the honour I would most wish for, a sign that I was always part of his fundamental reality.

For the next three days I worked steadily and when I wasn't working walked the streets of Moscow. I told my bosses that I was concerned about my relationship with Finn, that he was getting too close. They just laughed and lewdly told me to enjoy it. But they didn't ask me any awkward questions.

Finn and I had prepared a special drop, a dead letter box to use in an emergency and which only Finn and I knew of. Neither of us, I think, had any intention of ever using it but even its existence was precious, a private thing between the two of us, away from all the surveillance around our relationship. He trusted me to keep it that way and, I suppose, this was another instance of our personal attachment beginning to take precedence over our duty. But as long as we had never used it, it was just that, a lovers' secret, and no more.

Finn had chosen a place for this drop that was usually crowded in the daytime with tourists, both Russian and foreign. It was a bookshop on the corner of a cobbled street dotted with old Moscow shops and another road with street stalls and bureaux de change, behind Moscow's Savoy Hotel. The Savoy was where Finn sometimes went to play roulette and where he claimed to have won over $20,000 one night a few years before.

The bookshop was a few yards from the Lubyanka, the old and notorious KGB headquarters, until Yeltsin transferred its operations outside the city. I visited the Lubyanka sometimes in my first years, before I went to the Forest. I still remember with dread the netting that hung over the stairwells to prevent prisoners throwing themselves to their deaths before interrogation. The KGB owned the Savoy Hotel back then and we would go across the street sometimes to drink.

Along this cobbled street behind the hotel there are a number of bookshops, a shop that sells maps, and some new cafés that now spring up almost weekly in the centre of the city. In one bookshop Finn had identified a dusty corner with some second-hand books. Behind a Bulgarian translation of Jeffrey Archer's *Cain and Abel*, there was a piece of wood that looked like the upright back of the shelving and that Finn had somehow managed to fit unnoticed. It came away by pulling out two books and pressing hard on a third. In this space I looked, at different times of the day, for three days. But there was nothing. And I had heard nothing from Finn since we had met at the Baltschug Hotel.

On the fourth day I received a message from my boss and the controller of Finn's dossier, General Kerchenko. It was an order for me to come immediately to the Forest. It was not an unusual summons. In the KGB, urgency usually meant that a senior officer was angry because he had been diverted from some other, more profitable, personal activity, not that the matter itself was urgent. Kerchenko, for example, had many private and personal activities, some of which I've witnessed. I was once present at his dacha outside Moscow, when he met with two mafia bosses from Tashkent who were bringing him his share of the clan's profits.

I dressed smartly in the kind of outfit that I knew made Kerchenko, a cruder version of my father, happy. With a pair of high-heeled shoes, I looked the typical female object Russian men were so enamoured of.

I have sometimes wondered how much my elevation to the rank of colonel owed to my looks. I have received several frank offers from Russian billionaires and, though I say so myself, in the right fur coat I can hold my own with any high-class whore in the lobbies of Moscow's swanky hotels. Oligarchs have offered to dress me from head to toe in white sable and fly me around the world for non-stop beauty treatments while they discuss the price of oil or the flotation of their companies.

My friend Natasha says unkindly that my rank owes everything to how I look. For my part, I am content to play with the fragile egos of such men, while not denying that it gives me more than just a sense of power.

I drove along the motorway south of Moscow to the Forest and while I waited in the café in the main block of the huge intelligence complex I ran into Vladimir, my old school friend and the man my father had wanted me to marry. I hadn't seen him for nearly ten years.

'You still here?' he said, grinning. 'I thought you were better than that.'

This casual remark struck right through me, disengaging the hold on my job that I was clinging to so tenuously. Vladimir's remark took me back to a comment of Nana's on the day I became a colonel. 'Just be who you were meant to be,' she had said. 'Be who you want to be, it's the same.'

Like that comment of Nana's, Vladimir, too, had exposed everything that I hated about myself: my job, my position – everything I was still unwilling to give up in order to go with Finn. I was suddenly reminded of my father and his anger, and his inability to change. I was reminded of the grip of the past on him. And, now, it seemed, the past had its grip on me.

We drank a coffee together. Vladimir told me what had happened to him back in our new dawn of 1991 when we were promised our freedom.

He had been encouraged to speak out, he told me, as we all were back then in the era of perestroika and glasnost and Yeltsin's ascent to power. At the Forest they had asked him to voice any concerns about the way the Forest was run, anything at all that struck him as wrong or wasteful or outdated.

Foolishly, Vladimir took them at their word. He told his questioners that he thought it was wrong for senior officers to use official cars for their own private business, a common practice in the nineties and today. He was praised for this honesty, and then summoned the following day to his observer's office, where a lieutenant colonel was waiting for him.

'We're sending you to the Cape Verde Islands,' the officer told him abruptly.

Stunned, Vladimir replied that he didn't speak Portuguese.

'Don't worry,' the lieutenant colonel told him. 'We'll blind you, too, so you won't be able to see anything either.'

And so Vladimir had spent nearly ten years in Cape Verde, in exile, effectively, doing nothing apart from learning perfect Portuguese. They hadn't actually blinded him but such a fate as Vladimir's, I was suddenly reminded, was and still is today the result of the self-defeating vindictiveness of the organisation I work for.

We said goodbye and arranged to meet the following week.

After waiting for nearly two hours for this 'urgent' meeting, I was finally called up to Kerchenko's office.

There were three of them there, including Kerchenko. The other two were the case officers who also worked on Finn's dossier. Yuri, one of the 'new KGB' Russians from Petersburg, lounged in a corner with his feet up as if to make it clear he didn't take orders from an old-timer like Kerchenko.

I knew Yuri took a cut from a logging business

out in northern Siberia and had become rich from the new black market run by the nexus of security officers and mafia *buzinessmen*.

The other one, Sasha, like Kerchenko an old Brezhnevite, had a lined face and bushy eyebrows. He sat to the side of the room with his elbows on his knees and looked at the floor like a prisoner. The General sat behind the overlarge desk so favoured in former times by self-important bureaucrats.

Before I had even sat down Kerchenko asked me where Finn was. He used our codename for Finn, which was Markus.

I didn't reply until I'd sat in the empty chair in front of the desk.

'I haven't seen him for more than three days,' I said.

I knew immediately that I was under suspicion; a cross-examination began, questions flew from all three of them, from all sides simultaneously.

I calmly and clearly told them about our last meeting and, in particular, everything that Finn had said about Putin. It was all stuff that was in the report I had made the day after he and I had met. I always made a report after every encounter with Finn.

I recounted Finn's anxiety and his anger with his own people. I didn't tell them the whole truth, nothing about his invitation to me to go with him but just enough, I hoped, to manipulate the manipulators who see betrayal and falsehood everywhere. What I really wanted to know was what had caused them to call me in so suddenly, but I concealed my interest in the reasons for their inquiries as well as I could. Of course they weren't satisfied.

'Why didn't you tell us he was leaving Moscow?' the bald Yuri barked eventually, and simultaneously snapped the buckle of his expensive watch. He looked at me with all the lust of assumed conquest.

My shock was evident.

'You didn't know?' Kerchenko said accusingly.

'No, I didn't.'

There was a pause while they watched me.

'When did he leave?' I asked, in an attempt at professional, rather than personal curiosity.

'This morning. On the British Airways flight to London. With two officials from London,' Kerchenko said.

'You didn't know,' Yuri sneered. 'You didn't know.'

I ignored him, looking at the watch on his wrist and thinking how brashly our new officers now wore their illegal wealth.

'Why didn't he tell you he was leaving?' Sasha asked so softly that I could barely hear the question. He still hadn't looked up from the floor.

'I don't know why. He doesn't tell me everything.'

'Surely he would tell you something like this,' Yuri demanded.

'Yes. Yes, I suppose he would. Normally. So I suppose it must have been a sudden decision.'

'Of his? Or theirs?' Sasha asked softly again.

'I can't say. Of theirs, I guess. Unless he's ill, or has family problems.'

'What was his mood?' Sasha said from under the bushy eyebrows which were all I could see of his face.

It was a question that was asked many times during that afternoon and evening.

'Just anxious. And, as I said, angry. He was very angry.'

'Did he say anything unusual to you at this recent meeting?' Kerchenko asked. 'Your last meeting. Anything that seemed too unimportant at the time, perhaps, to include in your report?'

I thought for a moment, giving them time to register this moment of contemplation. And then I smiled. It was Finn's instruction to tell them that made me smile, but they weren't to know that.

'What's so funny?' Yuri said. 'You've lost a British intelligence officer you're being paid to stay up close to night and day. What's so fucking funny?'

'What he said,' I replied coolly. 'That's what was funny.'

Kerchenko raised his eyebrows and Sasha looked up at last.

'Well?' Kerchenko said.

'He told me he loved me,' I said.

There was a moment of silence in the room, the first real silence since I'd arrived. For me, it was unnervingly a thing of beauty. Finn had invaded the room. I was thinking only of Finn.

It was Yuri, inevitably, who finally brought me back.

'That's funny,' he said. 'Falling for our whore.'

'I am a colonel in the SVR,' I reprimanded him. 'I am not your, or anyone's, whore.'

I looked at Yuri's face and saw the amorphous hate I'd seen so often in my father's face. To me it

came from a fury that anyone was capable of independent thought.

'So,' Sasha said, recapping my words, 'you said
that this was funny.' I liked Sasha for that.

'Of course,' I said. 'To me it is funny, yes. For a
colonel in the SVR to be told by a British intelligence officer that he loves her – yes, that's funny.
He's been out of control for some time,' I continued.
'It's in my reports. But this was a new low. It seemed
such an obvious, ridiculous thing to say to me. Apparently he's lost it.'

'And you've lost him,' Yuri said.

'Why isn't it in your report that he told you he
loved you?' Kerchenko asked, turning a page in a
mannered way so as not to meet my eye. I wanted to
laugh at his pomposity next to the question.

'It meant nothing. It was just one more symptom
of his loss of discipline. It's not an important piece
of information.'

'Maybe you were embarrassed?' Kerchenko said.

'Embarrassed, no,' I replied. 'Disgusted. It was
laughable. As I say, it was a complete collapse of discipline and I've reported on his loss of discipline ex-
tensively.'

'Yes,' the General said heavily. 'We were hoping
you would take more advantage of that than you
have. We've been expecting some results for some
time from his apparent disintegration; something
that tells us what he's been doing in Moscow for so
long. Far too long. But now he's gone.'

'It's something that's been discussed in this room
many times,' I agreed. 'But on the instructions I was

given I didn't want to alarm him, scare him off. He's been quite unstable for some time. He could do anything, in my opinion.'

'So you've said,' Kerchenko replied, leafing through Finn's dossier. 'Do you believe that he . . . he loves you?' he said squeamishly, as if he'd just discovered some chewing gum attached to the underside of his desk.

Yuri snorted.

'I don't know,' I said. 'I doubt it.'

'But he said so.'

'Yes.'

'And he's never said so before.'

'No.'

At this moment, Patrushev entered the room.

11

WHEN I'D GOT OVER the shock of Patrushev actually appearing at the Forest, it was clear that the FSB chief, our new boss of the renamed and airbrushed KGB, had been sitting in an adjoining room, wired to ours. But at the moment he entered the room, I was completely taken aback. The others, while making their respect obvious to Patrushev, looked even more astonished.

Patrushev didn't come to foreign intelligence territory, to the Forest. He and the SVR chief were fierce rivals and there was no precedent as far as I knew for the two agencies entering each other's ground. Foreign and home intelligence waged a low-key war against each other. It was said that three of Patrushev's agents had been arrested in Paris a few months before while following a group of Chechens in the French capital. The Forest, angry that their rivals were performing a foreign intelligence function, had tipped off the French security services.

I had seen Patrushev a few times before, but only from afar. He had spoken at KGB functions and afterwards worked the room, vodka in hand, but I had never been introduced.

On this afternoon Nikolai Patrushev was dressed in his trademark grey suit and red tie. A tall, hawkish man, his receding hair was brushed over a balding patch and his thin nose appeared to hover over thinner lips. His eyes had a hard, mesmerising stare that ensured you met his gaze. He was Putin's close ally, which might explain how he could appear at the Forest on the territory of his rival. I suppose Finn was a moving target between agencies but Patrushev's presence could only have suggested Putin's personal interest in the case.

Patrushev had come with Putin, like so many of the president's acolytes, from his St Petersburg clan, the gang Putin collected around him from the time when he was deputy mayor of the city. Like Putin, he had collaborated with the KGB since he was a student. The two of them were practically born to the profession, but by nature not background.

Patrushev's job was to guard the President's back while the new order was being put into place before and during Putin's rise to power. His personal guardianship of Putin was all in the name of national security, of course.

He stood in silence for a moment, instilling a sort of cold quietness into the room. A military man, tall, erect and proud of the military achievements in his family, he is the perfect KGB clone.

His fitness from playing the favoured KGB sport of volleyball was evident from his lean strength. I knew he chaired the sport's national organisation. From gossip among acquaintances over at the FSB headquarters in Moscow, I also knew he read thrillers and spy stories obsessively, after a personal assistant hired for the purpose recommended the best ones. Otherwise he attended the Bolshoi regularly, but only to listen to Russian composers. And he hunted, drank vodka and collected weaponry.

After the surprise and then their oleaginous deference to the KGB boss, the three men in the room were silenced by his arrival. I stood automatically and he looked me over with what is normally called a practised eye.

There followed a complicated procedure, as there were only four chairs in the room. Kerchenko gave up his seat to Patrushev and took Yuri's. Yuri took Sasha's and Sasha was told to get another chair. I sat back down where I was.

Patrushev leaned his elbows on the desk, tucked the back of his hands under his chin and wasted no time.

'Anna, I want you to tell us what really goes on behind this man's ramblings,' he said in a clipped voice. 'I don't think any of us really believes that he is a drunk who rants on and on for nothing, do we? Or some obsessive at London's Speaker's Corner. His outspokenness about Vladimir Vladimirovich is a little hard to take at face value, don't you think?'

His use of my first name, rather than my rank, indicated that the meeting was to take a new turn and for the first time I felt nervous. In some walks of life, such intimacy is only menacing. Patrushev's presence had raised the stakes enormously. Whatever the reason Finn interested them, it was no longer because they believed they could turn him. Patrushev wouldn't be taking a personal role otherwise.

But I didn't see any need to reply beyond tilting my head in uncertain agreement.

'So. Why do you think he is so interested in giving us his thoughts on how much the West should distrust our president? What is he hoping to gain from this?' Patrushev then began to answer his own question. 'Unlike some, I don't think it was a prelude to him coming over to us,' he said, casting a withering look at General Kerchenko. 'You don't tell your girlfriend you hate her mother before you ask her to marry you, do you? Tell me your thoughts please, Anna, based on your very special position with him.'

'I'm sure that he never intended to defect,' I agreed and got cold looks from the General and Yuri. 'I think he genuinely dislikes the President, however, fears him perhaps, fears what Russia can become under his leadership. I think he is genuine in that.'

'But why is he so keen for us to know this?' Patrushev pressed me without a pause. 'There's barely a report of yours since New Year's Eve that doesn't contain his thoughts on the subject.'

'I don't feel that he is really talking to me at all,' I said truthfully. 'I believe when he tells me what he thinks about the President it is as if he is talking to his own people. He says it to me because of his frustration that nobody in London will listen to him. I don't think he has any motive for letting us know his thoughts. I think he's angry, frustrated, but he's not trying to give us any kind of message.'

'Maybe he's trying to get you to agree with him about our president,' Kerchenko said, with some accusation in his voice. 'To subvert you, perhaps, so that you'll help him get whatever it is he's after.'

Patrushev gave him a sharp look and then looked back at me again.

'I agree with you,' Patrushev said to me. 'He's not trying to give us or you any message at all. But now he has finally vented his anger about British policy to his superiors, where he formerly aired it only to you. He's stepped over the line, and they've recalled him to London. Would you agree?'

'I think he has committed professional suicide, yes,' I said. 'I think it's been coming for a long time. They put up with his increasingly undisciplined behaviour but now he's gone too far.'

'A spent force . . .' Patrushev said.

'I don't think so,' I said immediately, and I didn't know why I said it. Perhaps it was Finn's remark, 'I'm going feral.' Perhaps, too, it was the missing element in my conversation with Finn at the Baltschug – his assumption, the fact that he didn't think it mattered that I wouldn't go with him, *because it was inevitable we would be thrown together again.*

'Oh?' Patrushev said and there was a clammy silence in the room. 'A British spy is suddenly taken home for insubordination concerning the most fundamental level of policy and he is not a spent force? What will he do? Write a book, perhaps, exposing the limitations of Britain's intelligence service? Another David Shayler?'

'Perhaps the whole thing's a set-up,' I said. 'They want it to seem as though he's been sacked.'

'That's good. Yes, that's good. But you don't think he's another Shayler. Your valuable instincts tell you he's not.'

'They do.'

'Use them,' he said and leaned over towards me. 'Think independently. You are a good officer for that reason. Your progress has been noted with approval for some time. Think freely.'

'Thank you, sir,' I said, but I was thinking about my conversation with Vladimir earlier in the afternoon and how their encouragement to think freely had landed him a ten-year exile in the Cape Verde Islands.

'But be careful,' Patrushev said slowly, as if reading my thoughts. 'Remember where his independence, unbridled, undisciplined, seems to have got him.' For a moment I was confused as to whether he was talking about Vladimir or Finn. 'Independent thought is not anarchic thought,' Patrushev explained.

'No, sir,' I said, though that seemed to me to be exactly what it was.

'But first, let's get some tea,' he said to nobody in particular and Kerchenko gave the order with a nod of his head to Sacha who picked up the phone and called for tea.

'I like all your reports, Anna,' Patrushev said. The use of my name again made me increasingly wary. 'They are a mix of the factual and personal. They have insight.'

I judged that I had thanked him enough by now.

'But no one, no one can get everything into a

report. The apparently unimportant comment, the throwaway line, the nuance, the remark that seems to mean something but means something else. And, simply, the forgotten. All that could amount to a whole volume for a twenty-minute conversation, as I'm sure you're aware.'

He then went back over a dozen of my reports on Finn, apparently at random, which had been submitted by me over the past twelve months. The tea arrived, and it was drunk. Kerchenko looked impatient but also seemed to be struggling to control it. The other two were bored and looked as if they wanted something stronger than tea.

We must have spent two hours meticulously treading back over old ground, dissecting a sentence here, a glimpse of behaviour there. Patrushev showed no sign of tiring. Then he finally closed the files and put his elbows on the desk and looked at me. Was the meeting over or was this simply a change of tack?

Out of the blue he said, 'Let's talk about Finn.' He simply said Finn. We'd never used anything but Markus.

The other three men in the room looked aghast and then confused. Proper procedure had suddenly been obliterated and they didn't understand.

I felt my stomach drop and a horrible void open up in its place. I closed my eyes.

As Markus, Finn was always, to me, at a convenient distance in my reports. I was informing on Markus, not Finn. The two had become separated. To me, Markus was almost another person, Finn's professional doppelgänger. But I understood immediately why Patrushev had dropped this bombshell.

We were no longer to talk about a target of Russian intelligence, but about a relationship, mine and Finn's.

I remember, presumably when I had opened my eyes again, seeing Patrushev watching from the other side of the desk. His face expressed a non-committal curiosity.

'Yes,' he said, as if he had seen some answer in my reaction. 'Let's talk about Finn.'

And so, for the next hour or so, we talked about Finn, right back to the earliest reports on him, right back to the beginning.

Of course, much of it had appeared already in the dossier, both from before I knew Finn and from my own reports. But Patrushev wanted what was behind the facts. We strayed increasingly from the area of intelligence into assessment.

Looking only at Patrushev, I began to talk about what I knew of Finn's childhood.

Finn had told me about it on a trip to Irkutsk in Siberia. He was visiting the city to look over a British investment there in his Trade and Industry role and he asked me to accompany him. He had a surprise for me. We arrived in Irkutsk on a bleak afternoon in January when the temperature was minus twenty-five degrees and he went at once to the offices of a gold-mining company, a joint venture between British and Russian investors. It was a Friday. When he returned to the hotel, he said, 'Now we have the weekend to ourselves, Rabbit. I've booked a place up on Lake Baikal. That's the surprise,' he said delightedly.

He'd arranged the business trip in order to spend the weekend with me.

We stayed in an old wooden house by the frozen lake, the deepest in the world. The house had been bought by a tycoon in Irkutsk and then modernised, though the only real concession to the modern was central heating and a generator. At night, in bed, it was too hot under the bearskins.

The next day we walked along the cliff below the house and found a way down to the lake. Finn collected up some brushwood and made a fire on the ice.

'It must be six feet thick at least,' he said.

'Be careful,' I said.

We sat on blankets around the fire and then Finn began to tell me where he was born, about his family and his upbringing.

'I come from the island of Inishturk,' he said in a self-mockingly grand way, as if he'd owned the island. 'It's on the west coast of Ireland.'

Finn's Irish connection had always fascinated General Kerchenko as well as my two case officers. In their world view, anyone born in Ireland would surely wish to damage the British Government.

'The community I was born into was an experiment. I was born into a social experiment, Anna, just like you but in a different way. Inishturk back then was what is known as an "alternative community". It later morphed into a hippy colony. My mother and father were actually both British but Ireland was the venue for my conception and birth for the simple reason that it was as far from what they called the "rat race" or the "machine" as possible. It still provided some familiarity of culture, I suppose, if only in the climate and the rugged scenery of the North Atlantic.

'The idea of the community was that everyone played an equal role,' he said, and stirred the fire with a stick. 'There were no leaders. Whether your job was cultivating vegetables or chairing what they called community conscience meetings to decide where the community was going, or what was wrong, you were all equal.'

He looked at me with weary amusement and exhaled a stream of cigarette smoke. 'Sound familiar?' he said.

I smiled but said nothing.

'The children all belonged to the community,' he went on, now staring into the fire. 'They were not part of their parents. I stayed in most of the stone crofts, which had been renovated in a rudimentary way, at some time or another. The community was more or less under orders to be one happy family. I was taught that my family was the community, and my blood relations were like anyone else.

'When I was six I was put through an ordeal they called "shouting therapy", which was for my own benefit, of course. I was stood in the centre of a circle while the adults shouted abuse at me and hurled the most vicious personal insults they could come up with; what I looked like, how I talked, my pathetic desire to be close to my mother. It was a ritualistic humiliation. It was very frightening but very organised. I cried. I couldn't stop crying and they judged that to be good. The purpose of the process was to destroy my self-belief and make me need them more. Equality meant the equality of subjugation.'

Finn threw more wood on the fire and stood up.

'That, of course, is always the way with social engineering,' he said. 'You know that as well as I do, Anna. But hippies were supposed to be different. They're just human, as it turned out.'

He held out his hand for me and we walked away from the fire a little. The low sun had disappeared behind a clouded winter sky. The trees were frosted up above us, and it was completely still. Then it started to snow.

'My mother became the leader of the community,' he resumed. 'She was a tyrant. My father was weak, resentful, humiliated and did nothing to protect me at all. He became an alcoholic eventually and left the island. That was when I was about seven. I haven't seen him since. Then, slowly, an elite formed in the community, as it does in any community. In this case it was made up of the members who controlled the supply of drugs, mainly hashish in the beginning, then heroin. Opium for the people.'

We walked back to the fire and Finn raked it over unnecessarily. No spark could have lit anything on that bitter day. Then he put his arm around me and we walked back up the fishing track we'd found to get down to the lake.

'But when I was twelve, I was saved. My uncle, my father's elder brother, came to Ireland and took me away,' he said. 'I don't know how he managed it, it was totally against my mother's will. I expect it involved money. I went with my uncle to Cambridge and began school for the first time, proper school. My uncle was a biochemist at Cambridge University, my aunt taught Buddhism. For a while after they took me away, people from the community hounded us. They wanted me back and it was frightening. They came to the house outside Cambridge, sending my aunt and uncle threats and hate mail. But they tired of it and disappeared from my life. So my uncle had me educated. I won a scholarship to Cambridge. I haven't seen my mother since I was twelve. She disappeared to South America, I believe.'

We arrived at the wooden house and Finn hugged me for a long time before we entered. When he pulled away he couldn't look at me and I knew he'd told me something very painful to him. I think it was the first time I felt I loved him.

It was getting dark outside the windows at the Forest. I realised it must be late. But Putin's head of intelligence showed no signs of urgency. A bottle of vodka had finally arrived, apparently to placate the General, but Patrushev's fondness for our national drink is well known.

We could hear the traffic on the motorway into Moscow and I thought of Barvikha, which lay not far away in the forest in the opposite direction to the capital. I'd said I would meet Nana there, but she was used to me breaking arrangements.

Suddenly Patrushev shot a question at me.

'And did they?' he asked. 'Did they destroy Finn's self-belief at the commune?'

'In a somewhat misleading way, I've never met anyone with more self-belief,' I said. 'He has a certain confidence that finds it unnecessary to display self-belief in public at all. It is a peculiarly English assumption, in my opinion. He demonstrates self-belief without there being any outward signs of it. I would say that his regular undermining of himself, for example, of his background and of his country is a supreme sign of self-confidence. He told me that ever since the shouting when he was six, conflict, anger and aggression have all left him cold.'

'And all the time Finn kept something of himself back from them,' Patrushev said.

'I think so. Certainly since I've known him, apart from that one conversation he seems to have placed his childhood in a sealed room. Either that or he has come to terms with it.'

'He's had psychiatric help, perhaps. Maybe he's been in therapy?' Patrushev said.

'I don't know. He didn't say.'

Yuri sneered and knocked back the full glass of vodka that Patrushev had just poured. I admit it was strange to hear Patrushev utter the word 'therapy'. I wanted to smile, but stopped myself. Finn liked to call the repressive political measures of Putin's re-gime 'theraputin'.

Patrushev filled my glass and those of the others.

'What was his relationship with his uncle and his aunt?' he said as he was pouring the vodka.

'Gratitude, certainly. Respect, duty. He keeps in touch with them, sees them regularly when he's in England. His uncle is retired from a professorship—'

'Yes, yes. In biochemistry. But love, does he love them?'

Kerchenko looked shocked that the word had come up a second time in a single day.

'No, no, I don't think so,' I said carefully.

'He's a man independent of love,' Patrushev said, and I wasn't certain whether it was a question or not.

'He told me that he loves Russia,' I volunteered.

'Ah,' Patrushev exhaled and unclasped his hands and leaned back for the first time in the broad arm-chair. 'The English are the most fatally romantic people on earth. They're always falling in love with other people's countries. A symptom of something or other, eh, General?'

Kerchenko didn't know what he was talking about.

Patrushev leaned forward again.

'So, Finn has no parents to speak of,' Patrushev summed up. 'He doesn't love the people who raised him as their son, he runs from woman to woman during all the time we've known him, and he loves an abstract Russia.'

I didn't reply, knowing now what was coming.

'And now he says he loves you,' Patrushev said, rolling his tanks gently on to my lawn.

'He says so,' I said, emphasising my doubt about it.

'Apparently Finn doesn't tell women he loves them in order to get them into bed,' Patrushev said knowledgeably. 'Apparently he doesn't need to. We know that from several sources before you. And besides,' he said, looking at me in a strangely aggressive way, 'he'd already got you into bed, hadn't he? So why did he tell you he loved you? What do you feel, Anna?'

'Perhaps he told me because he knew he was going to lose me,' I said, 'and it brought out the romantic in him. In my opinion, Finn is the sort of man who tells you he loves you as consolation for him leaving you.'

I instantly regretted my reply.

'But he told you three days before he left Moscow that he loved you,' Patrushev snapped immediately. 'If he knew he was leaving you, he would have told you that too, surely.'

'Then perhaps I'm wrong about my previous thought,' I said, and felt the ground slipping under me. 'In that case, my guess is that he must have known he was being recalled, or something of the kind. But he couldn't tell me for security reasons.'

'We believe he left in an unplanned way,' Patrushev said sharply. 'He was bundled out of Moscow by his people. That's true, isn't it?' He looked at Yuri.

'He was practically frog-marched,' Yuri said.

Patrushev swung his head back at me. 'So it's odd, isn't it, that he knew he was leaving, even though it was unplanned. He tells you he loves you because he knows he's leaving. That is very plausible. But how does he know he's leaving?'

Patrushev leaned across the desk and fixed me with his stony eyes.

I had nothing to say. I was trying to recover myself.

'Perhaps the whole thing is a set-up,' I repeated. 'The British want us to think they've sacked him.'

'Perhaps so,' he said.

'Why would they do that?'

But Patrushev ignored my question.

'Do you believe he loves you, Colonel?' he asked, for the first time using my rank rather than my name.

I felt the other three focusing their gaze on me.

'Yes,' I said finally. 'Yes I do,' and I surprised myself by saying it. Suddenly, I felt light and happy, and as if the men in the room were from some other, unreal time and place.

Patrushev suddenly dismissed Kerchenko and the two officers.

It was very late by now, I don't remember what time it was, and I wanted to get away and to go home to Barvikha. But Patrushev showed no sign of leaving when the others had gone and suggested that the two of us have something to eat in the building. I felt uncomfortable that the night might be taking a turn for the personal. He couldn't take his eyes off me and I now regretted wearing the clothes intended to disturb the General.

But a deeper instinct told me that this wasn't the real root of my anxiety. This instinct was a feeling that Patrushev's interest in Finn and me wasn't over just yet and that I didn't know where it was leading.

He was now full of courtesy, which only put me further on my guard, opening doors and offering his arm to me. When we came to the restaurant in the Forest's recreation block, the staff and the other people still working in the building were wide-eyed that Patrushev, the FSB chief and Putin's close friend, should be here at all, let alone at this hour. I felt my status rising as we walked down the corridors and took the lift down.

Patrushev ordered a bottle of wine and from somewhere that certainly wasn't the staff restaurant, sushi was produced for us.

It was as I took a mouthful from the tray in front of me that he asked a seemingly casual question.

'Do you sometimes wonder about that conversation on New Year's Eve, Anna? When Finn talked about Schmidtke? You remember?'

I nodded.

'It's strange that he never talked about it again, never, ever alluded to it, don't you think?'

My pulse quickened as I thought of that night, of the look in Finn's eyes when he stared at me as he told the story of Schmidtke; of how there was a deeper meaning in the story that was somehow meant for me personally, unseen, of course, by any of the microphones that recorded every word.

'I believe he said it in relation to the President,' I said. 'It seemed to be some sort of back bearing that Finn was taking from the moment he first heard that Vladimir Vladimirovich had been appointed Acting President. The back bearing was East Germany, the end of the eighties, the President's former years of service over there.'

'Yes, of course. In a sense it was part of his obsession with the President,' Patrushev said. 'But I think the connection he was making was more than just a back bearing to those days and to the President alone. He seemed to be making some kind of link, not just of the personalities, but of the nature of their work, of a policy perhaps that connected Schmidtke to the President. On what basis is he trying to link Schmidtke to the President? Why does he think there is such a link?'

'I'm afraid I don't know,' I said. 'He said nothing more.'

'And then you both left the house, didn't you?' Patrushev pressed me now. 'You talked intensely by the pond in the forest. At least, he did and you listened. You're sure you remembered everything he was saying in that twenty minutes or so in your reports?'

'I think so. It was late. So much had happened that night already. Finn spoke in a wild way – I remember thinking he seemed almost possessed.'

'Possessed?'

'Yes. I remember wondering at the time what the General and the others would think of his words; that Finn was mad, perhaps.'

'But we agree that Finn isn't mad, that he doesn't ramble unnecessarily. Yes?'

'Yes. Yes, I suppose so, but everyone has their moments when they don't make much sense.'

'Do they?' Patrushev said coldly. 'Tell me again what was possessing him.'

'He was talking about history and the remaking of it, over and over again. He seemed obsessed by the recurrence of the same themes. This link between Schmidtke and the President seemed to be one of those themes.'

'So he believed that what Schmidtke was doing in Germany back then involved the President too?' Patrushev said. 'Finn is trying to change the good opinion the President enjoys in the West. He's looking for evidence. And then . . . Beware of Vladimir Putin . . . is that it?'

'I don't know. He wasn't specific.'

'Oh, I think so,' Patrushev replied quickly. 'Finn sees a connection somewhere between those times and the present. He believes he can make trouble from the President's past.'

I thought of Finn then, in the forest at Barvikha,

of how he had seemed infused by some external power. And I thought of my question to him, that he hadn't answered. What plan was he talking about?

He had mentioned the Plan again at our last meeting at the Baltschug, just once before he clammed up as he had done before in the forest. But perhaps from some instinct, I hadn't included it in my last report after our Baltschug meeting, and now Patrushev was really close to this omission.

Suddenly I felt very alert. The tiredness that had been washing over me for some time, and which Patrushev seemed to be enjoying, evaporated. I wondered why he was asking me this, after the other three had been dismissed. It seemed somehow to have a crucial importance because of that. Even the General and his case officers weren't to hear this line of questioning. I felt we were approaching the centre of power.

'I thought he was slightly crazy that night,' I said. 'As I said, I remember thinking then, what will my superiors think of Finn's great theme of history and so on? Will they think it fiction, bathos or madness?'

'I don't think it is any of those,' Patrushev said. 'Do you, Anna?'

'Finn believes in a theme,' I replied. 'That theme, which runs from the days of the Soviet Union right up to today, is that the KGB never wholly lost control and has now regained it in a way that is perhaps more dangerous to the West than ever before. He believes that perestroika was managed by the KGB.'

'Yes,' Patrushev said, ignoring the old initials of our great organisation. But I didn't know whether he was agreeing with what Finn believed or with the fact itself.

'Schmidtke, the President, Russia's reviving fortunes, our new stronger security service . . . what did he call this theme that night?'

'He talked about a plan . . .'

'A plan, yes. Have the General or your case officers ever picked up that comment of his from your reports? About a plan?'

'No. No, they haven't,' I said.

'So what is this plan?' Patrushev asked.

'Finn asked me if I knew what it was,' I said. 'But I didn't know what he was talking about.'

I had the uncomfortable feeling that Finn's monologue existed somewhere in our archives, recorded, though I knew that this couldn't be possible. Nevertheless, the fear drove me to be truthful.

Patrushev leaned in so that I felt the smell of alcohol on his breath.

'He said a plan. Is that exactly what he said?'

I recalled exactly what Finn had said that night.

'I think he said the Plan, actually, but I may be wrong.'

'He said *the* Plan,' Patrushev replied, more as a statement. 'He used the English pronoun, yes?'

'Yes, I think he did,' I said.

I began to realise that this simple change of pronoun explained the presence of Patrushev that day at the Forest. It was what he had come for, in fact. It told him that Finn knew something, or suspected something, however little, that was known only to a very small group of individuals. Certainly Kerchenko and the case officers didn't know anything, and neither did I.

'What is it?' I asked him. 'The Plan. What does it mean?'

Patrushev stared at me and I knew I shouldn't have asked the question. Eventually, he took his stare away and flicked his hand for a waiter to remove the empty plates. When the man had gone, Patrushev held me with his gaze again.

'I'll walk you to your car,' he said.

We left the restaurant and Patrushev waved away the staff who offered him help. We walked out into a dark, moonless night and strolled across the car park which was the size of a parade ground.

'Do you know why MI6 has kept Finn in Moscow for so long?' Patrushev asked when we were far away from the buildings.

'No, I don't.'

'I believe you don't,' he said.

I returned his stare.

'We have a great interest in Finn, Anna. It is a vital interest for Russia.'

'I guessed so. You wouldn't be here otherwise.'

'You're smarter than your colleagues, if I may say so,' Patrushev said and took my arm.

'I'm going to confide in you, Anna, because it's important for your work, for us, for your country. You understand?'

'This is not even for the others' ears,' I said.

'Exactly. Confidential isn't a strong enough word,' Patrushev said. 'This is to be buried at the bottom of the deepest ocean as far as you're concerned.'

'I understand.'

'We believe Finn has overstayed his welcome here for so many years for a very good reason. He has a source. An unusually important source, and one who will communicate only with him. We believe this source is so senior, either in the FSB or the SVR but probably the latter, that his identity can be restricted to a handful of perhaps ten people. We want to know who that source is, Anna.'

I didn't answer. I was thinking wildly of Finn and his amiable, frivolous, carefree front and the huge secret Patrushev believed it all concealed.

'You're a clever woman, Anna. You've made him fall in love with you,' Patrushev said.

I felt sick at that. I couldn't speak.

'And so you're now in the perfect position,' he said. 'We want you to help us to make Russia strong again.'

'Yes,' I said.

'There is a bright and modern future for our country. But there's someone very close to our hearts who doesn't want that. We want the identity of the enemy, Anna. You are in the right place. You have the right background. And you are a rising star yourself in this new Russia. You can make history, perhaps, if you find this insider who will do anything, it seems, to damage Russia. That's your job, and that alone. Find the identity of this traitor who has talked about the Plan.'

As I drove along the dark road to Barvikha that night, I felt completely joined to Finn, completely connected. He'd known we'd be reunited, and now I knew why. I was to be assigned to watch him again, sometime and somewhere else. And, once more, I knew that this future conjunction enabled me to postpone a decision to leave Russia for ever.

12

A **S I SIT** now in the vault at Tegernsee, I recall
how well Finn guarded his great secret from me
while he remained in Moscow. Had he been about to
tell me on those two occasions, by the pond on New
Year's Eve and at the Baltschug Hotel? He had come
close. But he drew back both times. And I know now
that it was for my sake that he had kept his secret to
himself. I doubt otherwise whether I would ever have
been able to act as ignorant in front of Patrushev as I
had.

Down in the vault below the little pink house,
the oil in the burner is low and I reach for a can, fill
the container, and the burner picks up. I stop and
listen. A footstep upstairs? People passing by in the
cobbled street outside? How much time have I got?
Where is Finn?

I'm certain that I'm the only person to have read

his record of that time. I can see, on this winter's night six years later, that everything here in the vault in Tegernsee is as Finn left it. It is here for a purpose and that purpose is to hide what happened, not just from us at the Forest, but from his own people in London too. He didn't trust them not to destroy the evidence.

I am reading an unread, virgin script and it feels appropriate to be reading it in a place that has been the refuge for illegal bibles, religious tracts, secret meetings and wounded fugitives from the religious wars that ravaged Europe five centuries ago. I am in a place of secrets.

Finn chose his hideaway at Tegernsee well. He found a small, pale pink wood-shuttered house, with a sharp-leaning roof against the snow. But evidently the most important reason he chose it was for the vault below. The entrance to the vault was behind a mantelpiece with a false gas log fire beneath it, its copper pipes unconnected. The whole mantelpiece and fire slid sideways. The entrance to the vault in the space behind the fire was protected by steel doors.

It was a modernised version of an old religious hideaway that existed beneath the site of the sixteenth-century house and, in recent times, someone had seen fit to improve on it. Finn had leased the building in the name of an offshore, brass-plate company in the British Virgin Islands.

But he also chose Tegernsee, the town itself, with his typical eye for the dramatic. Two streets away, the old bull-necked Stasi spy Anatoly Schmidtke lives out his retirement in the upstairs apartment of a wooden chalet, next door to a lingerie shop. The cameras of the BND, the German security service that made their deal with him and brushed over the tracks that could have embarrassed their masters, have long since gone from across the river at the back.

'But Schmidtke doesn't just live with his memories,' Finn writes. 'Tegernsee is the home of other interesting characters, Anna. They are people well known to Schmidtke from the past, some of whom play a part in this story. It is just as I told you and Nana on that New Year's Eve.'

These residents of Tegernsee are not old spies, like Schmidtke, but Western European financiers, businessmen from the former East Germany, wealthy and now ancient ex-Nazis, and a few retired politicians with multi-tentacled connections. There are people here, apart from Schmidtke, who played double roles in the Cold War and are a link to the extension of that war in this, the new millennium.

'Tegernsee is so beautiful, so perfect, so private,' Finn writes, 'that it is a place where the devil himself might choose to reside, hiding himself behind high gates in a multimillion-dollar chalet like so many of its other inhabitants. And from where, like them, he might choose to emerge in a Hermès jacket, silk polo neck and St Laurent slacks, perfectly tanned, immaculately silver-haired, his features, like theirs, appearing at any time of day or night as if shaved and oiled and pampered by some privately retained gentleman barber only a moment before.

'This is how these men always look,' he writes, 'wherever we see them in the world. They seem to have been briefly animated in order to step out from the pages of a retirement edition of *Harpers & Queen*, money and deceit oozing from their pores. The devil's most devilish when respectable. These are men to whom power belongs and, in their Faustian bargain, they themselves belong to that power.'

He lists them, these elite inhabitants of Tegernsee. They are politicians, bankers and financiers, industrialists, ex-Communists and ex-Nazis, and the grey capitalists who hide somewhere in the centre ground.

'I'm writing up this journal late at night, darling Rabbit. I'm a little drunk and maybe I'm emotional from the loneliness of it all. Loneliness is playing tricks on me, in fact. Last night I dreamed that all the world's a stage and I'm fighting some devil at the centre of it. *"And thus I clothe my naked villainy. And seem a saint when most I play the devil."*

'That's what some of these residents of Tegernsee are like, Anna. They seem so perfect.'

I close the book. That's how he signs off his night's work, quoting Shakespeare. I imagine him, from this distance in time of his writing, falling into bed, exhausted but fulfilled from choking up the bile of his anger.

Despite the renewed vigour of the burner, the cold drives me out of the vault and into these old streets and I do what I promised myself I wouldn't do for security reasons; I take with me Finn's book that recounts those summer months in the year 2000, after his sudden departure from Moscow. Lastly, I slide the handgun with its twelve-inch barrel into a shoulder holster and fill my pockets with shells. Outside it is snowing and a driving bitter wind rushes down from the Algauer mountains.

Tegernsee's charming medieval streets with their low houses and discreet, expensive shops weave around the lake. Tegernsee, I'm now beginning to see, is also perfect for its geographical position. A short road takes you across the Bavarian Alps to Austria or, a little further, to the old Communist East. A different, equally short route, rides over the Algauer Alps to Liechtenstein, and, further west, beside Lake Bodensee, to Switzerland.

Tegernsee is a place of crossings. It is like some petite and perfect geographical transaction, in which money and secrets are exchanged, with private banks and borders of every kind neatly close at hand.

I walk up the street, on to a pavement beside the frozen lake – the *See* of Tegernsee – and into the thick warmth of a *gasthaus*, Finn's precious exercise book tucked safely into my coat.

It is Saturday night and the place is full of locals. Loud Bavarian music is playing from a band on a small, improvised stage and there is dancing. Bavarian regional dress is everywhere: feathered hats, lederhosen, braces, big boots for the drinkers or patent shoes with buckles for the dancers, and the waitresses wear long white full dresses and colourful, embroidered waistcoats. Bavarian traditions are not reserved for tourists.

I sit at a table by the monumental stone fireplace, flaring its flames and heat from monstrous logs, and order food and wine. And then I open Finn's 'book of record', as he calls it.

13

FTER FINN'S SHOWDOWN with the embassy's head of station, he was confined to a room in the building while two thuggish escorts from the Service flew out from London to Moscow. They escorted him to Domodyeva airport to the south of the city and the three of them enjoyed a first-class trip to London, courtesy of British Airways.

They take Finn to a house in Norwood in south London, where he is questioned for nearly two weeks.

It is all routine stuff. First a man called Sanders who says he's from the Russian Desk, but whom Finn has never met, questions him.

'We want to know about your Russian girl, your Anna, Finn. She's had a very successful career so far, a shining career. She's shot up the ladder, it seems. A full colonel at her age! Does she know? How much of a threat is she?'

'She's very dangerous indeed,' Finn says. 'And I don't know what she knows.'

His reply holds up the process for a while and Sanders takes the opportunity to confer elsewhere. When he returns, Sanders is with another man, a junior Finn vaguely knows, and they repeat the question.

'Look,' Finn says, 'she's dangerous, all right, but only to a good night's sleep.'

'How do you feel about her?'

'Feel?'

'Do you miss her, Finn? Do you miss Anna?'

'You can't miss her.'

'For God's sake, grow up, Finn,' Sanders says angrily.

Then they all leave and some old buffer comes along and reels back the years, with questions Finn was asked when he first joined the Service.

'Have you or any members of your family ever held any extreme political views?' this man asks kindly.

It was a question that was asked of people who needed clearance for minor civil service jobs rather than clearance for the security services.

'Am I being prosecuted, then?' Finn asks. 'Is this some kind of prelude for doing me under the Official Secrets Act?'

'My dear chap, no, no, nothing of the kind.'

But then Finn tells the man he does have a member of his family who has extreme political views.

'Oh yes?' the buffer says politely, maintaining perfect calm in the face of this unusual statement. 'And who is that? What are his or her views, Finn?'

'My aunt thinks Blair is Jesus Christ,' Finn says.

At this they're very angry and don't see him for two days.

'Will you try to see her again?' Sanders asks when they all finally come back. But this time they've come back with the big guns, with Adrian, Finn's recruiter and handler and who's in line for the top job at MI6.

'As far as she and I are concerned, it was already ten years past our bedtime when we met,' Finn says. 'I was too late. But now it's finished. No. I won't try to contact her.'

Adrian then leans across the table and puts his hand on Finn's arm.

'She doesn't know the reason we left you in Moscow all that time,' he breathes. 'Does she, Finn?'

It is a blunt and almost threatening statement that has all the subtlety of a pair of thumbscrews.

Finn looks back into Adrian's ruddy face and answers truthfully.

'No, Adrian, she doesn't know that.'

'It would have been so much easier if you'd told us that at the beginning,' Adrian says. 'When we brought you in. You could have saved us and yourself an awful lot of trouble.'

Finn doesn't reply.

Adrian turns gentle now.

'You're home, Finn. You're home now. You've done a fine job. You'll get over her.'

But Finn doesn't feel he's home. And he doesn't feel he'll get over 'her'.

* * *

Finn's superiors and the interrogators who visited him at the house in Norwood never thought that he would defect, with or without the 'Russian girl'.

'They wanted to tidy me up, that's all,' Finn says. 'And to get me out of their way. They wanted me safely pensioned off. In their eyes I was a worn-out, washed-up, mentally and emotionally compromised ex-officer, and the only thing that really concerned them was that I would keep my mouth shut and how much I was going to cost them in retirement.'

And suddenly he's writing straight to me.

'Anna, I felt you with me in that room in London. I loved you then and I love you now.'

It is just a sentence, but it is the first love letter from my lover to me.

After Finn was let go 'on a long leash' from Norwood, he tidied up his affairs and visited his aunt and uncle outside Cambridge. Otherwise he kept a low profile so that the Service could be satisfied he wasn't about to do anything rash.

'There are enough dissatisfied former intelligence officers in the world,' he says, 'and I don't want to add myself to the list. I've seen them many times, the dissatisfied, men whose careers have ended in anger and resentment and demands for bigger payoffs from the Service, men who think they're worth more but whose real gripe is the fear of a wasted life for which they believe they should be endlessly compensated by other people, by anybody but themselves.'

In typical Finn style, having established this record of what *wasn't* motivating him, rather than what was, he then turns a new page and writes just two words.

The Beginning.

In the late autumn of 2000 Finn let it be known to the Service that he was taking a 'holiday'. But this holiday wasn't to a beach on the north African coast or to the cultural treasures of Italy or the Far East. It was to the unusual destination of Saarbrucken, the old coal-mining town, long in decline, on the German side at the junction of the three borders of France, Germany and Luxembourg. He was, as he'd warned me in Moscow, going feral.

Here on a dull, cold November day when the wind was blowing fine, freezing sleet down the River Saar and the grey town and the grey sky were fused into one, Finn met an old German acquaintance from the past, in a cheap Chinese restaurant under a grim post-war office building that ran for two blocks down the Goethestrasse from the river.

In this anonymous dead-end town in a backwater of Germany Finn chose the twelve-euro menu and his contact chose the same, and they kept their silence as two Tiger beers were brought across the grubby red and gold, dragon-painted room with its paper lamps that swayed whenever the door was opened on to the grey, damp concrete outside.

Finn doesn't trust the man who sits opposite him, but he likes him and would like to be able to trust him.

'A good German,' as Finn puts it, his tongue

firmly in cheek. And then, more thoughtfully, 'Dieter is someone who looks beyond the narrow tunnel walls of his job. He thinks for himself, he sees the world moving outside the avenue of his own efforts, and that is why perhaps, like me, he eventually lost his job.'

Finn has known Dieter since 1989, from the time when the British seized Schmidtke at Tegel airport in Berlin, and whisked him to London. Dieter was one of the BND intelligence officers who formally received Schmidtke back into the bosom of German justice when the British bowed to Germany's insistence that he was theirs.

I think Finn thought of Dieter as being an inappropriate introduction for me, unlike most of his sources. It wasn't just that Dieter was uninterested in women, but simply that it would have made him uncomfortable to sit down and break bread with an officer of the Russian SVR. Finn never said so, but I felt his reluctance in Dieter's case came from the fact that Dieter could not compromise with an enemy who had not only enslaved the East of his country but who had also corrupted so much of what was good in the West. Unlike the British and the Americans, Dieter had been fighting the KGB on the front line.

Sometimes I've thought that Dieter was an invention of Finn's. But here he was, written on the page; a ghost, but a living ghost of our past.

Dieter is a tall, slightly stooped man with black hair thinning and greying at the sides. He has a sharp, lean face, and a dark stubble shadows the pale skin of his jaw. He rarely smiles, but seems to carry a burden of solemnity that leaches from his expressionless eyes into the slope of his shoulders and the movements of his hands. He speaks tonelessly, as if giving a statement to disbelieving interrogators.

He joined West Germany's intelligence service, the BND, at the start of the long post-war years of reformation. While the world watched Germany rise from the ashes and saw its industry thrive and dominate, its foreign service, the BND, and its army, unlike its automobiles and electrical goods, were forbidden from going abroad. By constitutional decree, its spies could not spy beyond its borders.

And during all that time, for decades, the East loomed across the Wall, porous only to those sent specifically by us in Soviet Russia – us the West's enemies – to infiltrate, to corrupt and to threaten West German political figures and the country's financial and commercial institutions.

'For our allies,' Dieter once explained to Finn, 'for you, the Wall was the front line in the war against Communism, the stark divide. But for us West Germans the Wall was far less clearly defined and permanent. For us, it was not some remote battleground, far from home, but a false wall, a partition in our semi-detached existence as one country. The dream of unification, of a greater revived Germany, never died on either side of the Wall,' he explained. 'The desire for communication with the East was overwhelming. We were all Germans.'

Finn raises the bottle of Tiger beer without bothering to pour it into the glass and Dieter responds.

'Cheers,' the German says in English.

'Cheers, Dieter. It's been a long time.'

'More than ten years,' Dieter replies.

Finn studies the face of his old colleague. It is a lived-in face, the eyes those of a man who has taken in more than he has given away.

In his early years with the BND Dieter had seen the Wall go up. The enemy and his German cousins were one and the same. But as a German whose adulthood emerged from the shadows of the Nazi war, he'd learned reserve, kept his own counsel, and seemed to Finn shy and wounded.

'Nazism didn't just end,' Dieter had told Finn, 'like the curtain coming down on a play. The Nazi migrations after the war sought to keep the flame alive, not just in the well-documented places like South America and other remote parts, but closer to home too. An SS officer who was a friend of my father's went to Turkey, for example, because it was far enough away from retribution while still being close enough to get a decent bottle of wine.

'And closer than Turkey there was Liechtenstein, just across our border. Did you know the population of Liechtenstein doubled at the end of the war? Oh yes. It was largely a German and Austrian migration, for anyone from the Nazi regime who possessed the necessary loot and influence.'

For Germans like Dieter, determined to remove the stain of their country's recent past, the totalitarian mindset of the ex-Nazis, whether across the southern border in Liechtenstein or elsewhere, was closer to that of the East German regime than to the new West Germany. Ideological differences between Communist and ex-Nazi were irrelevant to the trade that could be done between two former hated enemies.

'Totalitarianism, like money, is not squeamish about whose bed it shares,' Dieter had said to Finn.

After the British had handed Schmidtke over to the Germans, Dieter had been one of Schmidtke's interrogators for the next two years, until the investigation into the old Stasi spy was quietly dropped and Schmidtke retired to Tegernsee with a good pension and the protection of his former enemies. Dieter wasn't happy with the deal and lost his job for being unable to come to terms with it.

A waitress brings menus to the table.

'I want to go back to the beginning, Dieter,' Finn says, when they've drunk half their beers. 'I need to see the unbroken line from back then, from 1961, to the present.'

'What makes you think the line is unbroken?' Dieter replies.

Finn doesn't answer.

The soup arrives, another beer is ordered. And then Dieter slowly begins to talk, as if he were having difficulty with the memories. But Finn knows he is like an old actor who's played a part so many times in the private theatre of his own head that the lines will never leave.

'When Kommerzielle Koordinierung – KoKo – was set up in East Berlin, just on the other side of the Wall in 1961, their motto was "Necessity has no law",' Dieter begins. 'It was a thieves' decree. Jewellery, artwork, stamp collections, antiquarian books – anything of value belonging to East German citizens – it was all on KoKo's menu. But this was state theft and, while some objects of value were simply stolen, in general the state and their Stasi agents applied the classic bureaucratic, totalitarian state methods of theft.

'To give you an example, Finn, people were told they had to insure their property, such as jewellery, for outrageous sums which they couldn't afford. When they failed to do so, the property was confiscated. That was one method. The value of a citizen's private property was hugely inflated by KoKo, in order to inflate the insurance value, simply for the purpose of rendering its owners unable to pay. Sometimes Schmidtke's men inflated the value by 1,000 per cent. Then, when the owners couldn't pay, or their persecutors simply tired of this longer bureaucratic route, the agents of KoKo would invoke the so-called Fortune Law that existed in East Germany and that said it was illegal to possess property of such a high value. The state could claim that the private citizen had broken the Fortune Law that regulated the private wealth of citizens.

'Huge numbers of private homes in East Germany were raided by the Stasi. I have walked with an old man after the Wall came down along the pawn shops and the second-hand shop windows of West Berlin, looking for a smart Swiss wristwatch that was taken from him right at the beginning of this grand theft. He never found it, but others have sometimes found their stolen property since eighty-nine, tucked away in a street market somewhere.

'The state raked in fifty million Deutschmarks a year from thefts like this and it went on for more than twenty-five years, though with decreasing returns, of course. The East Germans were hard up. There was an embargo in the West on the export of technology. In the East they needed to fund their own technological development.'

'And their own intelligence operations in the West,' Finn interrupts.

'Certainly, their own operations in the West, many of which concerned precisely the theft of technological secrets. And this theft was mainly from us, in West Germany. So, in the beginning, KoKo stole the valuables, sold them to West Germans and then used the money to bribe West Germans in particular for industrial secrets. But they also used *Raubgold*, this stolen wealth, to corrupt our bankers, politicians, even us in intelligence. A lot of money was available for bribing West Germans.'

'Schmidtke told us that KoKo used a holding company as cover, to keep up appearances,' Finn says, remembering. 'Art and Antiquities GmbH it was called, if I remember rightly. It sounded very sound, very proper. Dealers in London did business with it all the time. The company, one removed from KoKo, enabled buyers to turn a blind eye.'

'Oh yes,' Dieter says. 'The two Germanys proved that crime pays,' he says. 'To both sides.'

'And Schmidtke was the great bureaucrat in charge.'

'Schmidtke was the head of KoKo, he organised

this *Raubgold*. And, in doing so, he learned many more valuable things. He learned how companies worked offshore, how the lawyers handle that side of things, which lawyers could be tempted on our side, how tax worked and was avoided, how to launder wealth, which banks were open to corruption. We were complicit here in the West, or at least many, many individuals in powerful positions were complicit. And all the time Schmidtke had the Stasi and the KGB to back him up with threats if anyone looked as if they might step out of line on our side. Some were willing, of course, but others were compromised with threats and blackmail. Politicians, bankers and businessmen were sexually compromised in KGB sting operations, for example. And Schmidtke had lawyers in Luxembourg and Liechtenstein and Geneva; he had bankers in all three countries, and he had politicians, too, here in Germany and elsewhere.'

Dieter sips from his glass as the soup bowls are removed and he lights a cigarette.

'And this network of Schmidtke's,' Finn says. 'You spent two years investigating it.'

'Just over two years,' Dieter replies, as if remembering a bad holiday. 'But it was vast and complex, hidden behind wall after wall of trusts and false company names. Two years was what it took just to peel back the edge of the carpet on Schmidtke's network in the West. And then? Then my government didn't like what it saw appearing from under the carpet and covered it up again.'

'So . . .'

'So I was retired, along with some others, after a decent time lapse from the investigations. We were being wound up individually, just as the investigation was being wound up. They didn't want us around any more, with our knowledge, in the same room as them.' Dieter sniffs. 'And they were afraid of our indignation that the file was being closed. I finally left in 1992 and they rolled the carpet safely back over the rotting stench.'

Dieter looks at Finn. The handsome eyes in the lined, outdoor face sharpen.

'But of course you are not interested in the robbery of German citizens,' he says.

'I'm interested in their persecutor who sits in Tegernsee with a government pension,' Finn says. 'I'm interested in why the investigation of Schmidtke's network was wound up, and in the network itself. I'm interested in the unbroken line from those times to these.'

'I've always thought you were honest, Finn.' Dieter pushes aside a half finished plate of noodles. 'I've met some of the victims and they are, sure, just victims of theft. They haven't been murdered or put in camps, their relatives weren't shot going over the Wall. But they lost out too.'

'You did your job.'

'And you? Are you doing your job, Finn?'

Finn doesn't reply.

'I think not,' Dieter says. 'Or you wouldn't be talking to me, a retired intelligence officer, like this in private.'

They split the bill and walk to a car park across

the bare concrete *platz* outside the restaurant. The wind creeps through the thread of Finn's coat and into his bones.

'So you want the unbroken line from the beginning to the present,' Dieter says, demanding no reply. 'You believe something remains of Schmidtke's network. Of course,' he says, and Finn isn't sure what Dieter means.

They get into Dieter's old blue BMW and turn out through the car park's barrier and head west along the banks of the Saar.

'Let me show you what I've bought with my retirement bonus, Finn. Or is it my hush money?' Dieter adds. 'I'm not as comfortable in retirement as Schmidtke, but I like it nevertheless.'

Outside the town, when the decayed remnants of its mining past have disappeared from view and been replaced by the slow grey-green curves of the Moselle River as it meanders through wooded hills, they come to an unmade track that leads down to the river. Dieter drives the BMW carefully over the rough ground and pulls up the car in a courtyard of stone barns and outhouses, out on their own. They sit in the car with the engine switched off.

'Do they know, in London, that you're here?' Dieter says.

'No.'

Dieter seems to weigh the implications.

'Good,' he says at last. 'We shouldn't trust our masters too much, don't you think?' Then he snaps open the door and steps out on to the hard ground.

They walk away from the buildings and up the slope of a vineyard with a view down on to the river.

It is bitterly cold on the top of the hill and the vines have been clipped down for the winter and protected with straw around their roots. A small fire made from old vine roots puts up a plume of smoke a few fields away.

'I bought fifty hectares with my lump sum,' Dieter says as they walk. 'I sometimes wonder why I didn't do it back then, back in the fifties, when I could have made my life as a farmer perhaps, with my own wine label.'

A long, slow barge creeps upriver against the current. On the other side, the forests of Luxembourg cloak the hills.

'These things are better as dreams,' Finn says.

'Perhaps so, yes.'

Finn looks at Dieter but sees no resignation, no sense of failure, in the German's face. He sees someone who has fought the long, slow battle of intelligence all his life, has seen his enemies rehabilitated, enriched even, while their victims either lie dead or are impoverished. But he sees, too, a face which tells him that the battle has been worth fighting nevertheless.

They walk back down to the banks of the river, their shoes coated with heavy mud, and Dieter indicates that they should walk left up the bank and towards the outbuildings which are half a mile away now.

'Germany was divided, yes,' Dieter says, as if to himself, 'but it was divided only for its ordinary citizens in the practice of their everyday lives. That much I saw when we investigated Schmidtke and long before, of course. The Wall was a metaphor as well as a physical thing. It was a political statement. It hit hardest at the ordinary people, not at those with the power and deceit to use it. For those with power and money, and the matchless amorality to exploit it, the Wall was in some ways convenient. For them, the division of Germany was not an obstacle, but a challenge. They didn't try to physically overcome it, of course, like the many victims of the border guards, but in other ways, through banks and finance, with corrupt lawyers and secret trusts and secret contacts. The Wall sharpened the wits of these people. Over there,' Dieter points across the river to Luxembourg, 'and here in Germany and in Liechtenstein and Switzerland, the avenues of finance are always open, Wall or no Wall. In the battle between capitalism and totalitarian communism, capitalism ate its holes in this metaphorical Wall, like lice in the beams of an old house. Until the whole thing was rotten. Money – capital – is like water. It will always find its equilibrium. It doesn't matter whether it comes from the East or West, it will come together, and it did. It is the ultimate power. It was our weakness in the West, this primitive accumulation of capital, as Marx put it. It opened our doors to every dictator, every brutal regime in the world.'

'How did it come together, Dieter?' Finn asks urgently. 'East and West. What did you learn from Schmidtke?'

'What did we start to learn.' Dieter corrects him, and stops walking and turns to look at the river. The barge is approaching level with them, its small bow wave sending thin lines of brown water out from behind it.

'I can give you three things, Finn,' Dieter says at last. 'I can give you a man, a bank and a company. These are just a brief glimpse, a dirty peephole into a large network that is more complex, more closely bound than the guts of a golf ball. Some would say this network is inextricable. As my masters eventually decided,' he adds drily.

'But not you, Dieter.'

'Everything is possible,' Dieter says. 'Our enemies knew that and we should be proud enough to know it too.'

They walk back from the field towards the buildings and Finn realises they've made the detour so that Dieter can establish who he is now, a retired agent, a viticulturalist. Dieter is making a statement about his present life.

They reach the first of the outbuildings where the car is parked and then Finn sees that there is a small house hidden from the track between them and the river. He is cold and sees Dieter is too. The German fumbles with numbed hands for a key and opens the door to the house and they enter. It is too cold to take off their coats even in the small, low kitchen, and Dieter switches on the central heating and puts logs into a wood burner and lights it while the heating grumbles into action. He puts a pot on the stove and makes coffee and pours two glasses of good Napoleon cognac and, by that time, the wood stove is kicking out a good heat and they remove their coats.

'The name of the man is Otto Roth,' Dieter begins. 'Or sometimes he's Osvald Roth, or Rottheim, or any number of variations. What's for certain is that none of these is his real name. Even he probably hasn't used his real name for so long it's meaningless. We'll call him Otto Roth. Nor is his true nationality certain. Some say he is originally a Russian-German, like Schmidtke, but born on this side of the divide. Some say he is Scandinavian, but that his parents were from Russia and worked in the thirties for the NKVD, Stalin's secret police. In this theory, Roth's parents came to Western Europe before the war, maybe during the Spanish Civil War, and were placed as sleepers in the West, to be used some day in the cause of Russia. If so, it was their son who turned out to be the gold seam of Russian intelligence and the investment made in the thirties was perfect. So the Russians have always played a very long game, so long that Roth's obscurity was assured.'

Dieter lights a cigarette and sips from the glass of cognac.

'Roth was born in 1939, in Antwerp where his parents were passing through. At least that's what it says on his birth certificate. We believe he has four brothers, younger than him, and an older sister. A brood of sleeping agents, perhaps? I don't know for sure. If that is so, we don't know with absolute certainty if any of them are alive, what happened to them in the war, virtually nothing, in fact. We do have our suspicions, however, which I will tell you in a while. They are suspicions which were nipped in the bud when our investigation of Schmidtke was terminated. At any rate, now Roth is a citizen of Switzerland and lives in considerable comfort in Cologny, a very wealthy suburb of Geneva. They say the lawns around his mansion are clipped with scissors,' Dieter says. 'But you know of Roth, of course, Finn, so what about him?'

Dieter answers his own question before Finn can speak. 'At the beginning of the sixties he became a trader, mainly in sugar, and was based in London for a while. Then he disappears. When we next hear of him, he's trading small arms. He's in Africa, the Far East, Oman. And then it grows, this arms business of his, and Roth is connected to a shipment of artillery, then spares for warplanes, oil, armoured personnel carriers, you name it, but it all originates from East Germany, most of it with Ko-Ko's implicit stamp on it, exported out of Rostock. Rostock was Schmidtke's Stasi-controlled port. And Schmidtke had the goods stamped with false declarations and false destinations.'

Dieter looks hard at Finn. 'How much do you know of Roth?' he asks.

'Go on,' Finn says.

'All right. Roth and Schmidtke are by now as close as brothers,' Dieter says. 'Roth travels back and forth to the Soviet Union under the cover of a Swiss sporting organisation. The usual cover. He gets himself on to an international committee of Olympic target shooting. Roth's little joke. The cover is good for him, as it is for many others in the years of the Cold War.'

Dieter gets up from his chair and puts a pot on the stove for more coffee and pours two more nips of cognac, but now he continues his story without a break.

'That's Roth,' he says. 'We'll come back to him in a while.'

Dieter sees that the coffee has run out and scrabbles in a cupboard for a jar of instant coffee that has, Finn sees, congealed with age and dampness around the rim.

'And then there's the bank,' Dieter says. 'It is called Jensbank and it was founded before the war in a little town in northern Bavaria called Fürth; the town where Henry Kissinger was born, as it happens. After the war, and after the Wall went up, Jensbank was one of very few that operated in both East and West Germany. Most people don't know that there were banks operating on both sides of the Wall. Well, there were. As I say, the Wall was a metaphor, an abstract in many ways, certainly not as solid as people think.

'Jensbank had more than three hundred branches, on both sides of the Wall. Many were concealed under different names, of course, but they were all Jensbank. And Jensbank dealt in very large funds indeed. Our investigations were stopped when they reached one of the world's few clearing banks, across the water there in Luxembourg. Jensbank has over fifty secret accounts there, what they call modestly in the banking world unpublished accounts. And there are trusts over there,' Dieter waves vaguely across the river, 'and there are trusts of Jensbank in Switzerland and Liechtenstein too, some of which we found our way into, most of which we didn't. What we saw, however, were huge transactions in cash, before the shutters got pulled down on us.'

Dieter looks back at Finn as he turns the heat off and the pot sends out its steam into the room.

'Roth, of course, was – is – a big client of Jens-bank, its biggest, perhaps, even the reason for its existence in the first place. KoKo was wrapped up in Jensbank too, before KoKo ceased to exist. And what we believe is that two – at least two – of Jensbank's directors are these mysterious brothers of Roth.'

'What is Jensbank now?' Finn says. 'Since the Wall came down?'

'Very well connected,' Dieter replies. 'It has forty years of business with the East and the Russians behind it. And forty years of parallel business with the West. Since the Wall came down the bank has continued its activities, with a new twist. It has recently been raising hundreds of millions of dollars from Western investors to buy property that doesn't exist in the former East Germany.'

'So it's in trouble?' Finn says.

'No, no, there is a cover-up at some high political level. "Mistakes were made" will be the official interpretation, if it ever comes out at all. Maybe there are too many in the West who are too powerful to let it come out, however. No. What is most interesting, perhaps, about Jensbank is that it will probably no longer exist in five years' time at all. It has done its work. It kept the wheels of commerce rolling on both sides of the Wall during the Cold War. But now?' Dieter looks at Finn. 'Now the Wall is down, there is no need for it. The Russians, the KGB, black money from the East is so entrenched in the West now that banks like Jensbank are superfluous. When the Wall came down, the banks of Geneva and elsewhere were able to welcome the new Russia and all its money with open arms. You see, Finn, you have to ask yourself. Who did the Wall protect? Them or us?'

'The Wall had to come down,' Finn answers.

'It was inevitable, certainly. And it has done a great favour to all those in the East trapped behind it. But it has also done a great favour to the movement of capital. The complexity of Schmidtke's and Roth's and the bank's arrangements was a great strain on the enemy. Now that strain has been removed at a stroke. In Putin's Russia, the freedom of people will, no doubt, be slowly and incrementally curtailed, but the freedom of money from East to West is total. But where does that money come from and what is it doing? Do we, the ordinary citizens of Western Europe, get the benefit of it?'

Outside, the grey late November light is fading. A few dead leaves flutter across the weatherbeaten wooden sills of the house. Dieter fills the glasses with cognac and pours fresh coffee.

'You sound like an old-fashioned communist,' Finn says.

'Ah, we are both communists, but in the true sense, you and I,' Dieter says, 'and we both know it is also an impossible dream. It is something, as you said about my fantasy of being a farmer, that is better left to dreams. The twisted reality of a communist state in action is too dreadful as we have seen.'

'And the company?' Finn asks. 'You said a person, a bank and a company.'

'You're impatient, Finn,' Dieter replies. 'Yes, you want the company, don't you? That is the real heart of this. Roth and Schmidtke, they are just the backdrop. You know much about them, but not as much as I do, I think. Jensbank is the machine that made it all work.

'So. On top of Jensbank there is just one company I can give you, you understand. But it is one example of many hundreds, perhaps thousands of companies in Schmidtke's stable. But the company will give you what you're looking for. It is a piece of actual evidence that reveals the continuous thread from the past to the present. From the Cold War up to today, and the KGB's seamless transition from defending the indefensible to becoming a major player in the so-called real world, the world of money.'

Dieter leaves the room and Finn hears him go down some stairs, perhaps into a cellar.

When he returns he is carrying a small brown box the size of a shoebox, wrapped in heavy clear plastic and sealed with clips to make it watertight.

'It's damp down there,' Dieter says. 'Sometimes it floods when the river rises. But I have kept a few things from the past in a cupboard high up on the wall. I never expected to touch them again. I hope they are not damaged.'

He puts the box on the table between them, without unwrapping it and begins to talk again.

'We were investigating a company by the name of Exodi,' he says tonelessly. 'That was back in 1991, nearly two years into our investigation of Schmidtke. Nearing the end. It was one of many companies bound up with Schmidtke and had a complicated structure like all the others. It was a set of companies, actually. There was Exodi Geneva, Exodi Luxembourg, Exodi in Paris, Exodi in Liechtenstein, and other places. All were set up by the same *treuhand*, commercial lawyers. The various Exodi companies had a dozen or so structures behind them that led to two lawyers in the Cayman Islands. The whole thing was the usual set of Russian dolls, one inside the other, no ultimate beneficiaries named outside the lawyers.

'The *treuhand* who set up the first Exodi, in Geneva, were the same commercial lawyers who we knew had worked before for Roth. They are a Luxembourg-based legal firm, with connections all over Europe. They set up companies for some not-so-savoury Russian interests and we had watched them for a while before we came across Exodi. So we made our investigations and discovered that Exodi was set up in 1991. In other words, it was set up just six months before we came across the name Exodi.

'Obligingly, the Geneva finance committee sent us the relevant company documents that showed when and where Exodi Geneva was incorporated. 1991. It was all in order. So we went to Liechtenstein to look at Exodi there and it was the same story. Exodi in Liechtenstein had also been set up six months before, in 1991. I interviewed Hutzger personally. He's the big wheel in the principality's finance committee, works as one of the government's anti-money-laundering experts. He's impeccable where his background is concerned, and his various seats on worthy international committees that fight money-laundering.

'Hutzger told me that he had personally looked into the origins of this company and the date was correct and they had nothing on Exodi Liechtenstein that alerted them to any wrongdoing.

'So we closed off that avenue. But by now my government in Bonn was only too pleased when another avenue was closed off, the boxes ticked, the dossiers closed and filed. Our investigations had already revealed too many uncomfortable things about corruption in Germany that threatened to go very high indeed. I now realised Bonn was already intending to stop our investigations into Schmidtke.

'But I wasn't satisfied. I don't know why. You know, Finn, when an instinct tells you just to look again, even though you don't know why. Anyway, that's how it was. I wasn't happy. So I did. I looked again. And I found a very odd fact indeed. Yes, there was a company called Exodi that had been formed in Liechtenstein in 1991. But there was also a company called Exodi that had been formed in Liechtenstein in 1975. It was wound up in 1989. And I looked further. The same was true of the Exodi companies in Geneva and Luxembourg and Paris. They were all founded in 1975 and all wound up in 1989.'

They are silent and Dieter observes Finn like a doctor watching for symptoms.

'Exodi is two things,' Finn says at last. 'One is real and one is fake.'

But Dieter doesn't reply directly. He holds Finn's eyes with his and continues.

'So I checked back at other Roth companies where we'd closed our investigations and I found the same thing. These other companies had been founded in the seventies or late sixties, some in the eighties, but all of them had been wound up in 1989. February 1989, to be precise. I found twenty-four companies with the same history as Exodi before I realised that the pattern was going to extend to many more, perhaps hundreds more companies, all of which we connected in various clear or obscure ways to Roth.

'I looked back at our files, working on my own now. I saw that in the few cases – maybe half a dozen or so – that we at the BND had gone to Switzerland or Liechtenstein to ask about these other companies, we had been told by the highest officials that they had all been incorporated in 1991, the same as Exodi. They were clean of Cold War connections, in other words.'

Dieter shakes his cigarette packet to extract a cigarette, but it is empty. Finn throws two packs on to the table between them like a winning poker hand and Dieter takes one with a grunt.

'When the British arrested Schmidtke at Tegel airport in March 1989,' he continues as a match flares, 'he had just returned from depositing nearly one billion dollars in bonds into a bank in Geneva. This bank will be important to your investigations, Finn. It's a Swiss branch of Jensbank and it has a long, historic trade with the KGB. I will give you the name. But anyway, we know that, from now onwards, Roth was put in charge of that money. The Swiss accounts were to be controlled by Roth after Schmidtke deposited the cash. You see, Schmidtke knew that the writing was on the wall for him and he just managed to make these deposits before the British arrested him. The end was fast, the Wall tumbled earlier than they'd expected. But by the time it fell the decks were cleared. The past was erased. We were ready to close in on Schmidtke when the British arrested him.'

'And we missed our chance to get Roth,' Finn

says, 'at the moment when he received this money and before he had time to obscure its origins.'

'Just so. But to Exodi,' Dieter continues. 'The Exodi companies demonstrate two things. First that many or maybe all of the companies Schmidtke and Roth controlled were wound up in 1989 *and then reformed in 1991 under exactly the same names*. They were not formed for the first time in 1991, as the documents we looked at, courtesy of the Swiss and Liechtenstein authorities, showed. It was a nice deceit. You look into the origins of a company that you have concerns about and you see it was formed after the period concerning your investigations. It does not occur to you that it may have a history before that. You have nice, clean, official documents in your hands, from impeccable officials, that tell you the date of incorporation. Why look further?

'But the second thing Exodi demonstrated to me is truly alarming. This second thing is that two of the most senior financial officials in Liechtenstein and Switzerland were able to say, without openly lying, that Exodi was formed in 1991. It *was* formed in 1991. *But not for the first time.* Did they know they were lying, these two impeccable officials, Hutzger and his opposite number in Geneva? If they did, it was perfectly deniable.' Dieter pauses awkwardly, as if he has allowed himself to run on too long to an unwilling listener. But Finn is far from unwilling.

'Why did they re-form these companies in the same name, after they were wound up?' Finn says. 'Why not just make new companies?'

'For exactly that reason. When I found on my second search that the Exodi companies had been originally founded in 1975, I also found information from that time about the activities of Exodi that related to money-laundering, corruption, fraud. All these activities had KGB traces. But if you looked at the history of these companies, as it was given to us in the documents from Geneva and Liechtenstein, their history only began in 1991. So we must be wrong, that was the implication. Any information about Exodi and the KGB must be wrong. And that's what they wanted us to believe.'

'They wanted you to believe the fake Exodi,' Finn says. 'But you were right, Dieter. Exodi existed before. And the highest officials in Liechtenstein and Switzerland were covering it up.'

'Deniably. And without actually lying, yes. And my government in Bonn decided to believe it, knowingly or unknowingly. And again, deniably, without actually lying.'

'And Bonn closed the investigations.'

'Swiftly.'

'And you, Dieter? Did you take what you found to your masters?'

'It was too late by then and I guessed I would not be thanked for it. I saw which way things were going. The government was using us, its security service, to give it a cloak of respectable investigation into the past, but it didn't really want us to investigate anything to its end. The glimpses of the truth we'd already found were too frightening.'

Dieter begins to untie the watertight clips, takes off the plastic coat, and pulls the box out from inside it. He pushes it across to Finn.

'Take these. They're microfiches; perhaps a hundred and twenty companies of Roth's and Schmidtke's. They show their real history before 1989. They are your link from the past to the present, Finn. Look at the Exodi companies.'

Finn doesn't touch the box.

'Take it. I don't want them now,' Dieter says. 'Once, I thought I would use them, not any more. When you no longer trust your own government . . .' He pauses. 'Now I spend my time drinking the odd bottle of fine Moselle in the evening. And I'm writing short stories for my brother's granddaughters, just children's stories. You, Finn, it's your turn to keep this box safe.'

Finn takes the box, puts it back in its thick plastic sheath and attaches the clips back on to it.

'I don't want to be connected in any way with what you're doing,' Dieter says firmly. 'I'm retired and I live for my great-nieces.'

'I may need your help, Dieter,' Finn says. 'More help,' he adds.

Dieter sighs and stands up and walks to the window.

'How will we communicate?' he says at last without turning back.

Finn draws an old thin hardback book from his coat pocket. He places it carefully on the table. Dieter turns and walks back and sits down again.

'Lessons in English,' Finn says. 'Published in 1941, very few copies left.'

Dieter opens the book and reads: 'Long Live International Youth Day. Long Live the Communist Party. Long Live Comrade Stalin.'

'They're the stories of Sasha and Misha,' Finn

says. 'Fairy stories, too, in their way. Two kids from the Caucasus. Children's stories with a difference. They were written to turn children into good little communist citizens. We'll use this book for code work. No phone calls, no e-mails. This address is my contact.' He gives Dieter a box number address. 'What about you?'

'I'll send you a contact place,' Dieter says. 'I haven't done this for a while.'

Dieter closes the doors of the fire and clears the glasses and cups into a stone sink. They leave the house and walk around to the stone barns and talk as they go about how the coding is to work.

In the car, Finn gives Dieter a sheet of paper denoting the code's mechanism. The page numbers that Dieter is to refer to in the stories of Sasha and Misha are indicated by the names of fungi found in another book, *The Oxford Book of Fungi*. The fungus 'Witches' Butter' is page sixty-eight of Sasha and Misha, for example. The letters of the words on each page in Sasha and Misha change according to the description in *The Oxford Book of Fungi* of each fungus that is date relevant. And the whole thing shifts after each communication from either of them. It is a crude, old-fashioned type of code, but they've both worked with such codes many times.

14

THE HEAT OF BODIES in the *gasthaus* at Tegernsee was by now causing steam to rise from the dance floor. The band broke their set and everyone returned to long tables. They were red in the face, these round, jolly people who looked slightly crazed in the eyes from the dance. Trays of beers were ordered and they sat, splayed legs and rolled-up sleeves, their conversation filling the echoing stone ceiling with amorphous noise.

I tucked Finn's notebook into my coat and finished the remains of the coffee that had gone cold. I wanted to be outside in the street, my bones warmed now against the snow, which still fell and melted on the window panes.

I walked carefully back along the lake to Finn's pink house, taking a roundabout route and watching from a distance for a cold half-hour before I approached. I walked around the outside, checking the windows and the front and back doors, before I entered. It was as I'd left it.

I lit a fire in the ground-floor sitting room and poured myself a whisky. I was cold again but I realised it was now also the cold of loneliness.

Dieter's microfiches would be downstairs in the cellar somewhere and sometime I would have to find them. They seemed to carry the weight of some valuable artefact from a lost time, a missing link. But I needed something more immediate, something that would lead me to Finn.

I went down into the cellar and picked out Finn's second *Book of Record*. Deciding now that warmth had beaten caution I took it with me up the stairs to the chair by the fire.

Dieter drove Finn back from his farm to the railway station in Saarbrucken and they parted as the early winter afternoon receded into darkness. Finn boarded the Frankfurt to Paris train, and left it at Metz in France just across the border from Germany. There he waited for an hour and took a local train north to Luxembourg. On the short journey he turned over Dieter's story in his mind and wondered how reliable Dieter was after all these years. But he had the box with the microfiches and the man he was going to see in Luxembourg would know how authentic, how useful, these sheets of negatives really were.

* * *

He sits on the electric train, full of Luxembourgers returning home from a day's work in France, and as it meanders through the bare fields and woods towards the city, he ruminates on this city state he's visited many times and which he thinks of as a modern fairy tale.

'Luxembourg is that most modern of cities,' he writes. 'A discreet, hi-tech tax haven on a hill, but dressed in the pretty bows of its medieval past. Who would guess that the whole of the modern world's economy hums and whirs through its ancient stones and chiselled cornices? Or that the vast rock-hewn tunnels and vaults dug deep into the hill on which it stands, and which once housed pitted iron ammunition deadly to men on horseback and in armour, now contain the secrets of all multinational companies? Or that alongside the hundreds of miles of carefully filed microfiches and documents detailing the transactions of these, the world's banks and corporations, lie also the secrets of some less than savoury organisations – the mafias of arms and drugs – as well as the secret accounts of intelligence services? Luxembourg is an iceberg. Four-fifths of this illusion exists beneath the surface. Luxembourg is so modern in its fine deceit. How old Europe does disguise the new world.'

Finn arrives and takes a taxi immediately out of the city to the surrounding countryside and checks into a country inn, on the far bank of the Moselle River from Dieter's little farm, a distance of just a mile or two as the crow flies. He takes this circuitous route because he has not told Dieter of his destination, but it is also his habit to go in circles.

Finn carries the little box that Dieter has given up and that men would kill for.

'Luxembourg is a city on a hill, the Jerusalem of the god of money, the capital of capital,' he writes. 'The tinpot duchy of Luxembourg with its chocolate-box name and its kitsch shops and its prim citizens is like a fairy tale that starts out nicely with an innocent picnic in sun-dappled middle-European woodland and ends with a wolf in the bedroom.

'Today as I arrive in the main square there is an exhibition of life-size, brightly painted plastic cows that say to me, "If you believe this, you'll believe anything." The artistic endeavour of this travelling plastic cow show is a tribute to the withering of the human spirit, presiding over which is the god of the mountain – money – secret money.' Finn does not like Luxembourg.

He sits in a bedroom overlooking the Moselle River, with the bare vineyards on the far side, and feeds his dislike of Luxembourg – or at least of what the city represents to him. Looking out of the window of his room, across the dark waters of the river to the glowing embers of a vine-wood fire, he turns the 'No Smoking' sign to the wall and blows smoke through the window, and it re-enters at once with the breeze. Then he picks up his journal and his cigarettes and descends to the warm bar downstairs and begins to work up an anger that comes from somewhere he doesn't understand.

'Where did it all begin,' he writes, 'this new Luxembourg with its little duke? How did a small, near impregnable hilltop fortress in northern Europe become the smooth machine of international finance?

'There is an unknown truth in the origins of this modern Luxembourg. One man began its transformation, back in the dark years of the 1930s; he was a banker, an arms dealer, a twisted visionary who wrote down his vision of post-war Europe in a little book of thoughts, under an assumed name. The only existing copy I know of lies in the library at the University of Texas. This man is, perhaps, the key figure of twentieth-century history, whom nobody has ever heard of. He is so obscure that to Google his name reveals a blank.

'This man, this banker and arms dealer, first of all took over the management of the finances of Europe's royal families from the Rothschilds. Then he set himself up as a guest of Luxembourg – the nightmare guest as it turns out. Before long he was powerful enough to declare publicly and in mockery of the duchy that he held the keys to its succession. "The Duke will marry whomever I tell him to marry." And so he forged a marital alliance for the Duke with the daughter of a magnate, while he went on to sell arms to all sides in the Second World War. Another kingmaker.

'And after the war was over and America laid out its new world order to protect the West against the Soviet threat – a threat that shortly developed its own usefulness – this man was America's silent potentate of finance, and Luxembourg became the place of all transactions.

'Modern Luxembourg began at the dawn of this new world order after 1945. It was a Switzerland, but a Switzerland created and controlled by the Americans. Like the military outposts of American power in Europe and around the world, Luxembourg was founded in its modern form as a financial outpost of American power. A discreet, secretive, "offshore" tax haven where the requirements of normal, commercial secrecy demanded by big business provided good cover for other secret operations, the movement of money to and from people and places that Western governments responsible to democratic electorates would rather their citizens remained ignorant about.

'But Luxembourg also became the bank for the world's mafias and intelligence services, totalitarian countries included. Like so many other efforts to combat the enemy, this one came back to bite the West. You arm the Taliban to fight the Russians, the Taliban returns and fights you with the weapons you gave it. It was the same with Luxembourg.

'And when this financier and arms dealer died, like a king himself he appointed a successor to his arms and financial empire.

'I have actually met his successor,' Finn writes. 'In a restaurant near the American consulate in Berne in 2003. So I know that I am not imagining all this. This successor is a man who America planned to be the ruler of Iraq in the latest war, but whose misdeeds caught up with him too soon.

'One day,' Finn concludes, 'I will write the story of his and Luxembourg's creator, the most important man of the twentieth century whom nobody has ever heard of.'

I shift in my seat in the pink house in Tegernsee. Will I visit this country inn one day to sleep in the bed where Finn slept that night? Just asking that question makes me realise how weak I have become in the past ten days since his disappearance. Am I already planning in my head for Finn never to return? In this journey to find him, there are so many such places that hold a trace of Finn. Perhaps I will be defeated by the sheer numbers.

I get up from the armchair and put another log on the fire. A church clock chimes midnight. I'm thinking about how I never liked Luxembourg either, for all its medieval charm, and now I am beginning to understand why.

In the bar of the inn, as Finn works up the kind of anger he always needs before a job, he stubs out another cigarette and orders another whisky and soda.

'What is it that epitomises Luxembourg as the hub of the world's financial dealings?' he writes. 'It is one bank. But this bank is not like any other bank. This one in Luxembourg goes by the name of Westbank and every day it does business that is worth around five hundred billion dollars. Every day, five hundred billion dollars' worth of transactions pass through its system from all corners of the earth. If a company in South America wishes to buy an asset from another company in Malaysia, Westbank guarantees – or clears – the sum the purchaser must pay and the asset the seller is offering. For this reason, every bank of any importance in the world, and every international business, company or corporation must have an account at Westbank for its business to function.

'The clearing bank can check that the buyer and seller can provide what they have agreed to provide by holding the accounts of each in Luxembourg.

'According to the bank's constitution and to the legal requirements of Luxembourg, however, no entity may keep a secret, unpublished account at Westbank, unless it also has a published account. This is important for reasons of transparency. It is a law that is intended to combat illegal money, a law against money-laundering, against fraud.

'If a normal bank or company has a secret, unpublished account, it is for reasons of business confidentiality, but a trail still exists for the purpose of financial investigations, if need be, between its secret and its published accounts. If an entity could open only secret accounts, no such trail would exist.

'Yet such an entity is Exodi. Exodi with a long "i", as Dieter puts it. Exodi is a set of companies with *only* secret accounts. Exodi has no published accounts at all. Exodi breaks all the rules. How – with whose connivance – has it been enabled to do this?'

And this is the reason that Finn has come to Luxembourg. He's come to meet a man, an old contact, who has been investigating Westbank for many years.

But Finn is blessed with another meeting that comes from this first meeting and that he hasn't planned. Finn was always lucky. It is this other, unscheduled meeting that arises from the first which opened his eyes a little further to the Plan of Vladimir Putin.

* * *

He meets his old contact at a café in the square. Frank is not a former spy, like Dieter, but a private investigator Finn has known, and used, many times before. Finn has known Frank for a very long time, fifteen . . . twenty years, maybe. Frank is another of Finn's ferrets who hunts the enemies of the West through the warrens of their financial transactions.

Frank Reisler is a short, plump man with a reddish-tinted beard, and with an impish, cheerful smile that belies his life of private investigation. 'As my daughters say,' Frank chuckles, 'they never knew a time in their lives when I wasn't deep into some secret affair or other.'

In his youth Frank had been a computer programmer and had set up the computer system at Westbank. He knew the way that published and unpublished – or secret – accounts operated because he had worked them out in the first place.

And then he had seen how his own system was manipulated, how certain customers were allowed to open secret accounts without possessing the published accounts that were a legal requirement. And his life changed.

'Some potential clients,' Frank tells Finn over a cappuccino and a bottle of water, 'they went to Brussels up the road, to open secret accounts at the world's other clearing bank. They were turned away. My contact at the Brussels bank told me that these people were deeply unsatisfactory. You wouldn't touch them with a bargepole, he said. And so these would-be clients simply drove two hours down the road to Luxembourg, and were able to open secret accounts at Westbank without any problem at all.

Against all the rules of Luxembourg and of West-bank, they opened these accounts.'

Finn and Frank are sitting in a café in the main square of the city. It is a cold, sunny day and the plastic cows gleam with the night's dew that won't go away. Shoppers are dressed well against the cold, the cafés are half full; it is morning, between break-fast and lunch.

For exposing these illegal practices, Frank loses his job in the middle of the 1980s. And he finds that, even for a citizen, Luxembourg is a closed circle of interests protecting each other. He cannot find a job anywhere else until he eventually finds employment as a union official. But he keeps his contacts at West-bank well nurtured. He is obsessed. And to pursue his obsession he has taken the precaution of bring-ing with him out of Westbank thousands and thou-sands of microfiches that demonstrate the truth of his allegations – that some entities have opened se-cret accounts at the bank without having the nor-mal, published ones.

'They are my insurance, Finn, the microfiches,' Frank says, and sips from his glass of water. 'I have them safely locked away in an attorney's office at a secret location in France. If anything untoward hap-pens to me, they will be revealed.'

'What kind of customers, clients, are we talking about?' Finn asks.

'People with dirty money from all kinds of places. Colombia, Uzbekistan, Russia, Afghanistan – all kinds of places where, shall we say, normal com-merce is overlaid with the fruits of black money from ventures that are, to say the least, below the line.'

'Very nicely put,' Finn says.

Frank chuckles and his whole face lights up with jolly amusement. He is a man made for his kind of work, Finn thinks, someone who isn't ever going to descend into discouragement, let alone despair. He is an individual strengthened rather than weakened by the huge odds against him. Finn identifies with Frank a little, or tries to, as he does with all his closest contacts. But Frank is very special to Finn, like a father, a benevolent version of Adrian. Finn works best at the level of the personal and nobody is closer to him among his contacts than Frank.

'I'm looking at a company here in Luxembourg and in other places. It's called Exodi,' Finn says.

He lights another cigarette, of which Frank imperceptibly disapproves, and scrapes the froth from his cappuccino out of the cup with a spoon.

'Exodi?' Frank thinks and his eyes glitter at some memory from his vast archive. 'Yes. I think I have heard of Exodi,' he says after a pause.

'There are several companies called Exodi,' Finn prompts him. 'They're all connected to one another. One or more of them have secret accounts at Westbank.'

'I will have to look at my files, Finn. It will take time. But I have heard of Exodi, I think, in another context.'

Frank frowns, looking cross at the unreliability of a memory that contains thousands of pieces of numeric and alphabetic information.

'Ah yes!' The frown disappears; he beams again. 'There was a story I heard here, in Luxembourg . . . when? I don't remember, but not long ago, a few weeks, maybe. Wait.'

Frank takes a mobile phone from the pocket of his tatty blue woollen coat and makes a call. He speaks first in German and then is passed to someone else, to whom he speaks in French. He writes down a name and address on a scrap of paper. He ends the call with some small joke or other and replaces the phone in his pocket and looks at Finn with disappointment.

'It's nothing, I think. Just a kid, a twenty-two-year-old boy who worked here in Luxembourg for a company called Exodi. He serviced their computers or something, that's all. But he was sacked a few weeks ago and told to say nothing about the company. That's normal, I guess. But apparently they didn't pay him his final pay cheque. He told a friend of a friend of a friend that Exodi doesn't pay its employees' insurance here either. That's illegal, of course. It seems the company got to hear about his conversations on the subject. He was telephoned and warned to stop talking about Exodi.'

'Telephoned by whom?'

'I don't know.'

'Perhaps there's more, Frank.'

'Perhaps. If you are interested in this company, Finn, you must have a reason. Perhaps there is something to look into further. Here. Here's the boy's name and address.' He handed the scrap of paper across the table. 'Perhaps you're right. My friend just said that the boy is scared of something.'

Finn pockets the scrap of paper after a brief glance.

'The address is across the bridge, a street behind the railway station,' Frank says. 'Let me know what happens. I will look in my files over the next few weeks. See if we have any Exodi for you, Finn.'

15

F INN PREFERS TO WALK. Even when he was in Moscow in winter, when even the moderately rich and relatively rich don't go anywhere without their cars, he preferred to walk. While they kept their chauffeurs running car engines for hours outside bars and restaurants simply to imply the status of urgency, Finn walked. He likes walking. Walking is the appropriate pace of humanity, he says, everything else is too fast for the brain. He always liked the French word for 'day' – *journée* – because of its original meaning, the distance a man can walk in a day.

Like so much about Finn's own analysis of himself, however, this represents only part of the truth. He likes walking because, as well as giving him time to think, it also delays the moment when he arrives. For Finn the journey – the *journée* – is always more enjoyable than to arrive. As if somehow his expectations were never quite met.

Walking also delayed the moment when he needed to act. There was now a reluctance in Finn, as so often on a job. There is a period of time he needs in order to steel himself to act, even in the most trivial actions, even going to the shops or telephoning his aunt. This reluctance reflects the deepest, most concealed aspect of Finn's nature – a lack of simple, fundamental self-belief that comes from his childhood, from the shocking few minutes of being ringed with adults, the shouting, his childish tears. As an adult he overcame the rising fear by sheer willpower. Most people never saw it.

So he walks from the main square of Luxembourg's city and across the long, wide bridge over the gorge that once protected the ancient fortress, until he comes to the Rue de Grèves on the far side of the gorge, behind the station.

The address is a five-storey, grey-stone building that rambles a long way back. There are twenty or so bells at the main doorway with nameplates that for the most part have no names written on them; small flats or studios for the more modest citizens of Luxembourg, a building for students, perhaps, or older people who have fallen through the net of Luxembourg's wealth.

The flat number Frank has written on the scrap of paper is number ten. Finn walks past the door once and then retraces his steps and pauses at the steps leading up to the door. He looks at an estate agent's sign and copies down the telephone number.

He casually scans the street. He thinks about walking up the stone steps, but if he rings the bell now, he risks a rebuttal before he can even get inside. The boy is scared, Frank has said. Why would he let a stranger in?

There are few people on the street. Finn crosses back over it and studies a few signs belonging to other house agents. Then he settles on the far side of the street, half concealed down some cellar steps, and waits.

After more than an hour standing in the damp cold, and with several false starts, he sees a man who appears to be approaching the main door of the block that interests him. He is a young man and he carries a small brown bag of groceries. Slowing as he approaches the stone steps, the man fumbles in his coat pocket and halts completely as he reaches the foot of the steps up to the door of the building.

Finn crosses the road. He is leaping up the steps behind the man as the man reaches the door and, still fumbling, inserts a key.

Finn stands at the young man's shoulder, with a genuinely grateful and somewhat foolish smile on his face, and looks with all the charming appeal he possesses into the man's eyes.

'Thank goodness you've come,' he says, stamping and shaking with cold on the step below him. 'I've been waiting nearly an hour and I haven't got my key.'

The young man turns, the door half-open now as he juggles the key and the bag of groceries, and stares at Finn. He's a student perhaps, Finn thinks, a temporary lodger in the building, and with the care-

lessness of a student who believes no doors, anywhere, should ever be locked, he silently shrugs and
Finn enters after him. They climb the first staircase
one after another and then the young man peels off
down a corridor on the first floor without a back-
ward glance and, without pausing, Finn climbs up
further to the floor above before he stops to check
his whereabouts.

He must be quick. He looks at the first numbers.
Eight, nine. Ten is around the corner of a dingy corridor. He walks along a faded, worn red carpet until
he stands outside a door with '10' painted roughly in
white paint on its peeling blue wood. He hears music
playing from behind it, the muffled wailing lilt of a
female singer singing a Portuguese song.

Finn pauses, catches his breath. Then he knocks
twice before he detects the occupant of the room
walking towards the door across a wooden floor. A
lock is snapped, the door opens a few inches on a
chain, and revealed is a tired, pale face with a wispy
orange beard that looks like thin tumbleweed.

'I'm from the property agents,' Finn says. 'Come
to check the windows.'

'The windows are fine,' the boy says.

'I'm sure they are. But we're painting the outside.
If you wouldn't mind, I need to make my report.'

There is a pause while the boy thinks and makes
the decision between risking letting a stranger inside
and risking offending the property agents. When the
latter has overcome his evident reluctance, the boy
pulls the chain off its slide and opens the door.

The room has an old carpet that was once olive-
green, Finn guesses, but now wears the scars of many

tenants who've had no interest in the apartment's long-term welfare. Dirty net curtains hang off a pole in front of the windows, there is an unmade futon on the floor, a shelf of books above it, and the main part of the room consists of a desk covered with lap-top computers, papers, wires, boxes of software and coffee cups. Finn looks around.

'Comfortable here?' Finn says.

'The windows are over there,' the boy replies. Finn shuts the door behind him and stands still in front of it.

'Having trouble paying the rent?' Finn says.

'How would you know?'

'That's exactly what I would know.'

'Who are you? What's your name?' the boy says nervously.

Finn takes a small transparent plastic packet from his pocket and holds it out. 'That's three months' rent,' he says.

The boy doesn't move.

'We have about ten minutes,' Finn says, 'before anyone watching the outside of the building wonders what I'm doing here.'

He wastes no time now.

'You have a number to call if anyone asks questions about Exodi?' he snaps.

The boy looks like he's been hit.

'Maybe,' he says faintly. 'What's it to you?'

'The longer I'm here, the more anyone watching will think you've told me. It's in your interests to be quick. When I leave, call the number they gave you. Tell them exactly what happened. Say, of course, what I asked you and that you told me nothing. Say

I was persistent and that it took you ten minutes to get rid of me.'

Finn throws the money on to the futon but doesn't move from the door. The boy looks paler than ever.

'What did you do at Exodi?' Finn says. 'What was your specific job?'

The boy doesn't reply.

'I'm not from here,' Finn says. 'I'm not from Luxembourg. I'm nothing to do with them. But if you don't talk to me, I will tell them you did talk to me. Got it? You have a few seconds to start answering my questions. After that . . . it's up to you.'

The boy hangs his head and looks around for some escape.

'What did you do at Exodi?' Finn repeats. 'We're wasting valuable time.'

'I was hired on a salary to service the computers,' came the faint and angry reply.

'For what kind of business?'

'The company didn't seem to do much.' The boy sits down at his desk, apparently exhausted, and faces Finn.

'What *did* it do?'

'It didn't do anything that I could see,' the boy almost shouts.

'Why did they hire you, then?'

'I don't know. Maybe they thought they'd be busy and then weren't.'

'Nothing coming in or out of the office, nothing on the computers you serviced, no one visiting for meetings?'

'That was the thing,' the boy protests, and Finn sees that it is genuine. 'There didn't seem to be anything going on at all. It wasn't like a normal office. There was no business in or out. No one ever came. Just once . . .' The boy's voice fades out.

'What?' Finn prompts.

'A couple of guys came into the office. They said they were from Exodi in Paris. I was introduced to them. I don't know why.'

'Who were they?'

'I don't know. Like you, they spoke lousy French. One might have been from Eastern Europe. They looked rich,' he adds.

'Where in Paris?' Finn says.

'It was an address near the George V Hotel, I remember that, because one of them was staying at the hotel and said it was handy for the office.' The boy tries to find some strength. 'Why don't you leave. I'm nothing to do with them.'

'I'll leave when I've finished and that's up to you. But remember. Be quick, or they won't believe you.'

'You bastard,' he said, but the weakness behind his voice contained no threat.

'Who told you not to speak about Exodi?' Finn snaps. 'Who called you?'

'Oh Jesus.'

'Who was it?' Finn persists. 'If you're interested in keeping your skin safe for any length of time tell me now before I walk out and it's too late.'

'Oh Jesus,' the boy repeats and waves his head from side to side like a distressed zoo animal.

'Who?'

'All right, all right. I was called by a man called Philippe Poulain.'

'The MP?'

'Yes, here in Luxembourg.'

The boy looks utterly defeated.

'Give me the phone number,' Finn says urgently.

The boy wearily threads his bony hands through a pile of papers and finally finds and holds up a sheet of A4 with nothing but a number written on it. Finn walks across the room, memorises it and looks down at the boy.

'Just do as I told you and they'll know they can rely on you,' he says.

As Finn turns and walks quickly out of the room the boy doesn't move. Finn shuts the door and, without pausing, descends the two floors two steps at a time and exits on to the street. He doesn't look up, or in either direction, but walks fast to the left, his face to the pavement but his eyes looking carefully to the right. There is nobody sitting in the parked cars on either side of the street. After a hundred yards, he stops sharply, puts his hand inside his coat as if he'd forgotten something, and turns back. But there is nobody there.

'Luxembourg is run by a small, tight group of people,' Finn writes. 'It is a small, tight state. Its MPs are businessmen, financiers, their interests lying principally with the interests of the ruling elite rather than with their constituents' complaints about road-widening or the provision of extra waste bins for dog faeces. And the interests of the ruling elite – as well as of ordinary citizens, it must be said – is the furtherance and increase of Luxembourg's share of the world's wealth. That is what national legislators should be interested in.

'But in order to do this patriotic task, because so much of what Luxembourg does for a living is secret, all branches of the state must be tightly controlled. The press, for example, is often told by the chief of police to bury a story that might otherwise damage the image of Luxembourg as a guardian of wealth. Many of the stories the police chief has buried in recent years concern a prominent member of the royal family who has been cut out of the line of succession to Luxembourg's duchy. There have been stories the police chief has buried that show bombings in Luxembourg and arson at the national airport in the mid-eighties, for example, in which he was allegedly implicated. There are many strange allegations that are buried here.

'But the culture of suppressing press stories doesn't stop with the Duke's family. Luxembourg and its parliament are so small that everyone is bound closely to everyone else. They are in it together. There is much more to conceal than just the prince's antics. If Westbank, one of the world's two clearing banks, can behave illegally, nearly everyone knows about it – everyone in Luxembourg's elite, that is.

'And so now, what do we see? We have a set of companies – Exodi. Exodi with a long "i". They are Schmidtke's companies, bequeathed to Otto Roth at the demise of Soviet Russia, wound up in 1989 and re-formed in 1991. Their true origins back in the mid-seventies, however, have been disguised by senior figures in the financial administrations of both

Liechtenstein and Switzerland. And here in Luxembourg, thanks to this afternoon's work, we have the edifying sight of a Luxembourg MP telephoning this boy, a former employee of Exodi with its illegal accounts, to warn him to say nothing.

'And how beautiful is this? The father of this Luxembourg MP was a senior European commissioner. The father's term ended in a welter of fraud allegations, missing public money, and attempts to silence the guardians of the EU budget who tried to blow the whistle on him. Exodi must indeed be important to have such protection.'

Finn describes this as a classic case of the over-kill of secrecy I too know so well: when secrecy, for its own sake, reveals precisely what it is trying to conceal.

'This boy knew nothing about Exodi, apart from the relatively trivial detail that it failed to pay its own employees' insurance contributions.'

And so the attempt to keep the boy silent about something he knows nothing about has pulled back the carpet for Finn, to reveal that Exodi is not just a set of front companies which handle KGB money, first through Schmidtke and then through his successor Roth; not just a set of companies that has illegal secret accounts at Westbank, but a very deep and dirty set of companies which has the highest KGB connections to figures in the West who are central to the defence of Western Europe's interests. Does this lone Luxembourg MP know what he is protecting? And is he indeed acting alone, not a rogue figure at all who is divorced from Luxembourg's interests? Everything about the way that this city state operates suggests 'Yes, he knows' and 'No, he is not acting alone.' But that is not enough, not yet.

I am about to go to bed in the pink house. It is late, I'm tired and I haven't found what I desperately want. Can there even be a clue, from all these years back in time, to where Finn is now? I must not be disheartened. I may be Finn's only chance.

It's strange being here, with so many of Finn's things, in a place we never shared, but which has Finn everywhere. I look around the bedroom with its huge and comfortable bed – always Finn's first preoccupation in a house. There are some novels he has read and I study closely where he thumbed them. There is a second-hand French wristwatch I gave him, an Emerich Meerson – and that he rarely wore because he said it was too beautiful to wear except on special occasions. There are his things in the bathroom – a razor, used, an empty tube of toothpaste which he seems still to have been squeezing long after any toothpaste could be extracted, an airline spongebag. I see his hairs in the razor.

I'm too tired, but can I afford even a few hours' sleep? How much time do I have? Who else will find this house and how long will it take them?

16

FINN WAS BACK in London on the first Eurostar train from Paris the following morning. He was taken, almost forcibly, at Waterloo station by two look-outs from the Service who picked him up without breaking step and marched him to a car, the two of them standing a little too close to him all the way until they were sitting in the back, one on either side, and the man on the right had given the driver an instruction. Finn was caught off balance by the reception, but unsurprised.

They returned not to the house in Norwood but to another Service safe house in Hackney. They drive in silence, Finn making no attempt, for once, to poke fun or to undermine his own situation.

It is a once-elegant house with chipped white cornicing and broken steps that lead up to it, and with weeds sprouting from the basement steps. The neighbours are plumbers and poets, actors, waitresses and the unemployed.

Finn is escorted up the broken steps a little too fast for comfort and, once the door is secured behind him, down some stairs inside the house which have peeling white banisters, until he finds himself half pushed, half guided into a room with a steel door and without windows.

Standing behind a desk and talking into a mobile phone is Adrian, the head of the Moscow desk and always Finn's handler. He has been Finn's mentor since the beginning and maybe, too, his substitute father.

With Adrian is a new young Russia recruit just out of Oxford who reminds Finn of himself, back in 1989, being taken to witness the interview with Schmidtke at Belmarsh prison. There is also a woman whom Finn hasn't met but who, it transpires, speaks good German. The room is bare but for three chairs, the desk and a metal box containing routing equipment and perhaps a scrambling device fixed to the wall at the back.

Finn is offered a chair and the handlers are sent back upstairs, one to find a fourth chair. He is then told to wait outside the door 'in case we need you', as Adrian puts it ominously.

They sit down. Finn is in front of the desk, and his three colleagues sit opposite, almost like a respectful interview committee, except that Adrian is picking his teeth with a toothpick. The woman speaks first. She asks Finn in German where he's been, who he's seen, why he's gone to Germany.

Finn speaks of a visit to Frankfurt, on his way

to the Hartz Forest, where he's been enjoying the hiking.

'Why are we speaking in German?' he asks Adrian, but Adrian hasn't finished with his teeth, as though they may play a part in the proceedings.

They know much, Finn observes, but from the line of questioning, he hazards a guess that they don't know about his meeting with Dieter or his trip to Luxembourg.

'Been frisked?' Adrian suddenly asks. 'Have they gone through all your hidden pockets?' he adds sarcastically.

'Your boys took everything I have, Adrian,' Finn says.

'Which is what?'

'Nothing much except a Eurostar ticket and some money,' Finn answers. 'And a bag of dirty clothes.'

He has cached the box that Dieter gave him somewhere, before returning to England.

'No receipts from some nice *gasthaus* in the forest, then?' Adrian says. 'No train ticket from Frankfurt?'

'Nothing, no. I was on holiday. I only keep stuff I can put against tax.'

'Convenient,' the Oxford recruit says, and receives a look from Adrian of such histrionically exaggerated admiration that it mocks the boy and reduces him, as intended, to blushing silence.

They're angry that he's gone abroad against their friendly but explicit instructions. Adrian has an energy pumping off his body that would melt a small snowfield. Finn knows Adrian's rage without observing anything. Adrian feels let down, too, he guesses.

So Finn tells them he's been clearing his head,

walking in the Hartz Forest, near the old border, saying goodbye to his old life.

They didn't believe him, but what could they do.

'Why didn't you go walking in the Pennines?' the young recruit is emboldened to ask him.

'It's not next to the Iron Curtain,' Finn says.

'Neither is the Hartz Forest,' the recruit says, a little too quickly. 'Not any more. Not for eleven years, since eighty-nine.'

Finn shrugs. 'You wouldn't understand,' he says.

And then the real purpose of his abduction from Waterloo station enters the proceedings. In a carefully timed pause, Adrian, the Desk head, old friend, and Finn's long-time 'spiritual' adviser, looks up at him and loosens his tie, as if they are all enjoying a balmy spring morning. He snaps the toothpick in two.

Adrian, as Finn describes him, is a red-faced man of middling height, who wears an ordinary-looking grey suit, white shirt, red tie. Finn says Adrian wears red ties because they dampen the glow of his well-lunched face, which has the jolly ruddiness of the Laughing Cavalier, he says. Adrian is an abrupt, sharp and, on the face of it, jovial fellow, coming to the end of a long and distinguished career at the Service – with still the possibility of the ultimate promotion – and, before his Service career began, a leading figure in Military Intelligence. He's served in the SAS in several of the British post-colonial wars in Africa, the Middle East and the Far East, but still had the time after they were all finished to rise very nearly to the top of SIS, or MI6, whichever you prefer.

Finn told me once that early on in their relationship he'd asked Adrian what he did in his spare time
at his country house. Pheasant shooting, perhaps?

'When you've shot as many darkies as I have,'
Adrian informed him, 'banging away at the odd
pheasant doesn't really cut the mustard.'

But Adrian hides behind this façade of military
bluster. It is an artificial construct that lulls others
into a belief that his mind is less acute than he sounds.
For behind the barked sentences and the politically
incorrect sentiments lies a mind as sharp as a mussel
shell. And Finn agrees with this estimate. Finn has a
great admiration for Adrian's intellect, if nothing else
about him, and he wouldn't have had if his boss were
a fool.

Adrian recruited Finn and there exists between
them that special relationship that exists between a
recruiter and his subject; like a father Adrian has
sought to make Finn in his own image, but like a
proud father, too, he admires the differences between them. When Adrian recruited Finn, Finn was
Adrian's shapeless clay, whom he has sought to fashion into a worthy object of his attention. If Finn has
let Adrian down with his recent Moscow debacle,
Adrian doesn't show it.

But – so easy to forget – Adrian is also completely
ruthless. His generally jovial bonhomie is a convenient disguise for that. Finn was scared at the beginning of his time in the Service of getting on the wrong
side of Adrian and he has cultivated a sufficient, though
cunningly insubordinate, friendship with Adrian so
that finally Finn believes he has manoeuvred Adrian
into the role of older brother rather than father.

Either way, he has let Adrian down now and Adrian doesn't like anyone to let him down.

And so now, at the house in Hackney, Adrian loosens his tie, undoes the top button of his shirt and reaches the reason for his presence at this otherwise routine telling-off of a wandering ex-intelligence officer.

'You've been a good officer, Finn,' Adrian says, so gently it puts Finn on his guard. 'Very good. Exceptional. Your work in Moscow could have been done by no one else, in my opinion. Extremely sensitive stuff and well handled from start to finish. I'm very proud of you.'

'Thank you, Adrian.'

'Your style may not have been to everyone's taste, but it was to mine. But that doesn't matter. You achieved great results.'

This time Finn doesn't reply, but inclines his head slightly to acknowledge such unusually high praise from Adrian.

'Never mind the way it all ended. It takes nothing away from your achievements, my boy,' Adrian says.

'I'm sorry for the way it ended too,' Finn says, and in this room he means it. 'For what it's worth,' he adds.

But Adrian ignores this, either because Finn's regret is not actually worth anything to him, or simply because he doesn't like to be interrupted when he has the floor.

'So I'm sorry to have to tell you this, Finn,' Adrian says quietly. 'It's come as quite a blow.' Adrian sweeps back his lank forelock. 'Finn, I'm afraid Mikhail was a fraud. Has been all along, I'm sorry to say. It's come as a great shock to everyone and I know that will include you, above all.'

The young recruit nods slowly and looks down at the table, as if they're mourning a colleague, as, in a sense, they are.

Finn doesn't move, doesn't say anything. He is stunned. He knows exactly what Adrian is saying, who Adrian is talking about.

'Yes,' Adrian says cautiously and observes Finn closely. 'It's a confusing thing to hear, I agree,' he continues, injecting a note of sympathy into his voice that fools nobody. But Adrian doesn't look like a man who's ever been confused, doubtful or even in two minds about anything in his life.

'Mikhail has been very useful,' he continues. 'A very clever source indeed. And, to us, a very expensive double agent for many years now,' Adrian says.

Finn watches Adrian's fingers tap irritably on the table.

'I'm not saying Mikhail hasn't provided us with good material, you understand. From time to time,' Adrian says breezily. 'Of course he has. That's why he's been so bloody successful. He gave us - you' – Adrian flatteringly nods across the table to Finn – 'some very useful material, valuable both to us and to our friends in Grosvenor Square' – by which Adrian means the Americans. 'But the big stuff which we – which you too, I know, Finn – set such store by, all this turns out to be the fruits of so much KGB inter-clan warfare and, to be honest, it doesn't take much light to be shone on it to reveal the flaws.'

Adrian pauses for his peroration.

'I'm afraid Mikhail allowed this internecine intrigue in the KGB to cloud his judgement on the issues that were most important to us. Mikhail's been fighting his corner in an internal battle for one KGB clan's victory over another. In doing so, he's used us, rather than the other way round.'

Leaning back in his chair and at last stopping the tapping of his fingers by cradling his hands together across his chest, Adrian sighs.

'This part of Mikhail's intelligence – the crucial part – is, to coin a phrase, absolutely useless,' Adrian finishes with a flourish, joining his fingers in a Gothic arch.

Perhaps Finn is too quick in his acceptance of what Adrian has said, or doesn't break into the protest of anger or frustration that Adrian expects, for Adrian doesn't take his eyes off him for a second, searching to see how the news is being received. After all, to Finn and all the other people in the room, Mikhail is the apex of Finn's career, the source that has sustained him for so long. Finn should be devastated. Mikhail is the reason he was kept in place in Moscow for seven difficult, fraught and dangerous years. To the irritation of the Service's chiefs, Finn was the only person Mikhail ever agreed to communicate with.

But Adrian is sharp. He sees an uncharacteristic meekness in Finn's calm that suggests his humble acceptance of this momentous news. And Finn sees in Adrian's eyes that he doesn't believe that Finn has bought the story. Adrian knows or suspects that Finn is agreeing for the sake of agreeing and that Finn's complicity in this extraordinary story that he has just unfolded is not guaranteed.

So he asks Finn to lunch with him, and this is something that wouldn't have happened if it hadn't been pre-planned; Adrian's diary is stiff with lunches. Adrian doesn't believe that Finn is really in the loop at all, that he accepts the debunking of Mikhail.

Outside the terraced Hackney house, the two of them step into a waiting grey car that matches Adrian's suit and are whisked towards the West End.

'I didn't want to break this to you quite so abruptly,' Adrian says, and for once avoids in this statement his habitual abruptness. 'But you understand it couldn't really wait. It's too important. It draws a line under your excellent career, Finn, truly excellent career. I know now it must seem to be a deeply unsatisfactory line. But it's not. You're one of the best officers I've ever had, and I mean that as a friend, not just your boss. Right now, I understand, it must seem a terrible blow to you. You're thinking that those last years in Moscow were wasted. Well, they weren't. You got hold of a lot of excellent material for us. Perhaps Mikhail was too good to be true. I should have spotted that. That was my mistake, Finn, not yours. You did everything right, everything. You mustn't beat yourself up about it. I know you won't, I know you're too tough for that. You're one of us,' Adrian says at last, by which untrue flattery he means, Finn thinks, one of a notional group of exceptional superheroes like Adrian who, camouflaged and with their faces blacked out, go about Her Majesty's business in the darkest, most dangerous trouble spots of the world.

'Fancy a walk through the park?' Adrian says and, without waiting for a reply, barks at the driver to drive under Admiralty Arch and drop them just before the fountain by Buckingham Palace.

They walk up through Green Park, parallel to St James's in the leafless grey of a London winter day. Adrian is attentive, full of friendship, says how he really wants to see a great deal of Finn, that they have more than just the Service that binds them.

But Finn is still in shock. He says little. His defences are down. Because he knows. He knows that he is being fed a lie and Adrian knows he knows.

They turn into St James's and enter the white portals of Boodles.

'Thank God you're wearing a decent suit,' Adrian jokes. 'Some of our new recruits these days! I don't know if they even possess one.'

They walk through the sitting room of the gentlemen's club to the small, cosy bar and Adrian greets several other members along the way. Adrian lunches and dines at Boodles with regularity. He lives in the country, but stays up during the week in town and Boodles is his common room.

'I'll have a glass of wine,' Adrian tells the barman, who knows what wine he wants and in what size glass – large. 'What'll you have?' he says to Finn. 'Something strong, I should think.'

'I'll have a Moscow Mule,' Finn says and for a moment Adrian is knocked off the treadmill of his platitudes. To Adrian, a mule is a drug mule. Is Finn referring to a man with drugs hidden up his arse arriving by plane from Russia? But Adrian swiftly conceals his confusion.

'Something they feed you at one of your more louche clubs, is it?' he says.

Finn describes the cocktail and it causes quite a comical stir. One of Adrian's friends from a City bank says he'll have one too and then they tell the barman to mix a jug. And suddenly they're in a conclave, Adrian, Finn, the banker and some other financial big shots, Adrian at the centre, a real partygoer – a real goer, Finn thinks. He's seen Adrian in the office chasing skirt, but he's just as useful at rallying a bunch of all-male lunch-time drinkers around him.

Finn is knocked off balance and can't recover from what he's been told. Perhaps Adrian knows he will be knocked sideways. In normal circumstances, the throng of public school City board directors only makes Finn rise to the occasion, to be as public school, as City board director as the next man. He's lunched with Adrian here many times before, after all. But now he feels out of his depth, his focus is lost, the game is getting on top of him and he sympathises for a moment with one or two of the Service's senior but grammar-school figures whom he normally scorns for letting themselves be browbeaten by their public schoolboy colleagues. This, perhaps, is what snaps Finn out of his shock: the need to perform, to be as good as anyone.

'What about this Russian fellow?' the banker asks Adrian, in a break in the inconsequential chat. 'The aluminium tycoon, Pavel Drachevsky. Is he good for it? Will he make a proper company that can list here in London, d'you think?'

'More Finn's department than mine, I'm afraid,'

Adrian replies. 'He's been our Trade Secretary out there for donkey's years.'

'Second Trade Secretary,' Finn corrects him, and wonders what Adrian's cover is in Boodles, or if he even has a cover here. The crazy notion flashes through Finn's mind that Boodles is a sort of official dining room for MI6.

'What d'you think?' the banker asks Finn. 'We've got to watch these chaps now, they've snapped up everything of value in Russia.'

'Are you an investor?' Finn replies gamely. The throng laughs.

'Wouldn't know how to,' the banker says. 'But I hear Rothschild's are nosing around this chap,' he adds seriously, and there is clearly a reason for his interest. 'He must be better than some of the other candidates.'

'Rothschild's have a history in Russia,' Finn says. 'They're the only people who ever sued the Tsar, back in the 1860s. They got a lot of points for that.'

'And won, no doubt.'

'Yes, they won. Russians couldn't believe it. The Tsar, a god, had been successfully sued. Rothschild's balanced it out nicely by suing the Pope too.'

'If Rothschild's are interested in Drachevsky, they must be on to something, don't you reckon?' the banker prompts Finn.

'The Russian oligarchs are still sorting out what they legally own and what they don't legally own,' Finn says carefully. 'Pavel Drachevsky has half of Russia's aluminium, but he's sharing it with some other co-owners. One of the men connected with the company's gone to jail. Others aren't so easy to deal with. There's a guy in Israel who really holds the strings. And then there's Stepanovich, who has a finger in the pie. Maybe others. If Drachevsky can consolidate, my guess is he'll look to London for a listing. In time. The rules are more lax here than in the States.'

'That so?' someone says.

'Surely you mean "relaxed",' another Savile Row suit says. 'The rules are more relaxed.'

Everyone laughs at this.

'The Russians like it here,' Finn persists unnecessarily, and receives a warning shot from Adrian, 'because, unlike the Yanks, we don't ask them too many difficult questions. The City will welcome them with open arms when they start to arrive, no questions asked.'

It is the winter at the end of the year 2000 and London is fascinated by gaining access to the oligarchs, their raw materials and their unprecedented wealth. The City of London has spotted a gold seam for several years now and, despite the occasional warnings, London wants into Russia more than ever.

Adrian smiles warmly at his protégé's expertise, but nevertheless takes him by the arm and they steer through the throng like joined contestants in a three-legged race.

Once in the dining room they sit down at a white-napped table in a corner, away from other ears, and the menus are brought, Finn – and Adrian – as always admiring the waitresses the club gets on the cheap from Eastern Europe.

Finn has potted shrimp and Adrian agrees rather

than chooses. They order steak and kidney pie to follow.

Adrian leans across the table.

'Remember ninety-five?' he says, not wasting any time, Finn notices. 'Six years after the Wall came down? Russia was in a total mess. Yeltsin was all over the place, gangsters roamed the streets like wolves and the bubble was going to burst. Russia was going bankrupt and the Communists looked like they might win the next election, get back into power.' Adrian doesn't wait for a reply. 'What they needed was hard currency to save the nation. The rich were getting their money out of Russia as fast as they could because they feared the return of the old regime.'

'The KGB spirited out four hundred billion dollars, according to our estimate,' Finn says.

'Well, we like to say it was the KGB,' Adrian says vaguely. 'But it was business interests, organised crime, you name it. Anyway, what Russia needed was our help to save the situation. The oligarchs rallied round Yeltsin to keep him in power and Clinton got together with the heads of the world's three biggest aluminium producers and told them to fix a price. Completely illegal, of course. But brilliant. And the right thing to do. The price was fixed so the Russians could sell their aluminium at a good price and save the economy. That's what happened. Russia was saved from a return to Communism. Clinton rewarded the head of Alcoa, the world's biggest aluminium company, with a job running the US Treasury. There was a hell of a stink, the FBI got involved, all the letter-of-the-law sort of people were up in arms. But Clinton was right. He saw the big picture.'

This is a most subtle approach, Finn thinks. Adrian knows that Finn admires Clinton. Adrian has called Finn a bleeding heart liberal on many occasions and, once, even introduced him as a 'commie student type', to much laughter. The fact that Adrian, in his praise of the former president, actually despises Clinton for 'avoiding the draft' is, for the moment, forgotten.

So Finn knows that Adrian is getting him onside with this anecdote.

Adrian picks up the wine list and makes a big thing of choosing an extremely expensive Burgundy.

'Special occasion,' Adrian says. 'I want you to know there's no hard feelings for what happened in Moscow. Let alone your little walk in Germany,' he added.

'Thank you, Adrian,' Finn says, but he is thinking about Mikhail, his source, his *raison d'être* for seven long years.

'Well, right now,' Adrian continues when the waitress has gone, 'we're in a situation which is not unlike the one back then, in ninety-five. But this time we have a new president, Putin, who can really put the past behind Russia, get rid of the Communists for good. He's got terrific ratings with ordinary Russians. Which he needs,' Adrian protests, 'in spite of your harsh view of him. The point is, Putin can make a difference. Bring Russia into the community of nations at last.

'OK, so he's not whiter than white. Chechnya was – is – a bloody sham. But we're all grown-ups and we need to see that Russia has to be handled by a strongman for the time being.' Adrian looks sadly serious. 'They're not, actually, ready for a true democracy yet, Finn. It's too early, you know. You know that.'

Somehow Finn bites his tongue on a number of possible protest points. He suddenly feels he isn't hungry at all.

But Adrian is off on another tack, no doubt connected in some way to the Clinton and aluminium story.

'Those special reports you did for us a few months ago,' Adrian reminds him. 'One of your last reports, I believe. A round-up of the Russian oligarchs, if you like, and where they stand in the line of power and money. They're the people we need, here in the West, and we need them to have the support of Putin and, for that, we need to encourage Putin, not tick him off every time he sends an army into Chechnya, or bumps off a bloody journalist. There are bigger fish to fry.

'Anyway, those reports were bloody good, Finn. You really got beneath the skin. You showed us the oligarchs, warts and all. The mafia network, their KGB connections, the rough and tumble of the way business is being done in Russia today. Brilliant stuff. Most of all you showed us just how vast their wealth is. Well, we need that wealth, Finn, we need it circulating in the world's economy, making more money, not just stuck in trust accounts in the Caymans, bugger all use to anyone.

'What I'm saying,' Adrian taps the table, 'is that, while the reports you did were damn good, they gave us exactly the wrong message.'

Finn is momentarily taken aback by this hairpin turn in Adrian's line of thought.

'They gave us the true message,' Finn counters finally.

'The truth is not always the whole truth,' Adrian says abruptly. 'Those reports you did were compiled by us at the Office in order to be shown to our banks and our investors here in the City. UK plc, if you like. They were compiled in order to *encourage* our banks, our institutions, Finn, to go into Russia. What you wrote, old boy, though containing much truth, would scare off anyone in their right mind from ever investing over there in a million years. Not good.'

Adrian sips the wine and it is excellent. Their wine glasses are filled almost to the brim by the pretty Romanian waitress, and Adrian nudges Finn at her inexperience at pouring wine. But when she's gone with a nervous smile, he continues.

'We reviewed them, the reports, at Joint Intelligence and, I must tell you, they received high praise from everyone. The PM was very pleased. But. But. The PM issued an advice to us to tone them down. He knew we have to get our banks and big companies over there, into Russia. Blair's advice was right. Probably written by Alastair Campbell, though,' Adrian adds and laughs.

But he is not finished yet.

'So. Tone them down we did. For Tone,' Adrian continues forcefully. 'Because that was the right thing to do. Like Clinton in ninety-five, Mr Blair is doing the right thing with Russia. We can't get hung up on the *way* business is being done over there, we must get on with actually *doing* business over there. Get me?'

For Finn, this is a first. He has certainly never heard Adrian heap praise on Clinton and Blair in the same meal, or the same year for that matter. But Adrian has made his point about why Putin must be supported, at apparently any cost – even the falsifying of field reports – and now slices through his steak and kidney pie as if he is partitioning India.

'Vladimir Putin will be very pleased,' Finn says.

Adrian halts a second forkful of pie before it reaches his mouth. He puts his knife and fork back on to the plate and looks at Finn. Gone is the camaraderie, the *entre nous* style of his recent exposition of events, the car journey and the meeting at the house in Hackney. His eyes are black with anger.

'Be very careful, Finn. You're treading a very thin line indeed. Don't try me.' He leans in towards Finn and starts to jab his knife too close to his face. 'Remember Tony Cardonus? He was with the Office in Bosnia at the end of the nineties. Remember him, do you?'

'No, Adrian, I don't.'

'Yes you do. Married a German woman,' Adrian says, without taking his eyes off Finn's, without even blinking. 'We pulled him out for rather the same reasons we had to pull you out. Insubordination. We paid him off and he went to live with his German bint in Saxony or somewhere. Then he got chippy. Then he demanded more cash. Then he began to make threats. First of all we turned his house over in Saxony. We took everything we needed, computers, the lot. That apparently didn't work. So we had to go back and we turned his house over again and really made a mess this time. In fact, they couldn't even live in it. Then, would you believe it, when he still didn't back off, his kid got kicked out of the local school, thank you very much. Then Cardonus found he couldn't get another job. His German bint and their son left him. Know where Cardonus is now? Working behind a bar in the Hamburg red light district. When he can stand up straight enough. Get me? When we came back the third time, we didn't just do his house in. So don't try me, Finn.'

Adrian returns voraciously to his steak and kidney pie.

Finn describes how, at that moment, he saw the brute in his old recruiter properly for the first time: the ruthless, single-minded streak that had got Adrian through the Malaysian jungle or the Omani desert thirty, forty years before; not wearing a grey suit in a London club, but a breath away from death, and which has propelled him through the Service nearly to the top.

'Not hungry?' Adrian says to Finn between mouthfuls.

Finn picks up his knife and fork and eats so that Adrian won't know how sick he feels.

'You must come down to Wiltshire,' Adrian says when their plates are clean and he's pouring the rest of the Burgundy equally between them. 'Pen would love it,' he adds, as though it has been some third person who, five minutes before, stopped by the table and issued an explicit physical threat against Finn.

They adjourn for brandy as a late appearance by

the sun sends a streak of light through the windows at the front of the club.

'Pen's very fond of you, Finn,' Adrian says, returning to the theme. 'She and I think of you like . . . well, like family.'

Pen is Penny, Adrian's wife. At various times in the years since Finn has known and worked for Adrian, Penny has been described by Adrian's contemporaries as 'first class', 'a top girl' and, once, as the 'perfect woman'. This has not stopped Adrian philandering in London during the weekdays and maybe that is part of Penny's 'perfection', Finn thinks: her ability to overlook her husband's behaviour.

'I'd love to,' Finn says. 'That's a very kind offer.'

'I insist you come,' Adrian says. 'Pen will call and make a date. Absolutely.'

And they part company on the club's steps, a deal done, it seems.

I get up and walk around the pink house and look through the windows at the back. I check upstairs and look carefully from behind a curtain out on to the street at the front. There is nothing. It snows still, but there is nothing untoward, nothing that alerts me to the presence of unwelcome visitors.

I keep walking, round and round the house.

When Patrushev finally told me what my assignment was on that night at the Forest, it was to find our enemy within. So this is it. His codename is Mikhail. Within a few weeks of the evening I spent with Patrushev in Moscow, Finn, in London, is being told by his bosses that this enemy within our ranks at the Forest, Finn's great source Mikhail, is no good; that Mikhail is a mistake.

I pick up Finn's book again. At the end of this meeting with Adrian, he writes just two paragraphs.

'But Mikhail has always been the silken thread of truth. He is so far on the inside that he practically shits in Putin's bathroom. Mikhail is the greatest source the British ever had in Russia. It is Mikhail who has got me this far.

'It is Mikhail', Finn writes, 'who first told me about the Plan, Anna. He is one of them, one of the so-called Patriots, brought down from Putin's St Petersburg clan. Before that, way before that, he was stationed in East Germany with Putin.'

This denial of Mikhail by Adrian explains so much of the past seven years. It explains why Finn had to go it alone, go feral, as he puts it. He was fighting his own side as well as ours. Finn never stopped believing in Mikhail. I know that, and the Service didn't like it at all.

Most importantly, perhaps, Patrushev's personal interest in Finn tells me something now, as I read of Adrian's denunciation of Mikhail. It tells me that Mikhail was . . . is real, just as Finn knew he was. Why did Adrian lie about Mikhail back then? And what does it tell me about Finn now, wherever he is? Is the identity of Mikhail the key?

17

FINN RETURNS HOME that afternoon after his lunch with Adrian. He goes to his apartment in Camden Town, which he'd bought back in the early 1980s and which is now a decaying reminder of the area before it bloomed into its current, wealthy incarnation. For the neighbours, Finn's apartment is the irritating reminder of where the neighbourhood has come from.

He goes to bed as soon as he gets home. The drinking at lunchtime, coupled with his lowered defences, overcomes him and he falls into a deep sleep.

He doesn't expand on his mood in the days, weeks and months ahead. This period, until the spring of 2001, he deals with in a few paragraphs.

It is unusual to see Finn disheartened. It is as if for the first, and last, time he is daunted by the odds against him. Adrian has been cunning in telling him the Cardonus story. It is a searing demonstration of pure malevolent power, and that demonstration has come from Finn's own people.

He says he communicates with Frank in Luxembourg, who sends him details of the Exodi microfiches from Westbank and their authenticity. And he communicates with Dieter in these dead winter months, and the German adds information to that already supplied by Frank.

One winter afternoon, sitting at his kitchen table by the window that looks out over a school playground, Finn begins to make notes and this is the turning point. On this nondescript day, when London is reduced to a small grey room, he begins to rise above the contemplation of Adrian's threats that have shadowed him since their lunch.

The notes he makes are simple and clear: there is a Plan, conceived by the KGB and nurtured through the 'dark' years of democracy in post-Soviet Russia; Putin is the guardian of this Plan and Mikhail its nemesis; the Plan codifies an attack on the West, but one which could not have occurred in the days of Soviet Communism; Exodi, one instrument of this Plan, is a nest of companies into which billions of dollars of laundered money are secreted to the West; the Russians' agents in the West provide the financial know-how for the Plan; one of the world's biggest banks illegally allows Exodi to open secret accounts; at least one political figure at the centre of power in Europe protects Exodi. But for what reason does Exodi exist? What are the billions of dollars for? What kind of attack is contemplated?

I read some of Finn's coded messages to Dieter,

which he has casually left tucked into a book. There are the exotic fungi denoting the different page numbers in the Sasha and Misha stories. The names of these fungi, 'Emerald Deceiver', 'Wolf's Milk Slime', 'Witches' Butter', seem to indicate an almost comforting enjoyment in him, a retreat into the safety of fantasy. It is hard not to conclude that Finn enjoys writing these coded communications.

He stays at his apartment until just before Christmas, without communicating with the outside world.

He doesn't say whether he went for Adrian's weekend to Wiltshire, but he spends Christmas in Cambridge with his uncle and aunt.

Quietly he begins to work on his own plan as a result of Adrian's warning. He needs to be more careful now he's seen the great deceit of Adrian, and the threat behind it.

He mulls over offers of specialised jobs in the commercial world that suit his talents. There are offers from ex-colleagues who have left the Service in the eleven years since the Wall came down: people who have now set up in private business in smart offices in London's old clubland around Boodles and White's and Pratt's and other obscure gentlemen's clubs that are scattered through St James's. These companies are enjoying a rush of profitability from running commercial investigations for large and multinational companies who need privileged information on the ground, wherever they operate in the world. It is an ideal opportunity for a new career for an old spy. And for Finn, a job with one of these companies is cover for what he really means to pursue.

And so in the New Year of 2001, after talking

with various ex-colleagues who have set up these private commercial security companies, Finn finally accepts a job as the Russian expert at a small firm in Mayfair, off Shepherd Market, advising British companies who they are safe to do business with and where. He comes at the invitation of an old Service colleague who's worked at headquarters in Vauxhall until the middle of the 1990s, and then left dismayed by the lack of attention given to Russian affairs. And as this old colleague points out to Finn, he is now earning five times as much as the Government paid him.

But Finn is under no illusion that the Service will forget about him or stop keeping an eye on his activities in this new job. In fact, this is the reason for taking the job in the first place; the Service will know where he is, and Adrian will receive reassuring messages about Finn's new course in life.

He knows he's safer if he doesn't walk off into obscurity, avoid contact, and become a figure in need of special attention. As long as his name is mentioned favourably in the London clubs and at weekend parties in the British countryside, the heat will burn less fiercely.

And so, after six months' diligent work in London, with some sanctioned trips abroad for the company – all above board and noted – in the high summer of 2001, he decides to take a holiday.

But he goes by devious routes and to a part of his life that is secret from everybody – his friends, his uncle and aunt, his former and current employers; anyone, in fact, who has ever known him as Finn.

In the unlikely event that anyone is watching

him, they lose him somewhere near Bishop's Stortford when his car 'breaks down' on the M11, to be towed later to a garage near Stansted airport. Finn walks across open fields, where the harvest is starting to come in, to a lock-up in the Essex town. From the lock-up he takes an old Ducati motorbike and sets off for the Helford River in Cornwall, where nobody knows him as Finn.

In a quiet creek that slides off to the side of the river, he keeps an ancient, semi-restored wooden pilot cutter that lies in the mud at low tide. The cash hole in his bank statement that represented the purchase of this boat ten years before appeared in his annual accounts back then as 'gambling debts', and he was summoned by the Office at the time to receive a warning about it.

The boat holds some kind of magic for Finn, a man who believes in magic without troubling to enquire too deeply, relying only on some instinct, some sense of its benevolence. But the magic is also more prosaic than Finn cares to admit. He has managed to keep the boat's existence a secret from his employers, and that is the real magic for him. As his reputation at the Service for recklessness and loose talk grew, Finn was, quite naturally, considered verbally incontinent. How could he have any secrets from them?

'If you choose a mask,' he once told me, 'choose one which is demeaning to you, like drunkenness. No one believed Kim Philby was a traitor, because how could a drunk be a successful traitor? What they should have asked was, how could a traitor be a successful drunk? They should have looked at his drunkenness and asked how real it was.

'So if you choose a mask, for whatever reason, choose one which is unflattering, unprofessional, foolish even. Then no one will believe that you've chosen it, and no one, therefore, will believe it is a mask.'

'And how do you know', I asked him, 'when your mask, your pretence, possesses you and becomes who you are?'

But I was thinking more about myself than Finn.

'That's the hardest bit of all,' he said.

But thanks to the deliberate foolishness of his mask, Finn's employers missed the boat, as it were.

For three days, Finn stays on his boat. It is called *Bride of the Wind* and named after a painting he loved by Oskar Kokoschka. He rows ashore in the day for supplies from a farm shop situated above the woods along the riverbank and he occasionally visits the chandlery on the other side of the river. The boat is a totem for him, a symbol of freedom, an escape from his other life, from all his other lives.

I have seen *Bride of the Wind*, sailed in her. She is tall-masted, long-planked and with a cutaway stern called a lute; her beautiful lines a poem of craftsmanship. In the saloon below decks was a framed, salt-faded print of a poem composed by Oskar Kokoschka's friend, George Trakl:

> Over blackish cliffs
> Falls drunk with death
> The glowing bride of the wind
> The blue wave of the glacier.

During these days, Finn paints and varnishes where neglect and weather damage demand. He mends a broken pulley block, replaces some worn-out halyards and services the engine. Fuelled and watered, he leaves the river on a spring tide under the nearly full moon and sails to France, to a little fishing port on the Brittany coast where they love old working boats and where, if you sail in one, nobody bothers to ask for your passport.

He spends the evening with an old aquaintance, a red-headed Breton boat builder, in a tiny, black-tarred fisherman's bar up the hill from the harbour. After two o'clock in the morning there are just three of them, Finn, the redhead and the moustached *patron* with a fat belly, who is a grumpy old misanthrope, but who warms up slowly after midnight like a rusty night storage heater. It is into the *patron*'s spare room that Finn collapses into bed sometime in the early hours.

The next day he catches a series of trains that take him by late evening to the Côte d'Azur.

In August along the coast from La Napoule to Monte Carlo, wealthy Russians, both exiles and those close and loyal to the Putin regime, are displaying their riches and their women in the hotels and casinos, and in the private châteaux and yachts they have bought for themselves in the previous ten years.

But Finn isn't going south for a summer holiday. He writes just three words on this journey. Building A Network.

18

FOR TWO WEEKS Finn criss-crosses southern Europe, from the Russian châteaux on the Côte d'Azur to private banking halls in Geneva, to a small and poor canton in Switzerland. His final stop, before departing the mainland of Europe on *Bride of the Wind* as the equinoctial storms set in, is Tegernsee where he discreetly sets up his hideaway in the pink house under the name of a brass-plate company domiciled in the Caribbean, which he had quietly created for himself while working in London. He is laying the ground for the work ahead.

The network he sets up could be described as ramshackle. It consists of one or two angry, self-pitying Russian billionaires, both wanted for imprisonment in Siberia; of money-laundering prosecutors and Swiss bankers; disgruntled KGB agents engaged in clan warfare; foreign intelligence malcontents from various countries; figures from the political fringes of the European Union who've been passed over for promotion or who are afraid of where the European Union is treading in its relations with Russia; private investigators, like Frank, who know the ins and outs of Europe's clearing banks and offshore shell companies; and others on the fringes of the intelligence world, one or two of whom provide a small but significant insight into Finn's quest, and the rest who talk a lot and say nothing. Many of these contacts have private motives, or grander geopolitical ideas that either crush them under the weight or distort their reason. A few are good, clear, honest people. These Finn treats as family.

He begins on that August night, after a day on trains bound for the south, at a party in Antibes, thrown by an acquaintance from Moscow in the 1990s. Boris Berezovsky, until a little over a year before the senior figure among the seven bankers who ruled Russia, is now firmly in exile in one of his many homes in the West, the grand Château de la Garoupe, where he nurses his dreams of a triumphant return.

On this night, however, Finn isn't after information. He wants some of this cash that washes the Côte d'Azur more brightly than the phosphorescence on its beaches. What he wants is funding. Here, among the Russians disenchanted with Putin, he will find the cash that will pay for the lease in Tegernsee and fund the subsequent years of his investigations.

But he goes to Berezovsky's party for a second reason. He knows his presence in the house of Putin's enemy will filter back to Moscow, the Forest and the Kremlin. Even Berezovsky can't invite two hundred and fifty guests without there being an informer among them. So Finn goes along to lay the ground for his reunion with me. He wants us, at the Forest, to know exactly where he is. He knows that they will send me after him.

Whether he finds any of the funds he needs from Berezovsky or from one of the many other billionaires, multimillionaires and also-rans at this party – or whether he takes a hat round and gets a sub from more than one of them – he doesn't say.

But the next night he has dinner at the Hermitage Hotel in Monte Carlo with one of the guests from the night before. He is a Russian oil baron, Gennady Liakubsky, and Finn meets him along with one of Liakubsky's cronies from the Russian underworld, and another man.

And this is where we at the Forest begin to pick him up on our radar. One of our SVR agents on the Côte d'Azur is a real-estate agent who deals in many of the high-end properties the Russian rich are buying. He has been at the party where Finn appeared and has put a tail on him.

And so I knew Finn was dining with Liakubsky and his mob friends that night.

Within twelve hours we had the photographs of this dinner back with us at the Forest; Liakubsky, in the company of a Russian mafioso recently released from prison and known as Yakutchik – 'the little Yakut' – and another man, a Russian trader living in Geneva who calls himself Danny.

Finn is sitting at a private table at the Hermitage

in Monte Carlo with five waiters for the four of them, who are drinking thousand-dollar bottles of wine decanted and poured by a sixth waiter. Finn is laughing and toasting with a billionaire thief and the best of the Russian underworld.

He's in his element, relishing this role that will later that night or the next day engender that curious brand of guilt and sorrow that is always mixed with pride.

He's telling filthy jokes and indulging in the back-slapping bonhomie with the best of them. But it is an unhappy union of a disgraced British spy and two thieves and a murderer, disguised as a convivial supper between colleagues.

'I am taking their money; money stolen off the backs of the Russian people. These people stole it from other thieves and murderers, but ultimately it comes from the poor, the old, the veterans of war and Communist persecution. It comes from industrial production from the factories and mines and oilfields constructed from the blood and death of Stalin's slaves. The thousands of pounds' worth of wine we are pouring down our gullets like Coca-Cola is the blood of those men and women who worked under the lash fifty, sixty years ago to construct an industry which has been stolen from their children and their grandchildren.

'This is Putin's great public relations coup – to focus on such thieves as these – while silently seizing their ill-gotten gains, not for the benefit of the people who made it, but for a new set of oligarchs, the KGB, which is now taking shape in the Kremlin.

'And me? How different am I? Here I am taking

their stolen money in order to expose this new crime that I so passionately believe is now unfolding in the Kremlin. So, for me, the means justify the ends too. But do they? For me, but not for anyone else?

'Sometimes, all we need to guard against is our own pious morality. But it's hard to see that when you're sitting at the rich man's table with a bunch of crooks and killers.'

When I see Finn's picture at the Forest the day after the dinner, I can hardly contain my excitement. He seems so close and I can feel his plan unfolding. The company he's keeping doesn't matter. I forgive Finn more easily than he forgives himself. There he is, the man who a little more than a year ago told me I could say he loved me. I smile again at the memory.

The whereabouts of Finn and these photographs of the company he's keeping are so important to us that they arrive at the Forest a few hours later. It isn't Liakubsky we are watching. Or the Little Yakut, just released from an American jail. Or Danny, the Russian trader from Geneva. It is Finn. The Forest is watching Finn in the hope he will lead us to Mikhail.

Gennady Liakubsky is thirty-eight years old. He was born in Komi out to the north-east of Moscow in western Siberia where there is nothing but tundra and oilfields, great winding rivers and the herds of reindeer that are still taken from one feeding ground to the next by the dwindling ethnic peoples of this inhospitable region.

As a student in the Engineering School in Moscow, Liakubsky had been a part-time informer for the KGB before perestroika in the 1980s. But then he'd seen the opportunity of marrying his qualifications with the new business opportunities that arose in the nineties. He'd traded on the Moscow stock exchange in any commodity he could get his hands on, but always looked east, where Russia's money is born, to the oilfields and mines that are strewn across the vast, empty Siberian plains ten time zones wide that reach up eventually a few miles from America in the Bering Strait.

When Yeltsin began to auction off the state's industrial property in 1996, Liakubsky was one of those who seized their chance. He bought oil production in Komi where his local KGB and mafia connections ensured a smooth transition, then branched out into a gold mine outside Yakutsk, the place where he struck up his partnership with the Little Yakut. A coal mine in the Kuzbass region was added, then iron mines, steel foundries and more oil. Like the others, Liakubsky amassed whatever he could get while the going was good. And like the others, he took his profits out of Russia to the West in a financial drain that has cost Russia up to five hundred billion dollars, all told. Bleeding the country was their insurance against the future.

But when Putin came to power in 2000, Liakubsky, unlike Boris Berezovsky, was one of those who prostrated himself to the new power. His château in France was not an exile's home. He paid and paid the new administration in the Kremlin, he agreed to Putin's new injunction to stay out of politics, he repatriated Russian art to St Petersburg from all around the world, and supported Putin's pet projects in Petersburg. It is said he gave over twenty million dollars to the refurbishment of Putin's home city and its palaces.

But even after all this, Liakubsky could never feel safe, as long as there were new, more trusted acolytes that Putin wished to put in control of the country's wealth at the centre of power, in the Kremlin.

We knew at the Forest that Liakubsky, like all of his kind, spent a great deal of his resources amassing *kompromat* – black propaganda – against Putin and his clique. One day, who knows, possession of the President's secrets, and those of his allies, might be all that stands between Liakubsky and a Siberian prison camp.

But Liakubsky was not alone in this. They all did it, they all still do it, as long as Putin and his KGB clan tighten the noose around Russia's throat and are the power to be reckoned with. They support Putin's political party, United Russia, which is now, six years later, the only real party; they pay up when asked. But always, always they continue their search for insurance.

And Finn, for Liakubsky, is just one more agent of his insurance, one brick in the wall of the *kompromat*, the black propaganda the oil baron needs. His financial contribution to Finn isn't even petty cash for Liakubsky.

But we're not watching Liakubsky, back at the Forest nor the Little Yakut, with his yellowed Asian features pinched from generations of Siberian cold and his string of murders behind him. Nor Danny the Geneva trader. We are watching Finn and I am being briefed to join with him again and find Mikhail, the enemy within.

After some financial arrangement has been reached with Liakubsky, the next morning Finn takes a train to Annecy. But in Annecy, we lose him. As I read now, I see the trail of Finn's route at the moment it went dead for us.

Somehow and un-recounted by Finn, he makes his way to the Swiss border and, crossing without a passport through the deserted frontier post above Grenoble, he travels to Geneva.

19

ON A FINE CLEAR SUMMER MORNING, when the out-
lines of the mountains seem to have been painted
on glass, Finn walks up a pleasant leafy road in Cologny, a suburb of Geneva reserved for the world's
wealthy, and its diplomats and the lords of the international agencies and organisations that have taken
root in the city. Here they huddle halfway to heaven
on a rolling hill above the lake. Above them, neat
domestic vineyards embroider the fields all the way
to the sky, while below them the city of Geneva stands
at the head of the flat blue lawn of its lake.

Finn has parked a small white van at the top of
the street, killing the reverberating volume of Elas-
tica as he cuts the engine. In the stunned silence, he
walks across the road, turns into a cul de sac that
curves in an arc rejoining the road further down

from where he's parked. He wears old blue overalls and carries a metal workman's box.

He's already seen the car he is looking for as he drove by. It is a silver grey Lexus with diplomatic plates, parked on the kerb outside white wrought-iron gates. As he walks back up the hill, without breaking step he takes a roll of black electrical tape from the box, bites into the plastic-tasting end, and pulls off a two-inch strip. When the car is level with him he places the strip in a vertical position at the side of the curved back window and walks on, continuing up to where he parked the van twenty minutes earlier.

He throws the toolbox into the back, switches on the engine and with it the blasting music, and drives back down the hill and into the city. He returns the van to the hire company less than two hours after he's rented it for cash from a bored representative, and boards a tram by the shopping plaza on the west bank. The tram winds its way up and around a hill, offering glimpses of the lake through side streets, and on to another suburb, south of the city this time, called Chêne Bougeries.

Finn steps off the tram, along with some Scandinavian backpackers, just a few hundred yards from the French border. He walks across the road unchallenged by the border guards, and into the Bar des Douanes, where he sits at a table in the back and orders a black coffee.

It is just after ten o'clock in the morning and the striking blue summer day is visible like a cinema screen from the dark gloom at the back of the bar.

Five minutes later a short, tubby, bearded man

wearing jeans and a faded grey T-shirt, and carrying a battered leather knapsack slung over his left shoulder, enters the bar. When they see each other Finn rises from the plastic seat and they embrace in the surprised way the English have, no matter how many times they've embraced foreigners. The man grunts an indecipherable and half-suspicious greeting. He sits, orders a coffee and brandy, unrolls a newspaper and slaps it with the back of his hand.

'Read that,' he says and, as Finn reads, the man takes a pouch from the leather knapsack and rolls a cigarette from some dry Drum tobacco he grumpily scrapes up from the corners of the pouch.

'They're trying to get rid of Stelzer,' the man says, gesticulating at the newspaper. 'He's doing his job too well.'

Finn has met Jean-Claude many times in the past five years. He's a man at home in one environment and completely at odds with all others. His plane of existence is a dark bar or, best of all, the wreck of his windowless office where he sits on a swivel chair with a torn and dirty nylon seat and hunches over a plywood door that is his desk and is piled with paperwork, ashtrays, half-empty beer bottles, scraps of paper scribbled with telephone numbers, half-drunk cups of coffee and thousands of coloured paperclips he seems to collect like semi-precious stones. His beard is dappled with the white blossom of cigarette ash from the cigarettes he wedges, until long after they're burnt out, between two brown and very crooked front teeth. His bulbous nose is somehow fitted on to his face, red and greasy, and it doesn't appear to obey the normal physics of noses.

In any environment other than his office or a bar, Jean-Claude is diminished. Finn walked with him once into the mountains outside Geneva and up there he looked like an ugly troll, with his nose and straggled beard, who'd had his fairy tale ripped out from under him. He seemed to be struggling to come to terms with a landscape that once, in another world perhaps, was his, but had now been tamed by roads and bridges and gas stations and hotels and all the other human forces more progressive than his own.

But in the dark cave of a bar, or of his study, he lost the uncertainty, the unease he felt in the wider, brighter modern world. Finn is the only person who calls Jean-Claude 'Troll' to his face.

'And they've just killed my documentary,' Jean-Claude puffs while Finn finishes reading the article. 'Help me sell it in England, Finn,' he says. 'They're serious in England,' he continues, with a nostalgia for British investigative journalism that is at least thirty years out of date. 'Anyway, why are you here? What do you want?'

When he senses Jean-Claude has finished with his tirade, Finn looks up from the newspaper, the *Zürcher Zeitung*, and grins broadly. 'Hello, Troll,' he says.

'What the fuck is there to say "Hello" about?' Jean-Claude grumbles. 'You've read that, haven't you?'

'It's two years,' Finn laughs. Jean-Claude looks at him in astonishment, as though time is some devilish human construct which now even this, one of his few remaining and trusted friends, has fallen for.

Jean-Claude, Finn told me, would spend a year, two years – ten years, even – tracking one secret money trail through a hundred different destinations until he found where it all began, the hidden owner, the motherlode. He could follow a financial pipeline as a water diviner traces water. His fellow enthusiasts, who Finn imagined as a band of trolls, lived in other Swiss mountain towns, as well as in Liechtenstein, Luxembourg, the Channel Islands, the Cayman and Virgin Islands. Jean-Claude had spent nearly fifty years obsessed with secret money.

First it was Nazi gold and the stolen cash hoards that found their way out of Germany at the end of the war, then the Camorra – the Naples mafia – and their Sicilian cousins, and then the KGB and Stasi secret money pipelines from East Germany. He has been spending fifteen years by the time Finn meets him on this morning in the Bar des Douanes, looking at the financial networks of Russian front companies and banks which were said to have been wound up when the Wall came down, but which were constructed so intricately, bound so tightly, that no one could be sure – and Jean-Claude, for one, didn't believe – that they had really been wound up at all; companies like Exodi.

Time was nothing to him. Time, he once told Finn solemnly, was invented by the devil to clog the smooth-running machine that was God's natural world. 'And that,' Finn had told me, 'was when he was sober.'

'Well?' Finn says. 'What's new?'

'Nothing's new, you fucking idiot. That's the point. What do you want?'

'Maybe this is a good place to start,' Finn says smiling and looks down at the front page of the *Zürcher Zeitung*.

Jean-Claude orders a large brandy the second time around, as if the single one hadn't really done the trick, and he orders two more coffees and then he remembers he's forgotten he's out of tobacco and walks over to the counter and buys another pouch. When he is comfortably surrounded by these props, he looks at Finn balefully.

'Stelzer's the best chief prosecutor this country's ever had,' he says. 'So what do they do? Intrigue against him. They'll have him out by the end of the year. He's prosecuting the wrong sort of people. Rich crooks, in other words. He's trying to clean up this sewer of a country. The burghers are aghast. Stelzer's been stopping dirty money coming over from the East. Russia itself; Kazakhstan and the other central Asian republics; the Caucasus. Tens of billions of laundered cash is getting held up by Stelzer from joining all the other cash that the world's murderers and half-mad potentates and mafiosi and intelligence creeps like you wish to deposit in our beautiful vaults. Two weeks ago Stelzer said to the parliamentary financial committee – in other words, interested bankers who run the country – that if we accept all these huge, unprecedented sums of black money, we'll choke on it. They didn't listen then and they aren't now.

'Last week was the final straw. Stelzer had four

men arrested coming over the border from Liechtenstein with nearly four billion dollars' worth of bonds.
And you know what they're saying down at the border post? That Putin himself is a nominee for some
of it. I don't believe it, I can't believe it. Are they that
brazen in the Kremlin? Anyway, Stelzer had them all
arrested, along with that Russian mafioso Mikhas,
and locked them up and photographed everyone, as
well as the documents.'

Jean-Claude puffs his cigarette, which has gone
out a while before. 'Walking over the fucking border!' he says, amazed.

Jean-Claude takes a delicate sip from his brandy
glass, a gesture that is somehow inappropriate next
to his brutal verbal assault.

Jean-Claude only ever drinks less than half of
what he buys or what he pours. He simply likes to
know it is there.

'And do you know what I know?' Jean-Claude demands. 'Of course you don't. They'll replace him
with Hutzger. You know Hutzger. Harvard Business
School, the Swiss Economic Committee, then the
Principality's financial adviser in Liechtenstein. He's
been in charge of hushing up their criminal activities
in Vaduz – perfect training for Switzerland. You know
Hutzger, Finn?'

Finn pauses and looks at the surface of the table,
as if at some imaginary stain. Hutzger is the name
he's heard from Dieter a year before, the man who
laid the false trail for the German intelligence services in their investigation into Exodi.

'Yes.'

'Well, what do you know about him?' Jean-Claude asks sourly.

'We believe he has contacts with the KGB,' Finn says.

For the first time, Jean-Claude looks wrong-footed.

'What did you say?'

Finn doesn't reply.

Jean-Claude replaces the brandy glass on the table and stares at Finn.

'Show me that's true,' he says at last.

'Maybe I can, maybe I can't. But with your help I can do a lot more than that. Putin's personal funds are a sideshow. I need you, Troll. I need your help.'

There is no indication of assent or otherwise.

'I have a friend in the mountains,' Jean-Claude says. 'He makes one wristwatch a year. Just one. He spends ten, twelve hours a day perhaps, for a whole year and makes one watch. Then he sells it for two or three hundred thousand dollars. I love this man. He's a perfectionist, there is madness in him. Switzerland is a perfectionist country, if you hadn't noticed. It has perfected the art of looking after other people's money. There are more people employed in Switzerland with the sole purpose of hiding money than there are coal miners in Ukraine. The Swiss are genetically programmed to hide things. The lines of banks along the lake and all the ones dotted around the cantons are just the physical manifestation of what is going on inside their heads.'

He looks directly at Finn. 'Apart from my house, have you ever been invited into the house of a Swiss out in the mountains?'

'No.'

'You see. They hide everything, even when there's nothing to hide except IKEA furniture. They can't help it, it's a disease.'

'And where there are perfectly hidden things there are also people who are perfect at finding them,' Finn says.

'Exactly,' the Troll says proudly. 'You make one thing and you make its opposite at the same time. That is normal. Bullets and armour; missiles and radar; tax laws and tax evasion; life and death.'

'That's why I want your help.'

'But will you hide things from me too? I know you and your profession.'

'You'll have everything I have.'

'Then I'll help you.'

He doesn't question Finn's word.

Jean-Claude rummages in his knapsack and takes out a videotape.

'There,' he says. 'That's my documentary which Swiss TV has refused to broadcast. Look at it soon. But you must go to Liechtenstein. Speak to Pablo in Vaduz. You know Pablo?'

'I've met him with you.'

'He has an interesting story about Hutzger.'

'Is Pablo like us?'

'Maybe, maybe not. I think he can't help playing both sides. That's his disease.'

'Thank you, Jean-Claude.'

Once again the Troll looks at Finn in amazement. He has no concept of gratitude.

'I need something very specific from you, Troll,' Finn says. 'There's a set of companies. They're called

Exodi, and there's one of them here in Geneva. I want to know whatever you can find for me about Exodi in Geneva.'

'Exodi?' the Troll murmurs. 'No. I don't know it. Call on me in a week and we'll see where we are.'

'I'll do that,' Finn says.

Finn sits on a stone bench by the neatly landscaped quay reserved for Lake Geneva's pleasure boats. Here the lake narrows to the width of a bridge span and runs off through a lock and into the Rhone.

He watches the man in the light brown polo shirt and Burberry slacks who ushers two small children in front of him and on to the ferry. Sergei must have seen the strip of black tape on his car screen within an hour of Finn leaving it there.

The Russian has been waiting on the far side of the road from the quay, buying ice creams and balloons for the kids until the ferry is almost ready to depart. He joins the end of the now-depleted queue, so he will know there is nobody boarding behind him – or, if anybody does board, he will have a picture of a face clearly in his mind. And he will know to abort.

But nobody comes on behind him and the ferry churns the water with its bow propeller and, crablike, leaves the quay in a white wash, heading up the lake for several stops on the way to Vevey.

Finn notes the ferry's destination again, folds the tourist map he's needlessly carrying, stands up and tucks it into a back pocket. He walks across the intersection of three roads that filter towards the bridges that join Geneva's two parts at the lake's apex and picks up the one taxi that stands at the rank.

They wind out of Geneva to the east and pass through its satellite towns and villages that dot the lake. He pays off the taxi a few miles before his destination and takes a bus the rest of the way.

The restaurant stands on a sloping lawn that meets the lake in a grass beach. Nearby is a quay where the ferry stops on the way up the lake. There is a large worn-out play area administered by two young women, probably itinerant workers from Eastern Europe. There is plenty of brightly coloured plastic equipment to amuse the children while their parents eat or drink in a modest wooden building that opens only in the summer.

Sergei sits by the window, facing towards the road with the beautiful lake view behind him.

'You were quick,' Finn says, and sits down.

'You were slow,' Sergei says. 'We don't have a lot of time. Life here isn't so safe for me any more. Not since Dobby's been in power.'

Sergei uses the insulting KGB nickname for President Putin, a name taken from Harry Potter's goblin.

Sergei had come up through the Forest's training school at the same time as me. In 1992 he started a trading company in Moscow which imported sugar at first, then branched out into other foodstuffs. He became acquainted with the trading floors of Western Europe, made his millions and then moved to Geneva.

After Yeltsin had made Putin his prime minister and when the various KGB clans rivalled each other to put their man in position to win the elections, Sergei was working on behalf of one of Putin's opponents, one of the KGB's four or five chosen candidates to win the elections, before the list was finally whittled down to Putin. Sergei ended up funding a losing candidate.

A successful businessman, now worth several hundred million, Sergei continued his work as a KGB informer and reported directly to the KGB's officer at the Russian delegation of the United Nations in Geneva. Sergei was riding high in Geneva for several years, making millions from KGB-backed trading contracts and his own private business. But his one mistake – a mistake that was to cost him and many others dear – was that he had backed the wrong horse. His candidate was now an ordinary MP in the Russian Duma and Putin was president.

'Things will pass,' Finn says. 'Just ride it out, Sergei.'

'I don't know if I'm under surveillance but safe, or on the list and not safe,' the Russian replies. 'That's how they like it best. Keeping everyone in fear.'

'How bad is it?' Finn says.

'Terrible. The Petersburg clan are triumphant in their victory last year. Putin himself, Ivanov, Sechin – the lot of them. And now they're ironing out their enemies – or anyone they feel like ironing out. Not just in Moscow either. They're already turning to the outside world. Putin's Petersburg clan – these damn Peterski – they're even more ruthless than we thought.'

Sergei gulps from a plastic glass of transparent liquor.

'They're putting out contracts, for Christ's sake,' he continues. 'It's not enough that Putin's won, now they want to erase anyone who's got under their skin. I put nearly five million dollars on the losing ticket in the election campaign and now my whole fucking body's above the parapet.'

Sergei drinks heavily again from the plastic tumbler and leans across the table to Finn.

'I'm glad you're here. You know, I may want to come over. Maybe it's my only choice now.' He sits back. 'I hear you've left Moscow. You've got trouble too?'

Finn thinks about suggesting that Sergei go to the Americans as a safer haven, rather than the British. But he needs Sergei where he is for now, in the field, not in some CIA safe house in Connecticut on a two-year debriefing.

'No, no trouble,' Finn says. 'Just a change of job.'

A waitress comes and takes Finn's order for a glass of wine and another vodka for Sergei.

'We can take you in, of course,' Finn lies. 'But now's not a good time. Give it a few months when we can demonstrate more clearly what Putin's doing. Then my people in London will really appreciate your value. But I need your help for that. Right now you'll be coming up against my government's love affair with Putin.'

'I can't last much longer like this,' the Russian says plaintively, and Finn watches the alcoholic self-pity well up in his face. 'They're watching me, sticking pins in me, hounding me. An article appeared in *Izvestia*, naming me in some scandal. Inspired, of course, by the dogs in Putin's clan. There are people in his clan who hate me in Moscow.'

'But, as you say, Sergei, they're putting the frighteners on everyone, not just you. What they want you to do is run. That will prove your treachery. And then they catch you before you can get to safety.'

'I hope you're right.'

'I'll help you when it's time,' Finn says, lying easily again. He has no power to help Sergei or anyone else.

'Putin has spent a year gathering Russia's money,' Sergei continues. 'It's going to be a great harvest. He's put all his own people into the state economy, the state oil companies, where they drain a fat percentage for themselves on the inside. And the oligarchs, our once-new independent businessmen, are now cap in hand. They're all afraid, even the most powerful. Putin has told them they must share their wealth. Share it with the KGB, with the Forest, of course, but not with the country. Geneva, you wouldn't believe it! It's crawling with operatives. Back in Moscow they're activating agents who've been asleep for years. There are sting operations against certain banks . . .'

'Which banks?'

'Which ones? There are half a dozen. All old KGB sympathisers who have long fallen into disuse. Asleep.'

Finn says nothing.

'A month ago,' Sergei says, leaning in towards

Finn again, 'the president of the Banque Leman was invited to Moscow. He has a weakness from a long time back. But this time they photographed him indulging in this weakness – for underage girls – in an apartment in the city. Now they use the pictures to tell him what to do.'

'What's new?' Finn says.

'This is what's new. The regime isn't only interested in funding the Forest's operations abroad any more. It has very big plans, very big money from business, mafia sources, billions. There are accounts being opened up in the Banque Leman in the name of foreigners who hold very senior positions in the West. So they say. Bribe money is bottomless. That's just one bank. There are others.'

'Why's it different from their normal Forest operations?' Finn says calmly.

'This time they plan to use their vast capital like the West does,' Sergei says. 'They're in a no-limit poker game with the markets as the pot.'

The small children Finn has seen with Sergei on the quay earlier run into the restaurant and look at Finn.

'What's the name of this bank's president?' Finn says.

'Naider. Clement Naider.'

'Can you get me the pictures, the photographs with these underage girls your side has of him?' Finn says.

'You ask too much,' Sergei says. 'I tell you, I'm watched.'

One of the boys tugs his arm and his brother comes in to join them.

'I'm taking too big a risk just by being here. I have to go,' Sergei says. 'You will help me?'

'Soon. When it's time. I need the pictures, Sergei,' Finn says. 'Naider and the girls.'

'No more now please.'

Finn stands up as Sergei does. 'I'll help you if you do this,' Finn promises. 'We'll have you in a nice big house in Surrey, near Boris, all yours, with a brand new passport.'

'There isn't much time for me,' Sergei says, and drinks back the tumbler of vodka. 'I'll see what I can do.'

Finn leans in to the Russian.

'No one's interested in helping you, Sergei,' Finn says harshly. 'Not us, not the Americans. They're in bed with Putin. If you want me to get you out, find the pictures.'

Beads of sweat break out across the Russian's forehead. Then he takes the boy's hand and leaves the restaurant without a word.

Finn watches the small boy looking back at him. Who's that man, he seems to hear him say. They step out on to the warm lawn, and Finn wonders how much grace Sergei really does have left with the Kremlin.

20

I **WAKE EARLY** the next morning unable to sleep, the worst night since Finn disappeared ten days ago. It is Thursday, the beginning of the third day since my arrival in Tegernsee, and outside the town fills with market shoppers.

At first I don't know where I am, then I see Finn's journal and then the mountains beyond the window. My first thought is of Finn, and then of Mikhail.

Apart from the pink house, Mikhail was the one secret Finn had kept from me, and I thought the clue to Finn's disappearance might lie not just here in Tegernsee, but in the identity of Mikhail.

Somewhere down in the cellar, I am sure, Finn would have left something that explained Mikhail. Until I have searched for this, the deepest secret of Finn's, I know I can't concentrate on anything else.

I take the book back down to the cellar, lock

everything, and leave to find breakfast. There is nothing to eat or drink in the house except some half-empty liquor bottles. I walk to a small café, up near Schmidtke's house on the Graubstrasse, a few hundred yards away, and try to eat a croissant, but eventually I can't postpone my sense of rising anticipation. I take the croissant and a cup of coffee and return to the house, buying a few supplies on my way back.

I descend to the cellar again, shutting everything up behind me, and light the oil stove. First I take the pile of Finn's books that I have yet to read and flick through them, but I don't expect Mikhail to be so easily discovered. Mikhail would be special, separate, if Finn had acknowledged Mikhail at all in his records. Mikhail would not be someone anyone could discover when they eventually found the pink house. How would Finn leave a record of Mikhail?

The cellar contains very little: a table where Finn seems to have edited some of the books before depositing them here, a small, empty metal filing cabinet, a rolled-up carpet that looks as if it hasn't been moved for years, some odds and ends from a plumbing job – offcuts of plastic pipe and a tub of hardened white paste – a waste-paper basket filled with screwed-up paper, a rickety chair with a reed seat, dust, endless dust, and an empty picture frame.

I begin to look at everything and the more I look the more I know that Mikhail won't be here. If Finn had written about Mikhail at all, there would at least be a clue here. And the clue, I knew, would be something that I, and only I, would understand.

I check the cellar completely and am covered

with dust, then finally I empty the waste-paper basket and begin unscrewing the paper. It is mostly old envelopes and scraps of paper torn from his books with a single word on them, or a sentence, or nothing at all. I examine each one and can get no answer from any of the scribbled notes. When I unscrew a piece of paper near the bottom of the basket, a single sheet, I see that one line is written on it.

It is underlined, like a title, and reads *Bride of the Wind*. I stare at it. There is nothing else. I swiftly turn out the rest of the basket, unscrewing all the remaining paper, but they are all blank. There is nothing else as clear as this one sheet.

I turn off the oil heater and ascend the wooden steps again, open the metal door and shut it firmly behind me. I draw the false wall across it, with its built-in fireplace, check the ornaments on the mantelpiece, and assure myself that all is as it should be.

Then I put on my coat and woolly hat and, clutching the paper in a ball, leave the house again for the second time in two hours.

Down along the path by the lake where I'd walked the night before to the *gasthaus*, a brittle layer of ice creeps a few feet into the water. There is a clear sky, it is bitterly cold, and the snow on the path has frozen into crusts. I walk fast to keep warm and because it suits my sense of urgency.

I come to the first of three lidos, closed up for the winter, the water frozen solid in the man-made harbours. There is a metal rail fence around the lido, and inside the fence plastic covers are pulled over some refreshment stalls.

By the path, there is a low metal gate in the

fence, shut with a chain and padlock. By the gate is a wooden pillbox to fit one person to take the money and dispense the tickets when the lido is open. The stand is closed up with padlocked stable doors.

It is easy to step over the gate. The fence and the gate are there just to deter summer visitors from entering the lido unnoticed, without paying. I walk past the pillbox ticket office, across the icy wood surface and past the boarded-up refreshment stands.

Behind them, on a broad wooden slatted deck area, are several dozen upturned rowing boats, sailing dinghies, tenders for larger boats anchored in the lake for the summer – anything that their owners had too little space or too much money to bother to take home with them at the end of the season. Most are covered, but the blue plastic covers are stretched across the hulls in such a way that I can pick out the boats' names written on the bow or on the transom.

I walk up and down the rows of boats, pausing to look at names, and lift the flap of a hanging cover, here and there, for a better sight. I translate the mostly German names, the type of silly, fond names that people give boats: *Our Boys, Jaws, Titanic, Beautiful Melinda*. By the time I reach the end of the last row, I have spent nearly an hour and am cold again. Every name I stop to study; I turn them this way and that, trying to see another meaning, another message from Finn. But it is no good. I leave the lido and hurry further up the path and into the *gasthaus* for warmth and coffee.

There is a solitary girl behind the bar at this quiet time of the day. I ask her about the lidos that dot the shoreline. She says that only local people kept their boats in most of them, including the one I had randomly chosen, and that if I am from out of town, the only place I can keep a boat is at a lido in the next village of Rottach-Egern. There, she says, they allow casual visitors to leave boats over the winter. I finish my coffee and take a bus for less than a mile along the lake.

Rottach-Egern is all but joined to Tegernsee by the scattering of houses and small inns between them. It lies at the edge of the lake and its lido stretches out a hundred metres from the shore.

It is built in a similar way and there is nobody to prevent me from getting inside, nobody around in winter at all. There is nothing to steal, except boats, and nobody in their right mind would wish to take a boat out at this time of year, even for a prank.

Again I walk the rows of upturned boats, checking the names. Finally I come to a sailing dinghy, perhaps fourteen feet long and made of wood. I look at the bow and there is no name written there. Its winter cover obscures the stern. I cut the string and lift up the thick plastic. The boat is called *Windsbraut, Bride of the Wind*. I see that the writing covers another, previous name that has been painted out.

I untie the rest of the blue plastic cover and peel it away and see a smooth, blue-painted hull with a slit in the centre for a daggerboard. I lift the boat up from the side as far as I can, but it is heavy and I can't hold it and look inside the hull at the same time. So I let it down and look around for something to prop it up.

There is the heavy concrete base of a parasol

near one of the covered refreshment stalls and I half drag, half roll it over, placing it close to the hull and managing to lift the boat about two feet off the wooden decking to place it precariously on the metal tube the parasol slots into. I get down on my back and worm my way underneath.

The daggerboard casing takes up most of the centre of the boat, there are coiled wires and a plastic bailer tied on to a thwart. Around the insides of the cockpit are ballast tanks built into the hull. They have four circular black plastic screw tops about six inches across that give access to the tanks. I begin to unscrew each one of them and to pull out the inflated yellow plastic ballast sacks inside. I pull them out one by one and when I've finished I worm out from under the boat. There are six ballast sacks in all. I pick up each one until I find which of them contains an object that I can feel sliding up and down inside. The rest I kick back under the hull. I lower the boat back on to the decking, put the parasol base back where I found it and cover and tie the boat again with its plastic sheet.

I let the air out of the ballast sack until I can fit it, and the solid object I can feel it contains, under my coat.

I find a taxi and take it to the market square in Tegernsee and walk, carefully again – watching for other interested eyes – until I approach the pink house.

In the kitchen I study the yellow ballast bag. I see its plastic seams have been carefully parted in order to store an object inside, and have then been melted together again. I rip it open with a knife.

Inside is a watertight package and, inside that, an exercise book. I open it up and, from the first lines, see that this story begins with Finn's alternative history lesson.

I take it into the sitting room, light the fire, and sit on the sofa.

'Vladimir Putin took up his KGB posting in Dresden,' Finn begins, 'in 1980, the year that Oskar Kokoschka died. He occupied a KGB residence two streets away from where Kokoschka held the Professorship of Arts at the Dresden Academy between 1917 and 1924. There the similarities end.

'Putin was one of the guardians of Yuri Andropov's post-Soviet vision, in which the outmoded, outdated methods of all the years since the Russian Revolution were to be reconfigured, under the watchful gaze of the first KGB president, Andropov. But then Andropov died prematurely. His successor, Chernenko, was a throwback to the Brezhnev era and lasted little more than a year before he, too, died.

'And then they ushered in Gorbachev, who would always have the KGB at his shoulder.

'Putin ran a large network of agents in East Germany. The most important of these was a man named Klaus-Maria Sudhoff. Sudhoff was another Russian-German, like Schmidtke, who had been stationed in Dresden for five years before Putin arrived. Sudhoff, apart from being the conduit between Schmidtke and the KGB, was also the main contact between all of them and Otto Roth.

'Sudhoff knew where all the skeletons were buried. Sudhoff was involved in KGB arms and drugs trafficking and he worked with terrorist groups in the West, particularly in West Germany. His friendship with Putin was described as instant. They hit it off like old friends.

'In January 1990, Putin began to sign contracts with all his operatives in East Germany which promised them, only a few weeks after the fall of the Berlin Wall, that the KGB would look after its own. Contracts were written and toasted in Sekt, Putin's favourite wine while he was based in Dresden. Plans were drawn up to give his network new identities, send them to other countries or simply bring them to live in Russia. The deals were sealed with a handshake from Putin.

'But as so often with such plans, the promises were never kept and some agents began to make threats and feel threatened at the same time. Some disappeared, Sudhoff among them.

'One of Putin's agents, Klaus Zuchold, finally went over to the BND, West Germany's secret service, and gave the names of fifteen spies in West Germany working for Moscow. But the West Germans decided not to pursue the names he gave them, and they buried them in their attempt to obliterate the complex past, just as they were to sweep Schmidtke under the carpet during the same years.

'Klaus-Maria Sudhoff was among those names. And he disappeared sometime in 1990.

'He was finally found face down in a canal in Berlin in March 1992. He'd consumed a great deal of alcohol, no doubt, but that was only partially responsible for his death. The official record claims the cause of death as "drowning".

'But I must digress for a moment from Sudhoff to look at the organisation you and your father were assigned to, Anna, Directorate "S". As well as your job, darling Anna, training subversives – *nelegali* – to engage in terrorist activities in their own countries, Directorate "S" was actually charged with a far more important role. That role was no less than the preservation of the KGB itself. When Gorbachev was President and before the Wall came down, Directorate "S" was assigned to hold the Soviet state together through the organs of the security services; to put the KGB on ice.

'Independent groups of senior officers in Directorate "S" set about preserving the clan loyalties that ran deeper than any loyalty to Communist cliques or even to the Politburo. In fact, one of the main aims of Directorate "S" in these years was to sweep these fusty, inefficient Communist cliques aside, right up to the Politburo itself.

'Directorate "S" operated with a cell structure, an underground formation, with no centralised control. Central control would have been too risky. Look at what happened in 1991. Kryuchkov and his other KGB associates staged their disastrous putsch against Gorbachev for control of the Kremlin and nearly ruined all the plans Directorate "S" had so carefully laid. It was its cell structure which ensured its preservation. The putsch was a setback for those who knew what the deeper, longer plan was. The

Plan. Directorate "S" was playing a far longer game than Kryuchkov and the rest of his dreamers realised.

'When Yeltsin stood on his tank in 1991 and the putsch was defeated, the Plan was disrupted by a chain of events that began with the coup Yeltsin overthrew. The cell structure buried itself still deeper, and waited. Yeltsin could have destroyed the structure by unmasking all Russia's operatives and all its illegals in the West. But he was afraid to do that, and who can blame him? Yeltsin, however, the one hope for democracy, did gain the upper hand for a while, and the Plan was postponed.

'So their organisation became even tighter. And then slowly, as Yeltsin weakened, these disparate cells began to join together, firstly through the KGB's reconquest of the Ministry of Defence and then, as Putin's power grew at the end of the nineties, through other ministries. Shebarshin and Drozdov helped the movement gather strength and to coordinate itself. Then Leonov promoted Sergei Ivanov to Minister of Defence. Once Ivanov became a minister and Putin became head of the KGB, the wagon began to roll at last. As you know, they called themselves – call themselves – "The Patriots".

'But Directorate "S" was the core, always the core. In the hard times, it was Directorate "S" whose access to vast numbers of illegals abroad – as well as hard cash – held the movement together. In 1991, Directorate "S" was, in effect, a separate country within Russia, funded by the new businessmen they controlled, and by Russians in the West. But they were also funded with even greater quantities of cash by the illegals who were already in positions of great financial power – in private banks and private companies in the West – men like Otto Roth.

'Directorate "S" was integrated on an international level, like any independent country. There are thousands of you out there, Anna. Like you, they have the best education, years of experience in the field. Each officer has up to a dozen illegals at his disposal somewhere abroad; operatives who are self-sufficient and who pay back when told to pay back.

'And they worked in cells, just as they did when it all began before the Revolution, before Lenin returned to Russia in 1917, the year Kokoschka, as it happens, took up his professorship in Dresden. These cells were in the same mould the KGB has always favoured. Even completely cut off from the KGB body, deprived of state financing, left out in the cold, the structure would still survive and prosper.

'And Ivanov and Putin, and the others Putin gathered around him, they knew this – they were, of course, part of it – and when they took power they began to fold Directorate "S" and all its hundreds of cells back into the mixing bowl of Russian politics like cream into a soufflé. They owed their positions of power to Directorate "S" and Directorate "S", like some precious Holy Grail buried during the dark years of democracy, was ready to change the world when it re-emerged.

'And so, slowly, from 1991, the Patriots have built the economic structures they needed; they have suborned the notionally independent businesses that came to power under Yeltsin, and they have brought the various mafias in under their wing, killing those crime bosses who opposed them. It is the biggest nationalisation of mafia and gangster groups in history.

'And with all these methods, the Patriots have created an over-arching state super-business that controls half the world's energy supplies. The state's energy supplier, Gazprom, the largest company in the world, is of course at its head. And the Patriots have elided the guiding hand of the Communist Party out of existence, out of history. The Patriots sit at the head of this new economic machine they have created.'

I get up and put the kettle on the stove but I forget to fill it with water. Then I catch myself and take it off and hold it under the tap until it's full. I leave the tap on and wash my face with my hands while the kettle heats and I can try to think. Who is Mikhail? Where is Finn?

I make tea, with a lot of sugar, and sit down at the kitchen table, stirring the tea while I look at how Finn continues.

'Mikhail is very senior in Directorate "S", Anna. In fact, he is one of the few who knew the structure well enough to bring it all together when the time was right. It was Mikhail who, behind the scenes, raised Putin from being Deputy Mayor of St Petersburg to becoming head of the KGB, then prime minister, before finally helping to elevate him to the presidency.'

I feel Finn pausing for thought, or perhaps to pour himself a drink, or simply to walk away from what he's writing and to gaze through a window. But his words continue on the page without pause.

'And so, back to Sudhoff. Whatever body was found in the canal in Berlin, it wasn't the body of Sudhoff. Sudhoff – his working name in East Germany – was someone else before Sudhoff, and someone else after Sudhoff. He's been with Putin right from the beginning, long before they "met" for the first time in East Germany. And he was with Putin afterwards. Mikhail is Sudhoff. Codename Mikhail is also codename Sudhoff. He was with Putin in St Petersburg when Putin worked under the mayor, Anatoly Sobchak. He was there when Sobchak met his mysterious death. He came with Putin to Moscow and, I hope with all my heart, he is still with Putin now. I hope his wife still lunches with Lyudmilla Putin. I hope this because Mikhail is one of very, very few hopes we have in the West of seeing what Russia has become and what it will grow to be.'

I can almost feel Finn's pen pause in mid-air.

'I can tell you that Mikhail has seen this monster he has helped to create. And he doesn't like what he sees. If the Plan succeeds, and Mikhail remains undetected, his statue will probably be outside the Lubyanka one day. But Mikhail is working to stop it and he cannot survive for long.

'And if the Plan does not succeed, it will be because Mikhail has tried to alert the world to what he helped create. He is, you might say, a pivotal figure in history, as great a double agent as there has ever been.'

There the writing abruptly ends.

I sit back in the chair, frustrated. He's dangled a lure, but he hasn't told me what I want to know. He hasn't given me the fish.

I tear the little notebook into pieces and burn them one by one in the fireplace. Then I put on my coat. I exit through the back of the house on the lake side, and I walk until darkness falls.

What game is Finn playing? He's explained Mikhail to me under yet another codename, Sudhoff. Why? Why doesn't he give me his real name? So his wife lunches with Putin's wife, but that doesn't narrow it down much further than Patrushev had already narrowed it down in 2000.

And then, as I stand and stare at the stars that glitter over the lake on this ice-cold evening, I see what Finn is doing. In the past six years he has already offered me my freedom once. Now he is offering me my freedom again, but this time in Putin's totalitarian Russia. For me to know the real identity of Sudhoff, I will have to take the name to Russia, to tell Patrushev, who will know. I will absolve myself of my sins with the Forest by giving them the name of Sudhoff as my passport back to Russia. Finn is offering me a way to save myself – at the expense of Mikhail, at the expense of the destruction of the Plan. It is Finn's way of giving me a way back, a way that I thought was closed for good. It is his ultimate trust in me.

But the fact that he doesn't give me Mikhail's

real name still keeps me at a distance from the truth, so that if I choose to stay here in the West, I will never be burdened with it.

For the moment I put aside the name of Sudhoff and turn Finn's thesis over in my mind and compare it with what I know Russia has become in the years since Putin came to power. I run over in my head the iron grip in which Directorate 'S' holds Russia in 2007.

Four out of every five – eighty per cent – of political leaders and state administrators in Russia are now members of the security services. Most of them have been appointed to these posts by Putin since 2000. They are known as the *siloviki* – the men of power. They are everywhere: in the presidential administration, in government, the deputies in our parliament, regional heads of Russia, they are on the boards of all of Russia's top corporations. They are the four out of five.

Under Putin, politics and business have become one. And all is under the KGB imprimatur, Directorate 'S'.

This has not happened anywhere else in the Communist countries of Eastern Europe.

And when you add it all up, this power, what does it come to? What are all the oil and arms and steel and aluminium and gold and diamonds and uranium and coal and copper and titanium and tantalum, and everything else worth? How many trillion dollars? And all is controlled by the KGB, the *siloviki*, the men of power. The four out of five. Directorate 'S'. It is the biggest heist in history.

It no longer matters if Vladimir Putin is again

'elected', as we still choose to call it in Russia, in 2008. It no longer matters if he overturns the constitution in order to remain in the Kremlin. One of the four out of five will become president, that is all that counts.

21

AT THE BEGINNING of September 2001, just after we lost track of Finn as he crossed from France into Switzerland after his meeting with Liakubsky, I was summoned to the Forest by General Kerchenko. The General told me I was to be put through two weeks of intensive retraining. It was routine stuff, he told me, and there was no explanation beyond that.

There was no sign of Yuri or Sasha, my case officers on Finn, and no explanation for that either. Instead, I was assigned Vladimir as my new case officer.

I noted a new deference towards me from Kerchenko. He himself also seemed to have been gently sidelined from Finn's case and was acting merely as a messenger. I never saw him again.

Vladimir and I spent these two weeks barracked at the Forest. We worked sixteen-hour days and in the late evenings I was given new instructions in coding, separate from Vladimir. I knew I was being prepared to rendezvous with Finn again. My excitement was tempered by exhaustion, but mostly by caution. It was one thing for them to know that Finn loved me, but I knew it was necessary to establish that I had no such feelings for him.

Vladimir was very attentive towards me. Our long acquaintance made the time together as relaxed as it could be. One evening, we had a drink together in the compound after my coding instruction ended. It was nearly the end of the two-week training and we both felt good. I was happy that the time for meeting Finn was near. We sat in a log house in the forest, away from the others, and drank beers and talked and laughed about how my father had been so angry that I'd refused to marry Vladimir.

'Might you have married me if your father hadn't wanted you to?' he asked me.

'I don't know,' I said. 'Maybe.'

He looked pleased.

'Why haven't you married?' I asked him. 'You should be married. You're the marrying type.'

'What does that mean!' he protested, and then he laughed easily. 'Anyway, you can talk.'

'One day I want to settle down at Barvikha,' I said, 'with four children and a good Russian husband.'

'You'd better get on with it, then,' he said. 'You'll be over the hill.'

I punched him on the shoulder and caught him right on the nerve and he bent over in pain hugging his shoulder.

'Thank God I didn't marry you,' he said through gritted teeth.

Later we were sitting very close on the porch, facing each other on two stools, elbows on our knees and each cradling a bottle of beer. I saw a gleam of tenderness and excitement in his eyes.

'I've always liked you, Vladimir,' I said.

I saw he couldn't speak. Then he looked down, unable to hold my eyes.

'You're the only woman I've ever asked to marry me, that's the truth, Anna,' he said. 'I never wanted to marry anyone else.'

I put my hand on his arm and he looked up.

'Maybe . . . ?' he said, and he let the question hang in the air.

'Let's go inside,' I replied.

For our remaining days at the Forest, we shared a bed and I told him that when this was all over, we should get married. I don't know if this was the cruellest lie I've ever told in my life. I don't know, because I don't know what his motives were, whether he was genuine or whether he was one more hook they wanted to plant in me before I went to Finn. I trusted nobody. Why should I? We were in the Forest and I was being prepared to find the thing the Patriots most wanted to find, the enemy within. But for my purposes, it suited me for them to believe I was committed to Russia and that Vladimir was my personal route home.

On the last night at the Forest, lying in bed, I told Vladimir I loved him.

'I've never told any man that before,' I said.

I don't know if we were both play-acting, or if it was just me. All I know is that, a few days before my rendezvous with Finn, I'd told another man I loved him, and I'd never told Finn that.

On a hot day at the end of September, I was summoned to Patrushev's dacha, to the north of Moscow and across the lake from the dacha where Putin entertains world leaders. When I arrived in the car that Patrushev had sent, I saw that it was a meeting to be attended only by Patrushev, myself and Vladimir. I justified my great lie by the presence of Vladimir on that day. If he were so far on the inside, then how could I ever trust that his feelings for me were genuine either?

Patrushev made a stirring speech at the dacha about my importance to my country and the crucial role I had to play.

'And we'll keep an eye on your grandmother for you,' he said. 'I know how much you care for her.'

It was the usual threat. Despite my training, my job, my father and heritage, despite my visible attachment to Vladimir, they knew the only place my heart had always been, with Nana.

When it was time to leave, Patrushev stood and we toasted Russia. He took me by the shoulders and looked at me with his penetrating eyes.

'Remember, Colonel,' he warned me, 'his only interest in you is to use you. All the rest is fake.'

Vladimir came to the airport with me and we – or was it just I? – made a great false show of hugging and kissing each other.

22

AFTER MORE THAN A YEAR without contact between Finn and me, our reunion held all the anticipation – principally the fear and doubts – that any lover would have felt in the same position.

How would we feel about each other now, I wondered, away from the familiarity of the surroundings where our intimacy had grown? Was our affair a thing of a particular time and place? Would the spark between us still exist? Would it need rekindling?

Too much expectation risked disappointment, too little risked failing to rise to the occasion and, perhaps, missing the moment, the opportunity, for ever.

I felt awkward and out of place at the airport in Marseilles, coming through the sliding glass doors beyond Immigration. There were groups of my fellow Russians already brimming with enthusiasm for a summer holiday away from Moscow's more anxious heat. My own arrival brought me face to face with a task that now seemed impossible: to love Finn and satisfy my masters.

I didn't see Finn at first. And then something drew my gaze towards a figure leaning against a car rental desk by the exit. He was reading a newspaper and it covered most of his face. Between us was a throng of taxi drivers and private chauffeurs holding cards with names on them.

I looked idly across the airport's concourse and wondered who was from the Forest here, who had travelled with me on the plane, and where they were placed in the hall now.

The reason I didn't see Finn at first was because he'd almost completely changed. He was very tanned and hadn't shaved for several days. His hair was long, down to his shoulders, and he'd dyed it a sort of dirty blond. He was wearing a light blue canvas jacket and jeans and, I was startled to see when he flicked the newspaper over briefly, he had no shirt under the jacket. Around his neck I saw a necklace of blue stones, lapis maybe. It was his feet I finally recognised. He wore a pair of old deck shoes with paint on the left shoe. I remembered them from his flat in Moscow.

In a split second our eyes met and then he looked away, still holding the newspaper. He walked with measured swiftness in the opposite direction and exited through automatic glass doors into the azure heat. I didn't follow him but exited through other automatic doors straight ahead of me. We found ourselves thirty yards apart, on the pavement where the taxis and buses pulled up. We were separated by travellers, their luggage, drivers, porters and airport staff. There was a convenient pandemonium of greeting, and the loading of vehicles.

From the corner of my eye I saw Finn walk quickly across the road, dodging cars, and I followed parallel, keeping the thirty yards between us. Madly, I was briefly irritated in the heat that he wasn't carrying my heavy case.

I saw him weave into a car park. I watched him look around lazily, behind and in front, and automatically made the same scan myself to see if anyone on foot was tailing either of us. For me in the crush, it was impossible to know, but he seemed to be clear. I saw him flick a switch on a bunch of keys and the lights on a white Renault flashed. I stopped on the far side of the slip road.

He got into the car, reversed out and drove slowly down the slip road towards me. I watched to see if other cars did the same. He stopped the car and threw open the passenger door and one of the rear doors. I manhandled my case on to the back seat and stepped in beside him.

I had forgotten it would be like this. Because it was Finn I was meeting, I was unprepared for it. His first words to me were matter-of-fact.

'What's behind?'

'A dark blue BMW about twenty yards away and a white Mercedes behind that.'

'Ahead?'

'Green Peugeot and a taxi.'

'Let's go,' he said, and grinned straight into my heart.

We drew up at the automatic barrier and there

were queues at all the barriers on either side. Finn put the parking card into the machine and the barrier rose. Before he accelerated through, he slid a thin metal card into the machine's slot. We drove under the barrier, I saw him watch it fall in the mirror behind us, and then he grinned. The blue BMW couldn't get the machine to accept its own parking card and was trying to reverse out, but there were at least four cars behind it. We drove out to the sound of angry horns.

'There'll be at least one ahead,' Finn said. 'They're watching you, not me.'

'There,' I said.

A green Peugeot was pulled over on to the grass fifty yards away and as we passed, it slipped on to the road behind us.

'Look out for others,' Finn said.

We turned westwards out on to the motorway. I watched in the side mirror for what was behind us, the green Peugeot and whatever else might be following. Finn drove fast so that when, some twenty minutes after we'd left the airport behind us, he suddenly pulled up on the hard shoulder, I was jolted forwards.

'Sorry,' he muttered, looking in the mirror.

The green Peugeot overshot by forty yards or so and swerved on to the hard shoulder also.

'There they are,' Finn said.

I saw the passenger talking into a phone.

Traffic passed us, but no one else stopped. I was watching the green Peugeot ahead of us further down the hard shoulder when Finn slammed his foot on to the accelerator and we surged backwards for thirty yards and then he slammed the gear lever into first and swung the wheel down to the left and on to a motorway works entrance that was so concealed I hadn't seen it.

We left the motorway in a squeal of tyres and crashed on to a dusty track that led to a quarry-like bowl full of road-making machinery.

Finn drove through this apparent dead end and out of the other side on to another dust track that led back in the direction we'd come from. I looked behind and saw the green Peugeot racing backwards along the hard shoulder.

Finn drove at breakneck speed for about a mile. I looked behind and saw dust kicking up far away as the green Peugeot finally found its way out of the quarry behind us.

The track we were on led back under the motorway and joined a small country road. Finn turned on to it and headed back again in the direction we'd been travelling on the motorway.

There was a distance of half a mile to the car behind and its occupants couldn't have seen which way we'd turned on to the country road. Finn accelerated and drove so fast I hardly noticed what we were passing. We turned off again twice, on to two more single-track country roads like the first one. When he was finally satisfied he had lost our tail, he slowed and turned off on to another dust road that led out southwards over a great expanse of dead, flat, bleak saltpans that stretched for miles in either direction.

There was no other traffic, not even the occasional slow farm vehicle we'd overtaken on the side roads. Finn drove the car out of sight into a gully and we waited, not speaking.

When we came back up on to the track he drove very slowly and on the grass edges, so that the dust didn't kick up. We must have driven for another twenty minutes on this winding track across the old, disused saltpans. And then I felt rather than saw the sea. We were so low that the dunes ahead obscured the view.

We seemed to be heading nowhere in a salt-and-sand desert. But when we finally reached the dunes and Finn pulled up behind them, I saw there was a dilapidated wooden shack, obscured from the road. It was a campers' restaurant, open only in the summer, which contained a few drifting adolescents sitting at rickety tables. Beyond the wooden structure of the restaurant were two more rickety wooden buildings, small shacks erected in a chaotic, haphazard fashion and constructed from what looked like bleached driftwood. Finn cut the engine and looked at me.

'Fancy a swim?' he said and grinned again. We got out of the car. 'And I think it's about time I carried your case,' he said.

We walked across hot sand – I'd kicked off my shoes – past the restaurant and up to the second of the two shacks built at an angle to the sea. We still haven't touched each other, I thought. The door to the shack was unlocked and Finn pushed it open with his foot and threw the case down. Then he took off his jacket and his jeans to reveal a pair of faded blue floral swimming shorts. He ran down the beach and into the sea, not stopping until the water became too deep and he fell forwards into it.

He looked round when he'd come up from under the surface and shouted.

'Come on, it's beautiful.'

I changed and joined him.

That was how it was, our first meeting in over a year. Finn never said hello. He didn't kiss me. He never asked me how the flight was, if I was tired, what my departure from the Forest had been like. It was as if I'd just come back from a visit to the shops, rather than that we hadn't seen each other for over a year.

And all this suited me, I realised. Everything I'd half prepared in my mind before our meeting, and that was so inadequate, faded away, and with it went all my awkward anxiety.

We drink beers sitting in the sand, swim again, and then go to bed in an extremely uncomfortable wooden structure that Finn tells me is the bed. Later we eat out at a table in the sand in front of what Finn insists is the restaurant as the sun starts to sink into the sea.

There is only fish, Finn informs me. The owner of the shacks is a Hungarian who came over in 1956 after the uprising against the Russians there failed. He'd taught himself to be a fisherman. Back then, when these things were still possible, he'd built the shacks illegally, constructed from driftwood in this isolated place where few people wanted to come and which he'd never left.

He is now seventy-odd years old, Finn tells me, and whatever there is for lunch every day depends on what he's caught that morning.

'I didn't tell him you were Russian, by the way,' Finn says. Finn has a curious, self-deprecating and ultimately deceitful habit of apologising for who he is and expecting others to as well. In Moscow, when anyone asked him if he was English, he would always say, 'I'm afraid I am.' It was a peculiarly English deceit, I thought.

'This is just about the only spot for nearly fifty miles that hasn't been developed at all,' Finn says. 'They can't build on the saltpans. There's nothing at all in either direction for several miles. To the left you eventually come to Marseilles' industrial wasteland.'

I can see the ugly belching smokestacks in the distance.

'To the right there's a tourist beach, empty of buildings, three miles along from here. Sometimes you see someone who's walked it but not often and they don't do it a second time. It isn't a pretty place except when you look out to sea.'

'Fast work to find it in three days,' I say.

'Yes, you didn't give me much warning, Rabbit.'

But of course Finn has known the place for years. I find later that the Hungarian, whom Finn introduces as Willy, has some connection to the Service. At any rate Finn persuaded Willy to throw out some hippies from our shack when he received my message that I was coming.

'We'll be fine here for a while,' Finn says later. 'And this place is always here when we need to get away.' And then, on our first night for fourteen months, he finally falls asleep with his arm around my stomach. I lie and watch the stars and listen to the thin-lipped waves that slip quietly on to the edge of the sand. Some gypsy music is playing from a hippy tent further down the beach. It is as if we've never been apart; as if we've known each other long before we ever met. It is the same as it was.

For nearly three days we say nothing about the reason I'm here and slowly the burden of it recedes. Finn ensures that we concentrate just on ourselves. We talk a lot about the distant past, about where we've come from, things that aren't recorded in Finn's file we kept at the Forest, things we never knew. And I respond with little stories of my own upbringing. It is like the games we used to play in Moscow, teasing each other with what we knew about the other, except that these are revelations, background that neither of us knew before, and we aren't taunting each other with them any more.

Finn tells me one evening how he was recruited, or at any rate how they made the initial moves towards his eventual recruitment. He speaks about the past, as we all often do, as if it is something from another life altogether and he was another person then. And I suppose, in Finn's case more than most, he was another person back then.

'At the beginning of my second year at Cambridge, I was invited to supper by a gay French professor who drank much too much whisky,' Finn says on this evening, and a smile plays around his eyes at the memory. 'I remember on one occasion he chased me round his flat begging me to allow him to beat me with a hardback copy of Balzac's *Passion in the Desert*.

'I didn't particularly want to accept his invitation to supper. But I was flattered to be asked, even though the reasons for it were fairly obvious. He was always inviting pretty men to his rooms. And I was always easily flattered, Anna,' Finn says, looking into my eyes so that I see right through them. 'Even alcoholic pederasts with only one thing on their minds had the power to flatter me in those days, as long as I sensed there was the prospect of mixing with those in high places, or of lifting myself away from my past, or of getting away from myself as I knew me.

'I was hugely impressed by the fantasy of Cambridge as it seemed to me then, and always in my mind I referred back to the commune in Ireland to reassure myself of how far I'd come. I was always looking for something and expecting to find it in the admiration of others. I needed people to be interested in me. So I accepted his invitation and went to high table at Magdalene College on a wet Friday evening, as usual looking for someone or something to tell me who I was.

'There was a full table, about twenty or so of us, and afterwards we went to the French don's rooms for a bottle or two of port. In our party there was the professor of Philosophy from Oxford, Freddie Ayer, the playwright Tom Stoppard, a Russian specialist from London University, the French don and me.

'The sixth person was Adrian. I remember Freddie Ayer and Tom Stoppard talked for nearly an hour about how far away from earth the Virgin Mary would be now if she'd been travelling at the speed of light. It was bizarre, funny, exciting, stupid, and, most of all, different. It was my fantasy of how university life should be.

'As usual I wanted to be like the people I was with. But all of them, not one individually. I thought I could piece myself together with bits of everybody, like a jigsaw. As usual I wanted to be everybody and felt nobody. I've always been good at being whatever the person I'm talking to at the time wants me to be. They like that, in the Service.'

Finn picks up a stone and throws it beyond the edge of the lazy surf and the ripples shimmer in the moonlight. It seems to me like a gesture of controlled anger, anger at his own behaviour when he was a young man and had been the blotting paper that soaked up the admiration and, perhaps worse, the suggestions of others.

'Anyway, I performed as usual,' Finn says. 'And as usual I felt I was at the centre of everything, of the universe itself, and at the same time completely apart. I immersed myself in the talk that went around the room, trying to impress, and apparently I did. At the end of the evening, Adrian offered me a lift back to my college, but we went and had a drink at his hotel instead. He asked me how I was enjoying my course and wouldn't it be better to do something rather more useful than Classics. Some living languages, for example.

'At about two in the morning, I walked home.

I had no idea who Adrian actually was, I realised, as I walked through the wet streets. But it didn't seem to matter. I was glowing at the memory of all these clever people who could make a conversation from anything, and I was impressed by Adrian's keen attention. "Someone from the Foreign Office" was how he had been described and I didn't think beyond that. I'd been invited to go on to have a drink with this incredible someone at the Foreign Office. Adrian had such power, Anna. He was the kind of man I'd been looking for. I thought he was someone who could tell me who I was.

'So, six months later I changed my course at Cambridge to Russian. No one told me to, it was almost a sixth sense. But I changed courses, I realised much later, to please Adrian, even though I hadn't seen him for more than that one night.'

'You were looking for a father,' I say, thinking of my own.

'I was looking for me,' Finn replies. 'I've always been surrounded by people, friends, lovers, anyone who cared for me. But the person who was always absent in the room was me.'

We come from different sides, Finn and I, in more ways than one. But this, perhaps, is the most influential difference between us. I have always been running away from my father, to the extent that I'd actually joined the intelligence service in my country as a means to be free from him through exceeding his expectations. Perhaps I fool myself. But Finn, I know, has always been running towards something, blindly, towards his lost identity.

'You were perfect for Adrian,' I say.

'Yes, Anna, that's the truth of it,' Finn replies, and there is silence for a while. He finally resumes. 'I didn't see Adrian for another two or three years, though. When I left Cambridge I had a first-class degree.' He speaks the words with some mockery. 'I travelled to all the places I'd read about, all around the Soviet Union. I wrote articles, short stories and a diary on my travels. I shot a bear with a university teacher in the Caucasus mountains, fished with the Mayor of Yugansk, fell in love with a prostitute in Magadan of all places . . . I wandered rather than travelled,' he corrects himself. 'But as Rilke warns, "Beware, O wanderer, for the road is walking too."'

'And then one day in Hong Kong, maybe three years after I'd left Cambridge, I was watching the Rugby Seven-a-Sides and there, suddenly, was Adrian standing beside me. I was overjoyed, or relieved, one of the two anyway. He filled up the empty years immediately. I'd have done practically anything for him.

'Two months later, I started my training and he was always with me after that. I felt like I'd come home.'

On another evening we are sitting at a table at the edge of the restaurant in the sand and Finn talks about Willy.

'He's helping me, Anna,' Finn says. 'Even at over seventy years old he's as sharp as anyone.'

'Isn't he reporting to London?' I ask him. 'Can you trust him?'

'Oh yes, I can trust him. Willy worked for us for many years. He was one of the best, went over the

Wall many times. When he first came to the West he was angry that we'd done nothing to stop Moscow in the Hungarian uprising. But he worked for us in the belief that we were all working on the same brief and that brief included the liberation of his country. But he slowly became disillusioned. He came to believe that no one in London gave a shit about Hungary. He became bitter. He came to hate the Service. But he's helping me now.'

'Is he your new Adrian?' I ask him.

'No, no.' Finn smiled and put his hand on mine. 'I'm finished with that now, grew out of it long ago. But I didn't know that until recently, until I met Adrian in London.'

Willy joins us and Finn tells him I am to be trusted, despite being Russian. And then, over plates of calamari and a bottle of excellent Condrieu, Finn finally edges on to the subject that has lain dormant for the past few days and which, from time to time, I've felt is only a bad dream, something unreal. But Finn speaks in a carefully low-key, non-dramatic way for once, so it seems like we are talking about something that is manageable, something normal. He is laying down what he has been doing in the past year when we've been apart.

'I need to tell you about some companies,' he says out of the blue one evening. 'They're called Exodi. They are the key to everything. They are the key to our freedom too, you and me. When we find what Exodi exists to do, this will be over. I promise you.'

He tells me – Willy obviously knew it all before – what he's found from Dieter, what Frank finally told him, with some additions from the Troll.

'Frank has done a lot of research into the companies,' he says. 'But first, perhaps, I should tell you the preamble.'

As Finn speaks he draws lines beside the table in the sand with a stick and occasionally makes a letter. Sometimes a bigger wave eradicates a national border, or a line of communication, and this is appropriate in the context. He is drawing a map of connections that stretch from Afghanistan to Uzbekistan, into Transdnestr – the independent territory inside Moldova that was, and is, still loyal to Russia – and then on to Bulgaria and Serbia and further still to a bank in Liechtenstein; the connections wind on from Liechtenstein to Luxembourg and the bank Westbank and then a branch line runs sideways into a box set of companies in the Cayman Islands.

'This small element of the story, the story so far, starts in Afghanistan,' he starts to explain, pointing his stick at the top of the map. 'General Baseer in northern Afghanistan is just one starting point of three, we believe, for Exodi's funds. Though I doubt he's ever actually heard of Exodi himself. Baseer's an Uzbek Afghan. Ally to the Americans, foe to the Russians way back. But that's just political manoeuvring. Principally he's just another warlord with interests that take precedence over any marriage of convenience with whatever great power happens to be passing his way at the time. The funds for his power and for his army come from the poppy, of course. With the Taliban in power in Afghanistan, Baseer and the other warlords are finding that their traditional business is hard; heroin is not on the menu under Taliban rule. But they still manage to produce a reduced crop of poppies, mainly in the inaccessible valleys in the north of the country, which is Baseer's area of control.

'Well, as an Uzbek Afghan he has excellent connections through family and clans across the border in Uzbekistan that are far stronger than any political line drawn on the map, or any alliance with the Americans. His chief ally there, as perhaps you know, is Uzbeddin Cherimov, the great trader and backer of the Uzbek president. Between Cherimov and the president, the Uzbek KGB was nicely finessed into doing what it does best, facilitating the drugs trade and taking a cut before the line of graft moves up further to Moscow's mafia and KGB interests.

'Cherimov is more the international figure in a small group, which includes Uzbekistan's president and General Meklikov, the old KGB general from Moscow who coordinates from the Forest all the drugs and arms movements through Uzbekistan. The three of them met, in fact, at the Silk Route Hotel in Tashkent last month, 15 August. That's a national president, Meklikov, a KGB general and Cherimov, a drug baron. Quite a useful gang. It was a regular meeting between the three of them for the division of spoils and future planning.

'But it's Cherimov who travels beyond borders the most out of the three. He always has. He's been a Russian Olympic representative for nearly twenty years; travels everywhere under the Olympic flag. He has a mansion outside Tashkent where all the servants are former athletes. He also has a cotton business that exports from the Fergana Valley in Uzbekistan out to

Western Europe and ultimately to America. The main port for the final leg is Brest in France. Originally the heroin went hidden in cotton bales, but now it uses different routes. Through Bulgaria, Serbia, Austria and down into Italy, it is now transported in refrigerated trucks, with the correct baksheesh chucked in the direction of customs officials. The trucks aren't opened at the borders, the excuse being that it would destroy perishable produce; it's tomatoes and fruit on the manifest.

'The northern route goes through Ukraine by rail. There's over a hundred thousand acres of farmland in Ukraine in a single block that's owned ultimately by Russian and Ukrainian mafia bosses and overseen by the KGB. In the centre of this land is a railway station, away from prying eyes. Here all the exports are repackaged and sent on under different bills of lading.

'Cherimov's been a target of Western agencies for years and I don't know why he's still free. He was thrown out of Australia at the last Olympics. Last month he was arrested in Paris, but here's the strange thing. He wasn't put in jail or charged with anything at all. He and his cronies were escorted to the Belgian border in three limousines in the dead of night by a team of French police motorcycle outriders. He walked free in Belgium. He is, it seems, untouchable.

'He stayed in Brussels for three days at a very nice apartment out in the diplomatic area, where the European Commission people can rub shoulders with the world's diplomats. The apartment belongs to a close friend of Putin, a Russian foreign policy adviser at the European Union.'

Finn pauses and Willy walks over to the bar and brings three beers and some bread and cheese he has bartered for his fish. Willy smiles at me, even though I'm Russian.

'The Exodi companies,' Finn continues, 'are a money-laundering operation for these drug sales. They are also laundering money for certain KGB-controlled arms sales that don't go via the usual KGB routes and, for one reason or another, need to be even further beneath the parapet. There's a lot of cash. In the Exodi companies and others we've yet to reveal completely, it seems we're talking about more than twenty-eight billion dollars.

'For drug sales in the West, there are a number of ways the cash is moved, then laundered. Exodi in Paris provides a security service for some less-than-mainstream national airlines. Each pair of security officers on each plane carries a bag for clothes to wear at the other end. Except the bag isn't full of clothes, it's full of cash. Suitcases full of cash that pass through airports all over the world, every day of the year, because they're being carried by airline security officers.

'Anyway, whatever way the cash is moved it's finding its way to Exodi in Liechtenstein which has an account in Vaduz under the name of Fartrust. It's a trust account with several signatories, including Cherimov's. The account has various companies behind it, registered in the Caymans.

'But here's the strangest thing: only a small proportion of the money goes to the Caymans. Of the twenty-eight and a half billion dollars that was in this Liechtenstein account at the start of this year, only about thirteen million has found its way to the Caymans. Hundreds of millions are going to the Banque Leman in Geneva and at least another hundred million has found its way either directly, or via the Banque Leman, to another Swiss bank in the poorest canton in Switzerland, the Banque Montana in the canton of Valais. The rest must be scattered in these banks or others like them; we don't know yet.

'Exodi Geneva is the mover of these funds, while Exodi in Luxembourg opens another account at Westbank but it is a secret account with no published account to back it up legally. Much of the money, I'm sure, is there. Frank, whom I told you about, has found that in one of the Exodi Luxembourg's secret accounts in Westbank there's another one and a half billion dollars, or thereabouts.

'And here's the great thing, the jackpot perhaps. Frank believes that a great deal of money also passes into this account from Russian state companies: oil and regular arms exporters, diamonds, and others. This money is being mixed with the mafia drug money from Cherimov. It's all in the same fund. Russian state company funds and Russian mafia money all in the same bed together.'

Finn claps his hands together to indicate this perfect marriage.

'You have been busy,' I say and he smiles.

'So. Now you're here we need to look further,' Finn says to me. 'I need your help.'

'They did tell me you only wanted to use me,' I reply.

'They're absolutely right. But first we have to talk.'

As if he has been silently asked to do so by Finn, Willy gets up from the table and goes over to the bar where he begins to busy himself with things his barman would normally have done.

Finn stands up and holds out his hand.

'Why don't we go for a walk,' he says.

We walk for maybe a mile up the dark beach in the opposite direction to Marseilles' industrial smokestacks. Finn holds my hand, a little too tightly I think. He is tense. Out at sea the lights of a big yacht imperceptibly move along the coast keeping pace with us. There is little wind and we can just hear its motor.

Once we are beyond the area around Willy's little enclave there is nobody apart from a couple of kids smoking dope and staring dumbfounded at the stars, and we soon leave them behind.

Finally, Finn loosens his hand from mine and gestures for us to sit down on the beach. We sit close together. The nights are nearly as warm as the days. Our knees touch and we look out at the yacht with its faraway lights.

'Did they tell you why they were sending you?' Finn says at last.

'Yes.'

'What did they say?'

'You have a source, Finn, that's what they said. It's the highest priority to them. To us,' I add, and wonder how I'm going to square all this with myself.

I look at him then.

'It seems you're not just the amiable joker you seem to be,' I say. 'It seems this source lies at the very heart of Moscow's plans and he's all yours.'

'The Plan,' Finn says.

'Yes. The Plan. Patrushev knows now.'

Finn pauses and picks up a shell and seems to study it.

'Do they know about Mikhail?' he says.

'Mikhail?'

'Mikhail is what we call this source in London. You must write that in your first report to them.'

He squirms his foot into the sand.

'So your job, then,' he says carefully, 'is to find out who Mikhail is. Perfect. We have breathing space. We can string them along for some time, keeping them waiting for that.'

'To find the enemy within,' I say.

'Well,' he says, 'that's why you're here professionally.' He turns and grins and then his face becomes serious.

'I've missed you, Rabbit. I'm so happy with you. Is it the same for you?'

'Can't you tell?'

'Can't you tell me?'

I'm thinking of Vladimir, of my deceit, and the foul taste it leaves in my throat now.

I put my hand on his face and we look at each other.

'I've missed you too, Finn.'

'Good. So that's all right then,' he says, and smiles easily.

'I have to tell you something,' I say.

He looks at me as if he knows what I'm going to say, but I go on anyway.

'You remember Vladimir?'

'Your old school friend? The man your dad wanted you to marry?'

'Yes.'

'You haven't gone and married him, have you?'

'No. He's my new case officer on you, Finn.'

'Very clever of them.'

'Yes,' I agree, and know that Finn is right. It is very clever of them and I have to be careful with Vladimir.

'We trained at the Forest for two weeks before I came out here,' I say.

'And you slept together.'

'Yes, we did.'

Finn looks at me and kisses me lightly on the lips.

'And that's very clever of you, darling,' he says.

There is no need to say more. He understands everything.

We get up and walk slowly back along the beach with our arms around each other. Finn talks in a businesslike way, but all his tension from before has gone. That is what the truth does, I think.

'You have your arrangements to communicate with them?' Finn says as we walk slowly.

'I have a contact in London,' I answer. 'Another in Geneva, whichever is closer. I'm supposed to check in every eleven days, even if there's nothing worth saying. We have our usual rules of contact,' I say.

'And Moscow?' Finn says.

'They'll contact me if they want me to go to Moscow.'

'Nothing set in stone, then,' he replies.

'In London there was a contact who kept in touch with one of the trade reps at our embassy there, but who's now been recalled,' I say hesitantly. 'A low-level Russian businessman working on the edge of the

City. His handler was one of our long-standing trade reps at the embassy, from the Forest.'

'This contact was arrested by your people a short while ago, however. He was released and he's been replaced by another "businessman",' I say.

'Why was he arrested?' Finn says.

'He'd been spotted by the Service coming out of a public convenience in Hyde Park,' I say. 'He was still doing up his zip. That's what alerted MI5, apparently. They'd found a package concealed in a cistern and were watching the place and saw this guy come out doing up his zip. You wouldn't believe the fuss at the Forest. He's really in the shit. According to us, the English don't come out of public conveniences doing up their zips. The Forest believes that's why he was spotted as a foreigner.'

I laugh and Finn joins me.

'So there's a new contact for you in London.'

'He's called Valentin Malenkov,' I say. 'Highly trained, very special to us, one of our very best, in fact. A perfect English speaker travelling on a Swiss passport under the name Franz Noiber. He's Forest to the core.'

'He'll know that he should do up his zip, then,' Finn says.

We walk on and stop, holding each other from time to time. It feels closer than we've ever been.

'We have to make sure you deliver,' Finn says.

'Yes.'

'Every ten days we'll compile your report, the two of us together,' he says. 'You have to be useful. You have to give them good stuff. That way we'll buy ourselves time.'

The last time we stop before we reach the huts, Finn holds my hands.

'Are you ready to leave?' he says. 'We can just forget everything but us, if you like. I'll stop this now if you're ready to come with me. We can start a pig farm. If you're ready to leave,' he says.

I don't reply. I can't make the leap.

'Patrushev told me they'd look after Nana for me,' I say.

Finn looks at me, with sympathy in his eyes.

'And what does Nana say?'

'She said, "Would you rather spend your time with Finn or with Patrushev?"'

Finn laughs.

'I want to come,' I say. 'I will come.'

'When you're ready,' Finn says, understanding my fears, and we walk back, stopping once to kiss each other for so long it was as if a premonition of bad things crouched over us and we clung to each other for shelter.

23

TWO THINGS HAPPENED in the following seven days that changed the bright colours of our briefly carefree existence to black. The first event altered the psychological landscape for the whole world but the second was more personal, it attacked our world directly – Finn's anyway, and therefore mine.

One late afternoon as the first cool September breeze blew in from the sea, Willy came running over to the shack where Finn and I were working on my first report to submit to the Forest. I had never seen Willy look agitated, let alone excited. He wore his past lightly and he took bad news in the same way he took good news, with tolerant equanimity.

'Quick, come quick,' he said.

Finn and I looked at each other, fearing that our hideaway had been discovered or worse, and immediately left what we were doing and followed Willy to the restaurant. He had an old radio that was screwed to the bar. It was a thing of great value to him, and reminded him of his youth when tuning into the BBC's World Service up in a friend's attic in Budapest could have had him imprisoned. He still treated a radio with reverence fifty years later.

One or two of the less stoned inhabitants of Willy's little enclave on the beach were gathered around the radio and their normal expressions of varying degrees of blankness were relatively animated. He pushed them out of the way so that he and Finn and I could lean in closer.

'A plane has hit a building in New York,' Willy said.

We listened to the commentary as the second plane hit and stories flew around the airwaves of other planes in America that were evidently aimed at American targets. I don't know how long we listened, but Finn and Willy must have drunk half a case of beer. It was an hour or more before we knew we wouldn't know anything more that day and Willy switched off the radio, as if it were a precious finite resource that needed to be rested. Then we sat down for an early supper.

'It's not events that change history, but the way people react to them,' I remember Finn saying, and Willy nodding with his mouth full of freshly caught red snapper, perhaps remembering Hungary again, back in 1956.

'Whoever did this did it in the cause of chaos,' Willy said eventually. 'The devil loves chaos.'

Finn said prophetically, if strangely in the circumstances, 'This will be good for Russia, for Putin.'

'Surely you're not going to blame it on Russia!' I said, and felt the gap yawn between defending my country as a place, as a people, and defending the clique who ruled it.

'No, no,' he said and gently held my arm. 'I don't think that. But it will open a window of opportunity for Putin.'

He was right. The benefits, from a Russian point of view, of the thousands dead in New York, and the subsequent chaos in Iraq and Afghanistan, was that the CIA and MI6 would cut their Russian operations still further. By the end of 2006 the British would devote only five per cent of their intelligence budget to Russia, instead of forty per cent at the end of the Cold War.

In America, George W. Bush said, in a bid to muster worldwide support for his military plans, that he 'had looked into President Putin's soul and liked what he saw'. Putin strongly supported Bush's second presidential campaign against Kerry who might have restrained the American invasion of Iraq. In Russia, and increasingly beyond our borders, we were free to join the amorphous war on terror created by Bush.

But it was the second event in those seven days that hit Finn far harder, being almost a fatal blow to his personal mission. Again Willy came hurrying over. We were putting the finishing touches to my report by this time. Willy was carrying a satellite phone. There was no mobile connection.

'Finn,' he said. 'You must call Frank . . .' He checked his watch. 'Call in about eight minutes.'

Finn took the phone and walked up the beach. He didn't come back for over an hour and when he did he was white in the face.

'The boy's dead,' he said inexplicably and sat hunched in the sand in front of the crates Willy and I were sitting on, and hugged his knees, rocking gently. 'They killed him.'

'What boy, Finn? Who?'

He looked me in the eyes and I saw how angry he was.

'There's a boy I spoke to . . .' he said. 'I put the squeeze on this boy in Luxembourg. About Exodi.'

'What do you mean, he's dead?' Willy said quietly. 'How is he dead? Killed, you mean?'

Finn picked up a handful of sand and let it slide through his fingers.

'Frank says he was found in a rental car in a lock-up in Metz across the border. Engine running. He was suffocated by the fumes. The boy couldn't have afforded to rent a car, for Christ's sake.'

'Did Frank say that?' Willy asked.

'No, he didn't.' Finn paused. 'He gave me the benefit of the doubt,' he added bitterly.

'You didn't kill him, Finn,' I said.

'This is what they do,' Willy said. 'You know that. That's why we fight these people. To prevent them from doing things like this.'

'A war of prevention,' Finn said mockingly.

'Back in the seventies,' Willy said, 'when I used to go over the Wall, something that concerned the British was Hungary's development of nuclear power. The Soviets used Hungarian nuclear facilities to provide Moscow with plutonium. One of my contacts in Budapest, a scientist, didn't like this arrangement. He gave me much information that filled in the picture for your people in London. The scientist was found in a vat of molten aluminium. It's a war, Finn.'

'Your scientist knew what he was doing and took the risk. This boy had no choice.'

'You say Frank gave you the benefit of the doubt,' Willy said. 'There's no evidence of anyone else being involved. The boy may have killed himself. We don't know.'

'They don't leave evidence,' Finn snapped.

Willy went to get a bottle of Scotch and we tried to talk to Finn but he was adamant. What Willy and I were both thinking, however, was that the boy's death confirmed the value of what he'd told Finn.

'We don't know what happened,' I said. I put my arms around Finn and held him close. 'You have a choice, Finn. You can choose to believe he was killed and you can equally choose to believe he took his own life.'

Finn had a child's attitude to his work, he'd always told me he had. Maybe we all do in this business. Finn once told me that he enjoyed putting himself in dangerous situations so that he could get out of them. He said that, for him, this was what made life worth living. But he also said it was the attitude of youth. It was the attitude of youthful pursuits, like mountaineering or any extreme sport, which normal people eventually grow out of.

The two of us walked up the beach as the sun

sank and merged with the orange sea on the horizon. We didn't talk for a long time.

The following day, we packed my things – Finn was travelling light – and Willy drove us to Aix-en-Provence in his car. Our farewell to Willy was sombre. Finn made no attempt to be cheerful, or even grateful, in the knowledge, I suppose, that we would be meeting again before long and that a new beginning was never far away. We caught a train and began a series of changes that slowly took us to the West, to Brittany, where *Bride of the Wind* lay on a mooring in a quiet estuary.

Finn could never be cheerless for long and rebounded from his grief with almost inappropriate speed. But somewhere, deep inside him, I knew that the boy's death had been filed away, fuel for future action and, perhaps, guilt.

It was a beautiful clear night when we sailed for England, but the cold of autumn was coming in off the Atlantic. I had never been on a boat before and Finn showed me what to do if he should fall off. We sat on deck for most of the night. Finn explained what he had to do from now on, and how he needed my help. It had taken him more than a year to get this far and he knew he was only at the beginning of a long journey.

As dawn broke on the English side of the channel, Finn said, 'What they'll do at the Forest in the coming months, years perhaps, is to try to drive a wedge between us. That's what we have to be most careful of.'

24

I MOVED INTO FINN'S LIFE and his apartment in Camden Town in the autumn of 2001 and so began a long game of manipulation and double lives that was to last nearly four years and in which the only constant, the only truth we knew we could rely on, was each other. Slowly, as we came to see we were both fighting our own sides to maintain our fictions, we became our own sole source of comfort and trust.

For Finn, his fiction, his double life meant diligently pursuing investigative work for the commercial company in Mayfair where Adrian and the Service could keep an eye on him. He cut his hair and wore a suit, he looked more respectable than I'd ever seen him, and we even went, once, to spend a weekend with Adrian and Penny at their country house in Gloucestershire, where Adrian flirted openly with me in front of his wife and asked me questions about the Forest and if there was anything he could do to make my life more comfortable in London – a comment that I took to mean him personally and not the establishment.

Finn and Adrian met from time to time alone so that Adrian could question Finn about my reasons for leaving Russia, and Finn I believe came as close as was possible in this secret world to convincing Adrian that I had left. And Adrian needed too some satisfaction that Finn no longer gave any credence to Mikhail.

Finn also took trips abroad for the company, and on each of these trips, he would fit another piece into the jigsaw, make the picture he was trying to illuminate a little clearer. His feral side now wore a dark suit.

Occasionally, one of his contacts came to London, on other business. Of all of them it was Frank whom I met first. He came over to attend the funeral of a retired ex-Service officer named Haroldson and Frank, Finn and I went together to Mortlake cemetery, where Adrian and a smattering of Service people came to pay their final respects. Adrian was more relaxed with Finn than I'd seen him before, and Finn's presence at the funeral seemed to reassure him that Finn had come back into the fold.

We took Frank out to dinner afterwards at a restaurant in Soho and I saw the closeness of his friendship with Finn that went beyond any professional necessity. We talked about Frank's daughters – his wife was dead – and about Frank's plans for retirement, which sounded similar to Dieter's, a bucolic dream that seemed to me like the postponement of regret. At the end of dinner, I saw Frank leave his copy of the *Evening Standard* on the table and I saw Finn pick it up. Whenever they met they were working.

For me, my fiction, my double life, was to drip-feed reports back to Moscow with sufficiently developing information to make my masters appreciate my worth in London. But my main task was to make them believe that Finn still worked for MI6 and that the Service itself, not just Finn, was avidly interested in Mikhail. This was absolutely crucial to my remaining in London. Finn and I both knew that he would become expendable as soon as the Forest believed he was on his own.

We designed these reports so that they would ask more questions than they answered. But of course they had to give away information Finn would rather not have given up. I slowly revealed MI6's progress with Exodi, with the Uzbekistan connections and General Baseer, with the Luxembourg MP and the secret accounts at Westbank.

The Forest was delighted with Mikhail even though it was just a codename. I heard that a new and special file had been opened on the case and headed 'Mikhail'.

In this period up to the spring and summer of 2005, Putin built up a hierarchy of power in Russia that harked back to Peter the Great. He won the presidency again in 2004, with such embarrassing ease that Grigory Yavlinsky, the head of Russia's Liberal party, said, 'And who invented this system? It used to take a slightly different form, but it was invented by Stalin in the 1930s.'

Slowly, power was drained from the executive, from parliament – the Duma – from the regions, the judiciary, the Federation Council, business and the media. It all found its way into the hands of the *siloviki*, the men of power, the KGB and its ultimate master Directorate 'S'.

The first breaths of democracy that Russia had taken in the nineties were stifled. Putin told Bush that Russia would have democracy, but democracy according to the traditions of Russia. As everyone knew, Russia had no traditions of democracy.

And Putin himself became an iconic figure. In a factory in the Ural mountains, furry rabbits were manufactured that sang a pop song about the President:

> *I want to change my guy*
> *For a man like Putin*
> *One like Putin who is strong*
> *One like Putin who won't insult me*
> *One like Putin who won't leave me.*

At the 2004 elections Putin backed his own invented party, United Russia, which was unconstitutional for a president to do. United Russia's election posters were portraits of Lenin, Stalin, Dzerzhinsky and those they jailed, Solzhenitsyn, Sakharov and Brodsky – as if they'd all been one happy family.

The world's leaders queued up to meet Putin and gain an entrée into Russia's oil and gas fields. And

Russia again began to push its power beyond its own borders, attempting to fix elections in the Ukraine and other former Soviet republics.

Two MPs were murdered after they questioned the KGB's actions, over thirty journalists were killed, and numerous others who never made the papers, but who got in the way of the regime.

'Putin made us an offer to exchange our freedom for bread,' one politician said, 'and many Russians accepted this trade.'

Just before Christmas in 2004, Finn suddenly re-signed from his job and announced he was going to write a book. He bade farewell to colleagues whose main role had been to parlay reports of his progress to Adrian in the preceding years and Adrian hosted a dinner for Finn in a private room at the Ritz – an overdue acknowledgement, Adrian said, of Finn's fine record of service. Adrian made a speech, but he was slightly drunk and told a risqué story of a trip he and Finn had made behind the Wall in '88. But Adrian, in his drunkenness, got it confused and, when everyone laughed at the denouement, most of them were laughing at Adrian.

A week later, Adrian took Finn for a walk in Green Park and questioned him about the proposed book. Apparently satisfied that Finn had 'recovered', as Adrian put it, from his delusions of four years before, Adrian gave Finn his imprimatur to write a story, as long as the Service got a look at it first.

And so for the next three months, Finn estab-lished himself as a writer and never travelled out of

London, quietening any fears that he might go off into the blue.

Meanwhile, I was able to tell the Forest that it was all cover, and they seemed to believe me.

In the early summer of 2005, Finn announced to anyone who would listen that he and I were going on a walking holiday in the Swiss Alps. And on 28 June, we took a flight to Geneva.

25

THERE ARE SEVEN OF US sitting in the Café des Douanes, a hundred yards over the border from Swiss Geneva in France. Finn is sitting at the centre of a long red formica table. The other plastic chairs are occupied by the team he has gathered together in the past four years and who will now stick with him until the end.

It is the same café where Finn and the Troll first met to talk about the Plan back in the summer of 2000. I am not yet officially included in the team, being simply Finn's trusted Russian girlfriend.

Finn persuaded, cajoled and, in one or two cases, even paid these members of his team to join him. He has at last come up with a plan of his own.

It is based on the work of all their efforts in the intervening years: digging into bank accounts, following money trails, gathering anecdotal and paper evidence from many absent sources, such as Sergei, who are outside the team. And, though only Finn and I are aware of this, all is being slowly guided by the hand of Mikhail, the ever-present ghost at the feast.

And there are others on this team of Finn's, like Dieter, who are not present but who still give this curious loyalty that Finn commands and that has got us all to this point.

As for me, Finn has never asked me to do anything that might compromise my relations with the Forest. And, though I don't yet know it, he will only ever ask me once.

Finn has named this meeting a partial 'family reunion'. Family, as ever, is important to Finn, even if it is just a word. The gathering is a two-day excuse for eating and drinking and enjoying each other's company. It is also a chance for Finn to praise and thank us, and to steel us all for the final push – to establish the purpose of Exodi.

Apart from Finn and me, there is Frank who sits solidly on one of the red plastic café banquettes, a slight smile playing in his eyes, wearing his old grey woollen coat even though it is hot inside the café. Frank is the immediate reason Finn has called us together. He rarely leaves Luxembourg but is making a rare trip to Geneva to attend an anti-money-laundering conference.

The Troll, just come in from the street where he's been barking into a mobile phone, is now wearing a russet beard that starts an inch below his mouth, like an Amish, and winds up on either side of his face like a hairy chinstrap. The Troll is cultivating this beard until the job is finished and this is some kind of ritual for him.

Then there is a man I haven't met before, a sixty-five-year-old Englishman named simply James. He wears a three-piece pin-striped suit and his boyish complexion, surrounded by coiffed silver hair, reflects a care for appearances. James lives in Andorra and is an old contact of Finn's. Former special services, SAS, I guess, James has run a security business for the past twenty years, bugging and debugging buildings, negotiating with kidnappers, sifting through rubbish bins, helping clients who are the victims of *kompromat*, as we say in Russia, and other, related activities. James can kill and apparently knows some interesting interrogation techniques. With a cheerfulness that disguises his squeamishness, Finn describes James as 'the blunt end'.

Then there is the Hungarian Willy, taking a summer break up in the mountains. Willy has come down from his hiking holiday to attend Finn's impromptu meeting. He wears a red cravat with white spots around his neck and chomps on a Villiger cigar.

The sixth person present is a Swiss woman, an investigative journalist. There is a slight pause when Finn introduces her by this description. She is called Karin and has long blond hair. I can't help wondering if she and Finn have had an affair in the past. I think it equally likely she is with Swiss Intelligence.

Karin is just finishing giving us all an account of her country's exploits in central Asia.

'Kazakhstan is known in Swiss banking circles as Helvetistan, so great is Swiss investment there,' Karin says and I note that she flicks back her blond hair at the end of sentences. 'Swiss bankers and politicians love Kazakhstan,' she says. 'It is rich in oil and gas and is run by the dictator Nazarbyev who conveniently answers to nobody but himself.'

Karin winds up her exposition with more flicks of her hair, which seem to irritate only me. 'Swiss money pours into Nazarbyev's coffers. The money is to buy his country's votes at international forums where the Swiss need support, particularly in the area of banking secrecy. Nazarbyev votes with Switzerland at these legislative gatherings when there is a Swiss need and, in return, the Swiss government has recently granted him permission to build a $20-million chalet in our poorest canton, Valais.'

A heavily mascaraed waitress takes the order for another round of drinks. Frank drinks coffee, the rest of us beers and wine. The Troll lights his umpteenth cigarette and Finn follows him in this, as usual, as if reminded that he smokes. When the drinks have arrived, Finn looks around the table at each of us.

'When I had just started in the Service,' Finn begins, smiling at this retrieved memory, 'I was asked to take the place of a more seasoned intelligence officer who was ill, during an operation in London. My task was to follow a Soviet embassy official and I was in the company of one of our occasionals called Kirill. Kirill was an old white Russian, nice guy, slightly mad, well into his seventies, and way past his sell-by date.

'The Russian embassy official we were interested in had previously been at the Soviet embassy in Kabul just before the coup in '79, and we were certain he was KGB,' Finn says. 'And now he had been posted to London. We decided to surprise him on his way home one evening and make him an offer.' Finn puffs on his cigarette without pausing to drop the long ash into the ashtray. 'It was my first face-to-face contact with a real Russian spy!' he says and he squeezes my knee under the table.

'Kirill and I were to wait in a pub by one of London's commuter rail stations. The Russian took either the 5.10 or the 5.35 train each day to Blackheath where he lived. But the target didn't show and Kirill proceeded to get drunker and drunker and angrier and angrier until I called back to base to say we should abort. They told us to stay where we were. When the target finally turned up after seven o'clock, Kirill was completely plastered. We followed the Russian on to the train and sat in the next carriage. Kirill had a bottle of beer and started walking up and down the carriage cursing and shouting about Russian spies. I thought he was going to be arrested as soon as the train pulled in.

'Eventually I managed to manhandle him into a seat and we got off at Blackheath and began to follow the target across the common, the old boy growling and swaying as we went. When we decided to make our move, the two of us came up alongside the man and I tapped his arm to ask directions. But as soon as we had his attention I told him that this was his moment of truth – either come over or we would fatally compromise him. Kirill was singing some old white revolutionary song and shouting something or other in Russian at a tree.

'The target just looked scornfully at the old boy and then right into my eyes. Then he said calmly, "Why don't you just fuck off," and walked away.

'I had to practically carry Kirill all the way home to Hampstead.' Finn finally grinds his cigarette into an ashtray and smiles. Then he gets to the purpose of the story. 'I'm telling you this to demonstrate that even our fine British intelligence service can conduct an operation of complete ineptitude.'

He looks around the table.

'So don't let anyone think we're not up to this task. We are as good as anybody, perhaps better. Who would believe that we had come so far already?' he says.

James, the blunt end, nods with soldierly approval, although he has no doubt heard better pep talks than this one on real parade grounds. Everyone is now looking at Finn.

'What happened to Kirill?' Karin asks.

'He was retired with honour,' Finn says, and arches an eyebrow at her. 'But in 1991 he decided to revisit Moscow for the first time in over sixty years. He arrived on the day of the coup against Gorbachev, saw the tanks on the streets and assumed they'd come for him, the idiot. He had a heart attack and died on the spot.'

The Troll laughs uproariously. He is full of black humour.

'Intelligence agencies usually overrate themselves,' Finn continues, when the Troll's rumblings subside. 'It's how they get their funding. If the British secret service makes mistakes like we did with Kirill, then all services do. All services anyway contain the inbuilt flaw of being forced to do what they're told by politicians.

'The KGB is no better, and in some ways it's worse. It's disorganised, bloated, overconfident and at war with itself. So we should not underestimate what we few can achieve.'

Karin raises her glass and we all toast 'the Italian job', as Finn has named the operation, and 'Italy', which is what we call Exodi.

The final push now, Finn says, 'is to find what the Kremlin plans to do with all this money it has clandestinely brought to the West. What is it for? What does Exodi exist to do?'

'There aren't enough football teams in the world . . .' the Troll muses.

'No amount of their intelligence operations in the West could possibly soak up these sums of money.' Finn pauses and leans back in his chair.

'The Russians are now the world leader in raw, brutal capitalism,' Karin says.

'Like America a hundred years ago,' Willy adds. 'There are no rules for them. The oligarchs have secret accounts all over Europe. It's unbelievable.'

'I've almost completed an investigation into one of them on just this theme,' Frank says.

'Which one?' the Troll asks.

'Mikhail Khodorkovsky,' Frank replies.

Frank is referring to Russia's richest man and the owner of its biggest oil company, who has just been arrested by special forces in Siberia, as his private plane prepared to take off.

Finn looks up at Frank and leaves his gaze hanging in his direction, but he doesn't respond.

'If we can find where Exodi's funds are going,' Finn says, bringing the conversation back, 'I believe we will find the answer to all questions of Russia's foreign policy.' He looks at Frank again and smiles. 'Frank, what do the illegal and secret accounts at Westbank exist to do? Where does the money go?'

'That would be difficult to find out,' Frank replies, and I sense he now regrets displaying his expertise a moment earlier.

'But possible,' Finn presses him. 'We know what's in the in-tray, but what's in the out-tray? What are the funds paying for?'

'Possible? Yes, it's possible,' Frank replies. But his habitual smile is no longer on his face.

Finn turns away.

'And can you' – he looks at the Troll – 'look at the same question from Exodi Geneva's point of view. With Karin perhaps? Both of you work together. What is going out of Exodi's accounts in Geneva and where to?'

The unlikely combination of the Troll and Karin escapes nobody. The Troll, so grumpily confident of his own skills, is reduced to an embarrassed boy by just appearing even in the same sentence as the beautiful Karin. His blush spreads downwards into the russet beard and he merely grunts his acknowledgement.

'Anna, James and I will be in Geneva for a while. There's an important lead here that needs following up,' Finn says. 'Our first move on to the offensive, in fact.'

'Oh yes?' Frank's smile has returned as he enquires, but Finn doesn't expand.

'I expect to make a start this afternoon,' Finn says, discouraging further questions. 'It's already in motion.'

'Oh go on, tell us,' the Troll says mockingly.

Finn grins.

Finn puts his arm around Willy who is sitting next to him.

'I have the name of a girl who works at a bank in Valais, Willy,' he says. He hands over a piece of paper to Willy, presumably with the name of this girl and the bank on it, but there is more writing than that. I see there are names and account numbers, but I can't read them, and Finn is careful to shield them from all but Willy. 'I want you to see if you can ask her these questions,' Finn says. 'Who are they?' He is referring to the unseen names, I guess. 'What is their history of payments, in and out. And why are the accounts under the control of the bank's president alone.'

'Sure, I can go to Valais.' Willy shrugs and takes the paper.

'There's good walking there,' Karin says. 'And excellent golf.'

'Thank you,' Willy says, and smiles back at her. 'But I don't play golf.'

When we leave the café half an hour later, Finn makes a point of taking Frank aside and they walk up the street towards a tram stop. Frank seems anxious.

'You need money, Frank?' Finn asks.

'Oh . . . you know,' Frank answers.

Finn has always said Frank has little or nothing. He has always worked for peanuts because of his messianic belief in attacking big, criminal capital.

'I can get you money,' Finn says. 'Just tell me what you need.'

'Thank you, then,' Frank answers. 'I do need some.'

They arrange how much Frank needs and, in the course of this conversation, Finn uses the moment to ask Frank the question that is really on his mind.

'If I give you what you need, will you stop investigating Khodorkovsky?'

I see by his tense stance and from his eyes piercing into Frank's how urgent this is for Finn.

'Why are you investigating him, Frank?' Finn asks.

'Khodorkovsky?'

'Yes.'

Frank looks uncertain how to react.

'I'm looking at his finances, that's all. Accounts all across Europe. Gibraltar, Isle of Man, Guernsey, other places.'

'Why are you doing that?' Finn asks gently.

'It's what I do, you know that.'

'It's the Kremlin that wants to know about Khodorkovsky's accounts, Frank.' I can see Finn's eyes gleaming from where I'm standing on the pavement. 'So you're doing the Kremlin's work. Isn't there a conflict of interest here?'

'Oh, you know . . .' Frank says.

'No, Frank. I don't know. How much do you need to stop this work?'

Frank looks across the street and is avoiding Finn's eyes.

'Finn,' he says finally, 'it's what I do, investigate big capital, you know that. That's the enemy. You won't like it, but I'm doing the job for German Intelligence. For the BND.'

'For the BND? And who asked them?' Finn is amazed.

'The German government,' Frank says stolidly. 'Who else could ask them?'

'Why is the German government interested in Khodorkovsky, Frank? He has no interests in Germany.'

Frank is silent.

'Khodorkovsky's the only Russian who's standing up to Putin,' Finn says. 'The only one who's capable of it!'

'It's a money-laundering issue,' is all Frank says.

'And German Intelligence is helping the Russians. That's right, isn't it?' Finn says, grabbing Frank's arm a little abruptly. 'The German Chancellor is helping the Kremlin. Is that it?'

'I don't know. That's not my business. That's politics.'

'We both know, Frank. Putin's asked Germany to help crush his personal enemy and the BND is doing Putin's work for him. Christ, Frank! It's against everything we're trying to do. It's for Putin to remove opposition to him in Russia, not for us in the West to do so.'

'It's an international crime issue,' Frank says doggedly.

'Putin's the crime issue here,' Finn practically shouts.

'I must go,' Frank says. 'Please.' He disengages his arm.

'Frank . . .' Finn says.

'I'll be late,' Frank replies, turning away from Finn and coming over to me.

He takes my hand with an intensity that surprises me, and lays his other hand over mine.

'We'll meet for dinner, I hope,' he says.

'I'd love to, Frank.'

And then he walks away, shuffling in his grey overcoat on to a tram that will take him back across the border to attend the conference's afternoon session.

I see Finn is furious and confused. For Finn, everyone must be against Putin. Putin is the enemy that justifies any action. Khodorkovsky is Putin's enemy and, for Finn, Putin's enemy is Finn's friend, no matter what.

We walk a few steps along the pavement and Finn takes my arm. I feel the energy from his hand. He kisses me on the cheek and says that he will find me back at the hotel after dinner. He has something to pick up, he says. Then he leaves.

The Troll comes up to me, perhaps seeking sanctuary from his forthcoming partnership with Karin. He asks me if I play billiards and, though I tell him I don't, he takes me to a billiard bar, a taxi ride away, and insists we play.

I am worrying about Finn as we order our drinks.

The Troll is at home in the dark, subterranean, windowless place, but I feel as if I need some air and, after sipping the drink, I leave the Troll so he can join three others and make a foursome for a game.

I walk through Geneva's grey streets, wet from a summer shower that passed unnoticed in the bar. It is the personal tone of Finn's urgent conversation with Frank that plays over in my mind. I see danger and put it down to Finn's uncharacteristic display of anger at a colleague. He is taking the job personally. And that is dangerous to all of us. Eventually, I let go of my anxiety and walk back to the hotel.

I take a bath and change and meet Frank at a small Italian restaurant on the north side of the lake where we have a convivial, relaxed supper and Frank treats me like a daughter. I almost forget the strangeness of Frank's and Finn's behaviour.

And when I return to the hotel, Finn's afternoon's work lies face up on the bed and all thoughts of Frank are obliterated at the sight of it.

26

THE PHOTOGRAPHS LIE SPREAD OUT on a burgundy-coloured coverlet that Finn has straightened for the purpose over the huge hotel bed. There are eight of them and Finn has neatly arranged them as if we were there to discuss the order of presentation. They are black-and-white pictures, taken from odd angles and with more than one camera, probably hidden in ceiling and wall fittings of the room where the pictures were made.

'Apparently there's also a videotape,' Finn says tonelessly. 'But we couldn't get hold of that, thank God.'

The cold orange light of street lamps enters the fourth-floor hotel room like a guilty, unwelcome visitor. But outside the window, the starry sky of a Geneva June night seems to set the city on display like subtle stage lighting. Couples stroll arm in arm and a few lonely people walk the streets, head down, heading for the late bars. The scene outside the window seems slow, staccato, apparently fragmented and disjointed like an old silent movie.

I turn away from the window and sit down again on the bed. I feel sick and wish that Finn would take the photographs away.

But Finn gets up and switches on a lamp beside the bed, three twists of the switch for the fullest glare, to augment the ceiling light. The orange light outside, and the moon's glow, are washed away with incandescent light.

'They come from your side,' Finn says, trying to be businesslike about the scenes on the bed in front of us. 'They were taken in March 2001 at an SVR apartment in Moscow. Evidently around the time Clement Naider, the man in the pictures, was threatening to step out of line – and Moscow was looking for insurance against some loss of nerve on his part. He's been chairman of the bank for over twenty years and my guess is he'd worked for the Forest for many years by the time these were taken. Perhaps he'd become afraid. Perhaps he was intending to go to the authorities, we don't know.'

'We?' I say.

Finn hesitates.

I realise now, years later, that he, too, was so disturbed by the photographs that he had been on the point of telling me about Mikhail. But he checks himself from taking such a fateful step.

'The knowledge is a burden,' he says. 'There are some things—'

'Some things we don't tell each other?' I say with a feeling of resentment spilling into my voice.

'It's not a matter of us. It's not about personal trust,' he says. 'This is separate from you and me, Anna. This is the job, not our life together. It's a matter of security, your security. How you will bear the burden of knowledge.' Finn gets up off the bed and throws his jacket on to a chair. It is a gesture of doing something to distance himself from any awkwardness between us.

'"We" naturally includes Mikhail, who procured the pictures,' he says with his back to me, confirming what I already know.

'It wasn't Sergei who got the pictures, then,' I say.

'No, it was Mikhail. He's going right out to the edge,' Finn says. 'Taking big risks.'

But Finn's perfectly reasonable argument, the protection of Mikhail, causes a flame of anger to rise in me. By now I realise just how big a toll the stress of being four different people is taking on me. Finn's lover. Finn's helper. The Forest's agent. And still, in some twisted form, someone who believes that Russia can be something other than the prisoner of the *siloviki*, the men of power. And I no longer know which of these four selves is credible. I maintain them all with equal conviction, comfort them, cherish them, look after their needs.

But most of all, perhaps, I need to believe that the two sides, the Forest and Finn, believe in me, despite my own clear deceit towards the former. It has become almost unsustainable, this split, and on this afternoon in the presence of the pictures I feel the unease rushing to the surface.

Naturally, I do not expect trust from my masters and so my need for Finn's total openness, complete trust in all things, becomes the greater. I feel myself like a child wanting to know who Mikhail is, just so I know that Finn has told me everything.

'He only wants to use you.' Patrushev's words run through my head.

The more I need the sureness of our relationship, the oneness of Finn and me, the more inconsistencies lie in the path I am following and the more fear I feel that Finn will be gone once, with my help, he has found what he wants. I don't stop to think for one moment that, in fact, Finn has never asked anything of me in the first place.

But my anger and despair are welling up at the sight of the pictures, not at Finn.

I begin to weep quietly. But I don't really know why I cry. Out of fear for Finn and me? At the content of the pictures? At the trap I'm in? I don't know, perhaps all of these. And eventually I cry for the reason that finally uses up our tears. I cry for all the evil in the world.

And when I know that I am crying for everyone and everything, I stop and smile at this great futility. Finn holds me and I feel in the closeness of his presence one of those brief moments of truth that I know we both gain from each other in times of chronic self-doubt.

'Don't worry, Rabbit,' Finn says after a while. Then he smiles. 'I'll give you more than enough to betray me.'

'Don't say that,' I reply.

'But that's the choice. Eventually,' he adds. 'I'd

like you to have the choice, Anna. Having the choice is what will bind us. Because I know of course you'll make the right choice,' he says. 'And leave Russia.'

I stand up and go to the bathroom. I look in the mirror to see if there are traces of four different people in my face. But I look as I always look, though paler, perhaps, from shock. And as I look at myself I think how easy life would be without choice and yet how such a possibility never exists, even when we are enslaved. I see my finely balanced act of doing my work and being so close to Finn, not as a brilliant exercise of skill and craft, but as simply a refusal to choose, to choose to leave Russia for ever.

When I return from the bathroom, I am ready for what we have to do.

'How do you plan to use them?' I ask.

Finn sits down on the bed and we both turn and look again at the pictures.

The sixty-one-year-old president of the Banque Leman, an elegant if bland nineteenth-century building artfully lit across the street from our Geneva hotel room, is dressed in various leather straps and thongs, studded or not with silver metal. His paunchy white stomach protrudes over a tight black leather strap above his naked genitals and in his right hand, in a studded glove, he holds a leather stick. There are open bottles of liquor everywhere in the room, some knocked over, their contents spilled over the carpet. In one picture white powder, possibly cocaine, is visible in a disorderly pile on a side table. In another picture there are stains on the wall – wine, blood, bodily fluids? The black-and-white photographs leave this to the imagination, which is some-how worse.

In some of the pictures the bank's president Clement Naider is laughing like a satyr, his prick fully erect. In others he is snapping or snarling and raising his hand and, judging from their expressions, apparently bringing it down from time to time, with its stick gripped firmly, on to one or other of the girls. Without them, without the girls, it would be almost comical.

But it's the girls who have broken me. They are no more than ten years old, twelve at the most. One of them looks as if she might be even younger. It is hard to tell how many of them there are – they are never all in one picture. One is lying on the floor like a dead body. But in each picture he is inflicting on them one or more depraved acts that outdoes the ones before, in an escalating gallery of foul and hellish images that threaten once again to break my composure.

The girls? They are provided for his purposes by my own people, of course, colleagues at the Forest. From where? I don't know. Orphanages, perhaps. Or off the street. One or two of them have central Asian faces, so they're from one of the southern republics, I suppose. Perhaps they are stolen from their homes, abducted in the cruel war in Chechnya. I don't know, I don't know who they are. But I realise it doesn't matter where they come from. They are just children inserted brutally into this torment of the Forest's making.

And it is at this moment that I decide the time has come for me to leave everything behind, to leave this – if this is what Russia has become again – for good. It is time to spend a life looking over my shoulder for the Forest's retribution. It is time to defect, and even Nana and all the memories of my childhood can no longer hold me. I wonder if this is why Finn has shown them to me.

Finn gathers the pictures into a pile and puts them in an envelope.

'Naider goes on Saturdays to visit his wife in a sanatorium outside Vevey,' he says. 'His wife has motor neurone disease. He has lunch with her there and then takes a walk alone through the woods if the weather's OK. I'll make contact with him then, when he's on his own.'

At last I snap my mind away from contemplation of my own situation and consider Finn's words from a professional point of view, glad to have something else on which to focus my thoughts.

'No. You have to go to the bank, Finn. It's more of a risk, but that's where the details are. Account numbers, names, whatever it is you're after. He won't have those in his head. If you force him without getting the full details, you risk losing him.'

'I have the photographs,' Finn argues.

'What if the photographs push him too far?' I say. 'He can't take it. He's trapped. He kills himself. No, you must hit him just once. It might be too late for a follow-up.'

Finn thinks for a moment, pacing the room, stopping by the window and, perhaps, looking across the streets at the bank itself. He knows I am right, but he doesn't like the prospect of entering the bank any more than I do. There are too many people inside a building, too many things that can go wrong. But he agrees.

Finn has prepared himself in all sorts of ways for what he's going to do. He has offshore financial vehicles tucked away, shell companies that Frank or the Troll have fixed up for him all over the world. He has an account in the Cayman Islands.

He also has a set of friendly lawyers, in Switzerland, personal contacts of the Troll and perhaps trolls themselves.

And he has a passport for the purpose, or more than one passport, for all I know. This one, however, is in the name of Robinson, and the Englishman James has acquired it for him.

He has painstakingly set up all the trappings of a privately wealthy international individual with strings of companies, but without the actual cash that would normally be concealed by such trappings. Concealment is his purpose but it is to conceal that he has nothing.

And so, on the following day, Finn drafts a letter from his Swiss lawyers to the Banque Leman which will be sent on their official paper from their true and verifiable address in Interlaken.

'Our client is a high-net-worth individual who wishes any contact with the bank to remain discreet for the time being,' Finn writes in the imagined hand of his lawyers. 'Our client wishes to put on safe deposit several tens of millions of dollars' worth of gold bullion, transferable to stocks, bonds or cash at short notice. For the time being our client has decided to amalgamate from disparate investments around the world a modest quantity of his total resources into gold to take advantage of a perceived upturn in the precious metal.

'Our client is seeking in the short term a major acquisition in Europe and other further investments over a short- to mid-term period. Our client wishes to secure the best, most advantageous rates of return for so high a deposit and in addition to know the security arrangements that he can expect from the bank are adequate.

'In the meantime, he also requests that a Swiss franc account be prepared for his signature, references supplied, so that, if favourable terms can be reached at this meeting, there will be no delay. Our client requests a meeting solely with the president of the bank at this delicate stage.'

All Finn doesn't write is, 'Are you interested?'

A warm reply from the bank's president arrives, via the Swiss lawyers, and then via the circuitous routes of Finn's mailbox arrangements.

'The president, Clement Naider, will be delighted to invite Mr Robinson to his office at a time convenient to him.'

Two days later, after what Finn considers to be an unhurried interval, Finn's Swiss lawyers telephone the bank and make his appointment for the following Thursday, just under three weeks since we were sitting in the hotel room with the pictures.

In the meantime, we watch Clement Naider. We follow him from his home, a smart bachelor apartment in Geneva's old town, to his bank and, on Saturday, out to Vevey to see his wife at the sanatorium.

In Vevey, I walk the same path he walks through the woods after lunch. We watch primarily to see if Naider is watched by others.

Naider has a driver who doubles as a bodyguard and after some time observing him I see that he is armed. He drives the banker to the sanatorium every Saturday and sits in the car while Naider lunches with his wife and then walks alone. In the weekdays, the bodyguard sits in the car behind the bank or, when he wants to smoke a cigarette, which is often, stands in a wooden hut that collects payments for a car park across the road from the rear of the bank. Here he stands chatting to the car-park attendant, jabbing the sports pages of the daily papers with his finger. He seems to have some kind of horse syndicate going, as far as we can judge.

Occasionally the chauffeur sits in the bank's fine entrance hall reading a dedicated sporting paper and every so often he drives Naider to a meeting elsewhere in town, or to a club overlooking the lake on the edge of the city where Naider takes a sauna and massage, and where he usually dines alone. To all, he is the respected Herr Naider, the martyr who has sadly lost his wife to a debilitating illness, and who cares for her regularly on a Saturday like a good husband.

Otherwise, apart from Naider's driver, Finn and I and James, and later the grumbling Troll, cannot detect anyone tailing the banker, either from my side, or the Swiss side or from anywhere else. We are, finally, sure of that.

But inside the bank, it will be a different matter. James has a detailed chart of the bank's internal security arrangements, which he has procured from one of his Geneva thieves. For a whole day he sits in a van in the car park at the rear of the bank, half a ton of concealed electronic equipment behind him, and 'looks' at the bank's circuits, trips and cut-offs until he knows them by heart. But, under Finn's questioning, he angrily acknowledges that there is little he can do apart from fuse the whole system, and that might cause more problems than it solves. James's role is now to disable the chauffeur's mobile phone – and the chauffeur too, if necessary. But once inside, Finn is on his own.

In the event of complete disaster, and if Finn is able to signal from the inside, we decide that the Troll will set off a fire alarm inside the bank, in preference to a general breakdown of security cameras which might automatically seal doors shut with Finn inside. To his dismay, it requires him to wear a suit and tie. The three of us spend an afternoon choosing a suit for the Troll. Finn calls it our 'family day out' and, at the sight of the Troll trying on ill-fitting suits, we laugh for the first time since the pictures arrived, and eat a huge tea.

But at least, with the Troll inside and able to set off the fire alarm, it will soak up the ground-floor security for perhaps a few vital moments.

James's job is to stay in the car park at the back and watch Naider's top-floor office window for any signal and then, when Finn exits, to cover him and remove anyone who follows him. James is adept at the management of chaos, Finn says.

It is the worst type of operation. Naider is on his home ground, Finn deep inside it. The banker might well panic and do something he regrets, but it will be too late for both him and Finn by then. There are too many open questions; Finn's insistence on meeting alone with Naider – will the bank's procedures allow it? And there is the possibility of an accidental or impromptu entrance by an employee or secretary. How will Naider react? An operation like this one contains what we would normally have considered, in our professional modus operandi, to be an unacceptable risk.

27

ON THE MORNING of the meeting, it is innocently bright, the sunlight dapples the street through the branches of the trees. On Geneva's bridges couples are walking, hanging around each other's shoulders, and tourists wander aimlessly or look over on to the huge fountain and Lac Leman.

Finn is staying in a different hotel now under his new name of Robinson.

On this morning Finn dresses, as he puts it, 'like one of your *buzinessmen*, Anna, like an assassin in a seventies TV show, rather than an investor'; by which he means ostensibly expensive casual, with one or two loud additions; he wears a polo neck and a blazer with 'yachting' buttons; a slightly ridiculous Piaget sports watch – like the one Putin wears, he says; a Swarovski solid gold bracelet. A set of Mont Blanc pens is tucked into an inside breast pocket. Liakubsky's funding has taken a serious knock.

He has ordered a chauffeured black Mercedes limousine, with darkened windows, and he has been to the barber.

At just after ten o'clock, he leaves in the limousine for a drive around town. He tells me he needs to settle his nerves. I take a car James has procured and pick up James and the Troll at a café in the old town. We park up near Geneva's railway station and the Troll sits drinking coffees and smoking cigarettes in the car, while James buys a paper and strolls back down the hill towards the bank. At eleven, the Troll and I drive past the bank to see James chatting at the car park's booth with the chauffeur and the attendant. Once they have become acquainted he will ask to use the chauffeur's mobile phone, and leave it unable to receive calls.

We see Finn stepping out of the limousine, his driver holding the door, and then he walks up to the bank's front entrance. The Troll gets out of the car and leans against it looking at a map. I watch James leave the booth, the chauffeur's phone disabled, and walk around to the far side of the car park nearest the bank.

The bank's doorman, evidently expecting Finn, nods to him and presses a buzzer and that is the last we see of him as he enters the building.

From the car where I'm sitting – a little too far from the bank for my liking – I scan the front of the building and look for anything unusual. The Troll is back in the car smoking incessantly and rattling through several puzzles in a newspaper before it is time for him, too, to enter the bank. As I watch him finally crossing the road, I think that nobody will believe he has ever worn this suit or any other suit in his life.

Less than three minutes after Finn entered the building he was in the lift to the top floor in the company of a dark-suited man Finn later described as the maitre d'hotel or butler. The Banque Leman devoted a sizeable proportion of its staff to the greeting and general welfare of its wealthy clients, rather than to actual banking.

The two of them emerged on to a thick-carpeted hallway, a private floor within the private bank, dotted with priceless antiques, Chinese vases, prints and paintings collected during the bank's illustrious history. Another uniformed butler appeared to receive Finn from the first man, who silently disappeared, and the butler beckoned him to an ornate Louis Quatorze chair. The butler made the quietest knock on a pair of black lacquered double doors, gesturing to Finn to step inside the president's office. The butler announced Finn like a hushed party greeter and silently withdrew, closing the doors behind him.

The room was in a different style to the hallway, decorated with early Art Deco masterpieces and French Empire furniture. A lion's head, the bank's symbol, was mounted on a wall to the far left of the room, and a drinks cabinet was tucked away discreetly in the opposite corner. In the centre of the far wall was a long, finely polished antique desk that looked as if no actual work had been done on it for at least a couple of centuries. In front of the desk was a broad guest's armchair designed to make the bank's fattest customers feel comfortable. To the left of the room was a seating area of comfortable softer arm-chairs, and to the right an aquarium, the bottom of which seemed to have been scattered artfully with real gold coins.

Finn noted two cameras; one was trained on the desk and the area around it, the other on the doors through which he'd entered. There seemed to be no coverage of the armchairs to the left.

Clement Naider stood up from behind his orna-mental desk and came round to the front to shake Finn's hand. White-haired, somewhere in his mid-sixties, he wore a three-piece pin-striped suit of the faintest chalk against dark blue. His hand was tanned, warm and manicured. He smelled of cigars and pol-ished leather. His face had the soft, bronzed craggi-ness of a well-pampered social skier, a face like those described by Finn of the wealthier inhabitants of Tegernsee.

'I'm pleased to meet you,' Naider said in a soft German accent and beckoned to the chair where Finn would sit. But Finn didn't sit. When Naider had already sat down on the other side of the desk and pressed a concealed buzzer underneath it, which Finn mentally noted along with the cameras, Naider saw him still standing and a look of mild consterna-tion crossed his face.

'I'd prefer the softer chairs, if you wouldn't mind,' Finn said. 'It's my back. I'm recovering from a recent car accident.'

Naider's expression immediately cleared to be replaced by one of unctuous understanding of his guest's requirements.

'Of course,' he said and, standing up, gestured to Finn to lead the way. 'Nothing too serious, I trust,' Naider said.

'A small injury in the middle lumbar region, that's all,' Finn replied. 'Certain chairs are easier on it. The doctor tells me I'll be fine in two weeks.'

'Good, good. But how very frustrating.'

Finn took one of the four chairs and Naider sat opposite him. A small round table stood between them.

The double doors to the room opened and a second butler, summoned by Naider's discreet buzzer, entered carrying an empty silver tray. Finn asked for a whisky and soda and Naider repeated the same for himself.

'How often do you visit Geneva, Mr Robinson?' Naider asked.

'Several times a year,' Finn said. Behind the desk across the room he saw a safe in the wall, and on the far side where the butler was pouring the drinks, a wooden filing cabinet with locks. The butler delivered the drinks in heavy crystal tumblers and left the room.

'We're delighted to be able to offer our services to you,' Naider said. He raised his glass. 'To your swift recovery.'

Finn responded and they drank.

'And after we've had our chat here, perhaps you would like to accompany one of my directors to the vaults,' Naider said. 'If you do us the honour of acting for you, I would like you to see the security that comes with our service.'

Finn nodded, only half listening now, as he reached inside the leather case he was carrying, withdrawing a brown envelope. He placed it on the table in front of Naider.

'I'd like you to have a look at some proposals which weren't in my lawyer's letter,' he said.

Naider seemed surprised but not unduly troubled. Perhaps he had a client with some very special request that could only be mentioned in a private meeting, it was not unusual. He replaced the tumbler of whisky on to the table and picked up the envelope.

When he withdrew the pictures, wrapped in photographic paper, he seemed interested. When he unfolded the thin sheet to reveal the first photograph, Finn had his hand in his pocket ready to press the agreed mobile number in the Troll's pocket, the signal to break the fire alarm downstairs.

But Naider simply stared at the first picture. His life seemed slowly and visibly to drain from him, leaving the soft flesh of his craggy features to sag as if into an empty carcass. His suit crumpled from its perfectly measured and ironed state into something Naider might have bought at a second-hand store. The tan leached down his face into the collar of his sparkling white shirt.

'There are six pictures altogether,' Finn said. He paused. 'I want you to move slowly to the safe. I want you to open it and retrieve the file marked "Dresden". Then you will close the safe and bring the file here. Go now.'

Naider didn't move, didn't look beyond the first photograph.

'Do it now,' Finn said. 'I have to be out of here in five minutes with the Dresden file, or the pictures will be wired right around the world.'

He watched Naider struggle with the enormity of the blow. How many years had he lived with the secret of his sexual perversion? And how many years had he lived with the fact that others, his Russian masters, knew his secret well enough to have finally trapped him?

The life of Clement Naider did not pass before his eyes. By this time, there was only one thing left in it. Locked inside him, the citadel of his terrible secret now protected only outlying areas of his being. The inside had been laid waste long ago, scorched to oblivion with nothing left alive. And as he had compensated for this empty interior by cultivating his fine exterior with each stroke of the manicurist's brush, each fine cut of the tailor's scissors, each expensive plucking of the barber's instruments – the pruning, the tanning, the aromatic oiling of Clement Naider, and finally the clothing of him in distinguished dummy's inch-perfect cloth – his interior had responded by withering still further so that now it lay untended, poisoned and finally devoid of human life. The Clement Naider Finn saw in the flesh had become an expensive mechanical doll and nothing else.

Finn wondered if the banker had even the strength to stand. But slowly, without letting go of the pictures in his hand, Naider got to his feet. He never looked at Finn. He walked slowly towards the safe.

'Touch nothing but the safe,' Finn said softly. 'If I'm not on the street in ten minutes, the pictures get wired anyway.'

He watched Naider move into the arc of the camera's view and stoop slightly to turn the dial on the safe. He watched Naider swing open the door and reach into the dark interior. He saw the file in Naider's hand as he withdrew it, closed the safe, and walked back across the room, clutching the file in one hand and the pictures in the other. Naider sat down in the same chair and placed the file on the table. Still he didn't look at Finn.

Swiftly Finn emptied the file of a sheaf of documents and placed them on to the table, flicked through them while keeping an eye on Naider, and then took out a small camera and photographed sixteen sheets in all.

'Sit still,' he said.

He walked to a window which was open at the rear of the office, slipped the camera into a reinforced bag in his pocket and lobbed it out. Somewhere below, James was there to break its fall. Then he replaced the documents and told Naider to return them to the safe. It took five minutes in all and Finn told Naider to hurry now or it would be too late. Naider still didn't speak or look at Finn.

Finn drank the remainder of his whisky and soda in one gulp and slipped the crystal glass into his leather case. The courtesy of Naider's servants in opening the doors did not require him to brush the surfaces in the room for fingerprints. He stood and walked to the desk.

'My envelope,' he said. Naider didn't want to part

with the pictures, his last hope being, perhaps, that there was just one set, and he held his safety in his hands. But he saw the pointlessness of this and let them fall on to the desk. Finn picked them up.

'Press the buzzer.'

Naider pressed it.

'Now sit back over there.'

Naider obeyed, a slave for so long to his secret.

And the butler appeared, ushering Finn from the room. Naider sat bent over in the armchair, speechless and dazed, as if he'd had a seizure.

The butler escorted him to the lift, pressing the buttons for the distinguished customer.

And as he stepped inside the lift, Finn heard the double doors closing behind him, as Naider attempted to place another layer between himself and the world and to shut himself away from its cruel glare.

28

THE DRESDEN FILE gives us five names,' Finn says. He pushes the small camera he used to photograph the file at the bank across the table towards me, leans back in his chair, and looks out of the window of the inn towards the mountains. 'Five names, five account numbers that correspond to the names, and monthly payments of twenty-five thousand euros into each account.'

I look at the names, clicking through the first five pictures he took.

'German?' I say.

'Looks that way. Maybe Swiss-German.'

'Twenty-five thousand euros a month paid to five people is hardly an explanation of Exodi,' I reply.

'On the face of it, no.'

'And yet it must be.'

'Mikhail says so,' Finn grunts. 'Mikhail said the file is the explanation. So it must be.'

I take a laptop from my bag and begin to Google the names.

When Finn left the bank, he and I took a taxi out of Geneva and then the slow red train from Montreux that heads up over the passes to the Bernese Oberland. There were a few hikers on board on their way to the small, rich resorts of Chateaux d'Oeux, Gstaad and beyond, and some tourists who simply wanted the thrill of seeing the high pass from the train.

The train hauled itself up to its highest halt, where it stopped to pick up and drop off the mail, and we looked over the great expanse of cragged mountains that stretched eastwards.

We got off the train in Gstaad after a winding descent into the high valley. A taxi took us a dozen miles beyond the town to the Bären Inn at the foot of the road's long ascent to the glacier of Les Diablerets. We ate supper in a wooden dining room with a slow log fire that crackled and spat its pine sap, and then went up to bed in another wooden room which had red-and-white chintz curtains with shepherdess prints and a faux wooden spinning wheel in the corner. We didn't talk much. Making love with Finn that night was a ritual of purification for both of us.

It is late on a fine summer's morning and we have eaten breakfast in the room. Finn then gently cuts the lining of an old, oiled coat that was so thick it stood up on the floor by itself.

From inside the lining he extracts the camera and mobile phone and places them on the pine table. The first five photos are the five names with their account numbers. A further four pictures of the Dresden file are a list of transactions, all of which consist of money paid into the accounts of the five names. Twenty-five thousand euros a month. The rest of the 'pages' are a long list of the names of companies.

'Each name receives his or her monthly payments from a bank affiliated with Clement Naider's Banque Leman,' Finn says. 'This bank is a small regional bank that deals with local agricultural loans, mortgages and meagre personal savings. Way below the radar, in other words. It's on the far side of the mountains from here, in the canton of Valais, and is called the Banque Montana.'

Valais, Switzerland's poorest canton, is free with handing out residency permits compared to the rest of Switzerland, particularly with permits for Russians since the Wall came down. And there was a KGB-owned ski hotel there, from long before the end of the Cold War. We used it to entertain officers from the American Sixth Fleet based in Naples.

'Clement Naider has a seat on the board of the Banque Montana,' Finn says.

'A bit below his status, isn't it?' I say.

'Exactly.'

'So Naider sits on the board of an insignificant bank in the backwoods . . .'

'. . . and his presence on the board is for just one purpose, to oversee these payments,' Finn says, completing my own thought.

'From an Exodi account?'

'I think the Troll will find that it's Exodi in Geneva which is making these payments,' Finn says. 'But it hardly explains the vast sums that Exodi controls.'

I have found the five names on my laptop. Four men, one woman. Each has a list of company directorships to their name, all German companies, some companies that Finn or I or both of us know – big, international names – others that neither of us have heard of.

Finn looks over my shoulder.

'Dieter will understand this better,' he says.

Finn sits on the bed and begins to compose a message for Dieter. He leaves the coding books open so that I can see his workings.

I'll give you plenty of opportunity to betray me. His words on the night in Geneva came back to me, and he is being true to them. How can he be so sure, I wonder, that I won't betray him? Or is it a leap of faith, a necessary passage on his intended journey for us to be one?

When he'd completed the message to Dieter, Finn wanted to get away from the room, the file, the names. We both did. He suggested we try some summer skiing up at the glacier and we eventually find some boots and skis for rent and take a taxi up to the cable car. It is a clear blue day and the cable car takes us to the top and we ski a few hundred yards and admire the view, the wind blowing out the intensity of the past few days and restoring some kind of sanity, clarity perhaps. We find a rock to shelter from the wind and Finn puts his arms around me.

'I love you, Rabbit,' he says.

'Thank you.'

'So you win the bet,' he says. 'I told you first.'

I look down at the snow beneath my skis.

'I knew I'd win,' I say.

'Sometimes I wonder what you feel.' He looks at me. 'Whether your feelings flit across your surface like a breeze on the sea, or whether they take a hold somewhere below the surface.'

I take his hand in mine.

'You have a glass wall around you, Rabbit,' he says. 'Sometimes I can get behind it. Sometimes you lower it a little, but you never lower it altogether. I want you to understand you can trust me. Telling you I love you is the freest thing I've ever done.'

'I've decided to leave,' I say finally.

'Leave?'

'I've decided to come over.'

Finn is silent and we listen to the wind whistling around the rock.

'Are you leaving Russia, or coming to me?' he says eventually.

'It's the same.'

'Not quite. You're leaving because of the pictures of Naider.'

'Yes. But it's everything at once. My past. The Forest. And you too, of course, Finn.'

'What about Nana?'

'She'll understand. It's what she'd want.'

'I'm very happy,' he says, and we hug each other. 'Me, too.'

'You don't have to tell me you love me, by the way,' he says, and grins.

'Well, I do,' I reply. 'I love you, Finn.'

He gets up and draws with his ski pole in the snow the words 'I love you, Anna'.

I hold his arm and look down into the snow, unseeing.

'Come on, let's go,' he says.

And we ski the several kilometres of the long glacier run and return by taxi when the light has faded
into black, and the mountains glow a dull grey-blue
in the moonlight.

We spend three days at the Bären Inn. On the fourth
day, two things happen that shatter the brief illusion. Finn had gone downstairs to fetch the newspapers as he always did when he got out of bed. While
he was gone I checked my e-mails and saw that I was
being summoned to Moscow. On the 'next plane'. It
was not a friendly message and it was the first time
in four years I'd been summoned at all.

Finn came back with the newspapers. He threw
them one by one on to the bed and I saw they all
contained the same story. The headline on the front
page of one of them, the *Süddeutsche Zeitung*, summed
up the story in all of them. 'Bank President Shot
Dead in Geneva Apartment,' it read, and there was a
wire-service picture of Clement Naider – head and
shoulders only – taken on a better day than the day
of his death.

Naider had been found dressed in a white towel-
ling dressing gown in the bedroom at his expensive
duplex bachelor apartment inside the walls of a con-
verted medieval building up in Geneva's old town.
He'd been shot three times, in the stomach, the
shoulder and in the head, to finish him off. It was an
execution Russian-style, but who else knows our
methods nowadays? The stomach and shoulder shots

were his punishment, the rest his death. One of the stories in a Swiss paper claimed that he had been tortured, and then his still-living body had been rolled around the walls of the bedroom, which were covered in blood. This story added that the body was then tossed over an internal balcony on to a white rug in the living room below. This may have been a sensational and untrue addition to the truth, but I doubted it.

The police were following several leads into the identity of the killer and were looking over the appointments Naider had made in the previous weeks. They had a letter written by Naider which, it was evident to me at any rate, had been extracted by the killer before Naider's death and deliberately left for the police to find. But the police were not divulging the contents of the letter to the press, not yet.

When we had finished reading it all, Finn said, 'They're getting very close, Anna, your people.'

'Naider must have cracked,' I replied. 'He thought that if he told them what happened, they'd give him credit for it.'

'Why torture him?'

'They probably thought he could tell them more about Robinson than he had,' I said. 'And he couldn't.'

I put my hand on Finn's shoulder.

'I've been called to Moscow,' I said.

Finn looked up from the chair to where I was standing behind him. There was a frown on his face.

'This?' he asked, turning back to the papers.

'I'm sure.'

'What do you want to do?'

'I don't know,' I said.

'If you do go back,' Finn said slowly, 'what will you do if they don't let you out again?'

'I'll find a way.'

'Maybe. You know what I want most of all,' he said.

'Yes, I do.'

'They'll go over you with a fine-toothed comb,' he said.

'I'll be OK.'

'Do what you feel is right, Anna.'

'I must say goodbye to Nana.'

'Yes,' he said. 'I understand that.'

'Will you tell me something?' I asked.

'What?'

'When this is finished, will we be free?'

'Yes, we'll be free,' he said.

We left the Bären Inn after breakfast and took the train to Basle, where Finn was to change for a train to north Germany. Finn carried my bag across the platform for me to board a train for Zurich and the flight to Moscow. When he'd put the bag down, he kissed me and wished me luck. Neither of us wanted to be the first to let go, until we each became conscious of the other's thoughts. Then we laughed.

Finn threw my bag into the open door of the train as the whistle blew.

'Don't be a stranger,' he said.

I didn't reply, just watched him as the train pulled away from the platform.

29

THE PLANE LANDED at Scheremetyevo airport north of Moscow at five o'clock in the morning. It was the first time I'd been in Russia for four years.

At the foot of the steps two thugs from the Forest took me in a car, its blue light flashing with unnecessary urgency through to a side entrance of the airport. Within a few minutes of landing, we were on Moscow's ring road.

They didn't speak, even to one another; we just raced at high speed towards the centre of the city. We weren't heading in the direction of Balashiha and the Forest, and I didn't know where they were taking me – the Lubyanka, perhaps, or a Forest apartment, or somewhere else. The fear they were hoping to generate by the speed of the drive served only to wake me up and make me more alert.

After half an hour of this breakneck journey, the

car pulled up outside the Savoy Hotel, just around the corner from the Lubyanka. One of the men opened the door for me, more like a policeman than a doorman, and they walked on either side as we entered the hotel and headed for the small downstairs bar.

The hotel was as I remembered it, a faded, scuffed reminder of its former empire glory before the 1917 Revolution, untouched by Moscow's real-estate boom. Upstairs above the bar there was the tiny casino where Finn claimed to have won so much, so long ago, it seemed now.

The bar downstairs was empty apart from one man. I don't know why I was surprised, but it was Vladimir. It put my mind at ease, a dangerous thing. But he was a welcome anticlimax compared to the reception I'd been expecting.

Vladimir kissed me four times in the formal Russian way and there was no attempt in here to remind me of our intimacy of four years before. He was now a colonel in the SVR, he said, but it seemed to me he had lost none of his old directness, simplicity, humanity even.

'You and I have much in common,' he said as he poured coffee. 'They need people like us,' he added, 'if Russia is ever going to change.'

He was effusive, asking me genuinely innocent questions about my time away, what I liked about Western Europe, if I'd ever like to settle there for good.

He wanted to know about the Russian scene in the ski resorts and on the beaches over there. What was London like? And Geneva? And Paris? Meeting

Vladimir was like coming home to a brother who has never left home. And for all I knew Vladimir had never been anywhere but Moscow and the Cape Verde Islands. I was aware, however, that the men with the car, whom he'd told peremptorily to wait outside, could in a moment take me elsewhere, to a place where the welcome wasn't so warm.

Vladimir ordered breakfast for us both. At one point a hotel guest entered the bar and Vladimir sharply told the barman to tell him the bar was closed. On the television, screwed to the ceiling above the bar counter, a violent Russian gangster film played out, the Russian hotel equivalent of the wallpaper classical music in a Western hotel.

When breakfast and coffee had arrived, Vladimir switched the conversation to the reasons for my return.

'They feel the British have stepped over the line,' he said. 'This death has made everyone very angry.'

I was relieved that they seemed to believe the British were still involved, rather than just Finn, but I felt uneasy that there would now be a change in their approach to Finn.

'But you are truly the returning hero,' he said. 'I'm told Patrushev is pleased with the way things have gone.'

His use of the past tense – 'the way things have gone' – sent a shiver through me. Was it over? Was I not required any more, would I not be ordered to return to Finn?

'It's good to see you, Anna. I've missed you.'

I kissed him on the cheek.

'Are you married yet?' I said.

'No.' He grinned, and returned my kiss.

Vladimir said that I had an unscheduled meeting with Patrushev before I was to be debriefed at the Forest. The men in the car are FSB, he said, not SVR. Then I would be taken to the Forest and Vladimir would meet me there and we'd begin work together.

But first he had thoughtfully booked me a room in which to bathe and change. Half an hour later I rejoined him in the bar where we had another cup of coffee and talked about the quiet things, an apartment he was hoping to find with his newly elevated rank, and the latest movies coming out of Russia that never made it to the West. I was grateful to Vladimir. He had made what he called my homecoming more comfortable than I had imagined it would be.

As we left the bar and walked into the foyer, I picked up a copy of the day's edition of *Novaya Gazeta* which was being delivered as we waited for my coat. On an inside page there was a story about a leading Swiss banker, brutally murdered in his home. The police, it said, wanted to interview a man called Robinson in connection with the murder of Clement Naider.

I was driven the hundred yards or so to the Lubyanka and was then escorted through its forbidding entrance.

Patrushev's office was at the top of the building and, once again, the view from inside the KGB's fortress made me forget where I was. The Kremlin's towers and the onion domes of St Peter's Church – the fairy tale of Russia's greatness – shone in the early morning light.

Patrushev welcomed me in his customary grey suit and red tie, and he smiled his thin, purse-lipped smile that was more a recognition of another's presence than friendliness. Yuri was back, no doubt with a new promotion and a more expensive watch. He glowered in a chair to the side of Patrushev's desk.

'Welcome home, Colonel,' Patrushev said.

'It's been a long time,' I replied.

'Oh, four years is not so bad,' Patrushev said, never taking his eyes off me. 'You're hoping to go to Barvikha tonight?'

'If that's possible,' I replied.

'We'll see, we'll see,' he said, and I felt that Yuri sneered at my hopes.

Patrushev spoke about the reports I'd made in general terms, praising their 'level-headedness', and told me I was a valued officer and more would be needed '. . . if I was capable,' as he put it. 'You must be getting tired,' he said.

I told him I was tired, but I would do whatever was required of me.

'Of course. Finn hasn't told you what we need,' he stated, and looked at me, apparently for confirmation.

'No, sir.'

'For your sake, perhaps, for his own sake, and for the sake of Mikhail himself.'

'That's exactly what he tells me,' I agreed.

'He said that?'

'Yes.'

'Then I'm getting too far inside his mind,' Patrushev said. I didn't follow his meaning.

'Four years. He's difficult to nail down, isn't he?' Patrushev said. I watched Yuri's face and could imagine, in a picture of horror, Yuri actually nailing down Finn.

'He may have seen Mikhail,' I said. 'On maybe one or two occasions. But I don't know. They obviously have a way of communicating without meeting.'

'You gave us the dates of these supposed meetings, but we haven't been able to match them with any movements of senior figures here,' he said.

'I can't be sure that he actually met Mikhail on those dates either,' I said, 'rather than simply picked up a communication from him.'

'And his meetings with Adrian in London?' Patrushev said. 'Are there any more of them than you've reported?'

'No. You have them all in my reports,' I replied.

'They meet often. Is this an attempt to make us believe that they are now just social friends? That Finn has left the Service?'

'In my opinion, the job he does at the commercial investigation company in Mayfair is just cover,' I said. 'It's very easy for him to meet with government officers behind the closed doors of this company, Adrian included. So, yes, I think Adrian hopes that we are picking up on their frequent lunches together in order to impress us that they are now just friends who meet in public from time to time and that Finn no longer works for MI6.'

Patrushev paused and watched me coldly.

'He's difficult to nail down in other ways, we've found,' he said at last, ignoring my explanation. 'There is the question of his childhood, for example,' he went on and threw a closed file across the desk to me without suggesting I open it.

'His story, the one he told you and the one we had from our other sources, does not seem to be correct. How well do you really know him, I wonder?'

I didn't understand what he meant, but he clearly wanted me to listen to him rather than to look into the file.

'You can look at it later. At your leisure,' he added. 'It seems Finn went to an English boarding school called Bedales, and was not brought up in a commune in Ireland after all. His parents lived in Berkshire, near London. His father was in the civil service, something to do with the coal industry, and his mother was a nurse. Two ordinary, middle-class parents, apparently. It's all in the file. From this new evidence, Ireland seems to be a fiction. Is Finn a fantasist?'

This, at first, seemed a small point.

'One of them's fiction, evidently,' I said. 'Maybe this second version is his fiction,' I continued cautiously. 'His fiction made for him by MI6. I don't think he's a fantasist, no.'

'But he was so convincing when he told you all about his Irish background out at Lake Baikal, wasn't he? This was his story as told to you, the woman he loves.'

'Yes,' I agreed. 'Yes, he was convincing.'

'If the story of his Irish upbringing isn't true, I

wonder what else he has convinced you of that isn't true.'

He paused dismissively, as if this was a minor issue but I felt the walls were closing around me.

I reminded myself of what Finn had said years before, as we sailed on *Bride of the Wind* back to England. 'They will do anything over the months, maybe years, to drive a wedge between us. That is what we must be most careful of.'

And these words of Finn's were also exactly what he would say if he were lying to me.

I was dismissed after nearly an hour, but as it turned out only from Patrushev's office.

Walking down two floors with Yuri in front of me, all I could think of was the file in my hands. This fiction, if it were fiction, was something so unimportant, so obscure, that I couldn't understand why Finn would have lied about it, to me at any rate. So it must be the file that lied, I thought. But I found that I couldn't keep that certainty in my head.

In an office below Patrushev's, there were two men I hadn't met, and Vladimir. But it was Yuri who was clearly in charge. The large desk was covered in documents illuminated by the one light in the room, a desk lamp that flooded the mess of paperwork. The four of us sat around the desk with Yuri in an old wooden swinging chair behind it. He lit a cigarette from one of several half-empty packets strewn across the desk and exhaled loudly and stared at me.

I placed the file of Finn's supposed deceit on a

mess of ash and screwed-up sweet wrappers – where it belonged, I thought.

Yuri continued staring at me. Then he looked away, affecting boredom.

He addressed one of the men I didn't know. 'Let's start with the photographs,' he said. The atmosphere was unfriendly, threatening even.

The man picked up a document case from under his chair and unzipped it. He withdrew a brown envelope, extracted a fistful of photographs from it, and gave them to Yuri. Yuri made a play of looking at them one by one, raising an eyebrow now and again, exhaling smoke, clicking his teeth. I wondered with a sinking feeling who the subjects of the pictures were. Finn and me, perhaps? I doubted it. The one thing we were careful of was our own, personal privacy. But this performance of Yuri's was designed to unnerve.

He picked them out one by one and placed them in turn on the desk in front of me. The first photograph was a shot of Finn and me boarding a train.

'Where's that?' Yuri said.

'Bourg-en-Bresse in France,' I said.

'What were you doing there?'

'Finn was meeting a contact. Then we changed trains for Geneva.'

'Who was the contact?'

'I didn't meet him. Or her,' I added.

It wasn't the start I was hoping for and Yuri made a great play of allowing an expression of deep doubt in my story to settle on his face.

The pictures came in quick succession, sometimes pausing over one for further examination and extrapolation from me. They were external shots of Finn and me, travelling, until we came to a picture of Finn, Frank and me, sitting in a café in Luxembourg.

'Who's that?' Yuri demanded, pointing at Frank.

'His name's Frank. He's in my reports.'

'Frank what?' Yuri said, implying I was withholding information.

'I don't know. I was introduced to him as Frank. If you have a picture of him, presumably you know.'

'What's he doing?' Yuri snapped, ignoring me.

'He's a private investigator. Specialising in banking, particularly in his home town in Luxembourg. He seems to be an old contact of Finn's. More than that. A friend. Finn admires him a great deal. There's a bond between them.'

There were two pictures of Willy, taken perhaps on a trip to Marseilles which the three of us had gone on, but these seemed to be the only pictures they had of us together. Then we came to pictures from the day before.

They weren't taken at the Bären Inn, but at the railway station in Basle, Finn and I embracing, saying goodbye.

'Two lovers,' Yuri smirked.

'That's the idea,' I said and he shot me an angry look.

'It looks real enough to me,' he said, and laid out the four shots of our parting on the desk.

'Then I'm pleased,' I replied.

'Where was Finn going after he left you?'

'He was taking a train north to Germany. To Frankfurt.'

'What for?'

'To meet a contact. A German. I've never met him and Finn has never mentioned his name.'

The more I tried to banish it, the more the name Dieter forced its way into my mind.

'There's quite a lot you don't know, isn't there, Colonel? After God knows how long with him.'

'It's a long game.'

'It certainly is. The way you're playing it.'

'Those were my orders.'

'You're taking for ever to find simple facts.'

'There are plenty of facts in my reports,' I said, and I felt anger rising up in me. 'We've learned a lot. Without me, there'd be no Exodi.'

'What makes you think that's so important?'

'Because Finn does. That's why I'm there, isn't it? To find out what Finn's doing. Exodi has been Finn's main achievement.'

'That you know of,' Yuri added.

And then Yuri threw one of the few remaining pictures on the desk in front of my face, just as he'd done with the others.

'Who's that?' he said.

I looked at the picture with the same care I'd looked at the others, but I knew when I saw it that I could not conceal the colour draining from my face. I felt the eyes of the four men in the room boring into me. I couldn't change the feelings I felt rising up in my eyes and throat.

'She's called Karin,' I said, trying to put some strength in my voice. 'She's a Swiss journalist.'

'No,' Yuri responded triumphantly. 'She's called Brigitte and she works for Swiss intelligence.'

The picture showed Finn and Karin, or Brigitte, boarding another train. Finn was wearing his old oiled coat, the one whose lining had concealed the camera. He carried in his hand a holdall he'd bought the day before we left the Bären Inn. He had his arm around Karin's shoulder and they were laughing.

'It was taken last night just before the train departed from Basle to Frankfurt,' Yuri said, his eyes gleaming with vicious pleasure. 'You were right about Frankfurt at least.'

I looked blankly at Finn with the Swiss girl.

Then Yuri moved relentlessly on to Clement Naider.

'Finn shot Naider,' he said bluntly. 'When did Finn meet Naider? Finn met him and extracted the Dresden file, didn't he?'

Something in his insinuating tone gave me the tiny hope I so desperately needed. They weren't sure – they didn't know – that Finn had met Naider at all. It was a glimpse into their doubt or ignorance of the fact and it was vital for my own story, my fiction. If they didn't know for sure about the meeting between Finn and Naider, then I could keep to the story Finn and I had worked out. My feelings were numb from the photograph and that played into my hand. It had the opposite effect they'd no doubt hoped for.

I told them that Finn and I had been in Geneva – which they knew anyway from my reports. I said that I had no knowledge that he had met with Naider. That I would surely have known, even if he had kept it from me. I told them that Finn couldn't have killed Naider, as he was with me outside Geneva, on the day when it had taken place.

'Besides,' I said. 'This isn't just Finn. The British and, for all I know, the Americans and the European agencies are crawling all over Exodi by now. They know how important Exodi is to their own security. Finn is just one individual. He's not everywhere, all of the time.'

And then Yuri leaned in towards me.

'He shot Naider, if you say he did,' he said. 'You are the witness.'

'I see,' I said.

Ever since I had read the newspaper reports I had guessed that the Forest was attempting to frame Finn for Naider's murder. Naider's murder removed a traitor and would now, perhaps, remove the unwelcome investigation of Finn's into Exodi, and send a warning, as they believed, to British intelligence. They wanted to kill both birds with one stone.

The letter the Geneva police had found no doubt implicated 'Robinson', as it was intended to do. But one thing I hadn't anticipated was that they might wish to use me to bear false witness in the framing of Finn. My final job for the Forest, perhaps.

Why didn't they murder Finn now as they'd murdered Naider and assassinated countless others? Why the need to frame Finn so elaborately? I believe, for their own reasons, they were reluctant to assassinate a British citizen who they believed worked for MI6. That was a last resort.

After nearly eight hours in this room I was allowed to leave the Lubyanka. But they had sown their seeds of doubt and discontent well. Half consciously, I had left the file Patrushev had given me on Yuri's desk. But it was restored to me before I was able to leave. I had this file, with its supposed evidence of Finn's 'real' childhood, I had the image in my mind of Finn and Karin boarding the train for Frankfurt the night before, and I had Yuri's unmistakable suggestion that, if the circumstances arose, I would make a fine witness in the framing of Finn for Naider's murder.

What did I feel about these revelations of Finn's childhood and the picture of him and Karin? In my head, I knew them to be untrue. I knew that the whole purpose of the day had been to undermine my trust in Finn. The file, which I hadn't read, would surely be one of their forgeries. The photograph of Finn and Karin technically could be a forgery.

Yuri had gathered all the pictures up off the desk after showing me this one. He had not wanted me to dwell too long on it, perhaps, no matter how expert it was.

But to know a thing is not true is not necessarily to accept it. Knowledge is not always the final arbiter. Belief, acceptance, these are the things that knowledge relies upon – most of all, acceptance. The trick itself was crude, if it was a trick. Of course, the Forest used forgeries like this all the time. I did not believe that either Patrushev or Yuri would expect me to fall for these things. What they did expect – and what they got – were seeds of doubt that I could not completely banish.

No matter what I thought I knew, I could not forget the image of Finn and Karin, nor the possibility of Finn as a fantasist with a self-dramatising account of his childhood.

Vladimir accompanied me as we left the building and walked up the street, past the Bentley show-rooms, and into a small cobbled street that led to Red Square. We found a café and ordered two coffees. Vladimir couldn't persuade me to eat. Vladimir, the Forest's velvet glove, I thought. He himself suggested the possibility of forgery in the café, so that I'd believe he was on my side. He was kind, attentive, eager to bend over backwards to understand my feelings.

And all I wanted was to get away from him. I went to pay for the coffees but he preceded me. Nothing was too much or too little for him when it came to taking care of me. He offered a car to take me to Barvikha, before our meetings and further debriefings the next day, but I declined. I wanted nothing he had to offer.

I walked alone down towards Red Square and wandered idly through the expensive shopping precinct that was once the GUM store reserved for the nomenklatura in my youth.

There were mostly young couples, newly enriched, looking in the windows and buying handbags, fur coats or jewellery.

The irony was that, in the Communist years, my family was able to shop here because we were the elite. Now only the new elite, the wealthy and corrupt, could afford to come here. My father, who had always existed happily on his salary, had lost his savings in the crash of '98 and was reduced to eking out his meagre state pension.

I was looking aimlessly through a shop window at a mink coat when my phone rang. It was him.

'Anna?'

My father sounded old, tired, and I felt an immediate sense of guilt that I had not contacted him once in four years. I'd had nothing to say to him. I spoke to my mother, very occasionally, and Nana often, even though she couldn't hear most of what I said on the phone.

'I know you've only just arrived,' he said, 'but I would like to see you when you have the time.'

This was not like my father, who'd always ordered me to do what he wanted. I detected no anger any more in his voice. I asked him where he was and he gave me an address of an apartment in a street on the far side of the Kremlin from where I was. I was immediately suspicious of his manner. Would he, too, turn out to be another agent of the Forest's slow demolition of Finn? For the first time, I felt like an alien in my own country. I realised that there was no one in Russia, apart from Nana, whom I could trust. But I told him I would see him in half an hour.

His apartment was in a block reserved for loyal subjects of the Forest in their retirement. The block was close to the Kremlin and had recently been repossessed from one of Moscow's rapacious property developers. They were all Heroes of Russia in this block. It was a Madame Tussaud's of ageing intelligence officers, a gallery of rogues who'd served their country well, committed its crimes without question, and were honoured for the mayhem they had visited on different parts of the world.

They were all Soviets at heart who cursed the past for bringing their country to a dead end and cursed the present for its capitalist 'American' ways. Putin brought some sense to their confused and bitter world. He had brought their old service back from near annihilation and elevated it to supreme power. After the shame of the nineties, at last their deeds were respected again. They were the fathers of the new elite, myself included.

When I stepped out of the lift on my father's floor, I saw his door was open and that he was waiting on the threshold. I was shocked at his appearance. He looked an old man, completely grey, and the lines caused by the anger and anxiety that had carried him through his career had deepened into leathery gullies and crevices that made him look like one of those bodies which are found in peat bogs from twenty thousand years ago.

He was wearing a grey suit, white shirt and red tie, as if he were still going about the State's business, and his breath, when I let him brush my cheek with his lips, smelled of a long acquaintance with vodka and stale tobacco. Once upon a time, they made men like him president.

'Anna, I'm glad you came.'

'You've got yourself a nice place,' I said. 'Does Mother come here too?'

'Sometimes, sometimes. She is . . . she stays away often. She still does her charity work.'

'The Sakharov Foundation,' I said and saw the old glitter of anger pass across his eyes.

'Is that it?' he said, but I knew he knew it perfectly well and that my mother's work made him ashamed and furious.

'Sit down. You'll have some tea? Or some vodka?'

'I only have a few minutes,' I said. I had nothing to say to him, I realised.

'I know, I know, you're busy. You're doing great work, I'm told. We'll have vodka.'

He walked with surprising strength of purpose to an inlaid Iranian wooden cabinet I remembered from Damascus days. He took out two glasses and filled them both. I sat on the only chair and left him the sofa.

'I have a fine view of the Kremlin from here,' he said, handing me the glass. He raised his own. 'To Russia!' he said. He made the toast still standing, drained his glass without waiting for me to drink, and poured another from the bottle in the crook of his arm. I sipped the vodka.

'You don't drink to Russia?'

'To Russia,' I said and he smiled wolfishly.

He sat down across the low table from me and refilled both our glasses.

'We are a great power again, Anna. Sure, some heads have to roll, but that is normal. You think the Americans and the British don't do the same?'

I didn't reply. I didn't know why I had agreed to come but it certainly hadn't been to talk about politics and violence. I felt as if I were in one of his drinking sessions of old and I saw a man who couldn't express himself without pouring liquor down his throat. And even then, his mind only worked in some impersonal world of power. More power, more control; it was all he and those like him were capable of.

'Just make sure you don't lose your head in all of this,' he said.

I felt suddenly exhausted, after nearly twenty-four hours without sleep. The day had already been filled with innuendo and insinuation, always with some veiled threat in the background.

'To Vladimir Vladimirovich,' I said and drank my glass in one to Putin.

He followed me, delighted to be drinking to Putin, and refilled the glasses again. Neither of us had anything to say to the other outside the sterile rigmarole of empty toasts.

I looked around the room out of embarrass-ment, the need to look anywhere but at him. I re-alised I hated him. I had hated him for a long time. I wanted to leave but my exhaustion and the vodka begged me to rest a while longer. I took in the tall lamp by the door with its pinkish fabric shade, the low table between us, some bookshelves empty but for a few photographs of men in uniform, a small corner table with curved legs in the shadow of the room, and then found myself staring to the left of him at the sofa on which he was sitting, leaning slightly forward. I felt him watching me. My unease was no longer controlled by the vodka in my stom-ach. It increased steadily into a thumping heartbeat, a hot flush, and then fear. The room began to take on the aspect of another room, another room much the same as this room of my father's. It was the room that I had seen in the pictures of Clement Naider.

I don't remember how I left him, or how I got out into the street. I had to vomit into a cardboard box beside a rubbish bin that overflowed with garbage before I was aware of very much. I remember an old woman laying her hand on my shoulder and clucking sympathetically, offering me a handkerchief and asking me if I was OK, if I needed a doctor.

I took a service car out to Barvikha. Nana was standing at the top of the three wooden steps that led on to the veranda of the dacha. She had watched the car's lights as it swung on to the track that led to our home. We embraced as the car left, its driver telling me pointedly he would be back at six-thirty the following morning to pick me up.

Nana was much frailer now, nearly ninety years old, but still able to hobble about with a pronounced limp where her hip had given up. The first thing she did as we entered the dacha was to put her finger to her lips and point to the ceiling. The Forest had bugged the house again in time for my arrival. It was too dark to go outside and a driving rain had begun to fall.

We chatted about Finn as we made ourselves supper. Nana said, 'Have you married each other?'

'No.'

'Why not?'

'He hasn't asked me.'

'Then ask him,' she said and we both laughed, me for the first time that day.

After supper, I crawled into bed and slept.

30

I DON'T KNOW what time it was – sometime after midnight certainly – when I was woken by the sound of hammering on the door of the dacha. It blended with a dream until I was awake and realised it was real. I put on a dressing gown and came out of my room. In the dark I could make out Nana already standing in the living room. No lights were on. She seemed frozen, in the middle of the room, stiff as if at some memory of other night-time awakenings in her distant past.

'What is it? Nana what is it?'

'I don't know,' she said. Then she turned towards me. 'Anna, darling,' she said. 'Come here.'

We embraced and held each other for a minute perhaps. But the knocking on the door resumed louder than before.

'Goodbye, darling Anna,' she said, and squeezed me as hard as her old arms were able.

I broke away from her finally and switched on a table light and we embraced briefly again. I felt tears coming to my eyes, but hers were clear. She just watched me, watched every movement I made.

'Get dressed,' she said, and moved towards the door. 'I'll let them in.'

As I dressed quickly, I heard from my room the door open and the voice of Vladimir.

He was standing in the centre of the living room when I came out. Nana was fetching something from the kitchen.

'I'm sorry for the time,' he said calmly. 'Please. Don't be too alarmed. I expect they're being deliberately antisocial, that's all.'

But I didn't believe him.

'Where are we going?'

'The Lubyanka. But first we'll stop at my place.'

Nana emerged from the kitchen carrying something wrapped in a cloth.

'Take this for breakfast,' she said, and glared at Vladimir.

'I'll wait in the car,' he said sheepishly.

Nana and I held each other.

'Don't worry,' she said. 'I haven't told you before, darling Anna, but I haven't got long to go. It's good. I'm glad. It's time.'

I cried openly.

From the pocket of her dressing gown she took a silver amulet that I saw was very old.

'It's a Tartar charm,' she said. 'Made five centuries ago. It will keep you safe.'

With tears in my eyes, I left the dacha and saw her standing in the hot night against the light of the door.

Vladimir drove out of the forest and on to the motorway towards Moscow. We didn't talk. I sat numbly in the seat beside him and slowly gathered my thoughts. And as I did so, I began to regain some calm. This was routine, I told myself, at least in the perverse world in which my employers operated. If I were being arrested, it would not be Vladimir. They'd have sent their own militia.

We crossed the Moskva River and drove to Vladimir's apartment near the botanical gardens. He pulled the car into the kerb and put his hand on my knee.

'Let's have a coffee before we go,' he said. 'And maybe something stronger.'

Upstairs in the apartment on the seventh floor, he made coffee and put a half-empty bottle of vodka on the table in the kitchen. I sat and watched him.

'I think it's OK,' he said. 'I think they're just trying to put you on the wrong foot. But you might as well be fortified.'

He smiled at me, poured two shots of vodka, and I drained mine at once. Once more, against my better judgement, I was grateful for his courtesy and care.

And then all I felt was him catch me as I swayed and slipped from the hard wooden kitchen chair.

* * *

All I was aware of at first was noise, but I couldn't place the noise, its origin or its identity. It hummed and throbbed and ground in my ears as I tipped from consciousness and back into unconsciousness. Slowly I realised why my only sensation was the noise. I felt the blindfold across my eyes first, before I realised I couldn't see. Then I felt the hardness of the place where I was confined, the bruising pain as my body thumped against its surface. And then I felt the bonds around my hands and feet and legs.

I tried to lift the top half of my body but my head immediately came into contact with a hard surface. I was in a box, a metal box that thrashed around as if it were being thrown down a river. My hearing came and went, so that now from time to time I could hear something more distinct, not just amorphous noise beating in my ears. And then I smelled rubber and, after that, the faint fumes of a car's exhaust. Then I knew I was being taken in the boot of a car.

I tried to move my legs, but they were bound too tightly and finally I lay still as every movement I made caused me pain as I was thrown around the small space. With my fingers I felt a small handle that I could get two fingers into. Perhaps it was something that would have held the spare tyre if there'd been one, and I held on as best I could to stop myself from being shaken. Then I felt the bumpiness of a rutted road turn into the tipping wave motion of an unmade track and finally the car stopped with a jerk that threw me against the back of the seats.

I listened in the silence. A door opened, but there were no voices. I heard the door slam again. And then I heard the latch pop on something near my head and the whining of an unoiled hinge and I felt the cool air on my face.

Hands untied my blindfold. I was staring straight into the sun and could see nothing. I turned away and shut my eyes in pain and then I heard Vladimir's voice.

'Easy,' he said.

He lifted me up and out of the boot of the car and when my eyes had finally adjusted from the darkness of the boot to the brightness of the sun, I saw we were in a forest of pine trees. He untied my hands first. Why untie my hands to shoot me, I thought? Why show me my executioner at all? But then he untied my feet, knowing, I guess, that long confinement would have made my limbs too cramped to run or put up a struggle. He gave me a bottle of water.

'Drink this,' he said.

I drank thirstily while he spoke with matter-of-fact urgency.

'You're in Finland,' he said. 'We're eight miles or so across the border. We were just in time.'

'Why . . . ?' I said feebly. My head throbbed from the drug he'd given me, and from the journey.

'It doesn't matter. You're out, that's all that matters. There's money, a passport, and other things in this bag. There's some food, more water too.'

I struggled to stand up, but he gently restrained me.

'Why did you drug me?' I asked him.

'Because I knew you wouldn't believe me,' he said. 'I knew if I told you that I had to get you out, you'd think it was a trap.'

Then he helped me to a tree and I sat leaning against it, sipping from the water bottle. I suddenly felt euphoric, from the drug perhaps, or from a reprieve from the fate I was sure awaited me.

'They would have arrested you this morning,' he said. Then he pointed. 'Five miles in that direction is a village. There you can take a ride and get a train to Helsinki.'

'And you?' I said at last.

'Goodbye, Anna.'

He turned and stepped into the car. It reversed over the rough ground and the dry twigs snapped under the wheels. Then I watched as he turned back towards the Russian border.

'Goodbye,' I said. But he had gone.

31

INN CAUGHT THE TRAIN to Frankfurt, with or without the blonde Karin, on the night I left Switzerland for Moscow. He arrived around midnight and checked into a seedy hotel in one of the few remaining old parts of the city that hadn't been destroyed in the war.

On the following morning, he walked down Berndtstrasse to a workman's café, buying several German newspapers on the way. As I'd seen it at the Savoy Hotel, he sees the Naider story on the front page of a German paper, also with the addition of the name 'Robinson' that the police had released.

He read through the stories and came to the same conclusions that I had: the Forest was trying to frame him for the murder. Despite his care, there was a possibility that he, as Robinson, existed somewhere on the bank's or hotel's CCTV film, but it was unlikely. He knew better than to show his face to a camera.

Finn drank two black coffees and ate a stale cheese sandwich that looked as if it had been on sale from the day before. He was ordering a third coffee when the little bell that hung on the café door tinkled loudly and a short man entered.

He was dressed in a black donkey jacket, like a workman, but incongruously wore a green felt hat that was too large for him, so that it came down over his ears. Finn couldn't see the man's face completely. He wore cream-coloured loafers. The man walked slowly until he was next to Finn at the counter and, in German that was as poor as Finn's, addressed the Turkish woman who was spooning coffee granules into a mug from an unlabelled tin.

'I'll have a large black coffee too,' he said.

Finn recognised the voice and turned. He saw the neat moustache visible beneath the low hat brim.

'What on earth are you doing in that silly hat?' he said.

'It seems I have a small head,' the man said in heavily accented English. 'At least by German standards,' he added in the morose tone Finn knew.

'Don't they sell hats in Israel? You look like you've just arrived.'

'Just off the flight from Tel Aviv,' the man replied.

Finn paid for their coffees and returned to his table by the window, where a thin June light filtered in and he could see the newspapers better.

'How did you know to find me here, Lev? Your people, the Russians, who else is following me around?

Maybe you should all divvy up the cost and hire a bus.'

'We're better than the Russians, Finn. Luckily for you.'

They sat down at a table by the window.

'What are you doing here, Lev? I'm not in Mossad's bad books too, am I?'

'Let me drink this first, for Christ's sake.'

'How did you know I was here?'

'What does it matter, Finn? I'm here. And I have a message for you. From our side.'

'Your side? Is that the same side as my side?'

'The sooner I can be out of this damn place, the better,' Lev said, ignoring the question.

'Twenty years in Israel and you've forgotten the charms of a north German summer,' Finn said.

Lev put his hands around the hot mug of coffee and warmed them.

'I could do with your help, Lev.'

'First of all, there's nothing I can do to help you. In Tel Aviv we know all about what you're up to. Adrian, as far as I know, doesn't know. Yet.'

'Long may it stay that way,' Finn said.

'We think the same way as you about Putin,' Lev said. 'We're following the same trail. That's why we've been keeping in step with you. In a few years' time one-sixth of our population will be of Russian origin, so Russia and the Russians who come to our country are of national interest.'

'You were Russian once, Lev.'

'That was a long time ago. These are the new Russians,' Lev replied. 'They're different from us thirty years ago.'

'So. Why? What have you got for me?'

'I've come to this damn country to give you a message, that's all.'

'Are you with me or against me?'

'Could be either. It depends. I don't know. That's up to you, I guess. All I can say is that we're interested in what you're doing.'

'Well?'

'Someone – not us – wants you to stop your inquiries. They say they've gone far enough. Time to back off.'

Finn leaned back on the plastic bench and lifted the coffee to his lips.

'I wonder who that could be,' he said sarcastically.

'You're being offered ten million dollars to go away,' Lev said.

Finn slowly put the mug down on the table. He looked in blank astonishment at his old friend. Lev was now casually engaged in stirring another spoon of sugar into his coffee. He still hadn't removed his hat.

'You're kidding, Lev,' he said. 'Aren't you?'

'Like I said, it could be very helpful to you, I'd have thought,' he said drily.

'Who's offering me that kind of money?'

'I don't know.'

'Come on! For Christ's sake, Lev.'

'I tell you, I don't know. That's the truth, Finn. I'm just the messenger. Presumably someone up high in Tel Aviv knows, General this or that, I don't know. The message was parlayed to Tel Aviv from God knows who and I just have the job of passing it on, that's all.'

'Ten million dollars.'

'I don't know what the exchange rate is, but it seems generous, yes. Unusually generous. Whatever you're up to from now on, I'd drop it. Take the money. Marry your Russian.'

'The Russians really are entering the modern world,' Finn said.

'It looks like they're treading carefully, I'd say,' Lev said. 'If it is the Russians. But whoever is offering you this kind of money is making you a decent offer. On the one hand you have this little incident in Geneva the Russians are trying to hang around your neck. On the other, you have ten million dollars. It looks like an easy choice to me. I know which one I'd take.'

'You think so?' Finn said. 'If they're offering me ten million bucks, it looks to me like they're worried they can't frame me for Naider's murder.'

'I wouldn't risk it,' Lev said. 'Here's a number where you can get me.' He handed a card across the table with a name Finn had never heard of printed on it, and a company title underneath. 'Don't take too much time deciding,' Lev says. 'Apparently they want to know soon.'

'The Russians?'

'I repeat, I don't know. My bosses in Tel Aviv tell me "they", that's all. Presumably you know who "they" are. If you know what you're doing that is,' Lev added.

'More coffee?' Finn said.

'Yes, why not. It's delicious,' Lev replied facetiously, now apparently sunk into a permanently disenchanted alternative world where words had become the opposite of their meaning.

Finn got up and went to the counter and got himself a glass of water and a coffee for Lev. When he returned to the table, Lev leaned across to him.

'The Russians who're coming to Israel now,' he said, 'they're buying everything. Some of them are on the run from Putin. Others, it's hard to say. The ones we're really interested in are those who we're sure are just an extension of his *siloviki* rule. We don't mind Russians buying things, we just don't want Russia buying them.'

'Is that the Kremlin's policy?'

'Could be. They have the money now.'

'Tell me what you know. Tell me about Exodi.'

'I can't do that. We're interested in what you're doing, that's all. Take the money, Finn.'

Finn knew he wouldn't get anything more from Lev.

'How's the family?' he said after leaving Lev's offer hanging in the air.

'All fine, thank you. The boys are going to college in America. I'm guessing they probably won't come back.'

'You happy about that?'

'It's best for them there,' Lev said.

'And you?'

'I will stay in Israel. I don't know why. Like I say, this new wave of Russians who've arrived since Putin came to power are a different bunch compared to us. We came with nothing. They bring billions. Billions. Some of them are making big donations, you wouldn't believe. Not just to the usual charities. To us, to Mossad.'

Finn laughed. 'You guys will take money from anyone,' he said.

'And you? Will you take the money?'

'I'll let you know, Lev.'

Finn takes the train from Frankfurt to Saarbrucken. The flat north German countryside changes to rolling hills of wheat and pasture, tree coppices dotting the tops of the hills with new season's green.

His mood on this journey takes him to the depths of the sadness that lives inside him, no matter what his outward enthusiasm suggests.

But his sadness comes from the knowledge that it is not beyond his control to stop and to walk away. He has a choice.

I've seen him sometimes in the early mornings, when he wakes and hasn't had time to prepare his mask for the world. I've seen the sadness in his eyes, which disappears as soon as he knows he's being watched. Finn never accepted that this sadness existed, and never addressed its causes. He could not or would not change.

Finn meets Dieter in the same Chinese restaurant where they had met four years before. They order the same inflation-proof twelve-euro menu and two Tiger beers.

Dieter has aged, Finn thinks. The short span in time has added a decade to Dieter's face and he looks like an old man suddenly. But his eyes are still alert, still searching, calculating.

'Who are the five individuals, Dieter?' he asks, referring to the Dresden file. 'Why them? Why are they being paid? What connects them to Exodi?'

'I'll do what I can, Finn. We are near the truth, just as I was fifeen years ago.'

'Maybe we'll get a different result this time,' Finn says.

'I have something for you too,' Dieter tells him and leans in across the narrow table. 'I may have turned up one of the brothers. One of Otto Roth's long-lost brothers.'

'Where?'

'Not at Jensbank, but it may be something more interesting than that. This man is said to be the owner of one of Germany's biggest trucking firms.'

Finn thinks for a moment and shakes his head.

'What's interesting about one of Germany's biggest trucking firms?' he asks.

But Finn knows the significance of one of Roth's brothers owning a company that transports goods across borders.

'The trucking company was set up in the mid-sixties,' Dieter continues. 'It was founded by this man, this brother as I believe. He is a prominent ex-Nazi, and today the company he set up is one of Europe's largest. It's a world leader in transportation, in fact, and was originally run by ex-Nazis. Roth's brother – if it is him – is using a different name now, of course, one unconnected to those times, to the Nazis.

'In the sixties, when Schmidtke appeared on the scene, this trucking company was helped along the way, shall we say, by the Stasi and the KGB. Otto Roth sorted out the financing and the money movements from East to West, and this brother of Roth's headed the company. The story is, they began to bring all kinds of contraband across the borders. A great German success story, built on a foundation of Soviet trade.'

'Are they trading with Russia now?' Finn asks.

'It's not as straightforward as that. In fact, the odd thing is that such a big firm doesn't go to Russia at all. Some of the fleet make frequent trips to Moldova. But they don't go to Moldova itself. They continue into the Russian enclave of Transdnestr, inside Moldova, which the Russian 13th Army has refused to leave. They also run trucks in and out of Abkhazia on the Black Sea. Since the civil war there a few years back, Russia's left troops behind there too. Just like Transdnestr, Abkhazia offers the Kremlin another safe haven for its criminal dealings. This trucking fleet doesn't go to Russia, but it goes to places where Russia exerts its influence.'

'How do you know this and not know any names involved?' Finn says.

'It's an underground rumour,' Dieter replies.

'With the details conveniently absent.'

'Well, OK . . .' Dieter is suddenly angry, either at Finn's response or his own inadequate information, or both.

'I'm sorry, Dieter,' Finn says. 'You think you can get any further into this?'

'I don't know.'

'So this firm transports goods to and from Russia's favourite offshore illegal trading havens,' Finn says. 'What do your sources say they're bringing over?'

'The routes are disguised, they say,' Dieter replies. 'The logs are rewritten. But my sources believe they are bringing cash. Black money. Millions, maybe billions. This is the operation that physically brings the laundered cash from General Baseer's drug sales and no doubt other illegal sources across Russian borders and into the West.'

'To Exodi?'

'Maybe yes. If we can provide evidence of what this company is doing the German government may be forced to unravel it all at last. They will not be able to hide behind the veil they have drawn over this. The BND would have to reopen investigations, Schmidtke or no Schmidtke, to threaten them.'

'If one of the trucks were stopped and taken apart at the German border . . .' Finn says.

'That would be necessary to nail it properly, yes. It would be a huge scandal. It would be proof of KGB involvement at the highest level, with German politicians and businessmen playing their part over many years. The head of the trucking firm, who I believe is Roth's brother, has very high connections in our government.'

They leave the restaurant and walk along the banks of the Saar River with its concrete embankments and cracked paths. The occasional cyclist or jogger passes along the narrow pathway and a mother wheels her children in a twin buggy ahead of them and stops in the shade of a tree.

'There is an alternative, Finn,' Dieter says, nodding at the woman as they pass.

'What's that?'

The path opens out into a wide field where boys

are kicking a ball and a young family is trying un-
successfully to fly a kite.

'Like I told you before,' Dieter says, talking more
urgently now, 'when you first came. I could have left
it all behind twenty, thirty years ago. I could have
bought my vineyard, lived a quiet life without the
fight. You have more than twenty years on me, Finn.
You can still choose to do what I delayed doing.'

'Yes I can,' Finn replies.

'Why not do it, then?'

Finn stops and leans on a parapet and watches
some boys throwing stones into the river up ahead.

'The same reason you didn't. I'm not ready yet,
Dieter,' he says.

Dieter stands behind him, his hands in his pockets.

'You're right, I wasn't ready,' he said. 'But for what
purpose did I carry on? To prove something, maybe?
To make something happen? To make a difference?'

'Yes, exactly that,' Finn says, turning and looking at him. 'To make a difference.'

'Make a difference to yourself instead, Finn.
The world is too big and this world we've spent our
lives in is too powerful for us.'

'We're too close to stop now,' Finn says.

'And the closer you get, the harder it will be,' Dieter replies. 'Either you can live a real life away from
this, or you can fail, perhaps even die in the attempt,
or you can succeed. I don't know any more than you
what will happen. But look at the choices and see
which is the obvious one. What do you have to gain
by enslaving yourself – and Anna – to the greed and
craziness of others?'

'Who asked you to persuade me, Dieter?'

'Nobody, damn you!'

'Have they asked you?'

'Who's they?'

'The BND. I don't know. The British, the Israelis, the Russians, anyone.'

Dieter frowns, whether out of incomprehension or frustration, it is impossible for Finn to guess.

'Listen to me. No one has asked me anything, Finn. I've spoken to nobody about this work. But I speak to you now as a friend.' Dieter suddenly grips him by the shoulders. 'Turn away, Finn. Give up while you have time. Do what I should have done.'

'Find the name of the trucking company,' Finn says, looking back into the German's face. 'Please, Dieter. And please, find why the five names in the Dresden file are being paid by the Russians.'

32

I RETURNED TO LONDON two days after Vladimir had
taken me across the border. I was exhausted,
beaten, but I didn't want to rest until I was at my final
destination.

Finn picked me up at the airport and on the way
back to his flat I told him everything.

'I've left,' I told Finn. 'Vladimir turned out to be
the good guy.'

'He saved your life,' Finn said simply. 'And he
saved us.'

I bitterly regretted that I'd never trusted him,
that I'd used him and that, in return for my callous-
ness, he'd rewarded me with his ultimate goodness.
I was ashamed and inside I cursed the course of my
life and I cursed myself.

But when we reached his flat and Finn tried to
hold me, I pushed him away. It wasn't just the mem-

ory of Vladimir. There were other matters to deal
with, not least the pictures of him with Karin which
the Forest had shown me. I knew them to be false,
but again my knowledge was no defence. I needed to
confront him. We were sitting on the balcony of his
apartment and watching the last of the tired, grey
leaves fall from the trees across the street.

'The night we left each other in Basle,' I said,
'did you take the train to Frankfurt with Karin that
night?'

'Karin?' he said.

I could have thrown him off the balcony.

'The Swiss girl we met in Geneva, Finn,' I said.
'That Karin.'

'Oh, that Karin,' he said.

It was such a typical response of Finn's and always
a fall-back position for him, even if he had nothing to
hide. He did it in order to ponder any question, no
matter how trivial.

'Well, did you?' I asked.

'That's what they say in Moscow, is it?'

'They showed me a photograph of the two of you.
You had the bag with you you'd bought with me the
day before in Gstaad.'

'Christ Almighty.' Finn looked up at the sky,
then scratched some peeling paint from the balcony's railing.

'So did you?'

He looked me straight in the eyes. 'Of course I
didn't, Rabbit.'

'Why, "Of course not"?'

'They faked up a photo, that's all,' he said. 'Isn't
that the answer you know to be true?'

'Yes.'

He tried to put his arms around me but I pushed him away.

'Come on,' he said. 'This is exactly what they want.'

'That's convenient, too.'

'Come on!'

'That wasn't all,' I said. 'They also provided me with a new background for you that denies everything you've said about yourself. Everything you've said to me.'

'So what do they say I am now? A trust-fund kid with a stockbroker father and a charity-worker mother living in a Queen Anne hall in Surrey?'

'Pretty much, yes.'

'So their fakes aren't getting any more convincing at the Forest, then.'

'Which is true?'

'Everything I've told you is true.'

We sat in silence and the first specks of rain began to fall. 'You're going to have to think about this,' he said. 'You know the answer. Just think about it. Think what's preventing you from accepting what you know.'

'I know,' I said. 'I know.'

I thought about how our profession allowed the lies and deceit to creep through the rest of our lives until it was hard to know what was true and what was a lie. For a moment I almost wanted my relationship with Finn to have been a fantasy, just to stop the uncertainty.

'Everything is so convenient,' I said.

'How do you mean?'

'What they say, that's convenient, of course, from their point of view. And your denial, that, too, is convenient. It relies on us both knowing that they are more than capable of faking everything.'

I let him take me by the shoulders then.

'I love you, Anna,' he said, and I looked deep inside him. I felt our lives come together with the contact of his hands.

'I love you too,' I said.

He grinned.

'Well, that's all right, then,' he said.

We sat in the rain and held each other awkwardly. I knew I couldn't bear to be without him then.

In the silence, with just the patter of the raindrops and the steady drone of traffic which becomes, in a city, like a kind of silence, he echoed my thoughts.

'I can't bear to be without you,' he said.

'That's what Nana always said was the only test of love,' I replied.

Finn and I went to bed just before midnight. He turned to me in the bedroom, looked me in the eyes, and asked me to marry him.

It was the most direct question he'd ever asked me and I said yes immediately, without thinking. It was as if someone had asked me if I wanted a glass of water when I was dying of thirst.

And so Finn and I got married, just as the year 2006 began.

33

AT THE END OF APRIL, Finn told me we were to travel to Liechtenstein. He said we should go by separate routes, as we usually did, but I thought that now it seemed like we were two parents who travel separately so that their children aren't left orphaned.

I flew to Zurich and Finn to Munich. We were to meet at the Café Sacher in Vaduz, Liechtenstein's capital, at 4.20 p.m. on 4 May. Failing that, our fall-back plan was to return at staggered hours over the next three days. I don't know why Finn made these complex arrangements, he never had before, but I should have guessed that he knew he was getting close to danger. I never saw him making a call, do-ing anything that concerned the Plan, but I guess he was setting up what was to be the final act, out of my sight.

* * *

We met at the time appointed in the Café Sacher, an ancient building which sagged over a cobbled street off the main square in Vaduz.

Finn had rented a car and after we'd had coffee and some pastries he'd bought at another café – which irritated the proprietor – we walked down the hill to a car park, the closest a car could approach the square. It was a beautiful day though, as Finn said later, there was still a hint in the Alpine evenings of the winter just passed. There'd been a huge snowfall in the middle of April.

We drove out of the city in the last warmth of a bright, clear afternoon and headed up into the mountains that bordered Germany. It was a beautiful drive. The fair-skinned cattle were cropping the early grass on the Alpine pastures where they would remain until the September transhumance, the ancient tradition which brought them down to the lower slopes. We saw few people, hikers mainly, and one or two farmers in the distance. When we passed two seriously equipped hikers, Finn looked at them in astonishment.

'Whatever happened to stopping for a drink?' he said, and gesticulated at the hoses connected up to their mouths from their backpack water bottles.

After driving for more than an hour we were very high up and there were fewer barns and even fewer farmhouses. The road we were taking had now become a dirt track and still we climbed until, in the lee of a ridge, we saw a very old wooden barn, with a wooden house attached to it, made in the days when animals and humans lived together.

Finn had talked for most of the way. He explained that we were on the last lap that would connect the money that came into the Exodi accounts with its destination, and thus the Plan would be laid out for a child to see, let alone Adrian and the Service. He called Exodi's purpose, the funds paid from Russia and their destination, the in and out trays. As we approached the last few miles towards the distant farmhouse, he began to tell me why we were here.

'Pablo is a very bad Italian,' Finn said as he drove, in his usual obtuse way, not explaining who Pablo was. 'In the early seventies he smuggled dope in a yacht he'd stolen. His regular route was up from Morocco to Holland. He made himself a lot of money and lost most of it gambling and drinking and whoring. But he learned some skills that have been invaluable to us . . .' by which I assumed he meant the Service '. . . and, no doubt, to anyone else who paid him the right money. Pablo is a Venetian merchant of secrets. When he was finally arrested by the Dutch police, they made a deal with him and he happily turned in his old drug-running comrades to save his own skin. Then the Dutch appointed him their police drug expert. He was a good choice. Pablo was dealing drugs from the sixties and was the first person I ever met who owned a mobile phone. I remember it. It was the size of a radio set.

'So Pablo was living in Holland, under arrest within its borders, until he'd served his time as their drug expert. The last time I visited him at the end of the nineties, he was testing all the drugs that came into police possession, to check their quality in order for the correct prosecutions to be made. The Dutch had also let him cultivate his own marijuana in greenhouses in the east of the country – legally and for medical purposes only.

'I remember Pablo's kitchen in Nijmegen, something his police employers never saw. It was full of jars of every kind of drug, and every quality of every kind of drug, that he'd skimmed off the top of the smuggled goods the police had seized.

'But then in 2000 Pablo changed. He'd run his term of being legally confined to Holland and he came to Liechtenstein. His knowledge of how and who to bribe in national police forces turned out to be even more useful than his knowledge of drugs. Somehow he infiltrated his way into Liechtenstein's financial authority and he is one of the few outsiders who dines regularly with a member of the committee. Pablo's the reason we're here.'

'He doesn't sound very reliable,' I said.

'He's completely unreliable,' Finn laughed. 'And that's why he's so reliable. If you shout down the stairs to Pablo "Where are you?" and he says, "The kitchen", you can be sure he's in the bathroom.'

'So why is he so important to us, to where we're going?' I asked. 'Why are you trusting him?'

'Oh, I'm not trusting him,' Finn said. 'He's told me he won't say a word until I'm out of the country, that's all. I believe that. But I know that what he's given me is so important he must be desperate to pass on to someone else my interest in it. So we'll go straight into Germany after this.'

'Why would Pablo give you anything?' I asked.

'OK, not given, exactly, of course not, no. He's the great Venetian merchant. We've exchanged what each of us wants with the other. I've given him some very valuable knowledge. It would get me thrown in jail if they knew in London I'd done it. No, Pablo never gives anything away. He'll already be selling my information now, I should think. It's taken me a long time to set this up,' Finn added.

I didn't ask him what state secret he'd sold to Pablo in return for whatever information brought us here.

'So we've come to meet Pablo, have we? Up here?' I said.

'No. The man we're meeting is part of the information Pablo's given me,' he replied. 'According to Pablo, the man we're seeing has hard information that links the KGB and the Russian mafia with their agents in the West. This is where we will find how Exodi works.'

'From a farmer in a barn in the Alps?' I asked doubtfully.

'That's right.' Finn grinned.

Finally, we came around a wide sweep of track near the top of a grassy mountain which brought us up to the wooden barn and the house we'd seen a while earlier. The track ended here. It was as remote a place as you could find in Western Europe.

Finn and I got out of the car. There was an old Toyota truck in front of the barn house and a small tractor parked on a grass slope that had animal dung on a rickety wagon behind it. From the open doors of the barn section of the building, we could hear the sound of a welding torch.

When we walked up to the entrance we saw a man with his back to us, wearing pale trousers, covered in grease and motor oil, and a blue shirt. He was crouched over a piece of red-painted metal on to which he was welding another, similarly shapeless piece of red metal. When the torch stopped and Finn shouted, the man turned, but his face was obscured by a plastic visor. When he lifted the visor I saw he was a man in his late fifties with a face so brown and lined that he looked like part of the old carvings on the barn's wooden walls.

He stood still. Then he walked unhurriedly away from the workbench, seemingly unsurprised to have visitors – or maybe unsurprised by anything at all. He came towards the barn entrance, slotting the welding torch on to a metal trolley that held the gas bottle. When he stood in front of us, he slipped the visor off completely. I saw he had a big face; he was a big man, but completely quiet in himself.

'Missed the road?' he said, in thick, placeless German.

'No. We came to see you,' Finn said in English and I translated.

'Oh yes?'

'It's a lonely spot up here,' Finn said.

'Maybe you want to rent it,' the man answered in a mocking voice.

'I want to know who rents it,' Finn said. 'We're passing through to the lakes on the other side.'

This, I knew later, was the phrase which identified Finn to the farmer.

On hearing the words, the man stiffened and his

air of quiet self-sufficiency deserted him. He walked past us, a little closer to Finn than was normal, like a big dog that wants its presence felt among potential rivals.

He said nothing and Finn and I followed him. He threw the visor on to a table by the door of the house and opened the door on a latch. He left it open and we followed behind him.

The light was dim inside – the place had been built against the winter – and we could barely see after the sunshine outside. When my eyes grew accustomed to the gloom, I saw on another wooden table which looked about a thousand years old, a rifle that was halfway through being cleaned, a hurricane lamp, likewise, and a few empty bottles of beer. The single large room was otherwise sparse. There was no kitchen, or any obvious room at all which could be described as such by an estate agent. There was no electricity. The place was bare but for half a dozen chairs in various states of repair, an old sofa on which a huge wolfhound was lying, and some artfully placed oil lamps.

'You have the money?' the man asked.

'Yes.'

'Bring it.'

Finn left the room and walked to the car. I saw him open the boot and bring out a black plastic briefcase which shone unnaturally in the dying rays of the sunset. As Finn walked back, the man disappeared through a door and by the time Finn was in the gloomy long room, the man was coming back through the door again carrying some beers in the crook of his arm. He snapped the tops off with a Swiss army knife and put them on the table. The beers were very cool, and came, perhaps, from a deep cellar.

Finn put the briefcase on the table and picked up one of the bottles. The man sat down, without asking us to join him. He opened the case and I could see from the angle at which I was standing, that it was full of bundles of cash. The man counted each row of bundles out in front of us and put them back in the case before counting the next row. When he'd finished, he snapped the lid of the case shut and picked up a beer and sat with his elbows on the table, sipping from the neck of the bottle.

'Sit down,' he said at last, and gave a low whistle. The wolfhound which had apparently been sleeping came immediately over to the table and sat on the floor beside him. Finn and I pulled up the chairs most likely to survive our weight and sat opposite him.

'So. Who's this Pablo?' the man asked, and I translated for Finn. 'How does he know of me?'

'I don't know how he knows you. He's a cheat and a liar,' Finn said. 'That's why the British employ him,' he added.

'The British?'

'And others,' Finn said. 'Anyone who'll pay him enough, in fact.'

'How does he know about this place?'

'I don't know. He makes it his business to collect valuable information, that's all I know.'

'Maybe my father spoke to him once,' the man said vaguely.

He pushed the briefcase to the centre of the table, as if he hadn't yet decided whether to take the money or not, but Finn didn't react. He just said, 'I've told Pablo that if any accident happens to you, he'll be dead in days.'

I looked at Finn in astonishment and saw that he was serious. It made me scared. But the man also saw he was serious and made the decision that Finn wanted.

'I'll show you something, then,' he said.

He got up and walked through the door where he'd gone to get the beers. He was gone a long time, as if what he was bringing was buried very deep somewhere. Outside the sunset was now turning into a dull glow. I saw stars through the open door and a chill air was creeping into the house.

When he returned he was carrying an old leather knapsack of the kind one of his ancestors might have worn while sitting out on the mountain, guarding his flocks against wolves. He sat down and undid the one buckle that still worked and withdrew a water-proof plastic folder; from inside that he took out a buff A4 reinforced envelope for photographs.

He put five photographs on to the table, looked at them keenly, then pushed them across the table to Finn. He got up and fetched a bottle of some home-made mountain liqueur with what looked like a sprig of rosemary inside the bottle. It was dark now and he shut the door. He lit a fire already laid in a rough brick fireplace in the corner of the room.

Finn looked at the pictures. Three were faded and were older than the other two, which looked very recent; different paper, sharp and with a glossy look to them as if they'd recently been developed.

The farmer poured three shots of the liqueur and raised his glass.

'To what are we drinking?' he said.

Finn and I raised our glasses.

'Let's drink to your father,' Finn said.

The farmer levelled his eyes at Finn.

'It's a good toast,' he said finally, and we drank. Then the man began to speak.

'In the spring of 1989,' he began, 'my father was working this farm. I wasn't here back then. I was working in Switzerland. An intermediary, who my father later discovered was acting for one of the men in the pictures, came to him and requested that he rent this house for a weekend in that June. In return for the rent of the farmhouse here, he offered my father a hundred thousand dollars and also a week in the Canary Islands for him and his wife, which they were to take over the period of the weekend when the farmhouse was rented. My own mother died many years ago and this was his second wife,' the man explained.

'My father accepted the deal and the money was paid into an account set up for him in Vaduz. The two of them were given air tickets and a room was booked at the most expensive hotel on an island called Hierra. Very remote, even by the standards there. But my father didn't go. Instead, he called me. I was working at the time on a dairy farm belonging to a distant relative over the border in Switzerland. I hadn't been up here for many years at the time. I didn't like his wife.

'I met my father in Vaduz and he asked me to go with his wife on this holiday instead of him. We had the same first names and it would be easy for me to simply substitute myself for him. I didn't want to. The idea of spending a week with his woman was repugnant to me. He offered to buy me a new car and I accepted. I was broke. So I went to Hierra and had a horrible time, drinking too much and trying to get away from her. We had to share a room to make it look right on the bill that the intermediary was paying. It wasn't an enjoyable week.

'And my father stayed behind in Liechtenstein. He told nobody but me and his wife. He kept it a secret. He hid out in an old shepherd's hut a few miles over the mountain from here. He came up here in the early evenings of the weekend these men rented the place and stayed in the cover of the trees over there.' He waved vaguely in the direction of the door. 'There was a lot of security, he told me later, and that was as close as he could get. And he brought a camera with him. These are the pictures he took.'

The farmer separated the three older pictures and turned them round to face Finn.

'The man on the far right you know. Most of the newspaper-reading public knows him.'

Finn and I bent over the first picture and looked at a tall, grey-haired figure. I recognised him immediately: a very senior, long-serving German politician from the political elite. Then I looked at the third figure from the right and recognised a KGB general, the SVR's central Asian boss, who liaises with the Uzbeks and their drug cartels. In between these two was a man I didn't know. Nor did I recognise the others. But Finn seemed to know everyone in the picture.

'Quite an interesting weekend,' Finn said.

'These three pictures were taken in 1989,' the farmer repeated. 'And these I took earlier this year, when there was a second meeting here, between the same men.'

The two recent photographs were indeed the same group, shiny in the newness of the pictures.

'They rented the farm up here for another weekend, fifteen years after they first took it. Maybe they've had other meetings, I'm sure they have, elsewhere. But this is what I have.'

He poured another shot of liqueur for each of us and raised his glass.

'These are the kind of people who run our countries,' he said. 'To freedom from such men.' Finn and I echoed the toast.

'I don't know why my father took the original pictures,' the man mused quietly. 'It was completely out of character. But I knew I had to do the same this year when they came back after all this time and, if only in memory of my father, I did.'

We left the farmer with the case of money and drove back down the track until we reached the road. Then Finn turned left, towards Germany, and we drove in silence for a while. I had the pictures on my lap, inside the stiff photograph envelope, inside the waterproof bag.

'I wonder what he'll do with all that money,' Finn said, breaking the silence briefly. I guessed at how much of it there was from watching the farmer count the bundles and I was stunned by the cost.

'He'll probably hoard it up somewhere like all the mountain men,' he continued. 'The Troll, for example. I bet he turns out to be a multimillionaire when he dies.'

Once we were over the border and in Germany, Finn began to talk quietly about the men in the pictures.

'There's the German politician. He's someone who might even become chancellor of Germany. And of course you know the KGB general, Anna. Then there's a citizen of the former East Germany, a man called Dietz, who's now a billionaire from his supermarket chains. And next to him to the left is a Swede called Bengsten. He's an arms manufacturer. The old guy on the far right is an ex-Nazi, former SS. His name's Reiter. He's in his early eighties now and still running his business with the same efficiency as he ran his SS unit in 1945. He owns, lock, stock and barrel, the third-largest trucking company in Europe. But Reiter isn't his real name, of course. He's one of the brothers of Otto Roth. And finally, the last figure in the picture is Otto Roth himself.'

34

F INN AND I FLEW to Bucharest one early morning in July. He seemed to have very detailed instructions about how to enter Transdnestr undetected. I asked him if it was a route he'd ever used himself, but all he said was that this was one of Willy's entry points into the Ukraine, through Transdnestr, from many years before when the Wall was still in place. And just a few days before we arrived, Willy had been back to check his old route still worked.

We stayed the night in Bucharest and watched a film and ate at a café in the vast Stalinist square that Ceausescu had built to glorify his empty rule; empire architecture without an empire. On the following day we took another plane, this time to Chisinau, the capital of Moldova.

The whole operation Finn had planned depended on the arrival and departure times of Reiter's trucks.

If our, or Dieter's, information was correct, we knew the date of the next shipment that a truck of Reiter's would be taking out of Transdnestr. What we needed to find out was where it would cross the border into the European Union.

I was accustomed to Finn's disappearances and he left the hotel in Bucharest at nine o'clock that evening because he'd 'run out of cigarettes'. The trip to buy them eventually took him over an hour. 'They didn't have my brand anywhere,' he complained when he returned.

Maybe he had met Mikhail there, in Bucharest that night, or perhaps there was a drop arranged between them somewhere in the city.

Over supper that evening, Finn told me what little he knew of Transdnestr and I filled in the large gaps in his knowledge.

'In London, we call it the Cuba of Europe,' he said. 'But I bet it's much worse than that. Hardly anyone's even heard of the place. It's far more obscure than Cuba. Transdnestr doesn't even officially exist. Even your people in Moscow who support it don't recognise it as a country.'

The Russian puppet regime, which runs Transdnestr, issues its own currency, but it is not recognised anywhere else; it manages its own borders, even though no borders officially exist. It needs our army, which it calls a peacekeeping force, to maintain control.

'It's about the only place left that still looks like the Soviet Union did fifty years ago,' I told Finn. 'The 13th Army's there, but we actually use the place as a secret training camp for the *spetsnaz*. I've trained there myself. But its real importance – its *raison d'être* – is as a marketplace for illegal arms deals, and as our "offshore" money-laundering centre.'

Up in the bedroom after supper, Finn laid out various maps of the region on the bed. Google Earth was of little use and he had an air map and another map of Willy's from 'a hundred years ago', Finn said, which was probably the most useful. They showed a flat plain. To the east was the Ukrainian steppe, with Odessa on the Black Sea a mere seventy miles away: to the west was Moldova, to which Transdnestr actually belongs by international law, even though it is ignored by those who run the enclave and by Russia itself. Hence the Russian 'peacekeeping' force.

'The way we control the place is by giving it free oil, gas and electricity,' I told him. 'The army's there to exercise control and to ensure the necessary muscle is there if needed. Essentially the enclave's run by our own people: former Russian special forces and KGB officers. Most of them were stationed in the Baltic republics before eighty-nine, before the Wall came down. And most of them are wanted by Interpol for crimes committed before the collapse of the Soviet Union. They've all changed their names now, of course.'

'Another bad fairy tale,' Finn said. 'A make-believe state.'

'Make-believe but real. There're two thousand square miles of flat steppe and cultivated fields, from which everyone except the *nomenklatura* chisels a meagre livelihood for forty dollars a month,' I said.

'Essentially the SVR runs the economy. There are two main companies and they control everything. They're both overseen by the self-styled "president" of the enclave. The boss of the first company is a senior commander of the MVD branch of the KGB. The second company makes arms and is controlled directly from Moscow, mainly from the Russian Ministry of Defence, but it also makes arms on the side for illegal export.'

'And Reiter's trucks go to one of these two companies?' Finn asked.

'They have to. Apart from these two companies there's nothing else in the place except second-rate vegetables.'

We studied Willy's map and Finn traced with his finger a small road back westwards from the so-called 'capital', Tiraspol, a city with no airport, towards the River Dniester, which separates the enclave from Moldova.

'The river protects its borders, and Willy says the bridges are well guarded,' Finn said. 'But a river's a river. It's porous. This is where we cross.'

He pointed to a lonely stretch midway between two bridges.

'There are patrols along the banks, of course, but Willy has a good record. He's crossed here half a dozen times in the past when it was more closely guarded. He's given me an updated study of how their patrols behave, what we can expect.'

Finn and I left Chisinau at midday and took a bus to within six miles of the river on the Moldovan side of the border and began to walk. It was a beautiful afternoon, larks sang, motionless, over the cornfields, and we stopped and ate a picnic we'd bought before we left. Then we set off again in the late afternoon.

When we were little more than a mile away, we sat on a small grassy hill surrounded by fields planted with sunflowers. It was pleasantly warm; the summer temperature lulled us.

A woman working in the fields, or maybe she was a gypsy from a camp nearby, stopped and offered us some *kvint*, the local brandy. We drank and exchanged nods and smiles. I didn't want to speak Russian in front of her. We told her we were *Ingliski*. When she'd gone, we took the precaution of walking in the opposite direction we'd been heading, until nightfall. Then we retraced our steps to the river.

About two hours after darkness descended we reached the river and walked along the bank of the Dniester for another four and a half miles southwards, along the Moldovan side. Finn saw the small hut disguised with branches for the purpose of duck shooting that Willy had used in the past. Next to the hut, under a small cover of woven branches, was a skiff that was tucked into the bank and tied to a wooden post. It was just as Willy had described it to Finn. Two oars tied by a new rope were attached on the inside of the skiff.

There was no moon and in nearly complete darkness I slung my small backpack into the skiff and untied it from the post. Finn said the current would take us automatically to the centre of the river. I lay down inside and Finn lay on top of me. He pushed us off from the bank with his foot and we were away.

Willy was right. The current bounced off this side of the river and took whatever floated into the centre of the stream. Once we'd reached the centre of the river, we'd have to propel the boat, and using just one oar, over the stern like a gondola, Finn fought for several minutes to push us beyond the fast-flowing central stream to where the current moved us slowly over towards the far side. After about a mile, with us both lying in the bottom of the boat and Finn struggling with the oar, I sensed we were heading slowly towards the opposite bank to the place where we intended to land.

Here, the river curved away in the opposite direction and the current was in our favour again, taking us towards the bank. We drifted with our heads below the sides of the skiff.

On this bend in the river, there was thick woodland and, according to Willy, no observation post for half a mile on either side. We drifted until the skiff bounced along a high bank and Finn grabbed an overhanging branch. We lay in the boat and waited, listening for dogs or shouting or warning shots, and catching our breath. Slowly, Finn crawled over the side of the skiff and half swam, half pulled himself with the branch to the bank. I threw my backpack to him when he'd climbed up the bank and followed him. We collected stones to put in the skiff and sank it. Finn tied the painter on to a branch that dipped beneath the water; we'd be returning another way, but it was a good precaution if things went wrong.

We waited at the edge of the wood under cover until we could be sure no sentries were close or troop manoeuvres were taking place nearby and then crossed a dust track into some fields of vines. They provided the cover we needed to reach a road on the far side of several fields, where we could wait out of sight for a bus that came sometime after dawn.

It was a short journey by bus to the border town of Bendery. By mid-morning we had reached the town, with its statues of Lenin still in place, fifteen years after the Soviet Union collapsed. We were two British backpackers, fascinated by this frozen piece of history, on a walking holiday.

The town of Bendery lay further north back up-river from where we'd landed. The capital Tiraspol has some modern buildings paid for with mafia money, and a huge new stadium, but Bendery has very few modern structures. Both cities are museums of Soviet architecture, but thanks to its border position with Moldova, Bendery's few modern buildings are paid for from legal and illegal cross-border traffic.

The two companies we were interested in, which are effectively Transdnestr's economy, were both based in Bendery. The first place Finn wanted me to look for Reiter's trucks was located in the barbed-wire fenced yards of Pribor, Transdnestr's arms manufacturer, controlled by the shadow state company Salyut in Russia.

We knew we were at the point of no return, illegal entrants into an illegal country, one of us an SVR officer, and the other a British spy. There was nothing we could do now if things went wrong. I'd be escorted to Moscow. And Finn? I didn't know what they'd do with him, but I doubted he'd choose to be captured alive.

It was in a café, about a mile or so from the Pribor factory, that Finn and I went our different ways. His job was to find a car, mine to enter the factory. A car hire company, if one existed in Transdnestr, was out of the question and he'd have to buy a car with cash.

Both of us were nervous. I saw the rationale behind the practice at the Forest – and I'm sure at MI6 – that two people in an intimate relationship were never sent together on an assignment. It was distracting me now. Leaving Finn was uppermost in my mind when I should have been thinking about the job.

'We could have a coffee, if you like, Rabbit,' he said. 'Or we could just go home.'

I put my arms around him and whispered in his ear.

'I love you, Finn.'

He kissed me, squeezed my hand, and we both turned and walked in opposite directions.

I walked towards the depot without looking back and found a café a few hundred yards from the entrance. It was hard to clear my head. We had several rendez-vous, depending on my timing. If I found what we were looking for at Pribor, there followed one set of rules between Finn and me: we would meet in the main square at Tiraspol. If I had to go to the second factory, there would be another day's work at least. In this event, and with the increased possibility that the authorities would be alerted, we would head for the mountains to the north and wait for the hue and cry to die down before crossing back to Moldova.

I sat and drank a greyish coffee and watched the movement of trucks in and out of the depot's gates, observing the procedures followed by the drivers and military personnel who checked their papers. After half an hour I had what I needed and I left. Any strip searches of the trucks must have taken place at the border.

I took a bus back a few miles or so along the main road towards Moldova and disembarked at a stop where nobody else alighted and walked towards some trees in a copse away from the road that offered some cover.

When I knew I was unobserved, I took my SVR Colonel's uniform from my backpack and changed into it. Then I walked back to the road until I saw the truck-stop café just on my side of the river, the Transdnestr side of the border, that Willy had told us about.

There were only trucks in the car park behind the café, no other vehicles. I entered the dingy jerry-built truckstop and found more grey coffee. I took it outside to the area at the back and studied the truck plates and any logos that were visible.

There were three German trucks, all with blue tarpaulins covering their sides and obscuring anything that might identify them easily. Trucks entered and left the park every quarter of an hour or so.

I looked under the blue tarpaulins of the three German trucks but saw no insignia to say any of them were Reiter's.

I waited for nearly two hours watching trucks enter and leave. Their drivers waited aimlessly in the café, presumably for the right time to arrive at their final destination somewhere up the road into Transdnestr.

Finally I saw a German truck enter with the usual tarpaulins covering its sides, and a young man stepped out and walked across the park to the café. Again I looked behind the tarpaulin but saw no logo.

I walked into the café, had another coffee and watched the driver. He was reading a paper and sipping something from a cup that was too hot to drink. He seemed to be in his late twenties, though he looked Russian to me and it is hard with Russian men to tell how old they are; most Russian men look at least ten years older than their real age. He had an open face and he smiled at the silent woman serving coffee and asked for a *kvint*, just so he could engage her in conversation. He and I exchanged smiles across the room, too, and finally I approached the table and asked him if I could join him. He seemed unimpressed by the uniform or my papers and, as long as I only needed to show my papers to those outside the Russian security services, I knew they would carry all their old influence.

'What time are you going to the depot?' I asked him.

'To Pribor?' he said.

'Yes.'

'You know more than me, I expect,' he said, and laughed. I laughed with him and nodded in agreement.

I asked him about his life and he told me that he was scraping a living doing two or three jobs and had a wife and children in Moldova. They'd got out of Russia, and then out of Transdnestr, and he wanted to go west and make a new life for his family. I told him I could help him and asked him what he needed.

'Asylum and money,' he said and laughed again. 'That's all. I have a cousin in France, working on the roads, but we want to go to America. They say it costs ten thousand dollars to arrange a marriage there. I want to go south, to the heat. My wife, she doesn't like the Russian cold. The winters in Krasnoyarsk made her cry.'

'There are problems at the depot,' I said. 'You may know about them.'

'I don't know anything,' he laughed, and put up his hands. 'That's your business.'

'You may be able to help us.'

'And why should I trust you?' he said, smiling still. 'Because you're a woman, perhaps? But it's not just the Russian winters we want to leave. We also want to say goodbye to Russian uniforms.'

'You seem very confident,' I said, taken aback by his lack of respect, let alone fear.

'What do you want? I'll help you and maybe you'll help me too. But I don't expect it. That way, I am always happy.'

'I'm going into the depot, but I'm going in unannounced. You get me?'

'Sure.'

'How much do you want?'

'I'll trust you to do what's right.'

'You're not like a Russian.'

'I haven't lived in Russia for three years, thank God.'

'You'll have a thousand dollars. Meet me in two minutes by the truck.'

'No hurry. I don't need to be there for an hour,' he said, without reacting at all to the offer of what was so much money to him.

'Two minutes.'

'OK, OK,' he said and put his hands up again mockingly.

I went to a filthy toilet at the back of the café and took off my SVR uniform and put on some dirty overalls I had in my backpack. To my surprise and relief, the driver was by the truck when I returned.

'I'm Anatoly,' he said, and held out his hand.

I paused, then took it. 'Good to meet you, Anatoly,' I said, and he didn't ask me my name.

'I can put you in the toolbox in the truck,' he said. 'I smuggled three tiger cubs across the Ukrainian border six months ago in there. There'll just be room.'

We waited, drinking coffee and *kvint* in the truck's cab for another forty minutes or so. Finally it was time. Anatoly opened the big doors at the rear of the truck and climbed in and I followed. There was an upright metal box, like a filing cabinet and maybe five feet high, and it didn't look as if a human being would fit into it. But he cleared out some of the equipment and lashed it to the side of the truck and I stepped inside. I heard him snap the padlock and then the rear doors slammed shut.

Why did I trust him? Finn always said that most of his life was instinct and it had never let him down. I had never had so much faith in my own instincts but maybe I had never trusted anyone, except Nana and now Finn. It was easier than I thought to add one more to the list.

I listened from inside the box and felt the truck rumble along the uneven, potholed road and finally pull up at what I assumed was the checkpoint at the depot. I heard the rear doors open and felt no fear. I was committed and, of course, I had a story – not much of one but something at least – if I was betrayed. But the rear doors clanged shut again. I couldn't hear any of the exchanges, but I felt the truck move on again and drive in what seemed to be a wide circle, pushing me against the metal side of the box. It finally came to a halt.

There was a long wait. I imagined security guards lining up with guns at the ready for the box to be opened, but maybe Anatoly was waiting for the coast to clear. I was becoming more and more cramped and started to feel a panic rising. What if something happened to him? What if he was taken away? What if the truck was taken to a scrapyard? Fear of everything began to flood into my head.

Then I heard the rear doors finally clang open and a figure walking around inside. I heard the key in the padlock and suddenly the door of the toolbox was open and I was looking past Anatoly at an empty concrete space with a barbed-wire perimeter fence behind it and, beyond that, wasteground at the edge of the town.

'You've got about a minute,' Anatoly said in an unhurried way.

'The money's in there,' I said, and pointed behind me at the toolbox.

Without checking the money, he walked ahead of me and jumped out of the truck while I swung my legs over the side.

'I'll be leaving at five o'clock if you're coming with me,' he said.

'Maybe. What's your cargo?'

'Spare parts.'

I looked at him.

'Don't ask me,' he said. 'That's just what it says on the manifest.'

'For where?'

'Ultimately?' He shrugged. 'I don't know. I'm taking this load to Romania.'

'OK. You'll be here at five.'

'They'll be loading inside that warehouse over there. Wait for me to pull up the truck somewhere in this area.'

'Is there a room where the drivers go?' I asked.

'Yes. Round the back of that office building. It's a bare room with dirty calendars and dirtier coffee.' He grinned.

Finn always said that if you want something, the best thing to do was simply to ask for it. He said it worked for him nine times out of ten. I hadn't really ever believed in his straightforward method, but I was beginning to now.

There were four and a half hours until Anatoly left. It was far too long. I took a clipboard from the inside of my overalls and began to walk, head down, around the depot. There was no uniform working clothing here and I was relieved. I blended in well enough for a long-haired woman under a pair of baggy overalls.

I walked around to the back of the office block and saw the entrance to the driver's room. On the way, I saw a truck parked with its doors open and up against the open doors of a smaller warehouse. It was a smaller truck than the rest. Its tarpaulins pulled aside for loading, but the metal sides were still up. 'Reiter' was engraved on the side and there, finally, was the outsized eagle.

When I entered the room there were three drivers sitting reading newspapers and sipping from polystyrene cups. They all looked up and didn't return to their newspapers. Their expressions seemed to suggest I'd walked out of one of the pornographic calendars stuck on the walls.

I pulled my SVR identity card out of my pocket and flashed it long enough for them not to remember the name, only the message. Their attitude changed instantly from mild lechery to embarrassment.

'Which of you is the driver of the Reiter vehicle?' I said.

None of them wanted to reply, to draw attention. Eventually the man closest to me, whom I chose to fix with a stare, stumbled out the information that the driver I wanted was in the toilet.

'Show me identities,' I said. I wanted there to be some business for them all to do while I waited.

They each showed me their grubby identity cards and the Pribor pass. And then the sound of a toilet flushing announced the return of the man I was looking for. He appeared through a door at the rear of the room still doing up his flies. I could see he wasn't cowed like the others, and he stood looking at my SVR card without any reaction at all.

'Your papers,' I said.

He hesitated and then, with deliberate slowness, took them from an inside pocket. I looked at them and saw he was German.

'What do you want?' he said rudely.

'Show me your itinerary,' I demanded, ignoring his manner.

'That's confidential,' he said without moving.

'I'm a colonel in the SVR,' I reminded him.

'And I'm the King of Sweden,' he said.

I tried to imagine what Finn would have done in the same situation. I tried to conjure up the flip remark, the careless, throwaway line that helped people put their guard down, but I couldn't be Finn and I couldn't use the full force of my position. I was hamstrung by not wanting anyone outside this room to know I was in the depot.

'Yes,' I said, summoning as much of a threat as I could manage. 'It's confidential.'

'My papers,' he said.

'You'll get them back when I'm ready.'

He took a slight move towards me, just enough to show me some aggression, and I turned around until my back was to him. Then I simultaneously cracked my elbow back into his nose and kicked my left foot into his groin as his hands went up to his face. I turned back to watch the effect.

'Who the fuck do you think you are?' I said in a

quiet voice. 'I don't need help to break you in two, but I can call some up and we could really do a good job.'

He was sweating, blood poured from his nose and he could barely walk.

'Get in that chair.'

I looked at the other three men in the room and they were wide-eyed with shock.

'Find him some shithouse paper,' I said. 'And some water. Clean up that mess on his face.'

'You bitch,' the German muttered through his teeth as he sat bent over the table, clutching his balls with one hand and his face with the other.

'If you want to get back home this year, you'd better listen this time,' I said.

A look of fear crossed his face.

The other three arrived through the door at the rear carrying toilet paper and several cups of water.

'Clean up,' I said.

I took out a piece of paper and a pen and told the German to write out his itinerary. He did so, muttering at me and what he would do to me if he ever caught me in his own country. When he'd finished, I told him to get out separate papers from his pocket with the formal itinerary printed on them and then he began to look genuinely frightened. I could see he hadn't written the truth.

'Give me the printed sheet.' I placed my hand gently on his shoulder and this, I think, frightened him more than anything.

He reached inside his jacket and gave it to me. I studied the route he was to take and gave him back the itinerary.

'What's your cargo?'

'Spares.'

'Weapons spares?'

'How should I know?'

I watched him without speaking.

'You going to let me go now?' he said.

'When your papers have been checked,' I replied.

I told the others to give me their papers too.

'Don't leave until I return,' I said. 'Or your stay here will be indefinite.'

I took the only truck that wasn't being loaded or unloaded and got into the cab. I drove it slowly around to the back of the depot, away from the main entrance and where there were fewer people working, and parked it next to the fence.

Using the truck as a blind, I climbed up the side of the cab and took a look around while I was still invisible. Two men in uniform were walking towards the truck talking to each other, but they turned when they were a hundred yards away and entered a building. I climbed the remaining few feet on to the roof of the truck and, visible for only a few seconds, I jumped over the fence.

It was a fifteen-foot drop to the other side and should have been easy, but in my hurry I landed badly. I began to walk fast away from the depot, across some wasteland, the truck shielding me for the first few yards and then, when I was in the open, I dropped down into a garbage dump for cover and came out on the other side into trees and then a road where there were cars and buildings. I walked fast into the centre of the town and stripped off the overalls in an alleyway, replacing them with my SVR uniform.

There was a very old Mercedes parked near the second-best hotel in the town centre, which had the word 'Taxi' written badly on a piece of card in the front window. The driver was sitting on the pavement smoking a cigarette. With my colonel's uniform, it was a straightforward exercise to get him into the car to take me wherever I wanted to go. That's the advantage of totalitarian societies. Certain people make everyone afraid, unquestioning. Their own system can be turned against them far more easily than in a free country.

We drove to the nearest gas station and I paid to fill the car. Then I told the driver to head for the capital Tiraspol, further into Transdnestr, and to the rendezvous we'd arranged. Bendery and the border would be filled first with troops if the alarm were raised.

As I sat in the front seat, nursing what I feared was a fracture, I wondered whether any of this had been worth it; we had an itinerary of one of Reiter's trucks. But if the alarm were raised they would change it. I was relying on the German driver's unwillingness to risk admitting a mistake.

I left the taxi on the outskirts of Tiraspol. I gave the driver fifty dollars and told him there was another fifty in it for him if he went to a hotel in the city, stayed put in his room, and waited for me there for twenty-four hours. I didn't want him on the road when checkpoints began to go up, if that was what was going to happen. I knew he'd do it for ten dollars, but fifty was more than he made in three weeks.

I then doubled back in the darkness the way we'd come and put the overalls and uniform into my backpack and wore what I had worn when I arrived across the river, ordinary clothes bought in Moldova.

Finn was waiting at the rendezvous in the main square, leaning against an old grey Subaru and I climbed into the car without speaking. We drove fast to the outskirts of the town and beyond, skirting in a wide arc that took us twenty miles to the south of Bendery. We left the car on a dirt track which had a few ramshackle houses scattered along it.

'We should take the other route out,' I said.

'Fine,' he said.

He didn't ask me what had happened. He just held me for a few moments and then we walked towards the river.

There were barges plying the Dniester River down to the Black Sea. They stopped for refuelling by a wooden jetty on the bank. They carried grapes and other agricultural produce, scrap metal, plastic – anything that could get a better price in the Ukraine or further afield than here. Finn went and stood behind a wooden building that was boarded up.

I leaned on a fence and looked down at a man smoking on the deck outside the wheelhouse of a barge that looked as if it might make it the sixty or so miles to the Black Sea. He finally noticed me and made a lewd comment. I told him that for a couple of dollars I was his, whatever he liked. He didn't think for long. I descended a walkway on to the deck and brought my knee into his solar plexus. I could smell the drink on him and he began to retch with the blow to his stomach.

I dragged him into the wheelhouse, tied him up

to some pipes, gagged him, took his cap off his filthy head and put it on. Then I started the engine and climbed back up the walkway as Finn appeared. He cast off the two loose hawsers that secured the barge to the quay and pulled in the walkway. I took the wheel and we turned away into the current heading south towards the Black Sea.

It was getting dark and it would be as dark as it had been the night before when we had crossed the river. There was little river traffic at this hour, just the occasional barge pushing its way slowly up against the current in the opposite direction.

Finn took the wheel and we were making good way with the current in our favour. We had to be careful not to overshoot the target and become entangled with the guards who watched the bridge where the borders of Ukraine, Transdnestr and Moldova met.

I saw the pontoons first. They were over to the right-hand side of the river – to starboard, as Finn said – until I told him to talk in left and right. I realised how hard it was going to be to dock a 150-tonne barge against a pontoon with all the power of the current behind it.

Finn headed straight for the upright post at the far end of the pontoon and as we seemed to be about to hit it, he slammed the engine in full reverse and spun the wheel. The barge choked and struggled against the current coming up behind us and then slowly, its engine roaring, the barge hauled its stern towards the pontoon while the bow pressed against the post ahead.

I jumped on to the pontoon at the stern and Finn threw me a rope, which I secured, and then ran to the bow and did the same. The barge edged towards me, I hauled in the line and secured it again as we docked parallel to the pontoon.

Then I climbed back on to the barge and we picked up our packs.

As we stepped off on to the pontoon, we heard shouts from farther up the bank. I heard feet running along the pontoon from the shore and saw at least three men in uniform. We turned back, climbing on to the barge. Finn pointed into the fast-flowing black water and then we jumped.

The water was very cold, a start-of-summer temperature, and I gasped with shock. My leg hurt again where I'd fallen on it. I heard feet behind me on the wooden deck of the barge, then shouts. Finally there were gunshots ploughing wildly into the water. But we were travelling fast in the current and were soon fifty yards away, holding tight to each other, our packs gone.

Finn shouted at me to strike out for the shore. I saw, perhaps a mile ahead, twin searchlights that seemed to be coming from a bridge and which were shining their beams on to the river's surface. It was the frontier with the Ukraine, below which was the Black Sea. The bank we were striking out for was Moldovan territory.

'Don't let go!' Finn shouted, and we both struggled with one arm, inch by inch, working half with the current as we tried to cross it.

I felt nothing, no pain from my leg now, no fear,

I was completely controlled by adrenalin. And I knew that this loss of all feeling would last me as long as it took to get to safety.

When we were nearly at the shore and the lights on the bridge ahead seemed dangerously close, a broken branch stretched its dead wood out from the bank and we both grabbed it and held on desperately, too exhausted to do anything else. Finally we pulled ourselves along the rotting wood until we touched the muddy bottom of the river. I hauled myself out, freezing in the cool night, and Finn followed. Without talking, we ran straight into the woods that lined the bank, hoping to avoid the patrols from the right where the pontoons were, and from the left where the bridge loomed now, close up and fully lit.

The woods ran all along the Moldovan side of the river and for several hundred yards inland. It was completely dark now. There were shouts from not far off, and dogs barking in the distance, the guards trespassing now on to the Moldovan side.

And then we suddenly came out of the trees and into a field. There was some spring-sown crop that was barely visible above the earth. We ran down the edge of this field and heard the dogs in the wood behind where our pursuers had now come far into Moldovan territory. I saw a vehicle coming down a road a few hundred yards ahead. We ran faster. We were well into Moldova now, but I knew that it wouldn't make the slightest difference to our pursuers. I could still hear the dogs.

We ran on to the road before I realised in the darkness it was there. It must have curved sharply from where the vehicle was approaching and I fell with the shock of the drop in the ground. I heard a vehicle slamming on its brakes and then I must have passed out.

35

I WOKE UP IN BED. I didn't know where I was or how long I'd been here. I could remember the race across the border, the truck, but then nothing. My head throbbed.

I saw Finn sitting at a laptop on the other side of the room. We were in a hotel bedroom, I saw. The sun was pouring through open windows and net curtains puffed in a warm breeze. Finn heard my grunt and looked around.

'You're awake, Rabbit.'

'Mm.' I leaned on one elbow and he grinned at me frowning. 'It's quite bright, isn't it?' I said.

'It's a beautiful day in Chisinau.'

'Chisinau. So we made it.'

'Of course we made it.'

'You're very full of yourself,' I complained.

'It's nearly over,' he said. 'All this. We're nearly at the end of the road.'

He brought a room-service menu over to me and kissed me.

'There's a doctor who can look at your leg, if you'd like. How's your head?'

'Hurting.'

'Your leg's not broken anyway.'

'I'm fine. You choose something, will you?' I said, handing him back the menu and sinking back on to the pillows.

When I'd eaten half of what he'd ordered and pushed the tray away, he said, 'I'm going to Germany. Just for the night.'

'You're seeing Dieter?'

'Yes.'

I thought for a moment.

'Was it really worth it, what we did?' I said. 'Transdnestr?'

'What you did, yes. Every intelligence agency in Europe will have to act.'

'Will they? Act, I mean?'

'I've been waiting to give Adrian something like this for years. How can he ignore it? A high-profile German firm illegally running huge sums of illegal Russian cash across European borders.'

'I hope you're right.'

Finn kissed me again and told me he'd see me the next day.

Finn meets Dieter at a Spanish restaurant in Frankfurt at four in the afternoon, having persuaded the manager to stay open by the simple expedient of ordering two bottles of his most expensive Vega Sicilia wine.

'We're celebrating,' he tells Dieter.

The German, always less flamboyant than Finn, looks uneasy at the vast cost, and at the quantity.

'Come on, Dieter. Relax,' Finn says. 'You've found what you've been wanting to find for fifteen, eighteen years. You have the five names, you know what Exodi exists to do.'

'What difference will it make?' Dieter replies grumpily.

Going out to this chic, expensive restaurant is more than a celebration. There is something reckless about it, and Dieter, I believe, sees that too. There is an element of carelessness in Finn's exuberant mood. It's as if coming close to the end of the job for him means nothing more than beating Adrian.

It is tempting to wonder if he asked me to marry him as one last-ditch attempt to save himself; to give himself a new beginning, something to live for, a way to look beyond the job.

They eat and drink a great deal, but Dieter refuses to talk about his findings while they are in the restaurant.

They take a taxi away from the centre of the city to the Schwanheimer forest. Finn has bought a bottle of whisky, and Dieter knows a path that leads straight into the forest's heart.

'The five names in the Dresden file are linked to Exodi by the payments they receive, of course,' Dieter began. 'But it's the reason they're being bribed that shows us what the real sums, the huge sums Exodi possesses, are intended for,' he says. 'The five are all German citizens. They have many directorships in different companies, but they are all connected to just one company. This company is unique to all of them.'

'The Russians want information about the company,' Finn asks impatiently.

'Very special information, yes. The company's a defence contractor named Hammerein,' Dieter says. 'Based in Essen. It's one of Germany's biggest defence contractors. Hammerein has a large stake in Europe's defence enterprise, European Air Defence Systems.

'One of the five is on the board of the company,' Dieter continues. 'The other four – three men and a woman – are non-executive directors. One has access to a highly discreet department that is concerned with technological secrets. But this, I think, is a blind to suggest that it is technology the Russians are after. It isn't technology. It's something much bigger than that.'

Finn drinks the whisky on its own.

'And what's that, Dieter?' Finn says. 'What's the ultimate goal?'

'It's a typically complex, post-war German phenomenon,' Dieter says wearily. 'The whole system was designed so that no one could get their hands on all the vital organs of the German state as Hitler did. It goes like this. Every seven years, for one day only, the board of Hammerein resigns, including the senior government minister who sits on the board.

'On this single day, for a few hours and only

every seven years, it is possible for anyone to buy shares in the company, to buy enough shares to take control of it. This has always been just a formality, of course. The members of the board are always automatically reappointed by shareholders, and the day passes as it has done for more than fifty years, without anything changing. It is an old post-war construct in order to guard against any company from the military-industrial complex becoming a law unto itself.'

'And this special day? When is it?' Finn asks the German.

'In just over eight months' time.'

'And if Exodi is paying these employees, what is it buying? Not just the date?'

'The date is important. No doubt the date and this curious window of opportunity itself were unknown to the Russians. Nobody outside the board and a few key shareholders really know it. So, yes, the Russians bought that. But they're also buying the strategy. They plan to buy one of Europe's biggest defence companies on the one day it can be bought. They're buying the expertise to buy enough shares during the course of twenty-four hours before the government can react. Six billion dollars' worth. That would take inside knowledge. These board directors would be key to that. They can line up which shareholders will sell and which won't.

'So. To pursue the end of taking over one of Europe's three key defence companies, Exodi is paying large sums of money into Merrill Lynch in Paris and into Goldman Sachs in New York. These brokers will be the ones actually buying the shares, but of course in a client name set up for the purpose, which is impossible to trace in so short a time. It is a hit of enormous proportions.'

Whether it's because of the whisky on top of the wine, or because of the incredible prospect of Russia buying one-third of Europe's air defence industry, Finn doesn't seem to grasp what Dieter is saying.

'Exodi are trying to buy . . . ?' he says.

'The Russians are aiming to buy the European air defence programme,' Dieter replies. 'That's Hammerein's particular speciality. Effectively buy it, with Germany's third, anyway.'

'Christ. Dear, beautiful Mikhail . . .' Finn mutters.

'Mikhail?'

Finn nods vaguely and Dieter doesn't pursue it.

'But that's not the end of it,' Dieter says. 'Buying control of Hammerein you would think would be enough, even for the Russians. But Exodi has many more billions at its disposal than what is needed to buy just Hammerein. Buying one of Europe's main defence contractors is, incredibly, only the tip of the iceberg, Finn. The Russian strategy is broader than that and Europe's defence industry is just the beginning. The two hundred and fifty company names in the Dresden file? They are all potential targets. The Kremlin intends to buy whatever it needs in Europe to give it control over Europe. Principally, that's energy companies, pipelines – they have the product, the oil and gas themselves – but the Plan is to ensure that Western European governments will answer to the Kremlin for all their energy needs by 2025. They'll own the supply and control the demand. In a decade or so, the Ministry of Defence in Moscow would like to control the way the European Union works, through its very bloodstream.'

'And Europe's defence industry is just another company for them? Christ.'

To Finn, this is at last a vindication of everything he's said and worked to achieve for over six years. It's what he lost his job for, what the boy in Luxembourg died for, it's his revenge on Adrian, the other bad father in Finn's life. It's also the end. It's the way he's chosen that leads in his imagination to me – to us – for good. This is close to all he needs and he's barely listening to Dieter.

'The price of oil has given the Russians the thing they've always lacked; a very large chunk of the world's riches.'

And then Finn seems to snap out of whatever dream line he's been following.

'So Exodi is a secret fund that amasses Russian government money. It adds into this pot the billions from drug and arms sales, brought over the old Soviet borders in Reiter's trucks. Some powerful people in Luxembourg protect Exodi's illegal account and other powerful people in Germany protect Reiter, Otto Roth's brother. The five names are there to provide information to buy just one company – a huge company that has close to a controlling interest in Europe's defence industry.' Finn pauses. 'So who else are the Russians paying? What's next? What other industrial giant do they have in their sights?'

'Look at the list of the companies in the Dresden file,' Dieter says. 'That is the Russians' list.'

'I can go to Adrian with this,' Finn says. He looks at Dieter. 'And you'll have to tell your bosses at the BND.'

'Former bosses,' Dieter corrects him. 'No.'

'What do you mean? Why not? It's your government that's best placed to stop what's happening with Hammerein. You have to tell them.'

Dieter looks off into the darkness.

'We're close to the truth, Finn.'

'We have the truth,' Finn protests.

'Why don't we leave it at that?' the German replies quietly. 'Why bang our heads against a wall trying to get others to believe it, when it's evident that they know and that they're ignoring it? For whatever reason, I don't know, but they are ignoring it. You know what happened with Schmidtke, what already happened to me fifteen years ago. The whole operation was closed down. Do the BND want to hear this, do you think? Nothing's changed since then. Nothing. And that, you'll find, is true with London too. Our governments are either walking blindfold into this, or they know, and are conniving in it for some short-term gain in terms of Russian energy supplies, for access to Russian oil and gas. Finn, our countries don't want to upset the status quo with inconvenient facts.'

'Then what?' Finn says.

'Tell me about Liechtenstein.'

Finn shows Dieter the photographs from the farmhouse in the mountains and Dieter leans over the pictures to identify the figures.

And Dieter knows all the faces in the pictures.

I can feel Finn's childish triumph at this. He has

found in these pictures what Dieter has been looking for for fifteen years, what the German was close to finding when his investigation of Schmidtke was terminated by the BND. He has found a picture of one of Roth's brothers, who all along was at the head of one of Germany's great firms.

'With these pictures and your information, Dieter, the circle is closed,' Finn says.

'Yes,' Dieter says when he has struggled to put his reading glasses on and looks at the photographs a second time. He points at the German politician. 'Finn, you think I can take these pictures to the BND along with what we know about Hammerein and Exodi? The chances I would live – that either of us would live – are nil. The BND is not some organisation independent of political control. If this politician is involved, as he obviously is, who else knows? Who in our intelligence services, in government . . . ? This politician isn't acting in some vacuum.'

'It's really so bad?'

'Of course it is. All I know is how much was covered up fifteen years ago. I don't think anything's changed, do you? The German government is locking itself into dependency on Russian energy every day'.

'Then get a message to the company. To Hammerein itself. Give them the evidence.'

'Yes. I can do that. Anonymously. But will they believe an anonymous contact?'

'With this evidence, yes. Or take them to a newspaper.'

'That too. It's possible.'

When they walk back along the path through

the forest, Finn is heady from the approaching end, and I guess from the fuel of the drink. And Dieter is worried. Finn is not listening to anyone any more.

That night in his hotel room, Finn writes in scrawled biro: 'Exodi is the vehicle to buy what the Russians lost in 1989. Exodi overturns seventy years of their failed communist experiment, since the day Lenin arrived in Petersburg. And Exodi achieves what the occupation of half of Europe failed to achieve.'

36

FINN'S EXCITEMENT is so naive. The almost boyish enthusiasm he exhibits in the lead-up to the final meeting with Adrian is doomed to disappointment.

But he writes about the meeting in two sections: the first section he wrote before the two of them met and is exuberantly optimistic; the second section he wrote after the meeting, about the meeting itself, and I can feel his anger and despondency leaping out of the pages. I can't bear to record now what his earlier mood was, it's too painful to see the contrast. But this is how he tells the encounter with Adrian, between 12.45 and 2.35 on a Monday in June 2006.

'It's the same scene at Boodles, with the same crew braying about whatever it is today that they think they know better than anyone else. This time it's the French tennis championships at the Roland Garros, and the way they talk about the players you'd think they were all ex-Wimbledon champions instead of desk-bound, money-bound public schoolboys who, if you put them in a car park in the Gorbals without a set of car keys, would be begging for mercy to the first bag lady who walked by. When you scratch the veneer you find there's just more veneer underneath.

'In this closed world, uncertainty or change of any kind is unknown, anathema, disgusting even. They have inherited the progressive empowerment of generations of privilege; a superiority that is by now in their DNA.'

Adrian is waiting for Finn by the door of the club, as if afraid he might talk to anyone without him, out of his earshot. He takes Finn's arms in his big red hands and gives him a broad smile from his rubicund face. But Finn sees that his eyes are dead.

'Finn, I'm so glad you got in touch. Where the fuck have you been?'

But Finn is too full of his own impending victory over Adrian to see the menace behind Adrian's usual crude bonhomie.

'Can we talk in private?' he says.

'Don't you worry about that, old boy. We have a private room. I thought we should. I guessed. What have you brought me in that case? The head of Vladimir Putin?' Adrian lets out a big, unnatural laugh that makes him sound like a clown who, tired of entertaining children, decides to devour them instead.

'Come on, we're drinking first. Business later. Over lunch.'

And once again, just like the last time, Adrian takes Finn by the arm and guides him through this club Finn knows so well, as if he's making a gentle citizen's arrest, so as not to alarm the other lunchers, but it will turn into a brutal assault if Finn so much as twitches.

And there they are, the herd, all leaping over each other's sentences to trump the last speaker with some dreadful witticism about the awful state of this tennis player's forehand, or the magnificently revealing skirt length of that one. And Adrian comes in amongst them like a priest leading a sacrificial lamb to the slaughter.

'Finn . . . Philip, Richard, Andrew, Peregrine . . .' On and on, the introductions keep reeling out like some lost fishing line, and Finn feels their disinterested eyes wash over him. 'You pretty much know everyone, don't you?' Adrian says chummily, but with his eyes expressionless, and as cold as a fish on a slab. 'And you all know Finn. My best boy. My ex-best boy, I should say.' And now Adrian's eyes have changed to the narrow, pitiless look that bores into people. 'Or should I say my best ex-boy?' he says.

But Finn doesn't flinch or look away, because he knows he's got him this time. He knows he has the goods and Adrian can't squirm out of it. Not this time.

And so they all drink and shout and drink again, and the starched-white-jacketed barman, from Romania or Mexico or wherever they got him, keeps pouring the drinks like an automaton.

And to Finn, this herd is far more menacing than the herds that normally afright the citizens of England: the gangs of immigrants that hang around on street corners in Dover and Ramsgate, or the hooded yobs in the inner cities.

'I wonder . . .', Finn is thinking. 'If I feel as if I'm on another planet in here, what's it like for him, the barman, Marco or Rudi or Chico or whatever his name is? What's it like to be utterly ignored, to be treated merely as a drinks dispenser? Or does he just shut down until he gets home from all this money and jazz and glitz and privilege to his wife and kid and his semi-squat in Balham?

'Suddenly I know why I'm doing what I'm doing; for people like him, the guy pouring the drinks. It's that simple.'

And then he catches himself in this thought and remembers what his aunt once told him as he came home from some anti-missile march and was railing against some American president when he was still a student at Cambridge.

'Why don't you become the peace you're trying to create?' she had asked him.

But Finn didn't listen then and he's not listening now.

'Moscow Mules, that was it,' someone barks, and Finn realises they're looking at him. 'You were drinking something called a Moscow Mule, weren't you? Bloody hell.'

'Yes, that's right,' Finn replies, and gets a look from Adrian who notes the sneer in his tone of voice.

'We'll go in now, I think,' Adrian says, far earlier than usual and with the diplomatic nicety of a scalping hatchet. 'Drink up. We'll get something special at the table.'

So they down their glasses of chilled Chablis and

put them back on to the bar and the condensation runs down the sides over the wooden counter.

They enter the dining room, with its cute aproned Eastern European waitresses and, sure enough, Adrian has a private room on the far side, making sure they can talk openly – or that he can, at any rate. And the last ten years of Finn's working life, he now realises, have been building to this moment, to wipe the self-satisfied smirk off Adrian's face. Is that what it's all been about? Has it all been for this?

'Why don't you become the peace you're trying to create?' Finn says to himself, but it doesn't seem to be working in here. It's like trying to say the Lord's Prayer at a Motorhead concert.

'We'll have the Corton Charlemagne,' Adrian says to the non-English-speaking waitress who enters the room as they sit down, and Adrian prods the menu angrily until she can connect it with the wine he's prodding. 'We'll have the potted shrimps and the steak and kidney pud . . . that's steak and kidney pudding. Got it? Twice. For both of us, in other words.'

This inelegant removal of choice in what Finn eats is vintage Adrian. You're mine, it says. You're in my club, sitting at my table, drinking my wine, and you can reconfigure the word 'guest' any way you like, but to me it means you're here at my bidding. Got it?

Maybe, it occurs to Finn, Adrian no longer even likes human beings. Maybe he never did and that's the problem. They get in the way. Certainly if they're not part of the herd, of which he's the bull elephant.

'Give me what you've got,' he snaps at Finn, without any preliminary. There are no first names any more, no 'Come-down-for-the-weekend-and-Pen-would-love-to-see-you' preamble.

Finn withdraws a few sheets of folded A4 from the briefcase and puts them in front of him.

'Read that, Adrian.'

Adrian puts on his half-moon spectacles and angrily picks up the papers and reads them through fast, as if he's checking for spelling errors. Without putting the papers down, he looks over the half-moons.

'Well, you have been a busy boy, haven't you?'

Finn doesn't reply.

'What's it all mean, d'you think?'

'You know damn well what it means, Adrian.'

For a moment they stare each other out and then Adrian pretends to look back at the papers.

'It's everything, Adrian,' Finn says. 'Names, companies, banks, secret accounts, Roth's brother and the transportation of laundered money and arms. It's Reiter's, or Roth's, itineraries and where his trucks can be stopped by you and our German friends, and at which borders. It's a panorama of the corrupt and the corrupted. In Europe, Adrian, the Europe you love to hate. Well, here it is, on a plate for you. It's the whole scheme. The Plan. It's what the KGB does these days and what I've been saying to you for over five years. This is just a peek behind the curtain. I have a list here . . .' – Finn takes out another piece of paper with dozens of the biggest company names in Europe written on it – 'this demonstrates the sheer scale of what's going on. You can ignore it, Adrian, but if you do, how will you call yourself a patriot again? How will you be able to say with pride that you work for Her Majesty's government if you're prepared to look the other way while it's being sold down the river?'

This, as Finn anticipates, almost draws Adrian's physical wrath across the table, but Finn watches as the redness drains from his face and he keeps himself under control.

'And we haven't even had the first course yet,' Adrian murmurs.

'What are you going to do about it, Adrian? Pretend it doesn't exist? Just like you did with "Mikhail"?'

The waitress arrives with two pots of shrimps and goes to fetch the wine on Adrian's orders.

'Those buffoons in there,' Finn says, waving in the direction of the bar, 'your friends, Adrian, they seriously believe that the City of London is on the march to Russia, that the wealth of our old enemy is up for grabs, that Russia is like Africa or something. They can walk all over it, that's what they think, isn't it? They're going to be cut to pieces, Adrian. Surely you can see that with that big brain of yours. There's nothing in Russia of any importance that isn't controlled by the Kremlin and all the KGB spooks who inhabit the bloody place. And meanwhile the buffoons are being outflanked by the Russians. There's enough bent and laundered cash coming round behind them to buy their companies out and to snap up all their houses in the country and all their kids' places at Eton, I dare say. What are you going to do about it?'

Adrian gorges half the pot of shrimps in one go and the wine arrives. When he's swallowed his mouthful of shrimp, wiped his lips, tasted the wine and pronounced it 'excellent', he leans with one elbow on the table and gives Finn his special paramilitary murderer's look.

'You poor fucking fool,' he says. 'Drink up. This may be your last meal. How dare you let me invite you here, you little shit.'

'Do nothing. That's the new policy, is it? You and the Prime Minister. What's in it for you, Adrian? They going to make you chief?'

But Adrian is coldly calm now and Finn feels the ground sliding under his feet.

'We're going to drink this and then we're leaving,' Adrian says. 'I've got someone for you to meet. Should be very interesting. Might blow the lid off your fabulous ignorance. I'll bring forward the meeting.'

Adrian picks up the bottle and sloshes the wine glasses dangerously full and presses a button for a waitress.

'Get us the bill,' he says.

'But you haven't finished—'

'Get us the bloody bill, woman.'

There's a human being getting in Adrian's way again and now he's just the kind of brute you can find in any backstreet anywhere, but he's wearing a well-cut suit.

She begins to clear away the empty plates and Adrian almost shouts, 'Get it now, for Christ's sake!'

She flees from the room and Adrian drains his glass like some medieval monarch in a fifties movie. And then he fills his glass again and holds out the bottle towards Finn, but Finn hasn't touched his first glass yet.

'You're in a wasteful mood,' Adrian says. 'First you

waste your life and then, much more importantly, in my opinion, you waste this very decent wine. Never mind, I'll be glad to finish it alone.'

And he does just that.

They leave Boodles after Adrian has made a long, staccato phone call on his mobile phone from the entrance to the club. It has started to drizzle outside, just in time for Wimbledon, Adrian says cheerily to a passing member.

A doorman takes them down the steps carrying an umbrella, which Adrian, as the most formidable party, gets most of the benefit from, and they step into Adrian's car which draws up as soon as the surprised driver sees him waving his arms like a madman from the top of the steps.

There isn't far to drive, they could have walked, really; up to Piccadilly and past the Ritz to the entrance to Green Park underground station. The drizzle has set in as Adrian's driver opens the door for him, umbrella at the ready, and Finn slides across the seat and out on to the pavement.

The two of them enter Green Park and Finn sees the deckchairs that have been out for summer lunchtimes the day before are now packed and stored away in their wooden boxes.

There is the mist of light rain up in the summer greenness of the trees' leaves and Adrian's umbrella bounces against the umbrella of another who's travelling with equal purpose and equal lack of care. Adrian makes no attempt to offer Finn any shelter underneath it.

They take a right fork along another path and walk at a diagonal across the park towards the walls of Buckingham Palace and Adrian's Queen. Adrian is angry. He's angry that he ever hired Finn in the first place, angry that he doesn't control Finn, angry that Finn might even end up damaging his credibility. He's angry like those Russians, standing on the podium for the great march past of Soviet military might. He's angry that, no matter how much effort he puts in, how red his face gets, he cannot control everything. Human beings keep getting in the way. He's angry that he doesn't have a barren depeopled world to control.

They head towards the trees in the centre of the park. But as they close on a park bench away from the paths that criss-cross the area, Finn sees there's a man sitting there, with his back to them. He's wearing a kind of pork-pie hat and a black shapeless coat and Finn seems to recognise his back.

They come around to the front of the bench and Finn sees this is where they're stopping, to meet this man. And then Finn sees it is Lev.

'Hello, Finn,' Lev says, without moving, and ignoring Adrian.

'Lev,' Finn says.

Finn doesn't know whether to be disappointed that Lev has been talking to Adrian, even though it was inevitable.

'Tell him,' Adrian says.

Finn sits down next to Lev and Adrian stands in front, a little too close, and looks angry while the rain drips off the edges of his umbrella on to Finn's head.

'Are they offering me more money?' he asks Lev in an attempt at light-heartedness.

'No, I'm afraid not.'

'Ten million not enough?' Adrian snaps. 'More than I'll earn in a bloody lifetime, you wanker.'

'Well, it was only dollars, Adrian,' Finn says, and sees that Adrian would now really like to have him on his own, in a soundproofed room.

'I can tell you who's behind the offer, the bribe, the payment – call it what you like,' Lev says. 'It's not the Russians, not anyone from Russia, either.'

'Oh?'

'The offer comes from a bank,' Lev says, and he gives Finn the name of the bank and Finn's lost for a second in confusion. 'But this bank represents a whole consortium of banks,' Lev continues. 'All of them, like this one, are American. You were being offered the money by American banks to stop your investigation, not by the Russians.'

Finn notices the past tense.

'These all-American banks have deposits of Russian cash, some legal, most not, which amount to hundreds of billions of dollars. If the origins of this cash are brought into doubt, if the cash is shown to be laundered or illegal in some way, there will be big turmoil, Finn. The flies on Wall Street say that, if these deposits are shown to be of questionable legality, it could bring the whole edifice tumbling down. They talk of financial meltdown, the sums are so great. So the legality of this money cannot be questioned.'

'Get it?' Adrian says to Finn. 'The financial system of America tumbling down.'

'But what about Europe?' Finn asks Adrian. 'Isn't that where we live?'

'You're even more of a fucking fool than I thought,' Adrian says.

Lev puts his hand on Finn's knee.

'Listen, Finn. America is the hope, the future, for your country and for mine. It always has been and maybe always will be. Not Europe. Europe is all but lost. You know that from your investigations in Germany. Europe is riddled with collaborators, Europe's assets are being handed over to the Russians bit by bit. In Europe they'll be able to hold off the KGB for a while, but not for long. There's not the will. America is the only power strong enough, and willing enough, to stand up to the Kremlin. That's why we have to look to the Americans, not Europe. It's just about money, Finn, that's all. It's about the power of money and we can be glad that the Americans have the sense not just to see that, but to act on it. They hold the Russian loot in America, that's good. It's got to go somewhere, and we're better off that it's there. But if you or anyone tries to tamper with that, the flies are right. It will bring down the system, there's too much money involved. Your ten-million-dollar offer represents less than petty cash compared to the cash deposits we're talking about, deposits whose origins, if brought into question, can bring down the whole house. You don't want that, do you, any more than me or Adrian or our countries do?'

'It's the kind of thinking that makes a lot of sense when there are no human beings in the way,' Finn answers him. 'Let the KGB make mincemeat of the European economy and institutions, and in the process build up a richer, more powerful America.

'The Cold War's back on, that should please

Adrian,' he says, looking at Adrian. 'But this time the front line is really going to crumble, right? Europe doesn't matter any longer. Why didn't you tell me?' Finn says facetiously to Adrian.

But Adrian ignores Finn and walks to a nearby tree and makes a phone call. When he comes back, he looks at Finn.

'It only remains for me to decide what's to be done with you,' he says, as if he's the headmaster talking to a prep school boy who's posted a turd through his letter box. And then he stares back at Finn in his victory. 'I don't know if we can afford to have you wandering about any more. Not with all this shit you've managed to vomit up. Perhaps you'll turn out to be insane,' he says mysteriously, as if insane is a colour he's considering for his new bathroom. 'That would keep you quiet.' And now Adrian's warming to his happy thoughts of revenge. 'And then there's your girl, isn't there. Your wife, isn't she? The Russian hooker. I bet she gives good head in uniform. That what you like about her, is it?'

He looks at Finn, hoping he might lunge at him, so he can chop him down with some specialist move, and then kick him half to death. But Finn remains calm.

'Yes,' Adrian says nastily. 'We can always fit her up so it looks like she's ratted on her own people. They'll really give her a good time at the Forest, I should think. There won't be much of her left to fuck, that's for sure.'

Then he turns away without another word and walks back on to the path and up through the park to his waiting car. Lev and Finn watch in silence as he blurs into the rain.

37

IT IS JUST MORE THAN a week later. Finn and I are at Willy the Hungarian's little ramshackle wooden empire on the beach near Marseilles. Willy is absent for a reason I don't know. But we expect him any day now.

Willy drove Finn and me out to the cabin with its restaurant at the beach on a beautiful blue day. He hid us in the back of a van. Anyone watching would think that it was just a maintenance man going down there to do some winter repair work. He even put a ladder on the roof of the van to complete the fiction. But there was nobody about in the bleak, remote place Willy had carved out for himself, nobody to see who turned on or off the three-mile track to the beach. And if you looked along the track, across the saltpans from the road, all you saw were dunes, and even then only if the day was clear enough. The huts were always hidden.

Willy had brought books and told us there was wood in a store for unseasonably cold evenings and that, bearing in mind that this store would run out quickly, we'd better start collecting driftwood right from the start. There was plenty of it on the beach, he said, from last year's violent Mediterranean storms that scoop up debris from the land or sweep it from the decks of ships.

Finn and I enjoyed a week of being alone without the hippies who had not yet returned from wintering in India.

'For Adrian,' Finn explained one night as we sat by a fire on the beach, 'destroying me would be like destroying part of himself. He hates me, don't get me wrong, Rabbit; he loathes everything there is about me. But I'm the part of himself that he hates. Even if he's not conscious of it himself. He won't kill a part of himself.'

Finn pokes the embers of the fire, which has just cooked our supper. I hope Finn's instincts about other people are serving him well. And I wish that he would apply the same acute perceptions to himself.

'But you're not so protected, Anna,' he continues and stares into the red embers. 'He'd happily hurt you to hurt me, and leave himself untouched in the process. I know that. That's why you're in greater danger than I am, at least from Adrian. It's you we have to protect right now.'

'You really think you're safe?' I say. 'After what Adrian said?'

'I'm safe only from Adrian.'

Since the meeting with Adrian, there's been no contact. In the meantime, Finn put it out to the Team that he had given up his pursuit. It was over, he told them, and the team was broken up. Thank you, another time perhaps. He met a few of the team, informed others by e-mail. He wanted it known that he'd reached the end, whether it convinced anyone any more, or not.

We had silently slipped out of the country on the night after his lunch with Adrian. We left, thanks to one of Finn's French friends who came over in a sailing boat with no motor and gave me just about the worst ten hours of my life. The seas were heavy, and I thought we would either sink or I would simply die of sea-sickness. But Finn and his bearded French fisherman buddy thought it was great fun.

Abduction or worse was a real fear. At around this time, a retired British colonel was shot and killed in what was an unmistakable assassination that took place in a small English village in Buckinghamshire. He happened to share the same name as the judge who had approved the application for asylum in Britain of Putin's great enemy, Boris Berezovsky, years before. The judge lived in the same street. It was a case of mistaken identity, and though the colonel's death was reported only in one Scottish newspaper, with a single column inch, this to Finn and me was ample evidence that Russian hit squads were back on the streets of Britain.

And then the dissident Russian spy Alexander Litvinenko was poisoned in broad daylight in a London hotel, and whoever in Britain had tried to cover up the colonel's death couldn't keep this one out of the press. We knew that both of us were probably on a hit list somewhere in the Forest, where I've seen them use photographs of their targets for shooting practice.

By the end of the winter, Finn said he'd spoken to Dieter and that Dieter had contacted the German company Hammerein in an anonymous letter and had received information that they were putting their defences in place.

And then one day Willy turns up out of the blue and opens all the shutters in the restaurant and sweeps the sand away that has piled up against the doors in the course of winter storms. A posse of Polish women arrives and cleans up the rooms in the other huts and washes the cheap bedlinen.

Finn and I have lost weight, Willy tells us, but now he is doing the fishing things will be better.

Soon Willy's summer guests, the hippies, arrive like migrating birds, in twos and threes. They come loaded with huge stripy plastic bags full of Indian clothes and trinkets, which they will sell at various hippy markets along the coast during the summer, and which keeps them in hash and whisky. Willy treats them like his naughty children and isn't above cuffing them round the head if they get out of hand. Finn says Willy's place is like a holiday home for dysfunctional kids, and that he feels right at home here.

Willy and Finn spend hours drinking beers and

talking, while I start reading from the suitcase of new books that Willy has brought with him.

And then, on the third morning after Willy arrived, I realise that I am pregnant.

I don't say anything for a few days. But I go into the local town with Willy and buy a kit to test myself. We stop at a café further up the street and I take the opportunity to do the test. It is positive, and I come out of the toilet at the back of the café clutching my bag of cosmetics to fool Willy, but the look in his eyes tells me I haven't succeeded. He says nothing and neither do I. But when we get back to the beach and have lunch, Finn and I walk a mile or so along the edge of the sea and I tell him.

There is no hesitation, he literally jumps into the air with joy. If he had four legs, all of them would have left the ground. But I still ask him what he thinks we should do.

'What do you mean?' he says, and his joyful expression crashes for a moment. 'Of course we want a baby,' he says, then corrects himself. 'I mean, don't you, Anna?'

'I've never wanted to have children,' I say. 'Not before.'

'Well, of course not before, no. It would have been mad,' he says, slightly madly. 'But we're free now. We have no jobs, no money, no home, no prospects and pretty much nothing at all. It's the perfect moment.'

I laugh and then we can't stop laughing.

A baby. I can hardly get the word out of my mouth.

Finn takes me by the shoulders.

'Do you honestly think, darling, that you and I, of all people, can't find a way to provide for something that eats mashed apples and is less than a foot long?'

'That's not how people normally see a baby,' I reply.

'Well, OK, no,' he says. 'Most people I know put their kids down for some school ten years before they're born, they create Disneyland on one floor of a large house, then they sign it up for piano lessons, karate classes, swimming diplomas, extra maths, post-birth therapy, nannies and a nutrition expert. Other people seem capable of just having babies.'

'Maybe there's something in between,' I say.

'There must be.'

'We aren't safe, Finn.'

'We'll make ourselves safe.'

'We need to think about this carefully,' I say, and then I hug him. 'I'm glad you're so happy. I really am. Thank you.'

'Aren't you?' he says.

'I don't know.'

'You've always been a slow developer,' he says.

We have supper that evening with Willy and Finn tells him. Willy says that he'd like to have a baby too, by which he means in his environment, I think, rather than literally.

Willy says, 'He or she has a mother and a father and I'll be his or her grandfather and I have cousins who'll be cousins. How do you help a child to be happy, Anna? That's all you need to think about, believe me. The rest will come.'

I think to myself that there is something about having two men, Willy and Finn, that makes the whole idea seem more palatable.

Later, back at the hut, Finn explains that it is an opportunity; that here we are being given this blessing, which also gives us the chance to do for our child what we missed ourselves as children. He says we would be the best parents, precisely because our own childhoods have been a mess.

'We're just the sort of people who should have children,' he says. 'We know what not to do.'

'Either that, or we'll end up doing what was done to us,' I counter. 'That's pretty common.'

'How can you say that!' he says, genuinely aghast. 'How could we behave in the way our parents behaved?'

'Isn't that what all parents say?'

'I will love this child, Anna, in all the ways I wanted love,' he says and puts his hand on my stomach.

I want to believe him and I decide to believe him then. Totally. We hold on to each other on this cold April night, with the burner spluttering in the background, and I feel that nothing can ever stand in the way of such happiness.

We stayed at the beach until the hippies departed again and winter set in. Unusually, Willy stayed after the end of summer and into the beginning of winter.

One day in November, Finn announced that he was going away for a few days.

'Where?' I asked him, unable to keep the fear out of my voice.

'I have to see Frank. There are one or two things I still need to tie up,' he said, so lightly that it hangs in the air between us. 'Loose ends, that's all.'

'You want me to come?'

'Of course, come, yes.'

He said it genuinely. And so I declined, content that it was something he'd like me to have done.

On the night before he left, Willy had the cook whom he'd retained after the end of the season make us a special dinner.

Afterwards, Willy said goodnight, and Finn and I walked up the beach. He was very calm, I remember, serene even. I couldn't help noticing that. He was always like this before taking a risk.

But I took it to be the wine and us, that I was pregnant, and that we were beginning a new life. When we went back to the hut, we hardly slept all night. Finn said he didn't want to go. I said nothing. But he left anyway.

He left around six-thirty in the morning, and Willy gave him a lift, hidden in the back of the van, to the railway station in Aix-en-Provence.

38

FINN SAID HE WOULD CALL twice a day until he returned. We waited, Willy and I, for three days without a word from him. On the third day, we were sitting in the restaurant, looking out to sea, and our conversation had dried up. Everything that could have been said about Finn had been said. We'd exhausted every possible explanation for his disappearence and an air of panic enveloped me.

Finally, sighing, Willy got up from the table and went into his hut. After a while he emerged with an envelope and gave it to me.

'Finn asked me to give you this,' he said. 'But only in an emergency.'

I seized the envelope out of his hand, angry that it had taken him so long. Inside was a letter giving me directions, and a key, to the pink house.

* * *

So here I am, in the pink house, having reached the end of Finn's handwritten books and sitting down again in the cellar with its smoky oil burner and its secrets that nobody wanted. I've found nothing that tells me where he is now or why he disappeared. These secrets, they are what my life has become. They are so useless.

I am counting up the times when I believed I could have turned Finn away from his course and in my head I'm back in Moscow, at the Baltschug Hotel, hearing Finn say, 'Come with me, Anna. I want you to come with me.' And me replying, 'Ask me something else.'

But finally I came to him, I let go of the past, and we had an agreement; I'd changed, I'd made the leap, and I thought he'd done so too. But it seems he'd gone back, that he was unable to let it all go. And now he's disappeared.

Willy also had his instructions from Finn, it seemed. He'd gone to Paris. There, through some channel of his working life, whether past or present I don't know, Willy contacted an officer inside the French intelligence service, the DGSE.

It was established that Finn had gone to Luxembourg. On the first night Finn had arranged to call me, Willy found that an Englishman answering to Finn's description stayed at the Bretonnerie Hotel, in the Marais district of Paris. There was an 'incident' – beyond that, the French intelligence officer wouldn't expand. The hotel was sealed off by the security services and remained so. The Englishman's room was examined down to every last thread in its carpet. Men in protective suits tested the bedsheets and pillow cases, the curtains, the shower-head over the bath, the bottles in the mini-bar – everything. Again, there was no explanation for this that Willy could find. Finn was nowhere to be found.

And that was just last night, when I spoke to Willy from a call box in Tegernsee.

I'm wondering how much time I've got left, who else will find the pink house, and when will they find it. I gather up Finn's books and I eventually find the microfiches that Dieter gave Finn six years before. They are hidden behind a stone in the wall of the cellar. I put everything into a bag I've brought, turn off the oil heater for the last time, and ascend the wooden ladder stairs to the sitting room. I throw the bag down on the floor and close up the metal doors, pull the false wall with its false fireplace across the front of the metal doors and rearrange some ornaments on its mantelpiece that have fallen over in the movement.

I have Finn's record, and I have the microfiches that Dieter told Finn people would kill for.

I feel a sense of urgency now. I have to get out of here. For someone will find the pink house soon, either from Finn's or from my side, of that I'm certain. Whichever side it will be, the result will be the same; the evidence will be destroyed and anyone in possession of the evidence will be destroyed with it.

444 ★ ALEX DRYDEN

I walk quickly upstairs and throw the few belongings from the bedroom I'd brought with me from the beach hut into another smaller bag. I dust the surfaces of the room, the banisters of the staircase as I walk back downstairs, all the door handles, the fireplace, the kettle and the cup, the whisky bottle and the glass. I dust everything I've touched for prints and then I am ready to leave. And at that point, when there's nothing left to do to distract me from myself, I break down and cry. Finn has gone.

And as I'm crying, I suddenly feel a fear, a presence. There is something in the house. Is it too late? Have they come? I break off from my tears and look around, the hairs on the back of my neck standing up. And when I half turn, over to my right and standing in the middle of the doorway to the kitchen, I see there is a man.

I look all around the room in total shock, then through the window, looking for the blue police lights or men surrounding the house, German backup for their Russian friends. But there is nobody, just this man. I'm frozen in the chair, I'm waiting to die. But the man doesn't move.

'I'm pregnant,' I say. 'I'm pregnant with Finn's child.' It's as if I've given up. As if this will be a defence against them. To myself I sound completely lost.

'I know,' the man says, but he doesn't move towards me, or take his eyes away.

I look at him more closely. He knows? He is a Russian. Yes, I'm sure he is a Russian. He's smartly dressed, he has an easy air of wealth. His hair is black like mine and is thick and short and parted like some thirties movie star's. He has a tanned face. His hands are manicured, his skin is polished and clean, the skin of a non-smoker, I think. Will he kill me with those manicured hands? I have no strength at all. But if I can find my strength, I know I can kill this man.

'You know me, Anna,' he says, 'and you don't know me.'

I look at him harder, but it isn't true, I don't know this man.

'I'm Mikhail,' he says.

I sit in shock, speechless.

He walks slowly, unthreateningly, across the room, keeping well clear of the space I'm occupying and sits in a chair opposite me across from a low table. He reaches into the side pockets of his jacket and pulls out two plastic cups, a yellow one and a blue one, the type that pack neatly into a picnic basket. He puts them on the table and then reaches inside his jacket and pulls out a silver flask. He unscrews the top of the flask and pours a generous measure for me.

'A favourite,' Mikhail says. 'Basilica vodka from Georgia.'

'I'm pregnant,' I say again. It sounds so foolish, and I wipe my face and feel my strength returning.

Mikhail waits. Then he pours two drinks to show that we are sharing whatever he's brought in the flask. He seems to sense my reluctance and drinks from my cup too. Then he raises his own cup between us.

'To your child, then,' he says.

I pick up my cup and we toast his children and my unborn child and all children.

He refills the cups and lifts his again for another toast.

'And to Finn,' he says. 'Himself, in some ways, a beautiful child.'

And I hear myself repeat it. To Finn. And I drink to the bottom of the cup and cry inside.

A toast is the Georgian way of expressing more than a thousand words can ever express. It is a method of communicating the impossible in that country.

And then Mikhail downs his empty cup. He puts his hand inside his jacket again and withdraws a long dagger from a pocket, but I sit there with no thought of running. Just for a moment, I actually want to be released.

But Mikhail puts the knife on the table between us. It is a *kidjal*, a Caucasian dagger, and it has an inscription on it.

'Pick it up. Look at it,' Mikhail says.

I do so, and written on the blade is an inscription. 'I will protect you, both in the day and in the night,' it reads.

'Finn gave it to me,' Mikhail says. 'It is the dagger's word and it is Finn's word. He kept his word. And now I want you to have it. It's now my word. I'll keep my word to you too, Anna.'

Mikhail stands up and puts the flask and the cups back into his pockets. I pick up the dagger and place it in my bag and do up the zipper.

'We must go,' he says. 'I don't know how much time we have.'

He leads the way through to the kitchen and the back door and looks out over the lake. I follow him with the bag of Finn's books and the microfiches.

I've never opened the back door out from the kitchen, I don't know how Mikhail got to it, but I see there's a lawn outside the door that leads down to the lake.

When he seems satisfied with his observation, he opens the door and we walk down the lawn to a small launch tied to a post. He takes my bags and places them gently next to the seat that he guides me to. Then he gets into the launch himself and starts an outboard. I untie the painter from the post and the boat swings around gently with the motor idling and then he accelerates away from the pink house across the lake. I look back at the widening wake, and the pink house disappearing into the distance.

We reach the other side. He ties the boat up and puts my bags on to a jetty as I climb out. He lets me carry them then, so that I know he isn't going to take them away. Then we walk up the jetty and to a lock-up garage on the far side of the road. Mikhail lifts the door and unlocks a green car, a Cherokee Jeep, I think, inside the garage, and he opens the passenger door for me.

The back seats are folded down and Finn is lying with his eyes closed on what seems to be an inflatable camping mattress and he is covered up to his neck in blankets. I see a drip attached into his arm and smell morphine.

As Mikhail moves the car away from the kerb I see him look back across the lake and I follow his gaze. On the far side, where we've just come from, the lazy blue light of a police car is slowly passing along the road that runs by the edge of the water.

'We must go,' he says.

I look down at Finn and I see that he is alive.

'Why isn't he in hospital?' I demand. 'Why is he lying in this damn car!'

Mikhail doesn't reply.

'Are we going to hospital?' I hear the edge of a scream in my voice.

'He has a few hours, Anna.'

'Get him to a fucking hospital, then!' I scream at him, leaning over the front seat in rage. But he drives into the gathering dusk and I don't know where we're going.

'Finn stayed at a hotel in Paris,' he says at last. 'Days ago, eight, ten – I don't know. He hired a car. French police and security have taken his room to pieces and found nothing. That's because what they were looking for was in the car. They, our people, put a nerve agent on the steering wheel. We don't know what nerve agent it is. Even if we did, it was too late by the time I found him. If there is an antidote, we won't be able to find it. He knew that too. He asked me to bring him here.'

I don't say anything, but sink back on to the floor next to Finn and watch his upturned face and listen to his laboured, infrequent breathing.

'If he wakes, use the time well,' Mikhail says.

We drive in silence, in darkness. I am lying next to Finn, sometimes on one elbow looking at his face, sometimes on my back, like him, looking at the roof of the car. We might both have been corpses then.

'What happened?' I say after I don't know how long. We are passing under some street lights, I am

on my back, and the lights are beaming through the
window, illuminating the interior of the car like a
lethargic stroboscope.

'He told me he went to see the man Frank.'
Mikhail pauses.

'Yes?'

'It was to confront him.'

'About what?'

'Finn told me he'd looked back over months, over
years, and found a pattern. The photographs you told
him about, the ones they showed you in Moscow . . .
On all the occasions photographs were taken, since
Geneva, Frank was the link. In Geneva he was there.
In France, he was there. In Basle, when you and Finn
were taken together at the railway station, the only
other person who knew you'd be there was Frank.
Finn had telephoned him, if you remember. I think
he telephoned Frank back then to confirm his suspicions. To see if there'd be a photograph. And there
was.

'He tried to forget this, Anna. He tried to forget
because he was genuine about finishing with all of
this, about putting it behind him and making a life
with you. But one thing he couldn't forget was four
years ago, in Luxembourg, and the boy's death.
When he left the boy's flat, he'd been meticulous,
he knew his job. And he knew that he wasn't observed entering or leaving the building. Knew as far
as anyone can know, anyway. But with all the other
evidence, the photographs, he knew that Frank also
was the only person who knew he'd seen the boy.
He was certain of that. And therefore he was certain
that Frank was the cause of the boy's death. He

couldn't forget that. He couldn't let that go. He had
to hear it from Frank himself. That's why he went to
Luxembourg. That was the loose end he had to tie
up. He couldn't let it rest.'

I lie silently and put my hand under the blanket
to hold on to Finn's hand.

'So Finn hired a car in France and drove to Luxembourg. He didn't tell me what happened between
him and Frank. But he left the hired car in Luxembourg and took a train out, following all the field
rules. He hired another car when he thought he was
clear. But somehow they kept a tail on him, he didn't
know how. During the night in Paris, they got to
the car in the underground car park where he'd left
it, over a mile away from the hotel. That's how it
happened.'

I stay silent. I don't know where anything goes
from here. And I think that soon I will be the only
person alive who knows who Mikhail is.

'He knew he was ill the following night, but he
didn't know why,' Mikhail said. 'His heart was weak-
ening already. He knew they'd got him.'

'And you found him.'

'Eventually.'

I didn't ask Mikhail how he could find Finn
when I couldn't.

Finn died during that long night in the back of
the car. He didn't regain consciousness.

EPILOGUE

THERE IS ONLY one photograph of Mikhail in the public domain, and in it his face is so obscured that you'd have to know it was him in order to identify him. He is hidden behind the face of Vladimir Putin.

The picture was taken at a small service in the Kremlin's Orthodox chapel on an afternoon in late 2004. Mikhail is in the pew right behind the President; only his ear and a small fraction of his face are visible. He is in a place of high honour in this picture. Yet Mikhail is a minor official in the Railways Ministry in Moscow, on the export side, but he uses this cover to travel widely in Europe for his real work: overseeing the continent's SVR presence. Mikhail is at the centre of power. He was there at the heart of Department 'S' before Putin, and he has risen with Putin from the beginning of Putin's own rise to power. Mikhail is everything that Finn said he was, and that Adrian denied.

In the summer of 2007 the Service held a memorial service for Finn, six months after his death. I received an invitation from Adrian, via the roundabout mailing route that Finn had set up and which still seemed to be working. Once in a while, Willy picked up Finn's mail from a box Finn owned in Monaco.

But I didn't go to Finn's memorial. It wasn't a service for lovers or wives, it was a service designed to draw a veil over how they'd treated Finn in life, not in order to respect him in death. I believe Finn was awarded some posthumous honour to complete the fiction.

Our son was born a few weeks later. We called him Finn, Willy and I, and Willy was his 'father', he told me, in all but fact. He said that his family lived long and that he would live to see my son grow into his twenties. He would take care of me, he promised, as a father, as a friend, and as a guardian.

Willy and I married, in order for me to have a new name and French nationality, and despite the fact that Willy was always trying to get me to meet men my own age. It was a marriage of convenience, between friends. It was from necessity but it was a bond of sorts too.

In the spring and summer of 2007, Putin railed against the West. He cut off oil supplies to the EU country of Estonia, under the pretence of a broken pipeline, but in reality in revenge for the Estonians removing a memorial to Russian soldiers, Estonia's oppressors and occupiers. Russian jet-fighters buzzed European airspace and Putin announced a new weapons' build-up; what used to be called an arms' race.

The Europeans reacted feebly; America stood up to Russia. The Europeans became more and more afraid of Russia and its oil supply. Its leaders and former leaders cosied up to the Kremlin, either for personal gain or out of fear. And Putin, like Peter the Great in his written military statutes, now 'answered to nobody in the world'.

And Adrian, I thought, was right. The power of America would take care of its own, and if you were lucky enough to be able to hang on to America's coat-tails, it wasn't such a bad place to be.

We, Willy and I, and other emigrants from the East whom we met from time to time in Paris, seemed to understand this better than Western Europe's complacent or corrupt indigenous peoples.

Finn's romantic view of what was right, and what was actually possible, was designed for some other kind of world. But eventually, what broke Finn was his inability to change. I finally found the power to choose what was good, what was right, for me. But Finn could not quite bring himself to say: 'I'm on my side.'

The following is a sneak peek at

THE BLIND SPY,

another mind-bending tale of intrigue

from Alex Dryden

Coming March 2012 in hardcover

"Everyone imposes his own system
as far as his army can reach."
Joseph Stalin, April 1945

"You don't understand, George,
that Ukraine is not even a state."
Vladimir Putin, to George W. Bush, April 2008

THE BLACK S-CLASS STRETCH MERCEDES crossed beneath the Moscow ring road on Entuziastov at just after 5.30 in the morning. It was snowing harder outside the city, or maybe that was just how it seemed to the men inside the car. Away from the protection of the city's buildings, the snow was free to hurl itself across the open landscape and a whirlwind of large, fluffy snowflakes rolled out of the eerie, monstrous white void, only to disintegrate as they raced onto the car's heated windscreen.

With the ring road behind it, the official car kept up the same steady regulation speed and moved on to the M-7 heading northeast out of Moscow in the direction of Balashiha.

There were two Intelligence chiefs sitting on the soft, sweet-smelling black leather of the back seat and a military intelligence driver alone in the front. Both chiefs were the most senior generals, elevated to their positions by age, experience, duty, but most of all the supreme skill of the Russian political intelligence class—a ruthless animal instinct for supremacy in the power struggles of the Kremlin's internecine bureaucratic wars.

In their late sixties, they wore uniforms almost comically be-medalled from past campaigns—real wars—that made them resemble highly colourful performers from a travelling mediaeval pageant. These tiered ribbons of medals had been won mostly in Afghanistan after Russia's 1979 invasion of the country and its disastrous and debilitating war there that had finally emptied the Soviet treasury and heralded the end of the empire. They were the medals of defeat.

General Valentin Viktorov had personally been in charge of an Intelligence team which, with initially magnificent success, had prepared the ground for the invasion of the presidential palace in Kabul at Christmas of that year. But those were the glory days, before the Soviet effort descended into stalemate and retreat in the subsequent years of brutal conflict.

Afghanistan. It was never far away from either of the generals' minds, even now, decades after the war ended. Just as the Second World War—the Great Patriotic War, in Russia's lexicon—had been the foul crucible whose hellish alchemy gave birth to Soviet might and to the greatest empire on earth, so Afghanistan was the insidious chemical formula that finally ripped the whole shaky edifice to pieces. For both the generals—as for many of the military veterans of that disastrous war—Afghanistan was the defining moment of their and their Motherland's loss of pride. Afghanistan was the fault line that severed modern Russia from its glorious past. The actual collapse—that of the eastern European empire in 1989 and the subsequent folding of Russia's central Asian possessions after that—were just the inevitable consequences of the Afghan defeat. And it was Afghanistan that welded the psyches of the two generals and thousands like them into an overwhelming and unified desire for the recouping of all of glorious Russia's losses since then.

But despite this psychological link between the two generals, it was notable that they sat as far from one another as the seating allowed, each pushed up against their respective rear doors. They were rivals and, in Russia's medievally clannish political and intelligence world, they had often found themselves working against each other. General Viktorov was from the core of the SVR, Russia's First Chief Directorate and the successor to the KGB's foreign intelligence department. The other veteran, General Antonov, was from the GRU, Russia's Main Intelligence Directorate.

The two men didn't talk and spent most of the journey looking away from one another and out of the windows on either side of the car, though the view was obscured almost completely by the white-out conditions, except for the thin, bunched together trunks of birch and fir trees that took shape as they approached The Forest.

They also both wore tight-lipped expressions that suggested even sharing the same car was an imposition. But that was the way it had been arranged by the prime minister's office and they hadn't been given the choice to travel separately. It was as if this enforced journey together was a test of sorts in itself. "You'll be working together"—that had been the order. But they had never worked together in any commonly accepted way.

The relative seniority between the two men was hard to judge—not least by themselves—but their rivalry was evident in the tension that existed between them. General Antonov deployed five or six times more agents on foreign soil than the SVR and he personally commanded 25,000 special forces troops, or *spetsnatz*. But it was the SVR that considered itself the elite foreign intelligence force and it was the SVR headquarters in Balashiha—The Forest, in KGB parlance—to which they were going. General Viktorov of the SVR was also a central figure in the elite of elites—the directorate's highly secretive Department S. This inner clan of Foreign Intelligence officers was in charge of training foreigners to spy for the Kremlin, then to commit terrorist acts back in their own countries. Social Warfare, it was called. Viktorov's highly sensitive department had achieved several important assassinations in the past year alone.

But in addition to being at the heart of Department S, Viktorov had the vital advantage of having closer personal access to Prime Minister Vladimir Putin than his rival did. The two were actually friends outside the day-to-day business of the intelligence world, and skied and hunted together. In Putin's baronial court, where rank was often a secondary consideration after personal favour—and favours—this probably gave Viktorov the edge.

In the last few miles of their journey perhaps each was thinking about the purpose of this predawn meeting with Putin. But, more likely, each was contemplating his own strategy of personal pre-eminence to employ when they met Putin, regardless of the purpose of the meeting. And each was certainly in a state of anxious speculation that the other knew more, had been briefed prior to this journey, had been taken into the confidence of the prime minister more closely. The usual fear of some loss of favour with Putin plagued them both. And that was how the Kremlin played its games. You never got used to that, Viktorov was thinking. Rule was administered through anxiety and fear, just as it had always been.

The snow ploughs had been out all night to keep the vital road connecting the Kremlin and its intelligence heart clearer than any other in Russia and the car finally swung through the high gates, razor wire and gun turrets disappearing into the snow on either side. The generals' identities were shown and logged by the guards. The Mercedes pulled up half a mile beyond the entrance, outside a long, low building, most of which was concealed beneath the earth.

It was Golubev, the special assistant from the prime minister's office, who was there to meet them. A chivvying young man with a foolishly small moustache, Golubev was a product of the new post-Soviet era. He was a politician-lawyer rather than a soldier—let alone an intelligence officer—and therefore the kind of bureaucratic ministry man who elicited little respect from either of the generals. His youth allowed no memory of the defeat in Afghanistan or even of the later collapse of the entire Soviet Union two years later. Unlike the generals, Golubev looked to the future at the expense of nurturing the past and its humiliations. And, to the generals, he also looked to the future at the expense of redressing the balance that had been lost in the past twenty years since the Soviet Union collapsed. That balance—in the dreams of many like them—was the restoration of the Russian empire.

With a fussiness that disguised his fears, Golubev brushed imaginary dust from the lapels of his jacket, smoothed its sides, then led the generals through cream-painted concrete corridors to an elevator, which took them down four floors into the earth and finally into a brightly-lit room the size of a tennis court. It was one of many operations rooms in this core SVR building and Viktorov knew it well. It was here that many undercover missions had been planned, from the wars in Chechnya to foreign assassinations in the Middle East and Europe. Long, identical tables were laid out in neat rows, each with a harsh light over them, and at a casual glance the whole space might have suggested a snooker club.

Golubev proceeded to a table near the centre of this space and pulled up two high chairs for the generals that offered a view down onto the high table, then one for himself, which he never sat on.

At once, Viktorov looked at several maps that had been opened on the long table. The particular map that caught his eye—it was in the centre of the table which was at the centre of the room—was of the Soviet Union. It was a pre-1991 map in other words, from a time before the Soviet Union had broken up. Viktorov was pleasantly surprised, as if he were looking at a recently discovered family treasure that had been unearthed in the clear-out of an old attic, and he took a greater interest. He saw another map of the period and of equal size, next to it which was a close-up of part of the former empire. It had been titled "Little Russia," but only by a scrawl on a yellow Post-it note stuck to the top. The name on the map itself, however, was "Ukrainian SSR."

"When is the prime minister arriving?" Viktorov asked, looking down on Golubev from the high seat. Golubev fidgeted uncomfortably. Viktorov was a big, muscled man, despite his age, and he took care about his appearance and his physical fitness. His eyebrows were artfully shaped to eliminate the wild-growing hairs that age unleashed and the skin of his face had a polished, pampered appearance. General Antonov, on the other hand, was ruddy in complexion and had allowed the hairs of his advancing age to grow like weeds in an abandoned courtyard. The one general affected a modern, careful appearance, while the other seemed to seek the virtues of a rugged lack of vanity.

"You'll be meeting with some colleagues first," Golubev said. "The prime minister has been detained."

"Colleagues?" Antonov queried. "For how long?"

"*Patriotiy*," Golubev replied almost mutely, as if embarrassed at the mention of this informal, almost underground group, which was definitely not part of his modern Russian vision. "We are waiting for the prime minister's call," he added.

"Ah," Viktorov said. "Our *patriotiy* friends. That's the reason for the map then." He was pleased to be meeting with fellows and, no doubt, old colleagues too from the *Patriotiy*.

Golubev didn't reply. But the generals relaxed into their seats as the nervous ministry man ordered coffee to be brought.

The *Patriotiy* were the core, Viktorov ruminated as he waited for the coffee to arrive. They were the promise. They were like a rare seed preserved in one of Russia's frozen storage units that guarded the planet's ecological and agricultural future. Like these rare seeds, the *Patriotiy* were the guardians of Russia's past and the hope for its future. They were the only ones left with any power who were true to the memory of their own people where Russia's former might was concerned. And for a moment Viktorov felt a brief affinity for the GRU boss Antonov, a veteran like himself of Afghanistan.

The *Patriotiy* consisted mainly of these veterans from the Afghan War. Most importantly in this all-but-secret society of the new Russia, members of the *Patriotiy* didn't believe that the loss of empire was anything other than a temporary historical mistake. In any other democratic country, at any rate, they would have been way outside the political process, on some semi-lunatic fringe. In the Russia of the twenty-first century, however, they were at the centre of power, though invisibly so to all but a few. Afghan veterans like himself and Antonov, who had risen in Putin's Russia through the organs of the security services, the *Patriotiy* were now in control of several intelligence departments and government ministries and had brought their grudges of lost empire with them.

Coffee arrived, delivered by an attractive woman in uniform whom Viktorov smiled at with an avuncular look that didn't—and didn't intend to—disguise the lust that lurked behind it. And then the room began to fill up with a dozen or more men in their sixties or seventies and a few younger men. Most of them were in uniform; lesser generals, colonels, retired or not retired. Greetings were exchanged, old links renewed. Two more uniformed female assistants had now materialised to help Golubev distribute files to all the men. Viktorov gave his trademark smile to the woman who approached his table. He took a file and slipped a pair of reading glasses over his nose. The title in bold Cyrillic on the cover was "Reappraisal. The Weakness of Ukraine—Political, Economic, Ethnic, and Military."

Viktorov and the others leafed through their files without yet reading them closely. "Who wrote this?" Viktorov snapped at Golubev.

"A think tank at the Ministry of the Interior" was the reply. "Along with some of your own intelligence staff, General."

Behind my back, Viktorov thought. The prime minister's mind games had begun. He snorted loudly and confidently, though whether at the words "think tank" or the fact that Interior people were in part the authors was unclear. Not that he despised the Interior Ministry. The Interior Ministry was one of several important ministries now controlled by the *Patriotiy* and its chiefs shared the same aims as the people in the room.

For a moment, Viktorov removed his glasses and looked across the large room. He stared hard with unfocused eyes until he recognised his son, Dmitry. Or Balthasar—though only the two of them knew him by the latter name. He saw that Balthasar was talking to an older man—an officer in the Alpha

Group, Viktorov thought. Viktorov couldn't take his eyes away from his son.

Then Balthasar broke away from a brief exchange with the officer and began to make his way through the throng. He walked with expert precision around three tables and paused to nod a greeting and say a few words to two or three other men. He looked assured, smooth in his movements, somehow modern, Viktorov thought, in that his proper deference to senior men was never at the expense of his personal pride and individuality. He was a Colonel—also in Department "S"—and was now thirty-eight years old. But in this room he was a junior.

Viktorov saw Balthasar was clearly making his way towards him. With one hand he was lifting up a chair that was in the way, while the other hand shook greetings with colleagues. He looked directly into people's eyes.

Amazing—even now it amazed Viktorov. Such extraordinary power Balthasar had. Nobody who didn't know him would ever have guessed that he was blind. And, realizing that he was blind, nobody would have dreamed that he could be Russia's most senior-decorated intelligence field operative in all of the Muslim countries. Amazing, there was no other word for it. Sometimes his son's strange abilities discomforted Viktorov—but there was no denying Balthasar's extraordinary, if uniquely bizarre, powers. For not only did he have an unerring geographical relationship with the people around him and with his surroundings in general—sensing the chair, moving it easily, knowing precisely where there was a hand to be shaken, understanding exactly where to meet others' eyes with his own sightless ones—

but also, despite this supernatural power—to Viktorov's mind, Balthasar's real value was that he could do what no eye and no electronic device could do, no matter how sharp or sophisticated. He had the ability of seeing inside the minds of those he was with. He had a sixth sense and maybe—who knew—a seventh and an eighth.

Viktorov cast his mind back thirty-nine years. The brothers of Balthasar's mother who he, Viktorov, had rescued him from all those years ago had said he was cursed by God. This "curse" had turned out to be a most precious, a most unique weapon. God had given him something far greater than normal sight. As it turned out, God had blessed him.

Balthasar approached his father and, with the same direct accuracy, shook his hand, "looked" in his eyes, and exchanged a welcome. To Vikorov, his son's demeanour suggested he was in some official position in this room. He appeared to be at the heart of the purpose of the strange meeting. Viktorov wondered why he hadn't known before about Balthasar's presence. He was the chief of Department S, for God's sake.

So. This morning was the prime minister's party and his own position could be, and often was, usurped by Putin and a few others. Yet what did Balthasar have to do with the message on the table? The map? Ukraine was an Orthodox Christian country. Not Balthasar's area of operations at all. Balthasar was in Islamic operations, pure and simple. Ukraine was the birthplace of Russian orthodoxy, the origins of old Rus. Ukraine was Russia's spiritual heartbeat.

"Look at this," he said, pointing at the map, then

felt immediately foolish to be using a word that assumed working sight.

"I know," Balthasar smiled, ignoring the mistake. He put his hand on the map, as if he could actually feel the terrain it represented. "Ukraine," he said simply.

If Viktorov thought he would draw out his son's reasons for being here by referring to the map of Ukraine, he was unsuccessful.

A trolley was now brought in by the two women who had distributed the files. It was 6.45 a.m. and there were various bottles of flavoured vodka and shot glasses on it. Not Golubev's idea of the right time for a drink and the ministry man was showing it with anxious glances. Not Putin's idea either, for that matter, so perhaps that was why Golubev looked so uncomfortable. But the glasses were distributed solemnly—like some sort of pseudo-religious, regimental ceremonial—by a one-legged *spetsnatz* hero who was apparently determined to show that his infirmity made no difference. The toast, when it was raised by a fellow SVR general, was to "Historic Russia." All present drank and placed their glasses back onto the trolley, which was wheeled away. One drink for the toast, that was it. The party, such as it was, was over. And they all knew that historic Russia meant Kiev, the capital of a Ukraine which had been independent from Moscow now for twenty years, after centuries of occupation.

Golubev's phone rang. He walked away from Viktorov and Balthasar, who reminisced in quiet voices. When he returned, he looked only at the generals, Viktorov and Antonov.

"You'll have to read it on the road," Golubev said

to the two generals, nodding at the document, and he clicked the mobile phone shut. "The prime minister is delayed. He asks you to come to his dacha."

As the Mercedes swung out of the gates and took the autoroute back to the ring road, Viktorov thought that none of this—the apparently pointless trip to Balashiha, the meeting with the veterans, and even the enforced shared trip with Antonov—was unplanned. Clearly he would be expected to work with Antonov and the meeting at Balashiha was in the style of an underground regimental get-together, something like Nazi SS officers meeting in secret at inns in the depths of the Harz Forest after the war. Except that here it was official and government-backed. The *Patriotiy* were the establishment.

They were met at the imposing gates of Putin's dacha by a Kremlin car, which would take them up the drive to the dacha where Putin worked, swam, and practised judo. His family dacha was hidden further in the forest.

Inside the high reception room the two generals stood. Still they didn't talk. Finally after nearly half an hour, they were summoned to a long, lavishly furnished office the size of a small ballroom, where Putin was sitting at a desk under the Russian eagle. He motioned them to seats in front of the desk, then without preamble, leaned on his elbows, with his hands clasped together and stared his blank, unblinking stare.

"We need greater cooperation," he said. "This war between two great services has to stop."

Viktorov shifted uncomfortably in his seat. The latest skirmish between the SVR and the GRU had occurred just three weeks before in Germany. The

SVR had betrayed two agents of the GRU to the German intelligence service. Their reason was—from the SVR's point of view—that the GRU was transgressing on its own patch.

"We have important work to do," Putin said. "And I need full cooperation. Your jobs are at stake. Russia's future is at stake."

The generals inclined their heads. Putin didn't seek a reply. Then he leaned in closer. "The report," he said. "Read it closely. Elections in Ukraine take place in just over a week's time. The final run-off is three weeks after that. But the elections are irrelevant. Whoever wins, we want to make our arrangements with our friends in Ukraine. Redress the balance." He looked severely at them and Viktorov wondered, not for the first time, if Putin actually didn't have any eyelids, if he was like a snake. Putin leaned back in his chair and stared at the two generals. "We all know, of course," he said with finality, "that Ukraine is not even a state."